Seasonal
Fears

ALSO BY SEANAN McGUIRE

SEANAN McGUIRE

Seasonal Fears

A TOM DOHERTY ASSOCIATES BOOK

NEW YORK

SEASONAL FEARS

Copyright © 2022 by Seanan McGuire

Edited by Lee Harris

A Tordotcom Book
Published by Tom Doherty Associates
120 Broadway
New York, NY 10271

www.tor.com

Tor® is a registered trademark of Macmillan Publishing Group, LLC.

Library of Congress Cataloging-in-Publication Data

Names: McGuire, Seanan, author.
Title: Seasonal fears / Seanan McGuire.
Description: First edition. | New York : Tordotcom, 2022. | "A Tom
    Doherty Associates book."
Identifiers: LCCN 2022000333 (print) | LCCN 2022000334 (ebook) |
    ISBN 9781250768261 (hardcover) | ISBN 9781250768254 (ebook)
Subjects: LCGFT: Novels.
Classification: LCC PS3607.R36395 S43 2022 (print) | LCC PS3607.
    R36395 (ebook) | DDC 813/.6—dc23/eng/20220105
LC record available at https://lccn.loc.gov/2022000333
LC ebook record available at https://lccn.loc.gov/2022000334

Our books may be purchased in bulk for promotional, educational, or
business use. Please contact your local bookseller or the Macmillan Corporate
and Premium Sales Department at 1-800-221-7945, extension 5442, or by email at
MacmillanSpecialMarkets@macmillan.com.

First Edition: 2022

Printed in the United States of America

0 9 8 7 6 5 4 3 2 1

For Wes and Mary,
who stand where the earth bleeds red and still remember me.

And for Phil, in the corn.

Once, in a time that was earlier than it is now and later than it might have been, later than the great ages of heroes and monsters, when quests were taught in school alongside the subjects we still have today, literature and swordsmanship, arithmetic and alchemy, science and the art of finding and fleeing from monsters, there were two children who had lived in the same ordinary town since the day that they were born. They had lived soft, swift, utterly ordinary lives, days blending into nights without any hint of the untidy impossible lurking around the edges, and their parents had looked at them and dreamed wholly ordinary futures, devoid of magic or monsters or other complications.

These two children had lived their entire lives on the same ordinary street, but as their parents were not friends—would, in fact, have recoiled from the thought of friendship that crossed class and societal lines with such flagrant disregard for keeping to one's own kind—and as they went to different schools, on opposite sides of their ordinary town, where they made the kind of friends their parents would approve of, they had never met one another, nor even so much as said hello in the public square. Avery was far too stuffy and preoccupied with neatness to be a good companion to Zib, who was in many ways what would happen if a large bonfire were somehow to be convinced to stitch itself into the skin of a little girl and go running wild across the fields of summer.

So Avery Alexander Grey and Hepzibah Laurel Jones had grown up, day by day and year by year, blissfully unaware that the person who would be the best of all their life's many friends, the person who would someday unlock the doorways to adventure, was less than a mile away that whole time. And then one day, one of the large pipes which carried water to the ordinary town took it upon itself to burst in the earth, causing an artificial flood and quite blocking the route that Avery ordinarily took to school. It was the sort of inconvenience that could have happened anywhere in the world, but which had, until recently, mostly left their ordinary little town alone. Adventure was against the civic bylaws, and best avoided, after all. . . .

—From *Along the Saltwise Sea,*
by A. Deborah Baker

BOOK I

Season's End

Though we have spent our harvest of this king,
We are to reap the harvest of his son.

—William Shakespeare, *Richard III*

Wishes and candles and whispers and tears
She can't help them all, but she'll try
Oh, and seasonal weather brings seasonal fears—
And when hurricane season comes by
Her faithful keep watch on the sky . . .

—Talis Kimberley, "Underpass Mary"

Investiture

CALENDAR SEASON: MAY 15TH, 1730: WANING
SPRING, UNDER THE FLOWER MOON.

The chanting has died to a dull murmur, with only the people at the back of the crowd still saying anything at all. Most of them aren't even speaking English, as if their heathen incantations can have any meaning for a good Christian man! To be sure, this is a pagan ritual at best, but he tries not to think about the contradiction, especially now that his future is committed.

It would be different if he had been coronated in England, where his roots still lie; he would understand every spoken word and every aspect of the spectacle around him. He would be so much better prepared. Well, prepared or not, he is still the winner, and this is still his crown. He always knew he'd be a king someday. Just not what kind.

Some of the people in the crowd are staring at him as he walks toward the dais prepared by the attendants. This is where the crowning will occur. The people stare because they don't approve of his presence, he knows; they believe the seasons belong to them and with them, and not to upstart settlers like himself.

As if there weren't seasons the world over. As if it's so odd for a man of his station and breeding to have been inducted into the mysteries.

Well, these people will see, won't they? God intended this country for the use of England and the English peoples, and the Empire is eternal, even on these distant shores. He is proud to represent Queen and Country in this new land, to tie it more tightly to Empire through this most familiar of rituals. There was no bean in his bread, but he has always known the rite of seasons and where it must inevitably lead. When he felt his blood turn to ice in his veins and the frost coming to his call, he knew what that meant, even before that Irish boy who had to be taught proper manners and comportment came to claim him and lead him through the trials. There were no surprises ahead of him.

If anything, the real surprise is that the people here, natives and colonists alike, seem to know the rite of seasons as well as they do. They began chanting the proper rituals as soon as he slew the last contender for his position, cutting the woman down with a viciousness that seemed to shock the onlookers as much as it shocked her. Their ascensions were apparently less violent in the past, with the losers going easy to their fates. He was the last potential scion of Winter to enter the labyrinth, and the woman would not refuse her crown; he did what had to be done.

Well, those who wish to be damned will always find a way to be damned. He refuses to accept that ending for himself. He is the Winter King, chosen and blooded and preordained. He will live forever, ascendant and resplendent and manifest, and all who challenge his dominion will fall, swept away like shadows on the snow.

They are bringing out the woman whose progress matched his through the final trials. She is pleasant enough to the eye, stout and clear of complexion, untouched by the pox. Her hair is dark and her skin too ruddy for true wealth, but she carries herself with majesty enough to serve as his queen. And if there is one shame to the fact that the rites are the same in this place as they were at home, it is that he has no say in the matter. When the challenge began, all in range who might carry the crown and wished to go without destruction rose to face it, and to the strongest go the spoils. At least his counterpart is a woman. He will not be trapped inside eternity with no opportunity for companionship.

Then he sees the look on her face as they lead her toward the dais. She looks at him as a woman may look at a snake, or a stain upon her hem; her lip is curled, her expression revolted.

"Welcome," he says as she approaches, hoping she simply has one of those easily misunderstood faces. "How wonderful to see that my Summer Queen is to be beautiful as well."

"We should not be here," she spits. Her attendants help her onto the platform. He wonders what the natives called them before the settlers arrived to teach them the proper names of things.

"Of course we should. We won."

"You won through savagery and violence." She squares her shoulders, looks down her nose at him, and the flickering moonlight on her hair reminds him that her season is ascendant, while his is fading. If he had been allowed to choose his crown, he would have taken the summer's sweetness for himself, would have left this . . . this . . . this *witch* to the barren winter where she so clearly belongs. But there is never a choice for the seasonal ones. They are like the weather, pulled and pushed where the wind wills them, until they rise and take the power to choose for their own. But never for themselves.

No. His choices will always be made by the Wheel of the year, but he will be able to choose for others. He will be able to make them pay for costing him everything they have.

"As did you," he counters. "We have to fight to claim the crown."

"No," she says, sounding surprised for the first time. "The fight is not required. We are not so easily dethroned as all that. You fought, as these people do not, and so they were unprepared to stand before you. And when the contenders for the Summer saw what they would have to stand beside if they were chosen, they lay down their own potential and stepped out of my way. This is not our continent. This is not our *country*. These should not be our crowns."

"They will be."

"They will, because you have left no others to hold the Winter," she snarls, and in that moment, she is a beast, and he realizes that the color of her skin doesn't betray the content of her heart. He has not defeated the savages to take his rightful place. One of them stands beside him, to be yoked to him for all of time. "You will manifest, and I will manifest with you, because no one will stand by your side. They know the Summer must be held, but they will not hold it in concert with a killer."

"But you will."

"I will do what I must for Summer's sake, and endure your company long as our fates demand." She stands a little straighter, the malice not leaving her eyes. "Your reign will not be long."

William thinks of the alchemist who came to him at the start of the crowning, the one who offered him victory and a measureless reign if only he would consider the needs of the newly formed American Alchemical Congress in his choices, in his guidance of the season that is his birthright. He turned the man down at the time, but the situation, it seems, has changed.

His reign will be eternal.

Runaway

M elanie isn't feeling good again.

Harry's mom says it's because Melanie has something wrong with her heart, but Harry doesn't see how that could be so. His grandma had something wrong with her heart, so she went to see the doctor and they gave her a machine called a pacemaker that fixed the thing that was wrong. Now she's fine, even if she doesn't like to run in the park with him when she comes to visit. Most adults don't much like running, anyway. So if there's something wrong with Melanie's heart, she should be able to just go to the hospital and get herself her very own pacemaker, and then she'll be all right again.

And Melanie goes to the hospital more often than just about anybody else in the whole world. Near as Harry can tell, she's there almost every week. Sometimes she has to spend the whole weekend at the hospital, and not come home at all, and she can't talk to him on the phone even. He doesn't like it when that happens.

She missed two weeks of kindergarten last year, and when he went to her house, she wasn't there, not ever. Just her dad sometimes, and some of her dad's weird friends. All adults are at least a little bit weird. Melanie says it's because they pick up weird like layers of stickers. Harry has a rock he puts cool stickers on when he gets them, and his parents let him because it means he's not putting stickers on anything else. "It's practical," says his mom, and "It's useful," says his dad, and they leave his rock alone. It's about three times as big now as it was when he got it, and that's all because of stickers. So if weird is like stickers, he guesses it would make sense for adults to be weirder than kids.

Kids have their own kinds of weird. Harry knows that. Everyone's weird in their own special way, and it's sort of wonderful, because if everyone wasn't weird, then he'd be the weird one, because he can't really think of a world where he's *not* weird. His family's rich, for one thing, and he didn't have anything to do with that, but it still means sometimes he doesn't think about things the other kids have to think about all the time, like when he asked why Karen Nelson got free milk in the cafeteria and he had to bring quarters from home if he wanted a little wax carton for his own. His grandparents in Wisconsin live in a castle, for another thing, a real castle that was built on the other side of an ocean and then got moved over to America one piece at a time before the people who moved it put it back together like a house of Lego.

He loves going to visit his grandparents in their Lego house, even though his dad says it's a monstrosity and a waste of money that would be better served by going into something called a college fund, for if he wants to do more school after all the main school is over. Harry doesn't think that sounds like a good time, and anyway, the Lego house has a name, and it's not "monstrosity." It's called "Castleview," and he loves saying that, even though it *is* the castle, and you can't view any castles when you're there, not unless you're standing in the front yard and looking up so far your neck hurts. It sounds like something out of the Up-and-Under, something out of a fairy story, and in fairy stories no one ever has to miss school because there's something wrong with their heart.

In fairy stories you might get turned to stone, or fall down a hole and wind up in a whole different world, or have a lady made of smoke reach into your chest and turn your heart into an ember and whisk it away before you can blink, but you don't have to get a pacemaker, and you don't have to stay inside all the time, and you don't scare your friends the way Melanie's been scaring him.

That's the other thing that makes Harry weird: he has a best friend, and her name is Melanie, and he doesn't care if girls have cooties, because if Melanie has cooties, he wants to have them too. He wants her cooties all over him like ants at a picnic. He's going to marry her someday, when they're both grown up and old enough. Maybe twelve. Twelve seems like it's probably old enough to get married.

But not if she never comes outside again.

His family's rich and he's seven years old and these two things can occasionally combine in ways no one bothers to think through. "A boy should have a bicycle," his father said, and bought Harry the nicest bike the shop had, ideal for a boy his age who had an interest in long bike rides and riding off-trail, neither of which Harry has ever shown a strong inclination toward. "His best friend is a sick girl who lives a mile away, he'll have to ask for a ride if he wants to go see her, and then we can tell him she needs her rest," thought his mother, and she would have been right if he'd been on foot, but he isn't on foot.

He has an excellent bicycle.

If anyone takes note of the small boy pedaling his way through the tree-lined streets of suburban Portland, they don't interfere with him. Small boys ride their bikes, and small boys have friends, and if they don't recognize this small boy, presumably he's a friend of one of the local kids. Surely no parents would have misplaced their child so comprehensively as to let him ride his bike alone through the city. Surely he's someone else's problem.

Harry rides the wave of being someone else's problem all the way to Melanie's house, where her father is parked in the driveway. He stops on the sidewalk almost a whole house down. He doesn't know if he likes Dr. Cosgrove.

For one thing, he makes everyone call him "doctor" all the time, but he never wears a white coat like the doctors on television or the ones who helped Grandma with her pacemaker. He mostly wears suits and ties, and an expression like he's thinking about how fun it would be to strangle baby bunnies with his bare hands. It only goes away when he's looking at Melanie, and Harry doesn't like the way he does *that*, either.

Dr. Cosgrove looks at Melanie the way Harry's father looked at Harry's bike when they brought it home from the bike shop. Proud and sort of . . . owner-y, like it was something he'd *made*, not just something he'd paid for. The first time Harry hears the word "proprietary," he'll think of Melanie's father and not be able to articulate quite why.

He knows Dr. Cosgrove loves his daughter, and Melanie loves her father. But there's something wrong between them, something Harry can't name or explain, no matter how hard he tries. It's not fair, the way things are, and he knows that if he rings the bell, Dr. Cosgrove won't let him in.

For the most part, Harry is a good kid, unspoiled by his parents' wealth. Sometimes, though, believing that everything is replaceable can make him careless. Maybe that's why he props his bike against the hedge and leaves it there as he heads down the sidewalk on foot, reasoning that if Dr. Cosgrove looks out the window and sees him, he'll assume it's some other little blond boy out for a walk. He's smart enough to know he's not supposed to be this far from home without an adult. He just doesn't care.

Once he's past the house, Harry stops strolling nonchalantly and bolts into the yard, heading for the oak tree outside Melanie's window. It's perfect for climbing, with its broad, twisting branches, and he's seen Melanie climb it a dozen times during play dates when her father was inside and couldn't tell her she was too fragile for something like that.

Harry suspects Melanie isn't fragile at all. He thinks she's probably a lot stronger than anyone, especially her father, is ever going to give her credit for being, and he wishes there were a way he could make her understand that. Maybe when they're grown-up and married. Maybe when they're twelve.

Harry grabs the highest branch he can reach and pulls himself into the tree, not realizing as he climbs that the window he's passing belongs to Dr. Cosgrove's office, or that Melanie's father is there on his phone until he hears the man's voice drifting through the barely cracked window. He freezes, held in place by the snake-charmer's song of an adult voice. He knows he's not supposed to be here. He can't move.

"Of *course* I'm keeping you updated on her progress. You know I'm grateful for everything you've done for me. Without access to Asphodel's research—Yes, sir." There is a long and terrible pause. "Yes, sir. I know how much faith you've put in me by even allowing this attempt, and I feel I've paid enough to prove my loyalty. Please, allow me to continue my work. It shouldn't take too much longer before we know if both are capable of reaching maturity, or if one will have to be culled to rebuild the other."

The second pause is shorter, broken by the sound of Dr. Cosgrove's uproarious laughter. It doesn't sound like he's heard something funny. It's more like the kind of laughter that comes from something terribly frightening, the way Harry laughed the time one of his babysitters put on a movie where a man in a mask ran around killing people and there had been so much blood, blood everywhere, and it had been like something out of a terrible dream, something dark and awful and unfair. That's how Dr. Cosgrove is laughing now.

Harry can't move. He's never heard an adult make such a terrible sound, not ever in his life. Not even his dad when the hospital called to say that Grandma was going to need a pacemaker, and he had cried and cried and cried.

"Yes, well, yours are further along," says Dr. Cosgrove finally. "Further along, *and* designed to catch something that's never been caught before. Mine are more like natural pitcher plants. Melanie seems to be attracting the season she's intended for, but it's hard to say for sure, without a Jack Frost at our doorstep or a coronation in the offing. I don't suppose there's any chance of—No, I didn't think so. Pity. He's long since ceased to be useful, although I suppose I can understand why you'd prefer to avoid the competition."

Dr. Cosgrove's voice begins to get softer then, like he's moving away from the window. Harry stays where he is until he hears the office door pulled shut with a decisive click, and the ice in his limbs shatters. He starts climbing again, faster this time, less concerned about falling than he is about beating Dr. Cosgrove to Melanie's room.

If they lived closer together, this might be the first of a thousand times he climbs this tree to her window, the first of a thousand times he comes sliding in to find her sleeping. But they don't and it isn't: after this, Harry March will never come in her window again. He reaches the level of the frame and tests it carefully, relieved to find that it's not only unlocked but well-maintained enough to slide easily upward when he pushes, not forcing him to fight it.

There's no window seat or chair on the other side. Melanie is delicate; she shouldn't be encouraged to do things like crawling in and out of her bedroom window. So Harry boosts himself over the edge and hopes.

His hope is somewhat misplaced. Harry tumbles into Melanie's room, all legs and arms and newborn bruises, landing on the floor with a thump he feels sure will bring her father running. He holds himself in frozen stillness for a long moment, as if Dr. Cosgrove could somehow fail to see the open window and the unexpected boy upon coming into the room. When that doesn't happen, Harry slowly untenses and stands, brushing bits of bark off his hands. The room is dark, even though it's the middle of the day.

"Mel?"

She sleeps in a big canopy bed, like something that ought to belong to a princess, something that should be in Castleview. When he's grown up and owns the castle, her bed *will* be in Castleview, and she'll be there with it. They'll have sleepovers and watch movies every night, and whatever's wrong with her heart won't be able to hurt her anymore. His mom says machines are just helpers, made to do things people don't want to do for themselves. So he can be her pacemaker, and keep her heart happy so she doesn't have to stay alone in her room.

"Mel?"

Harry moves toward the bed, where the curtains are drawn and

Melanie is, presumably, asleep. When she doesn't answer, he pulls back the curtain.

For a long moment, he can only stare, expression absolutely solemn, not moving in the slightest. Neither is Melanie. She's lying perfectly still, like a statue or a carved soap doll. She's always been pale—she's the palest person he knows—but she looks like someone's stolen all the blood out of her body and replaced it with water, she's that pale right now. It's like there's nothing left of her.

She's not breathing.

Harry's eyes get bigger and bigger, and wider and wider, until the skin around them starts to hurt. Finally, when it's all too much, when he knows that if he doesn't do something, anything, to make things different than they are, he whispers her name again, her whole name, like he's a teacher calling on her during class and hoping she'll have the right answer after all.

She doesn't answer.

Harry leans forward and takes her hand. It's cold. Of course it's cold. He's only seven, but he knows a dead thing when he sees one, and Melanie's a dead thing. Dead things are only warm when they've been out in the sun, and there's no sun in this room. It's cold in here even for October, so cold. She isn't breathing and her hand is cold and this is the worst thing that has ever happened, this is worse even than the movie with the man with the knives on his hand, and he can't breathe, and this is the sort of terrible you can't even laugh at, because it's too big. It's too big, it's too big, it's too much, it's too big—

If he were older, or harder, he might think of fairy tales, the kind where the brave prince wakes the sleeping princess by kissing her, even though she's in no position to give him permission. But he's not older, and while he's not the softest boy in the world, he *is* seven years old and his best friend is a girl who hits harder than anyone else he knows. He would no more kiss her without asking her first than he would jump out her bedroom window and expect to be able to fly. Some things are possible and some things aren't, and kissing her for the first time when she can't say yes is impossible.

(Seasonal creatures are by their very nature linear: they run in one direction and not the other, one foot after the other, progressing ever forward into the uncertain future. In another story, they may have played out another way, may have followed a different set of rules and possibilities. If it seems strange that Harry knows what not to do when he's so young and so afraid, consider only that he has, on some level, been here before, as we have all been here before, over and over again, for so long as to beggar understanding.)

Still holding Melanie's hand (Melanie's *dead* hand), Harry starts to cry. These aren't little, delicate tears: these are the great, braying sobs of a boy who has just been betrayed beyond all reason, who can't understand how any of this can possibly be happening. Dr. Cosgrove comes thundering up the stairs only a few seconds later, slamming the door open. When he sees Harry in his daughter's room, holding her hand and sobbing, he doesn't react with fear or with distress: he reacts, immediately, with anger.

"Get away from her, you fool!" he thunders, and throws himself at Harry, slapping their hands apart. He glares at the boy, man in a rage. "Get out of this room *right now*! Do you have any idea the damage you could have done? Any idea how much research you could have just wasted?"

Melanie's hand, once dropped, dangles off the edge of the bed, taking her whole arm with it. She doesn't move. Of course she doesn't move: she's dead, and she's never going to move ever, ever again. Harry keeps crying as Dr. Cosgrove drags him out of the room and down the stairs, keeps crying as Melanie's father calls his parents, and is still crying fifteen minutes later, when the doorbell rings.

"Stay *right* there," Dr. Cosgrove commands, and leaves him sitting, weeping, on the couch as he crosses the room to let Harry's parents inside. His mother is the first through the door, distress clear and arms already open, and Harry doesn't need any further prompting: he flings himself into them, clutching her while he sobs.

"Baby, what's wrong?" she asks.

The look on Dr. Cosgrove's face is complicated and terrible, the face of a man who dreads the words he's about to hear. Harry barely notices. He looks into his mother's eyes, takes a deep breath, and wails,

"She's *dead* she's *dead* Melanie's *dead*!"

His voice is high and piercing and honest in its distress, as only a child's voice can be. Maybe that's why it does what it does. He's standing with his face buried against his mother's arm, sobbing his heart out as she demands to know what he's talking about, when he hears the impossible. There are only four people in the house. Three of them are in the living room already, and he hears feet on the stairs.

Harry jerks away from his mother's comforting arms and whirls to see a black-haired little girl in a red nightie standing with one hand on the bannister and the other hand rubbing her eye. "Daddy?" she asks. "Why's Harry crying?"

Harry doesn't answer her.

He's already on the floor, passed out in a dead faint.

Runway

The ground is too soft.

He knows that even as he hurries across the lawn, eschewing the paved pathway intended for passenger use. The ground is too soft. It sucks and tugs at the heels of his Italian leather shoes, trying to pull them off his feet, trying to pull him under. It wants to keep him, this ground. It wants to *have* him, in a way he can't articulate and will not allow. He hasn't made it this far by giving in to the senseless demands of *soil*.

He's not a worm. He's not even a man. He's a *god,* has been a god for more than three hundred years, since the day he achieved and seized his own ascension, and like any god, he refuses to go down this easily. This isn't his fault. This isn't fair. This isn't what he agreed to.

But the world has been changing while he's been standing still; the seasons no longer follow the exact pattern he remembers. So the ground is too soft, and when he steps onto a patch of what should be safely frozen grass, his foot sinks almost an inch into the muck before he can pull back, the dried-out fronds of last year's growth wrapping tight around his shoe. They remember him, somehow, even though he's never stepped on them before, and this isn't *fair,* this isn't *right,* Reed promised—

But according to his connections in the alchemical world, Reed is gone, like Asphodel before him. Like Milo before her. Like all those temporary, transitory people still tied to the yoke of the year, and not standing at the helm. Reed is gone, and most of the American Alchemical Congress along with him, all save those few masters who had failed to attend the meeting that destroyed their elders and, for the most part, betters. Their promises hold no weight any longer. America is defenseless.

He is defenseless, and the ground is too soft, and the thaw is coming. He's been delaying this moment for literally decades, and now, when it's finally arriving, he has nothing and no one to hide behind.

William Monroe has always been, essentially at the base of himself, a coward. When he realized none of the boys he went to school with could hear the snowflakes singing as they fell, he kept that knowledge to himself, not out of a desire for power or the strength that comes from having secrets, but out of the intrinsic understanding that to be different, to be in any way *other*, was to make himself a target. He was a fox surrounded by wolves, and like all successful foxes, he learned to make himself small, to play down the degree to which his very body was a red flag, his very presence a reminder of blood on the snow.

He carried that same understanding to the coronation, seeming small, seeming soft, until he was ready to strike, and then he struck, again and again, without mercy, to win his godhood.

All those lessons, though, all those years; all those alliances forged with larger predators, monsters who understood what it meant to move, camouflaged in bars of light and shadow, through the edges of the forest; all those hard-won battles mean nothing in the here and now, not when the ground is this soft. Not when the ice is retreating. He was supposed to have more time. He was supposed to have another two weeks, at least, before the thaw began!

He walks faster, and his feet hit the solid, safe concrete of the runway, gray asphalt under the hard soles of his shoes, mud smearing away and leaving a trail behind him by which any predator could track his progress, but there are no predators here. None except for William himself, and he's never been a hunter. He prefers the easy ambush, the long wait before a full stomach, and the lack of danger.

He's never had the nerve for taking risks he was able to avoid, and the more time he's had to solidify his place at the center of his own little universe, the fewer risks he's had to shoulder on his own. The symmetry of it has always appealed. It still appeals now.

The plane is waiting that will take him away from here, away from this undefended country with its too-soft ground, carry him to the sweet safety of the antipodes, where the cold still reigns. He'll miss the snow—it snows so rarely in the parts of Australia he claims as his home—and he supposes he'll have to renegotiate his treaties with the Australian Alchemical Congress once they realize he intends to supplant their pretender of a Winter Queen and stay on in her place, but he's sure they'll see the logic of his requests, the reasons he has to stay in ascension. This is so much better than the old system, the one he inherited from his predecessor. Change is another word for chaos, and chaos disrupts the best possible plans.

He's just grateful that those damn cuckoos of Reed's pulled their little coup in the middle of the summer, and in the presence of the corn. He's known about the situation for months. He had time to *prepare*.

He could have hurried, could have done this sooner—*should* have done this sooner, if he'd been on top of things, but he's not used to having deadlines anymore, didn't really think through what the change to the balance of things was going to do until it was too late to evade. Still, he had the bulk of the summer and all of the fall to brace himself for what he knew all along was going to be a hard spring.

It just wasn't supposed to get here so *fast*. Not with the worm moon still hanging ripe and restless in the sky, not with the hunger moon so close behind them. All the meteorologists he'd spoken to had given him a few more weeks to get things in order, and only the fact that he fell asleep at his desk last night gave him the warning to make it this far.

The plane that will take him from this rural little strip of nothing to the hub where he'll transfer to his plane for Melbourne appears on the runway up ahead. No security here, no invasive scans or troublesome examinations of his luggage; his are the privileges of power, and no one would dare. William Monroe rushes across the strip, past the silently waiting man in pilot's whites, and all but throws himself up the narrow stairway to the open door.

"Come on, man," he shouts over his shoulder to the pilot. William is a man of many skills, some developed out of necessity and others out of boredom as the years marched by, but he's never learned to fly a plane. Too many powerful people have died because they decided they were better than the sky.

He *is* better than the sky, has two of the four winds under his dominion by right and two more by conquest, but that doesn't mean taunting the oversized. Let people who still understand what it is to be properly humble control the planes, and he'll ride along, safe and protected and shepherded by the skills of others, as he always has.

The pilot, who has been flying Mr. Monroe's private plane for almost a decade, yet has never been referred to by name, manages not to sneer as he follows his employer into the overly opulent cabin, where two women in uniforms stolen straight from the nineteen seventies wait with cocktails in their hands. They shoot the pilot sidelong, sharp-eyed looks, which he acknowledges with a nod. This job demeans them all, but it pays well, and sometimes that's what matters.

His copilot is already strapped into her seat. She avoids contact with Mr. Monroe, who sees her as a glorified flight attendant, and cannot understand why she refuses to make herself equally available to his wandering hands. "Ready?" she asks.

"He's in a hurry today," he says, beginning to run down his part of the preflight checklist. It is shorter than it should be, every step that *can* be taken before their single passenger arrives long since taken, to minimize the amount of time Mr. Monroe spends on the plane.

"This is your captain speaking," he says, flicking on the intercom. "We have an approved flight path between here and Minneapolis, with little turbulence and clear skies predicted. Mr. Monroe, please take your seat. Crew, please secure cabin for takeoff."

Mr. Monroe will sit, he knows, but won't bother with his seat-belt. The man seems to think of himself as invincible, and while he knows it would mean his job, he's sometimes tempted to steer into turbulence, just to bounce his employer off the walls a few times and make him understand that money doesn't grant immunity from physics. He'll never do it: his flight crew doesn't deserve that. But oh, he wants to.

The ground crew has sent up the okay. He turns the engine on, moves the stick into position, and begins making the long, slow turn that will allow them to accelerate down the runway until they reach velocity and soar away.

The plane responds easily, even eagerly, and they're away, gliding down the runway, gathering speed, gathering momentum, finally reaching the point at which braking, even in a modern aircraft, becomes difficult enough to border on the impossible. Physics has the wheel now. They'll be obeying her demands.

His copilot reaches over, clutches his arm, and he sees what she sees.

"Mr. Monroe," he says, almost automatically. "We're going to be making a hard turn and hopefully stopping. There is a woman on the runway."

The door to the cockpit, which would be locked and bolted if they were flying commercial, to prevent exactly what is about to happen, bangs open, and their sole passenger rushes into the space. All the color has drained from his cheeks: he looks like nothing so much as a wax figure of Santa Claus. "No," he says, somewhere between a moan and a shout. "No, the spring's not here. The season still holds!"

Pilot and copilot alike look at him like he's been dropped in from another story, something far more dangerous and dramatic than a routine flight. He barely notices them. All his attention is fixed on the woman on the runway.

Diana.

She looks exactly as she did on the day they ascended, dark of hair and dark of eye, wearing a white dress that once would have made her seem like a maiden of the spring, and now resembles nothing so much as a winding shroud. She isn't holding up her arms, isn't making any dramatic gesture of defiance or triumph: she's just standing there like the risen dead, silent as the grave, unmoving in the face of the plane that barrels down on her.

William has had centuries of his own way, unfettered by the woman who was meant to be his opposite and equal.

"Turn, damn you!" he howls. *"Turn!"*

He lunges for the stick, and the pilot, unsure of what to do in the face of a woman clearly committing suicide by airplane, is too slow to stop him. The plane, which is tiny by the standards of the great commercial jets, accelerates.

It's small compared to its brothers, but it's big enough to do the job. Diana dies without a sound, smeared across the tarmac.

William's heart stops beating at the same moment Diana's does, and both of them are gone.

Zib had more experience with wells than Avery did. Her father had been born on a farm, and his parents still owned the property. She spent every summer with them, running feral through the fields of corn and strawberries, getting twigs tangled in her hair and stealing warm eggs out from under broody hens. She felt around until her hands found the handle on the well's side, and then she began to crank, reeling in the rope and the bucket at its end.

When it finally came into view, it was sleek and silver, with not a hint of rust or tarnish, and filled with water so clear and perfect that Zib knew even without tasting it how sweet it would be. She reached for it with shaking hands, as the others walked up behind her.

"This is a wishing well," said Niamh, sounding pleased. "They're generally harmless, and not home to misplaced river hags or unspeakable curses."

"*They grant wishes?*" *asked Avery, as Zib pulled the bucket toward herself.*

"*No, not at all,*" *said Niamh.* "*What a queer notion, a well granting wishes! Might as well ask for grass to set the table, or clouds to control the weather. No, wishing wells are wells that have been wished for. They go where they're most needed. Or where they're brought. I suspect the improbable road went and fetched this one for us.*" *She gave the bricks at her feet a hard look.*

The improbable road twinkled in the sunlight, silent and smug . . .

—From *Along the Saltwise Sea*, by A. Deborah Baker

. . . the Doctrine of Ethos, although it has never before been embodied in material form, is an underpinning ideal of the universe. It guides thought, memory, even creation. And as such, it must be assumed to play by the rules governing other such embodiments, which our world throws up of its own accord when given the space and opportunity to do so. Consider, if you will, the near-universal tendency to embody ideas such as death, nature, and the seasons themselves into human form. No alchemist has summoned these guiding principles, no hand shaped the vessels which contain them, and yet they are contained, they are summoned into being by the need and necessity of the world itself.

It is my argument that the world needs the Doctrine of Ethos in order to function as the universe intends, but that the Doctrine is so diffuse and integrated that the universe has never figured out how to force it into physical form. As the oyster learns the art of pearl-making from the presence of the sand, we must begin to change the world if we wish the world to realize it needs to change *itself. In that change, the Doctrine will be born, and our ascension can finally, properly begin.*

—Address by Asphodel D. Baker to the American Alchemical Congress, 1901

BOOK II

The Beginning

Fall, leaves, fall; die, flowers, away;
Lengthen night and shorten day . . .

—Emily Brontë

Nobody who ever gave his best regretted it.

—George Halas

Gardener

Pamela Covington—"Jenny" to her friends, and "Corn Jenny" to her colleagues, not that she has many of the former—closes her apartment door with a sigh, digging for her keys with one hand and holding the strap of her purse in the other. She's been called to the hospital again, another round of flu shots delivered months after best efficacy, children with crayons up their noses, and teens who fell out of trees and sprained their wrists. It's a living, and one she still enjoys, even after doing it for the better part of a decade.

Her candidate is sleeping. If the oracles are right, her candidate may die sleeping. Unless that changes, this is all that she can do.

She's still searching for her keys in the voluminous pocket of her coat when someone slaps a cloth over her nose and mouth, the paint-thinner scent of chloroform filling her sinuses. She wobbles, immediately woozy, but she doesn't fall down. Her reserves are slightly deeper than the average person's, after all.

The young man behind her, who has a smooth, handsome face that she would recognize if she could see him, leans forward and murmurs, lips right next to her ear, "Hi, Pammy. Let's you and me head back inside."

The door isn't locked yet. It's easy enough for him to push it open and shove her inside.

Her apartment is sparse and simple. Most of her materialism has been burned away by the decades. She has a theory that the elderly tend to become hoarders because they're trying to externalize their memories as much as they reasonably can, tying important moments to objects and artifacts as they sense, in some indefinable way, that their minds are growing close to capacity. That will never happen to her, who can offload so much onto the winter, and she was taught to fear discovery, whether by superstitious neighbors or, worse, the local alchemists, with their endless greed and conviction that everything can be codified and controlled. So she pares down, strips away the extra, and keeps herself as tight and efficient as she can.

The hand remains locked over her mouth as her assailant pushes her toward the couch, not letting up, even when he pauses to close the door behind them. There's a surprising delicacy to the gesture, like he doesn't want to worry anyone who hears a slam. It could be fear of discovery, but Pamela can sense a certain gentleness to the way he's holding her. That might sound like a panicked mind making excuses: it probably isn't. She understands human nature, and she understands malice, and she isn't picking any up from him. He's doing what he thinks he has to do.

"There are two candidates in this city," he says, pushing her harder toward the couch as he shrugs his backpack off his shoulder and crouches to pull the biggest pocket open without taking the cloth from her mouth and nose. She still hasn't seen his face. "You know that. Nod if you know that."

Pamela, struggling to breathe, manages to nod. It's a very small motion. If he weren't standing so close, he probably wouldn't see it. But he does, and he sighs, relaxing slightly. She recognizes him now, the sound of his voice, the feel of his hands. She trained the boy, and this betrayal . . . it *burns*. Oh, how it burns.

"Yes," he says. "You understand." He reaches into his backpack, pulling the cloth away from her face as he removes a small, silenced handgun. "Our Lady of Flowers is awake, and she intends to end the farce her reign has become. The coronation is about to begin, and there are two candidates. One of them is yours, and one of them is mine. But I don't like my candidate, and I know you've never been able to find yours—you probably thought they'd died when they were a baby. They didn't. So I'm going to take yours away from you, and leave mine without a guide. Yours will win, if that's any consolation. With me as a guide, they'll win."

Pamela stares at him. She still can't breathe properly. She should be unconscious, but she's been here for too long; if it weren't still so close to winter, he would never have been able to catch her unawares. She would have known he was coming long before he got close enough to drug her. She should have felt the Lady wake, should have felt the coronation drawing near.

"Not . . ." she manages to croak. "How this . . . works. Assigned but up to . . . them."

"Maybe so," he says. "But my girl will have the odds on her side here. I'm sorry, I really am. I wouldn't do this if there were any other way."

Then he pulls the trigger. The gun speaks once, soft as rain and loud as thunder, and Pamela is done. She stops trying to breathe. She stops breathing at all. She's finished, and what comes next will not involve her.

After more than a hundred years, Pamela Covington is finally free.

The young man who killed her, Trevor Worth, looks at her body for a long and silent moment, staring at her as if he still expects her to do something. When she doesn't move, he drops the gun back into his bag, slides it over his shoulder, and walks away.

Things are going to begin happening very quickly, very soon.

He wants to be there when they do.

Football

CALENDAR SEASON: FEBRUARY 11TH, 2017:
WINTER, UNDER THE WORM MOON.

The full moon is fading from the sky, leaving only murmur and memory behind. It will return tomorrow night before slipping away for a month, returning transformed and redefined as the fish moon, or possibly the pink moon, depending on who's doing the defining. So many things operate that way. But here and now, it is a beautiful February morning, unseasonably warm, the day of the Valentine's Dance, and the world has never been brighter or more beautiful.

The football season is over, but the team still swarms the field in their practice gear, purple and yellow like the heralds of the coming spring. Their coach blows his whistle, shrill and high and bright as the last gasps of winter wind, and this scene has played out before, and this scene is perfect in every possible way. Melanie Cosgrove wouldn't change a single thing about it as she walks onto the field, pom-poms in hands and heart beating far too loudly in her chest.

She hates the sound of it, hates the fact that she can feel it shudder through her skeleton, a drumbeat clasped and kept within her ribcage. She's been under medical supervision since she was born, doctor after doctor coming to study the poor child with the dead mother and the impossibly broken heart. She missed the last game of the season, missed her chance to yell and jump and shake her pom-poms with the other girls. They sent her letters in the hospital, sent their apologies, told her how much they missed her, but none of them came to see her, fearing, as her peers have done since they were old enough to understand that she was somehow intrinsically fragile, that if they got too close, that fragility would transfer onto them, and they would be tainted by it.

It doesn't work that way. It has never, not once, worked that way, but they fear it all the same, and in fearing it, they fear *her*. So when she collapsed during the homecoming game, her friends watched the ambulance take her away, blue-lipped and gasping, and the student body gave her the homecoming crown in a ceremonial gesture that cost them nothing but gave her absolutely everything. She still has it on the nightstand next to her bed, the curve of its base circling the medications she takes every day to keep her traitorous heart beating. She hates them and she loves them and she supposes, sometimes, that she knows how it feels to be an addict, because she's well and truly addicted: she's addicted to staying alive, to the little pills, some hard-coated and some crumbling and bitter, that she slips between her lips four times a day to keep everything doing what comes naturally for most people.

But none of that matters here, or now, or today. Here and now, today, she's an ordinary girl, and she's here to cheer for her boyfriend, for the ordinary boy who's going to go to college in a few months and never look back at the girl he's left behind. But he loves her *now*, and Melanie has had seventeen years to learn the value of *now*, the importance of putting her focus on the moment she's living in. Especially when that moment comes with an absence of pain, comes with breathing easy and living in a body that remembers it's supposed to love her, not destroy her.

Although she supposes those things have always gone hand in hand. What loves you is the best positioned to hurt you, because you let it in. You invite it through the front door, you drop your shields and bare your throat and tell it to feed if it hungers, because you love it, because you want it to be happy.

She loves Harry. She wants him to be happy. She sometimes supposes she wants that more than she wants anything else; more than she wants her heart to miraculously heal, more than she wants her name to come up on the transplant list, more than she wants a future of her own. She wants him to be happy and healthy and have a good long life filled with wonderful things, and she can want all that and refuse to even consider the thought of him with another girl, or eventually with another woman, someone who can help him be happy when she's gone.

She'll be gone very soon now. She knows it like she knows the long bones of her legs, like she knows the burn that settles in her muscles after cheer practice, on the rare occasions when she's allowed to attend. She can feel it in the way her heart beats, even medicated past feeling anything. The doctors say she's doing well, that if she stays stable for another six months, she'll be out of the woods her most recent incident thrust her into, but she knows her body from the inside out, and she knows something they don't.

She knows they're wrong.

So she walks onto the field with her pom-poms, a purple-and-yellow checked scarf knotted in her hair like a conqueror's flag, and she ignores the way the other cheerleaders stare and mutter behind their hands, judging every inch of her. The cold February air is a welcome friend; it bites the exposed skin of her legs, nipping harmlessly at the creamy stretch between the tops of her thigh-high socks and the hem of her thigh-high skirt. Somehow, even though both garments officially end at the same point, there's at least four inches between them. A conspiracy, probably one set in motion by the same person who decided bouncing teenage girls in skimpy outfits were somehow integral to the sport of football. She loves cheerleading, loves the freedom and the spectacle and the iconic Americana of it all (and if that sounds a little overtly self-aware, well, she's been a girl with a heart condition living in football country for her entire life. She's watched a *lot* of movies, and her eye for media theory is better developed than most critics'. She's allowed to be a little overtly self-aware if it makes her happy). She even loves the other cheerleaders, casually cruel as so many of them are, vicious as they can be when cornered. They've always treated her as a combination pity project and deadly rival, the mysterious beauty who could drop dead at any moment, who's simultaneously the virginal bride on the beautiful burial mound and the heartless harpy here to drag all their boyfriends down to hell with her.

They've never had anything to worry about, not really. Parts of her story are horrifically novel, the sort of thing that would never make a good movie, not even one of those John Green tearjerkers about the kids with cancer who die beautifully and leave each other alone. But she's come to think that every life is allowed one flawless cliché, and this is hers: she met Harry when they were both in preschool, chubby little balls of sweater and snow pants, their arms starfished out by the tension of their down jackets. He was the boy next door, and she loved him before she fully understood that other people existed distinct from herself.

And wonderful truth, beautiful lie, he loved her almost as quickly, and absolutely as well. They've been inseparable since they were four, hand in hand, weathering illnesses and disagreements and their own inexorably growing senses of self, which haven't always meshed as well as they would have liked. She's pretty sure they didn't even *like* each other for a whole year when they were eleven, and it didn't matter, because they loved each other enough to make it through. They always have and they always will.

She's only ever told him one lie: Harry still thinks he's going to marry her, still thinks he's going to spend the rest of his life rolling over to find her sleeping next to him, black hair spilled across her pillow like ink, maybe drooling in her sleep, but his, and beautiful despite everything, *because* she's his. Because he loves her.

Because for him, that's always been enough.

She hasn't told him yet how hard it's getting to breathe in the mornings, or how often her pulse oximeter shows her with a blood oxygen level verging into the danger zone. She hasn't told him how she feels like she's winding down, like the beating of her heart, while still clinically stable, is coming to a close. Maybe the transplant list will save her.

She doesn't think so, though. It doesn't feel right, doesn't feel like part of the cliché. She's going to be his lost Lenore, and he's going to be happy without her, and that's okay, because it's inevitable.

One of the boys on the field barks a command she's too far away to hear, and they scatter, dressed in practice gear rather than their uniforms—even among the cheerleaders, whose uniforms are less cumbersome, more playful, she's the only person on this field in full uniform—but beautiful all the same, so beautiful it takes her breath away for a moment, because they will never be this young or this beautiful ever again.

Tonight, she's going to put on a dress the color of wine spilled on white linen, and let him tie the matching corsage around her wrist. Maybe it's another cliché, wearing red to a Valentine's Day dance, but some clichés are worth it. Some things become iconic for a reason. He's going to pick her up wearing a tuxedo he rented from the shop downtown, and they're going to dance until the gym closes, and he's going to kiss her in front of the balloon arch, and it's going to be perfect.

They don't have many perfect nights left. No force on Earth is going to take this one away from her.

So when she woke up this morning, she got out of bed, checked the group chat to confirm the girls were still planning to hit the field for their own impromptu practice, took her pills, and put on her uniform. She brushed her hair until it shone, falling down her back in a flawless black waterfall, a stroke of ink slashed across the lines of her uniform. She put on just enough makeup to look like she was among the living and not one of the walking dead, and she walked to the school to meet him on the field.

It's already going to be a perfect night. She's going to make sure it's a perfect day as well, the kind of day he'll always remember, the kind of day he can hold close as they're lowering her into the ground. (She'd prefer to be cremated. Her father hasn't been willing to budge. Her mother and her sister were both buried, and the family is going to be together when they're gone. If it kills him, they're going to be together.)

The boys have finished running their play. They're coming back together on the field, smug and sweaty, laughing as they clap each other on the back and settle into their positions. Some of them will be here next year, juniors looking forward to their moment of gridiron dominion, when they're at the top of the high school food chain and the world is theirs for the taking. Others will be gone, off to college and the hope of greener pastures, every one of them believing their glory days are not yet behind them.

Some of them will be wrong. Some of them have already peaked, such as it is, and will see nothing from here but the slow erosion of their dreams and the slow loss of their childhood loves. She doesn't want that for Harry. She wants him to have a clean break, to walk away and not look back. That's why, if her name doesn't come up soon, she doesn't intend to see the end of the summer.

Suicide is easy when you're a dead girl kept walking by pharmacists and prayer. All you have to do is forget a few pills and let nature do the rest. She won't be the reason he never gets away.

One of the boys on the field has seen her. Not Harry, but she's a distinctive figure, she knows: she's always been pale, but a year spent almost entirely in hospitals and in her bedroom, where natural light is rare and fleeting, has pulled almost all the color from her skin. She's a Snow White girl, and she owns it, because what choice does she have? Her lips are painted red as blood, her fingernails buffed and polished to match, and she wears her uniform like nothing else has ever been appropriate.

The boy elbows the boy next to him, who says something, not quite a shout, not loud enough for her to hear, but loud enough for Harry. He looks up, sunlight glinting golden off his hair, and he's young and strong and perfect in his practice gear, no one has ever been more beautiful, and his heart is strong, not like hers at all. He'll survive this.

Somewhere two thousand miles and more away, William Monroe is grabbing the controls of his private plane, ignoring the pilot he pays to see him safely from place to place, and maybe he could have avoided the collision if he hadn't done that; maybe he could have stood idly by while the pilot steered the plane to a stop without hitting the woman on the runway. Maybe he could have survived. But he doesn't do any of those things, and time is a road that runs only one way for most people: they cannot negotiate with the past the way some others can, the way a girl with numbers where her heartbeat ought to echo once did. It is later than it has ever been before in the life of the universe. The clock has started running again, and the future is here.

Harry raises his hand and waves, beaming, and that smile is all for Melanie, that smile is *hers,* that smile belongs to her in a way very little ever has. It is the smile of a boy in love who will be a man all too soon, and that thought fills her heart with light and love until it seems like it must burst.

And two thousand miles away, a plane slams into a woman standing on the runway, and her death is swift and terrible and several hundred years too late. She dies with a smile on her face, despite the pain, despite the horrific damage to her body. She's been ready to go for a long, long time.

Melanie Cosgrove isn't ready.

She's seventeen years old and still fresh as the summer sun. She may have come to terms with the idea that she doesn't have forever, but that doesn't mean she's consented to it, ever once agreed to it. Her plans to die before September comes have been less about resignation and more about needing to feel like she controlled *something* about her life, like she did *something* on her own. She didn't choose her heart condition or her dead mother or her stillborn twin, didn't choose her veil of tragedy, didn't even choose the boy she loved. She could choose the moment that she died.

This isn't the moment she chose.

But when William Monroe collapses in the cockpit of his private plane, her traitorous heart seizes in her chest. The pain is immense. The pain is like a wave, crashing down so hard and so fast that there's no time to evacuate the people standing on the shore. And like any wave that comes that quickly, when it pulls back, it pulls everything in its path out to sea. She is snuffed out like a candle. One moment she *is*, bright and beautiful and raising a hand to return her boyfriend's wave, and the next moment she *isn't,* just a sack of bones and tissue crumpling where she stands, collapsing to the cold, dew-damp grass.

She never hears the other cheerleaders shout, never sees them throw their own pom-poms and their water bottles aside as they run for her. (One of them, Christine, keeps her phone in her hand, and it's her footage that will be on the evening news tonight, her breathless narration that will define a semi-viral moment for people around the state and world.) She doesn't see Harry bolting for her, running faster than he's ever run before; doesn't see him clutch his own chest and collapse. She doesn't see anything.

Her eyes are still open, but she doesn't see anything, because she's not here anymore.

Melanie Cosgrove is gone.

BOOK III

The Lost Lenore

But the silence was unbroken, and the stillness gave no token,
And the only word there spoken was the whispered word,
"Lenore?"

—Edgar Allen Poe, "The Raven"

Small minds cannot grasp great ideas; to their narrow comprehension, their purblind vision, nothing seems really great and important but themselves.

—Sir James George Frazer, *The Golden Bough*

"You're in a bucket," said Zib, with careful delicacy.

"Yes, I had noticed," said Niamh. "I got into it on purpose. You can come into it, too, if you would like."

"I don't think it's big enough," said Zib.

"This is a wishing well," said Niamh, patiently. "The bucket is exactly as large as we need for it to be."

"Oh, then, I've never been in a bucket before," said Zib, and pulled herself up onto the well's edge before reaching for

Niamh. The drowned girl took her hands and tugged her gently forward, and Zib tumbled into the bucket, finding herself seated quite securely on the lip, with her bare feet against the cool wood of the bottom.

It was quite the most comfortable seat she'd had in hours, and so she turned a sunshine smile on Avery, and said, "Come on, Avery. We'll all fit in this bucket if we try, and it feels so nice."

Avery, who had noticed the Crow Girl's failure to return from the bottom of the well, and who had a slightly more developed sense of narrative structure than Zib did, having always been rather more interested in staying in his room to read, bit his lip and looked at the bucket. "If I get in the bucket, will the rope break and drop us all to the bottom of the well?"

"No," said Niamh. "I promise, the rope won't break." . . .

—From *Along the Saltwise Sea,* by A. Deborah Baker

Heartbeat

CALENDAR SEASON: FEBRUARY 11TH, 2017: WIN-
TER, UNDER THE WORM MOON.

Because Melanie dies so fast, she doesn't see the way the others abandon her body as soon as Harry hits the ground, and she wouldn't blame them if she did. She's been waiting for this moment her whole life, and while she would be furious to know the decision had been taken away from her—while she would be appalled and disbelieving if someone tried to tell her she was dead because a woman named Diana had finally managed to shrug off the alchemical chains keeping her in a state of enchanted sleep, crawl out of her grave, and orchestrate her own demise—she would be more horrified to know anyone had bothered with her when Harry needed them.

She's the one who's here to go, not him. He's here to be the hero of the story, the man with the tragically dead girlfriend in his past, not another body on the field.

But here and now, that's exactly what he is.

One of the other players, a junior named Trevor who'll probably be one of the starters next season (he came to practice late and distracted, which he's never done before), drops to his knees and presses his ear to Harry's chest. He took first aid and got his certification last summer, as part of working at the local pool. He took his job as a lifeguard very seriously, and that's why no one says anything as they watch him work, despite the fact that Trevor's dislike of Harry is well-established enough to be something of a joke around the school. He was one of the unlucky boys who trailed after Mel in middle school, punch-drunk on his crush for her, what adults called "puppy love" and laughed away, as if the feelings of children don't matter, as if they never have the heft to hurt. When Mel didn't even notice his clumsy attempts at courting her, leaving Harry to make his preexisting claim clear . . . well, that had been bad enough.

But when Trevor had tried to tell Melanie she was dating a caveman who treated her like something that could be owned, she had laughed at him and said Harry wasn't being overly possessive, just exactly as possessive as she was. He was only doing what she wanted him to do. Trevor has barely spoken to either one of them since then, never even looked at Melanie twice in the halls, was the only person not to sign any of her get-well-soon cards when she went to the hospital earlier this year.

He's also the only one here who knows CPR. So the crowd doesn't object to what he's doing, just stands by silently, halfway holding their own breath as they wait for him to say anything.

Finally, Trevor sits up and says, "He's alive. He has a heartbeat. Has anyone called 911?"

No one has. Everything happened too fast, and the only person holding a phone is Christine, who has been far too focused on her potential career as an independent news consultant to think about contacting the authorities.

"My phone's in my bag," says another of the cheerleaders, and they scatter, glad to finally have something to do.

No one bothers checking Melanie's pulse. There's no need. She fell with her eyes open, and she's still staring up into the clouded sky, unblinking, motionless in a way nothing alive can sustain. She's gone, and they *know* she's gone, they don't need the proof that comes from laying hands on a corpse and calling it rationality.

So when she blinks, no one sees. No one sees her take her first, shallow breath, chest barely rising. The pain is still with her, a vast and incomprehensible presence that seems large enough to blot out the entire world, but she's lived with pain before. She's been in pain almost from the moment she was born, almost from the first breath she took. This breath feels like that one, the two of them joined in an ineffable, undefinable way that nonetheless defines absolutely everything. If she could understand the connection between them, she would understand absolutely everything. It feels like being born again.

Despite the pain that blankets the world, for the first time she can remember, the first time (ever) in years, her chest doesn't hurt. She's used to living life intimately aware of her own heartbeat, listening for any fluctuation with the focused intensity of a guard on permanent watch, but right now, she can't hear anything. All that comes from the cage beneath her ribs is silence. Her bones don't shake with mistimed beats. She feels . . . fine.

Melanie blinks at the sky, taking slow stock of herself. The pain is everywhere and all-consuming, but after that initial wave, no worse than what she's been living with for her entire life. She can push it aside and ignore it. She's on the ground, that much is obvious: the grass beneath her is wet and cold, and the dew is soaking into the polyester fabric of her uniform, making it stick to her skin. She can tell she's cold, but it doesn't bother her in the slightest: she doesn't shiver or try to roll away from it.

That's not as unusual as it might seem. She's always had a remarkable tolerance for cold, pronounced enough that her father used to find her outside in the snow in her bare feet, catching snowflakes in her hands and studying them intently. They never melted when she was a child. She remembers that vividly. They didn't start melting until she reached puberty, and her heart broke a little that winter, when she realized the snow melted when it touched her skin. She'd heard about unicorns only coming for virgins (patriarchal bullshit, as if a horse that was also a phallic symbol would give a damn about virginity), but she'd never heard about snow refusing to melt for girls who had yet to grow their first pubic hair.

Absence of a heartbeat: strange. Absence of frostbite: pleasant and not all that unusual. If she were just a little younger, or if her hair were any color other than absolute black, the other children would probably have called her "Elsa" instead of "Snow White" when they were still innocently cruel enough to taunt the girl with the fatal heart condition. Absence of Harry: unthinkable.

He should have been there the second her vision cleared, kneeling over her, trying to shake her awake. It's happened before when she collapsed in his presence, and while she hates to worry him, there's also something sweetly reassuring about knowing he'll be there when she wakes up. Slowly, she pushes herself up onto her elbows, blinking at the crowd of people, football players and cheerleaders alike, that's formed around something on the ground a few yards away.

Christine turns toward the movement as Melanie rises, phone still out and recording in her hand, and screams.

The sound is an ice pick driven through the heart of the world. Melanie hears a story in the sound, a tale of shock and collapse and impossible inevitability. She scrambles to her feet, heels skidding in the mud, and her body answers easily, leaving what feels like the bulk of the pain behind her on the ground. By the time she's standing, only her head and her rump hurt, and since both those probably hit hard when she fell, it makes sense. She's still feeling the impact. She's not hurting from anything else.

"Harry?" she demands. Christine, still screaming, doesn't answer. Melanie tries again, louder, almost in a shout, "*Harry*?!"

The crowd begins to part, leaving her with a clear line of sight to the boy on the ground. He isn't moving. Her heart, her traitorous heart, doesn't leap in her chest or skip a beat—it is, for once, following the rules everyone else seems to live by and simply beating calmly away, so distant and ordinary that she can't even feel it—but it feels like it's breaking all the same, because she doesn't have to see his face.

She knows him. Knows every inch of him, every line and every angle, knows it with an artist's eye, with the eye of the little girl who could stare for hours at snowflakes when she wanted to truly understand them. "Harry!" she gasps, and bolts for him, moving faster and more easily than she has in months, since the last time she came home from the hospital, since her doctor stopped looking her in the eye when he answered her carefully worded questions.

The crowd makes space for her. She's not sure she would have been able to forgive them if they hadn't, if she'd been forced to lay hands on a single one of them. She scrambles her way to Harry's side and hits the grass on hands and knees. He's still. He's so *still*, and this isn't him, this isn't her Harry, he's not the still one, he's never, ever been the still one. He moves because motion is his natural state of being, as natural to him as stillness sometimes seems to her. But he's not asleep, he's not breathing, he's not *here*.

The understanding of what that means hits her like a physical blow, like a thing she's been braced for all her life, and it hurts, it hurts, it *hurts*. Hurts like the wave that slammed down on her before, hurts like the first time she felt her heart stop beating.

"Don't you *dare*," she hisses, between teeth bared like a beast's, lips drawn back in the rictus of a snarl. "Don't you *dare*, Harald March, this isn't what we agreed to. This isn't what you signed up for."

She's supposed to go first. That was the deal. And yes, she knows, in a distant, abstract way that she technically did; knows she was dead when she hit the ground before, knows there's something wrong with the echoing silence where her heart is supposed to pound. But none of that matters now. What matters is Harry, silent and broken in front of her, and what matters is that this isn't what he promised her. She's never supposed to see his funeral. Never ever ever. And maybe that's selfish and maybe it's not, but it's one of the only things she's ever been promised in her life, and she wants it, wants it like a flower wants the sun.

"You can't go without me," she says, and slams her lips down on his. A few of the other cheerleaders gasp and mutter to each other about how she's *kissing* a *dead kid*, Melanie Cosgrove is *kissing* a *corpse*, and it doesn't matter that it's her boyfriend, or that he's still warm, or that Trevor says he has a heartbeat: this is too deliciously disgusting to ignore.

This is where Christine's video ends, in a flash of dazzlingly bright light, so white it hurts to look at, sudden and sourceless, overwhelming the camera and burning out the lens. One moment Melanie is kneeling over Harry's motionless form, and the next, everything is brilliant white, and everything is gone.

(When the news runs Christine's tape, they'll claim the battery died, cutting off the video before the paramedics could arrive. No one will contradict them. There's nothing they could say that would be believed.)

On the field, in the moment, under the bitter February sky, this is what they see:

Melanie kneels over Harry, fingers digging into the grass to either side of his head, kissing him like she thinks someone is going to take him away. The two of them making out is not an unusual sight around the school, hasn't been since ninth grade, but the sight of her kissing him without his arms around her is strange enough to be worth staring at. Maybe that's why he lifts his arms and wraps them around her torso even before he begins kissing her in kind, the two of them locked together in an embrace that will not end.

When he pulls away, it's only to stare at her, eyes wide and wounded, and say, "You fell down."

"So did you."

"I thought you were dead." What he doesn't say—what he doesn't need to say—is that he's had as long as she has to get used to the idea that he's going to outlive her, that barring a miracle or a cliché from one of the teen romances he likes so much more than she does, the ones she carries in her purse for him to read when they're alone and he won't be laughed at for it, he's going to see her dead and buried and be expected to keep going, alone in a world that no longer has a Melanie in it.

(She knows all that. What she doesn't know is that he had his tissue typing done years ago to see if they were a match, if he could be the donor she tries so hard not to hope for and won't admit she needs. He isn't a match. He can't save her. If he could save her, he would have done it already, would have found some means of suicide that let him give her his heart and keep her in the world where she belongs, even if they can never stay in the world together.)

Melanie looks at him with grief and resignation, and the air between them is heavy with the things they both know but never say. He knows she's planning to die this summer if the miracle doesn't come; that she doesn't intend for him to go off to college shackled to the dying girl back home. He knows she thinks she has to break his heart to keep her heart from destroying them both. He knows she's wrong, and he knows she doesn't know that, and so he doesn't say anything, because he can't stop her.

He'd give anything to stop her.

"You can't go," he says, and this time when he pulls her close, he sits up at the same time, crushing her against him, holding on so tight he can feel her ribs shift under his grasp. He'll hurt her if he keeps holding on this tight, and yet he can't stop himself. "You *can't*," he repeats, voice muffled by the side of her neck, by her hair, by the smell of her skin and the minty bodywash she uses.

"I'm right here," she says, and pats his back.

The blare of sirens tells them all the authorities are on their way: that Trevor managed to get someone to break out of their fugue long enough to dial 911 and summon the paramedics. Melanie's head snaps up, hearing the entire future in that sound, and she pushes away from Harry and up to her feet in the same gesture, so fast that for a moment he's left embracing the air.

"I can't be here anymore," she says hurriedly, not seeming to catch the irony of saying this right on the heels of her previous statement.

"The paramedics will make sure you're all right," says Harry, pushing himself more slowly to his own feet.

Melanie isn't all right. She knows she isn't all right, because she still can't feel her heart beating, can't feel the pains that have attended her every waking moment for years. And somehow, none of that matters as much as . . . "My father said I couldn't come to practice. If they call him—and they *will* call him, even after they check me out clean—he'll make me stay home. I'll miss the dance. I can't *be* here."

In the moment, despite everything, a high school dance is all she can think of, all the future she can see. No one stops her, not even Harry, as she whirls and runs away across the field—*runs,* really runs, the way she used to run when they were children, when "congenital heart defects" were just words adults liked to say and not real things that would ever have any impact on their lives. Harry hasn't seen her run that way in years.

He stares after her but he doesn't call her back, because he wants to go to the dance with her as badly as she wants to go to the dance with him, and they're both seventeen and not entirely clear on the concept of long-term consequences. They've been living their lives from heartbeat to heartbeat for as long as either of them can remember, and if they didn't know how to live in the moment, they wouldn't be living at all.

Then the paramedics are reaching them, and the other football players are pushing Harry forward, demanding he be examined, and he doesn't have time to watch his girlfriend go. He just has to hope her father doesn't find out.

(Her father *will* find out, of course, *will* be informed of what happened, by the evening news if nothing else. But that won't happen until it's too late for him to interfere with what has to happen next. His part in things comes later, when they understand more of what's going on. For all that he did a lot before the story started, he doesn't have the biggest part to play now that it's happening.)

Melanie runs under the gray February sky, the clouds concealing the fading rays of the worm moon, although she doesn't know its name, has not yet had cause to learn all the different words for the ways time can be marked and mapped, the different ways the seasons turn. The ground beneath her feet is softer than February ground is meant to be, already thawing, already preparing for the coming spring, and her heels dig down to mud again and again, squelching and sucking and almost getting stuck. But her legs have always been strong, even when her heart hasn't been; even when she's been reduced to sitting at her desk and doing physical therapy to keep her muscle tone from wasting away. She pulls herself free again and again, and she *runs*.

And at some point, it turns from running for the sake of getting away into running for the sake of running, for the feel of her legs obeying her commands and the wind blowing in her face, the ground beneath her feet and the sky overhead. Nothing hurts. Nothing hurts at all. She can't feel her heartbeat, but after a lifetime of pain, she doesn't miss it. She doesn't *want* it. She just wants to run.

So she runs.

She runs, and the school drops away behind her; she runs, and the paramedics are checking Harry over, declaring him a little warm, but that makes sense for a football player who's been exerting himself, nothing to be concerned about, not hot enough to qualify as a fever, no, no, nothing wrong here; she runs, and no one mentions that she was there, no one points out the extra pair of pom-poms or the spot where her falling body crushed the grass, no one gives her away; Christine has already posted the footage, will find the query from the local news the next time she checks her messages, but that's not *telling*, no, no, that's not being a *snitch*, that's just seeing the chance to go a little viral and grabbing it with both hands, like any sensible child of the social media age. Melanie won't mind. Melanie never minds anything, as long as it doesn't upset Harry. She runs, and there's her street, and there's her house, and there's her father's car in the driveway, and that's when she finally slows down.

It's not that Roland Cosgrove is a bad man, or a cruel man, or even a particularly strict father. It's that he's a man who lost the love of his life to a difficult pregnancy that ended with one of his daughters dead and the other living under a death sentence as her heart winds down like a piece of glass clockwork, unable to sustain life without the aid of an entire team of medical professionals. His life, for the past seventeen years, has been almost entirely bent to the task of keeping Melanie alive; it's clear he has no idea what he's going to do without her. Melanie regrets that she won't be able to see Harry grow into the man she knows he's destined to become. She rejoices that she won't have to see her father fall apart. Death will spare her from witnessing both of them.

Everything she's ever done with her life has been against her father's wishes, from kissing Harry to joining the cheer team—a sad list of accomplishments, but she is, after all, only seventeen; her peers aren't that far ahead of her, no matter how she feels when she looks at their Instagram feeds, packed with selfies and vacation shots and adventures she can only dream of. He just wants to protect her. He just wants to keep her safe, for as long as he can, because she doesn't have much time.

She's never had much time. When they placed her in his arms at the hospital, almost six weeks old and finally stable enough for him to hold, he had already been to speak with the doctor, two specialists, and the hospital counselor; he knew she wasn't expected to reach her first birthday, much less her fifth. Much less her seventeenth. But he's taken care of her, watched over her, kept her safe, kept her *here*. His little girl is a miracle of medical science working hand in hand with alchemy, and if she can't appreciate that, he'll just have to appreciate it enough for both of them, until the day she understands what he's done for her. What he's sacrificed, what he's paid for the sake of her peaceful, protected life.

Melanie moves carefully and quietly as she slips into her own yard, skirting the outline of the house, avoiding the windows looking in on the rooms where her father is most likely to be whiling his day away, heading for the perfect cliché that is the oak tree outside her bedroom window. Family legend says her mother loved that tree, which is why her father never cut it down. She's been climbing up and down its loving branches since she was six and old enough to slip away from sight for the precious minutes it took her to defy gravity. Her proprioception was built half on bouncing on her bed and half on swinging from the old oak, and she loves it like the babysitter she always wanted.

Her father has only seriously threatened to cut it down once, the year she was seven, after Harry used it to sneak into her room while she was home sick from school and scared himself into thinking she was dead. She begged him not to, begged and cried until he agreed that the tree could stay as long as neither of them went climbing anymore, and since she's pretty sure Harry's afraid of the tree after that incident, it wasn't hard for her to cross her fingers and agree. She still climbs it constantly. Harry has never climbed it again.

Hoisting herself onto the lowest branch, she pauses and waits for the warning twinge from her hapless heart. It never comes. There is still no pain, still no feeling of having something frantic trapped inside her chest.

Still no heartbeat, and she'll worry about that later, when it turns into a problem. Right here, right now, it's still a relief.

Silent as the grave, Melanie climbs upward, toward her bedroom window on the second floor, toward the peace that waits for her there.

Toward home.

M elanie has never been downstairs in her father's study when she was also going out of or coming in through her bedroom window. Try as he might, Roland has never been able to fully invert causality in his own home, and if he had, inviting his daughter to come and experience the proof that he always knows where she is would have been at the bottom of his list of good ideas. So she doesn't know, because he's never told her, that when she uses the window in either direction, one of the boards in her floor bends, ever so slightly, underfoot. It makes no sound in her room, cushioned as it is by carpet and muffled by the sole of her shoe. But *downstairs,* oh downstairs, the creak is plainly audible.

Roland looks up, phone pressed to his ear, and frowns at the evidence of his daughter's return. He knows she snuck out to attend Harry's football practice; she's not as subtle as she thinks she is. She's seventeen, and not being as subtle as she thinks she is is essentially a survival adaptation. He also knows, from the schedule pinned to the fridge, that practice won't be over for another two hours. She shouldn't be home yet.

If the boy had finally gathered up the spine and sense to break up with her before she could break up with him by putting herself into the ground, she'd be crying: he knows his daughter well enough to be certain of that much. She would have come in through the front door, sobbing like she thought she could expel her sorrow if she just tried hard enough, so the fact that she's sneaking it with what she believes to be silence means she hasn't been hurt that deeply.

So why is she so early? It is a mystery not of his own making, and he doesn't care for those: especially not today, when he has just received the second most distressing phone call of the last year. William Monroe, the Winter King, the man who has kept the crown safe and prevented it from passing for three hundred years, is dead. His counterpart somehow managed to wake from the slumber she had been forced into, and walked onto the runway where his plane for Minneapolis had been beginning its taxi. She died on impact. He died an instant after, unable to form a swift-enough connection to any of the available Summer candidates.

That's the trouble with the natural ones. They require a specific key to unlock them, a second side to their coin. The artificials will be better, more flexible, more equipped to bond in multiple directions. The naturals almost never manage to re-bond if their counterpart is lost, and so they go down as well, ships lost at sea.

William Monroe was a bottom feeder of a man, a coward who spent more time fleeing from his own death than he did living the life he fought so hard to preserve. But he was useful, and he was *known*. If the crown is in play again, Roland can't control where it goes.

He can't control whether Melanie is in the running. She is his daughter and his darling and his greatest failed experiment, because there's no way her body can take the strain of carrying the crown. He's tried, for the last several years, to undo some of the damage he originally did, tried to bring her back to what she should have been in the beginning, and this is the only way to know if he succeeded.

She's here. In her room, where she belongs, not bursting into his office and throwing herself into his arms as she tries to make sense of what's happening to her, so maybe nothing is happening to her. Maybe he did worse work in the beginning than he thought he did, or better work now, and she gets to be an ordinary dying girl.

He doomed her once. Maybe he saved her too.

It's a strange thing for a father to hope for. It has to be enough.

On the other end of the phone, a voice asks if he's still there. He forces himself to focus, responding, "Yes, yes, I'm still here."

"Good. The timing of this couldn't be worse. What we know is that Mr. Monroe was leaving the country because he didn't feel we could protect him with the Alchemical Congress decimated. He could have chosen to help us rebuild, and instead he ran."

"We've always known he was a coward."

"You mean we've always known that Reed said he was a coward. Well, Reed is gone, and he's not coming back."

Roland nods. "That's true enough. He's gone."

He went to the site of Reed's research facility in the fall, when the hunter's moon was in the sky, and sifted the ashes for himself. All Reed's work, destroyed. Reed himself, destroyed, and that mannikin monster he called a right-hand woman along with him. America will be stronger for the loss of those two beasts, but first they'll have to recover and rebuild, and they did *not* need this right now.

"I'm sorry. This was above my pay grade eight months ago."

"It's all right. We're all getting used to the new status quo." A status quo that includes two of the most powerful embodiments the world has ever known, both artificial and both ungrateful toward the people who made them possible, somewhere out there in the wilds, doing whatever pleases them.

Attempts have been made to find the incarnate Doctrine, something which shouldn't be difficult, given what little information Reed shared with the rest of them: they know the language side of the equation is likely to be somewhat reserved, resigned to their place in the cosmos, while the math side will be flashy and loud and unable to resist drawing attention. Combined with the power they wield when together, they should be a beacon shining on the horizon, leading their pursuers to the Impossible City.

Instead, there has been nothing. For months, nothing. Reed is gone, his lab destroyed, his research burnt, and the Doctrine is unleashed upon the world, uncontrolled and uncontained.

This is not a good time for a passing of the crowns that have been stable for three hundred years, even if the moment of their passing will unlock another path, however briefly, into the Impossible City.

The stability of those crowns was the only reason he agreed to be a part of this project, a project that has already cost him his wife and youngest daughter, that has been costing him his eldest one heartbeat at a time for seventeen years. If the crowns weren't stable, he would never have put her into harm's way.

(He can tell himself that as much as he wants to. He's still an alchemist, still a student of the American Congress, which prizes accomplishment at all costs, and would have thought him infinitely less if he hadn't been prepared to sacrifice what he claimed to love in the name of progress. Knowledge was the light, and the light would guide them to a glorious new age of logic and plenty. Maybe not Reed's Impossible City, but something even better. He would have done this even if the crown had been a normal harvest away from changing hands.)

"With Monroe dead, you need to be on your guard. There's every chance Melanie won't be in the running, and if she's not, you're to continue as you have been: the experiment in process matters more than a change to the situation. But if she's under consideration at all, if Aven wakes . . ."

"It's February," he says. "I know it's warm, but the month still stands, and the moon still shines."

"And we're still tidal creatures all."

"Yes. It will be a Jack Frost that comes for her, if anyone does."

Of the natural manifestations, the interstitials have always been the hardest to prove. The Congress knows they exist, because the literature is there, and because Monroe is so damned fond of exiling the ones that displease him, but they are so shallowly tied to their living seasons that they might as well be ordinary people with a little extra tolerance for hot or cold. The Congress has taken several of them apart, and learned nothing useful of the art of seeing them coming. Despite their ordinary natures, they are remarkably difficult to contain.

Roland doesn't know how to contain them, but he knows how to kill them. They've been coming for Melanie for the last ten years, one a year, like clockwork. And he's been doing what any good father would do, and destroying them before they can get to her. Her medication doesn't just keep her heart in tempo. It keeps her distinct from the season that seeks to steal her from him, the one he connected her to in the first place, and the Winter has been getting desperate. He still hasn't rebuilt his defenses after the last one to make the attempt.

If a Jack Frost comes for Melanie tonight, he'll have no way to stop it.

It's an alarming thought, but he can hear her moving in her bedroom above him; whatever brought her home early, it can't have been that bad, and there's no way both she and Harry could be candidates without their noticing something wrong. The crowns haven't passed in centuries, but there are older accounts, and Roland knows something of the shape of this. Melanie would feel it instinctively if she were under consideration, and she knows so little about what she is, what she has been crafted to be, that she'd come to him if she felt like anything was wrong.

Roland Cosgrove doesn't consider himself a bad man, just a scientist who has done a few questionable things—even now his mind shies away from the word "unforgivable"—in the pursuit of knowledge. He has always done his best to be a good father to the girl he made. But he doesn't understand what it is to be a seventeen-year-old girl kept under lock and key and suffering from a medical condition that will kill her before she sees adulthood.

The thought that she might keep things from him has somehow

never occurred to him, even though she's been going in and out of her bedroom window for years to avoid interrogation. He, like all men in positions of power, is intentionally unaware of his own biases, and will not see that he has created a culture of secrecy in which telling him that she suffers will only bring more suffering.

"If they come for her, I'll know," he says, with calm and absolute assurance, and only the fact that he has no idea how wrong he is keeps the lie from his voice.

Upstairs, silence falls as Melanie climbs onto her bed and stops moving around for the moment. Roland sighs and turns his attention fully back to the phone call. The crown is passed, but not to her. Never to her.

She was never really in the running.

Secrets and Stories

Melanie climbs into her bed, a ridiculous canopied confection of pink velvet and billowing lace that she outgrew years ago but hasn't been allowed to replace. The heavy maple posts conceal and support the hooks and attachment points for her IVs and monitors, which she has required more often than she likes to consider; she sleeps here almost as safely as she does in the hospital. Her father has poured thousands of dollars into having this bed rebuilt and retrofitted, equipped with a mattress that can be raised and lowered without compromising the frame, turned into the perfect place for his precious angel to die. She can't imagine how much engineering innovation went into her bed. She doesn't want to.

She hates it almost as much as she hates the pill bottles on her nightstand (safely contained within the circle of the homecoming tiara), waiting for the time when they'll be needed, whether it be an emergency or the predictable beeping of her phone alarm. She groans and flops backward, head hitting the pillow with the familiar feel of memory foam compressing, everything calibrated for her comfort, her confinement. This bed has been her coffin for years, and she's been buried alive over and over again.

Her legs ache pleasantly with the memory of motion, reminding her that her flight from the field really happened. It wasn't a particularly lovely dream. She *ran* today, really *ran*, and she isn't short of breath or light-headed at all. For a little while, she got to feel normal, and while she knows she shouldn't push herself, there's nothing she wants to do more.

Not pushing herself has swallowed most of her teens, a great and baleful beast whose belly is never full, that takes and takes and takes everything it can wrap its coils around. First it took her freedom of movement, locking her away from the world with more and more regularity. Then it took her art, making it harder and harder for her to sit up long enough to paint, much less carry her supplies anywhere farther away than her desk. It's tried to take Harry, but Harry fights back, and as long as he has the strength to fight, she supposes he'll be able to hold on.

That's good. If not pushing herself took everything, she's not sure she'd survive.

She wants to run around the room, wants to jump back out of this bed and run laps around the house before her heartbeat returns to drag her down, to jump and somersault and cheer and cheer and cheer. She doesn't do any of those things. Instead, she closes her eyes and breathes in the memory of running, of Harry waking up when she thought she'd somehow lost him, of *living,* at least for a little while, the way she wants to live. The way she would live, if her heart allowed it.

She has several hours and two alarms before she needs to get ready for the dance, step into her dress and paint her face to look like she's actually alive. She has time to think about what happened today, to decide how she wants to feel about it, what, if anything, she wants to do.

She doesn't notice when sleep looms up and takes her, pulling her down into the darkness behind her own eyelids. She only dreams.

To a normal girl, Melanie's dreams might seem boring, mundane, limited. She dreams of walking through a frozen wood, stepping so lightly atop the ice-crusted snow that the ice never cracks. Her feet skate along the surface, leaving it unblemished behind her. She walks, and the wood spreads its branches wide to meet her, and the cold doesn't touch her, and her chest doesn't hurt. She has never wanted anything more.

She has dreamt this wood over and over again, not every night, but most nights, for most of her life. It is as familiar as any part of her waking world, and as welcome. It isn't warm, but neither is she, and the cold doesn't reach her here, not even to the pale degree it does in the waking world. It may seem odd to dream of walking barefoot through the snow and not feeling the cold like it's the best thing imaginable, but it's life as she knows it, and some things aren't worth questioning. Some things never have been.

She's never been out of the country or seen the ocean, never climbed a mountain or spent more than a week's worth of nights away from home that weren't in the hospital. She has the wood in her dreams, and the bed in her waking world, and that's all.

She walks through the wood, snow underfoot and black trees all around her, and it's the landscape she was made for, the place where she fits in perfectly, perfectly designed to be part of this world. It's welcoming and, in its own way, to her, warm. She can smell flowers on the breeze.

So she keeps walking, following the scent of blooming jonquils and sun-warmed grass, until she comes to the end of the wood. Where the trees end, winter ends too. There is no snow past the shade of the branches, no ice past what surrounds her. Instead, there is a wide and sun-bathed clearing, blanketed with grass and tiny, blooming flowers. On the other side is another wood, this one lush and green and ripe with summer fruits.

And there, at the center of the clearing, is Harry. She stops for a moment in her dream, looking at him with an open longing that she rarely allows herself in the waking world.

He's not the prettiest boy in school, not the one who steals people's breath away or makes them think he should be on television, but he's *hers*, and that makes him better than all the movie stars and all the influencers in the world. He's naturally tan, a color that only deepens over the summer, when he's outside more often than in unless he's sitting with her in the approved safety of her bedroom. She may be the only girl in school whose father insists she stay *in* her room with a boy, rather than forbidding her to have one up there alone.

Environment and genetics have conspired to keep his hair golden long past the point when most of the boys in their grade have gone brown, and she's always liked that, the contrast they make when they go out together, the balance of it all. His eyes are as blue as hers, but the shade is altogether different: while her eyes are almost exactly the color of a glacial surface, so bright and pale that her father was concerned about her vision when she was younger, his are the deep and beautiful blue of the summer sky.

Harry's eyes are part of what got her into painting. When they were in elementary school, they had a teacher who tried to tell them sky blue was a bright and sunny color with no real depth to it, and Melanie had already spent enough time matching Harry's eyes to the sky to be distantly offended, in that way that is really only accessible to small children hearing something patently untrue from the adults around them. She requested and received her first watercolor set that same year, and began trying to capture the colors of the world as they were, and not as people wanted her to see them.

Even in her dreams, Harry is wearing the casual clothes he wears to practice, sweatpants and T-shirt and no real thought to how they go together. She has no idea what he's going to wear tonight.

"Harry!" she calls, and steps out of the trees, moving toward him . . . or tries to. The sunlight burns where it touches her, searing her skin like acid that leaves no mark behind, and she knows at once that the clearing is forbidden: the summer is not for her, is for the sun-kissed boys like Harry, for the golden girls like Chloe from the cheer squad, who has been far less than subtle about her intent to "comfort" him if something happens to Melanie before graduation.

She shrinks back, recoils, withdraws into the shadow of the wood. Too late: he's heard her and he sees her where she stands among the trees. Breaking into a wide grin, he jogs in her direction, and she wants to shout, to scream, to tell him not to come any closer. If the summer is closed to her, the winter is closed to him.

When he crosses the threshold, he collapses, and when she goes to him, he isn't breathing, and he won't wake up. He won't wake up.

Melanie wakes to the sound of her phone alarm singing a jaunty tune, and her own voice, sobbing.

Jack Frost

CALENDAR SEASON: FEBRUARY 11TH, 2017: WINTER, UNDER THE WORM MOON.

T he window is open.

That's wrong: Melanie *always* remembers to close the window when she gets home, lest it attract her father's attention and he looks closely enough to find the signs of her coming and going in scrapes on the windowsill. They don't live in a crime drama, and he's not an investigator, but she saw it once on an episode of *Law & Order* and hasn't been able to shake the fear ever since.

She sits up, intending to close the window, and realizes something else is wrong, something bigger and more fundamental than an unclosed entrance: maybe the reason the entrance was left unclosed, when she has always been so utterly, exquisitely careful to erase all signs that anything has happened. She's not alone.

Someone else is in her room.

Someone is sitting at her desk, flipping through one of her sketchbooks, and for a moment the offense of someone touching something so personal, so *private,* is a greater shock than the violation of having someone in her space to begin with. Only for a moment—only long enough for her to sit up and stare, and realize she still can't hear her heartbeat, still can't feel it trying to escape her body. Something's wrong. She knows something's wrong, knows she should tell her father immediately, but also knows she wouldn't be alive if her heart really weren't beating, so maybe this is normal. Maybe this is natural, and her body is giving her a much-deserved break.

Maybe.

The person at her desk looks up and smiles, teeth a white slash against the dimness of the room. That one expression puts the whole person better into focus, reveals details she wasn't catching before in the sheer shock of their presence: it's a child, maybe eleven, maybe twelve, dressed in bright yellow corduroy pants and a blue shirt covered in sparkling silver snowflakes. They have dark, curly hair, gathered into tight ponytails on either side of their head, and freckles covering what seems like every visible inch of their skin.

"I'm a girl, if that's what you're wondering," says the child, tone casually matter-of-fact. "That's what most people wonder when they meet me. The ones who try not to assume, anyway."

"I was actually wondering what you were doing in my bedroom, and how you got in here, and why you were touching my sketch-book, in roughly that order," says Melanie.

"It looked interesting and like the only thing in this room that hadn't been vomited up by the Disney Princess Collection, I got in here the same way I assume you usually do, Miss 'I have a big oak tree outside my window with suspiciously smooth patches worn into the bark,' and I'm here because I was the closest one when we realized what was happening," says the girl. She smiles again, white teeth in the darkness. "We need to have a talk."

"You need to be somewhere that isn't my bedroom," Melanie counters, sliding out of the bed and standing. She fell asleep fully clothed, walked through the forest in the dress she only wears in dreams, and she's prepared for this.

What she isn't prepared for is the wave of dizziness that sweeps over her, nearly knocking her off her feet. It isn't accompanied by a stutter in her heartbeat or any other feeling she can easily recognize; it's just dizziness, shaking the world to its foundations. She catches the bedpost, holding herself up until the wave recedes and she can stand on her own again.

When she looks to the girl, she finds her watching with sympathy in her eyes. She isn't smiling anymore. "That's just going to get worse," she says. "Means someone else is making progress. Maybe one of the others got around to their explanation faster than I did. I'm sorry. I just didn't want to wake you up."

Melanie frowns. "What do you mean, it's going to get worse? Progress toward what? And *why* are you in my *room*?"

"I'm in your room because everyone with a season's worth of sense knows who your father is, and there was no way he was letting me through the front door," says the girl. "I've had my ascension less than a year. I'm not ready to give it up yet. And I *had* to talk to you, because you have no idea about anything, and leaving you unprepared isn't right or fair."

Melanie doesn't think she's ever been this confused in her life. "Unprepared for what?"

"For everything."

The girl sighs and closes Melanie's sketchbook, placing it carefully on the desk before resting her hands on her knees and focusing on Melanie herself. "My name is Jack," she says. "It wasn't always, but it is now, and it's the only name that matters for me. I am the spirit of Winter Ascendant, which means I belong with you. I'm part of your household . . . if you win. If you make the most progress, the most quickly."

It's no relief for Melanie to realize she was wrong, because she's even more confused now than she was a moment ago. She's confused enough that it's giving her a headache, and with the thought of pain, she realizes she's committed one of the cardinal sins of her short existence: she's ignored her phone alarm.

"Wait!" says the girl, says Jack, as Melanie reaches for her pills. She sounds genuinely alarmed, like Melanie is making some terrible mistake. "Wait, okay?"

Melanie pauses. "Why? I need my medication or my heart stops beating, and I'm supposed to be meeting my boyfriend at the school for the Valentine's Day dance. Sorry, weird kid who broke into my room, but Harry is more important to me than whatever ridiculous thing you're here to say."

"Your heart can't stop beating, because it already did," says Jack. "You've been dead for hours, and you're still moving around."

Melanie stares at her. "Okay, cool, so I'm still asleep."

"No, this is really happening. You're as awake as I am."

"First up, not sure you exist, so make a note of that. Second, you're saying I *died*—I'm guessing when I collapsed on the football field? That seems like it would be the most logical time—and I'm still up and walking around, which would make me some sort of zombie. So shouldn't you be running before I get it in my head to eat you or something?"

"You're not a zombie," says Jack. "Zombies don't exist. You're the Winter Incarnate, or you have the potential to be, anyway, if you progress faster than the competition does. I'm rooting for you, if that means anything. Most of the other candidates aren't very nice."

Melanie blinks. "I thought you said *you* were the Winter whatsit."

"*I'm* the Winter Ascendant. *You're* the Winter Incarnate. They aren't the same thing at all, and I'm sorry, I should have told you all this as soon as I came to serve the crown, but I got the post because the last Jack in this region tried to get past the threshold, and your father made him go away. He's made a whole bunch of us go away over the past decade or so, and we don't always have time to tell each other what's going on. This is supposed to be a job you can do for a century, but my predecessor had less than six months. Do you remember him at all?"

Melanie frowns and shakes her head. If she can't break out of this dream, she may as well play along. "I don't know anyone named 'Jack,' I'm sorry," she says. But that's not true, is it?

There was the teacher's aide in her seventh-grade classroom. He'd encouraged her to experiment with pastels, and praised her art, and called her very clever. One day when she'd come to school exhausted from a weekend spent in the hospital, he'd talked about setting up a home visit to talk to her father about ways to balance her medical needs and her classwork, and he'd never come back to school after that.

None of the other students had even seemed to remember him. Melanie hasn't thought of him in years. She blinks, slowly, and is silent.

Jack looks satisfied. "I want to do this for a long, long time," she says. "I was only twelve when I became Ascendant, and that's in part because your father has been stripping and casting down so many of us. I should never have been up for the job. Well, now that I have it, I'm holding it, and no overmedicated cheerleader is going to take it away from me."

She gives Melanie a challenging look. Melanie, who has no living idea what's happening here, who is, in fact, so confused that she still isn't sure she's not still asleep, says nothing as she sits down on the edge of her bed.

"None of this makes any sense," she says. "What do you *mean*, you're the Winter Ascendant?"

"All right, this is where things get weird," says Jack.

"Things got weird a while ago," says Melanie.

"True enough." Jack doesn't sound bothered by that. If anything, she sounds pleased. "The world doesn't *need* humans to function. It doesn't even particularly want them. We're sort of a byproduct of the universe organizing itself, a natural form of static in the signal. Little bits of time and matter that organize enough to think for themselves, and *want* things, which is very inconvenient for the world, since it has to keep going while we wander around in it having all these desires and feelings and ambitions. It has to fit us in, learn to live with us."

"Okay," says Melanie, even though it isn't; even though this isn't helping things make any sense at all.

"So reality started tying humans to essential functions of itself. It keeps us busy and from making too much trouble. Issue is that once you give a human face to a function of reality, the function stops working right if no one represents it. There was a first person ever tapped to stand in for anything that embodies itself on a regular basis these days, and whatever that thing was, it did just fine before it learned how to be human. Once it understood the concept, though, it got addicted. Take the human away now, and you take the concept from the whole universe. You following me so far?"

"No. Not at all."

"I'd say it was going to get easier from here, but it's probably not, so." Jack shrugs. "Sorry about that."

"No, you're not."

"Nope, not a bit. I mean, I'm sorry I'm the one trying to tell you all this, since I'm still pretty new to it myself, but hey. The lady who explained it to me was a Corn Jenny, and she would have done a much better job with you. It's too bad she's not appropriate. I still have her phone number." Jack brightens. "I bet she's with your boyfriend right now, since he flared up the same time as you did. I bet she'll explain things real good, and he'll be able to help you understand. Won't that be nice? Because I also bet you're better at listening when you're talking to someone you actually care about. You'll care about me eventually, if you win. Until then, I'm just the weird kid in your bedroom without an invite."

Melanie frowns. "I am so lost."

"And you will be forever, unless you win." Jack leans forward, elbows on knees, and looks at her seriously. "Look, before the first Stingy Jack was called to serve, the fall happened just fine without a human face to show the world, but once it got tied into a human skin, once it knew what it was like to breathe the air and walk among the other men, it got addicted, and now, if you take Jack away, you take the fall away at the same time. Summer surges straight into the winter, and everything falls out of balance."

Melanie says nothing to that. She simply stares.

"The seasons ascendant came about one at a time, as the year figured out how to divide and subdivide itself. Jack in the Green shepherds the spring. Corn Jenny keeps the summer. Stingy Jack sees to the fall. And yours truly, the lovely and inspiring Jack Frost, takes care of the winter. But the longer we served, the heavier the year became, and finally we lost control of it. The two stronger seasons coalesced into the crowns. Winter and summer. And they became Incarnate as well as Ascendant."

"Meaning . . . ?"

"Meaning you've always gone outside in the winter without a coat, and even when you were so sick you couldn't hold your head up on your own, you forgot your socks and gloves. Meaning you don't know what brain freeze feels like, and until your father figured out how to medicate you away from your season, snow didn't melt on your skin." Jack smiles. "Meaning I was born with the potential to serve the season, but you were born with the winter in your *bones*. And now the old Winter King is dead, and you have the chance to claim the crown. You'll have to be quick, because you're not the only one in the running, but if you get there first, you'll live for as long as the winter wants you. And if you don't, you'll die."

"Oh," says Melanie. "Is that all?"

"Isn't that enough?"

"Sure, in crazytown." Melanie lies back down, head on her pillow, and closes her eyes. "I'm going to sleep until it's time to get ready."

Unsurprisingly, Jack doesn't argue, and the world slips away.

Into the Wood

CALENDAR SEASON: FEBRUARY 11TH, 2017: WINTER, UNDER THE WORM MOON.

M elanie opens her eyes in the wood, exactly where she was when she woke up last time, Harry sprawled on the ground at her feet. The snow beneath him broke when he fell; it's melting from the residual heat of his skin. She tries to grab him, to shake him awake, and recoils. He's so hot that touching him burns.

There's probably some deeper symbolism to that, but right here and right now, she just wants him to wake up and comfort her. She just wants to know none of this is happening, that she isn't dead, or a season, or anything else that doesn't make sense. She's just sleeping.

She doesn't have to do this. Because everything that Jack girl said sounded right, sounded true, sounded like it described the world she'd always almost understood, the world that existed alongside her world of doctors and pills and dying by inches. And she doesn't want it. She's sleeping, just sleeping, perfectly normal and perfectly fine.

Just sleeping, with the sound of her phone alarm buzzing in her ear.

Melanie Cosgrove opens her eyes, and this time she's alone in her room, and it's time to get ready for the Valentine's Day dance, and everything is perfectly normal.

Honest.

The pair struck down. The Crow Girl came tumbling after them, narrowly managing not to land on Zib. She squawked and spat water before turning to the human child and asking, "Did you pull me down?"

"No," rasped Zib, in a voice as waterlogged as a kitchen sponge on cleaning day. "I think the plant did that." She indicated the writhing green mass beneath them. It wasn't grabbing or pulling anymore, or trying to eat them. That was enough of an improvement that she didn't want to question it, not really.

Niamh crawled over to Avery, who was sprawled alongside the remains of the bucket. The rope had snapped at some point during his descent, and its frayed end rested on his chest, like a tether to nowhere. Reaching out, she gingerly shook his shoulder.

"Peace, Avery," she said. "I know drowning, and you're not drowned. Open your eyes and come back where you belong."

Avery remained still and silent for several seconds more before he coughed, water coming out of his mouth, sat up, and vomited into the bucket. He took a great, shuddering breath, leaned over the bucket, and vomited again.

"That's surprisingly tidy of you," said Niamh, in an approving tone. "Never throw up on anyone you haven't been introduced to. I would normally suggest not sitting on anyone you haven't been introduced to, either, but it's a bit late for that, and since this charming individual tried to drown us all, it seems like a little sitting-on is simply tit for tat."

"Individual?" asked Avery blearily.

Several of the nearest green fronds lifted up and waved gingerly in the air, for all the world like the fingers of a vast hand folding over themselves. Avery screamed.

Zib jerked around to face him, and followed his scream with one of her own, much higher and shriller. The Crow Girl burst into birds, all of them cawing loudly and franti-

cally as they flew around the cavern. Avery kept scream-
ing, and so did Zib. Niamh rolled her eyes.

"Screaming isn't going to help or change anything,"
she said. "No matter how loud you get, the facts remain
the same. I've never encountered noise-soluble facts, al-
though I suppose they must exist. If someone has a head-
ache, and you scream in their ear, the fact is that their
headache may get worse, and you may get punched, very
hard." . . .

—From *Along the Saltwise Sea*, by A. Deborah Baker

BOOK IV

The Rights of Spring

The promise of spring's arrival is enough to get anyone through the bitter winter.

—Jen Selinsky

For myth changes while custom remains constant; men continue to do what their fathers did before them, though the reasons on which their fathers acted have been long forgotten. The history of religion is a long attempt to reconcile old custom with new reason, to find a sound theory for an absurd practice.

—Sir James George Frazer, *The Golden Bough*

Waking Up

Not that far away, as high school students who only got their first cars last year measure distance (which is a means of measuring distance entirely distinct from the bicycle math of younger teens, or the walking distance of children, or the advanced driving distance of adults), Harry March is getting ready for the dance.

He's sometimes very glad he's not a girl. For a lot of reasons, but chief among them are the moments like this one, when he has to make himself look good for some social event where Melanie will expect him to look nice enough to match her. He knows she has a new dress, one she hasn't allowed him to see, and that she'll spend at least an hour on her makeup, blending foundation powders and highlighters until she looks less like a dead girl walking and more like the girl she wants him to see when he looks at his high school pictures in his college dorm. She'll be curling and twisting and styling her hair, and taking a thousand steps toward the kingdom of acceptable feminine beauty, where he has never been and never dreams of going. While he puts on the same suit he wore to Winter Formal, and to Homecoming before that, and runs a comb through his hair, and calls himself good. It isn't fair. It's the way things are.

He's told Mel before that she doesn't have to paint her cheeks for him, that he knows how much color her illness has stolen and he doesn't care, he still thinks she's the most beautiful girl in the world and he always will. She smiles and says he's sweet and goes back to swatching lipsticks on her hand, like she's competing in some grand pageant he can't see and won't ever be scored in.

The other girls can be cruel, although they mostly reserve their cruelties for each other these days. They used to target her the way they target everyone else, until the day someone whose mother worked as a receptionist for her cardiologist came to school with the news that Melanie had been admitted sometime after midnight, and they weren't sure whether she'd be leaving the hospital this time. She'd been back by the end of the week, but things had never gone back to normal. Not for either one of them.

He's seen this happen to other kids who got sick, the ones with cancer or who've been in a terrible accident. The ones no one's sure will be there for graduation. It's like the reminder that nothing lasts forever strips away the veneer of casual cruelty they've wrapped around themselves, destroys the shroud of bitter indifference, and turns them all back into children sharing juice boxes and playing pretend out by the swing set. Children can be cruel, he knows— Harry's sure he has some illusions about that, but he has fewer than most, thanks to a lifetime spent with the sick girl as his closest companion—but teens are so much worse, because they understand so much more about the anatomy of the heart.

It's like they all received shivs on their fourteenth birthdays, and instructions to treat their time in high school like the Hunger Games.

But Melanie has managed to exempt herself, through the simple act of standing on death's doorstep, and her exemption has taken Harry with her, almost as an afterthought. No one wants to bully the dying girl's boyfriend. It's like an interesting inverse of the ableism that assumes she can't do her own homework because she's on too many drugs, or says she shouldn't be allowed to try out for the cheerleading squad next year because of the potential liability.

Even though he knows, and Melanie knows, and Melanie knows he knows she won't be openly judged for whatever she wears tonight, he also knows she'll try her hardest to make the night as normal as she can, because she wants him to have that. Mel is probably the kindest person he's ever known, and sometimes he wishes she'd be less focused on him and more focused on herself.

The only thing he wants from her is the only thing he knows she can't give him, and as he checks his reflection and straightens his tie, he wishes for it more than anything. All he wants, all he's ever wanted, is for her to stay.

It's February, but the air in his room feels hot as a sauna, hot enough that he wants to take his jacket off, and so he does, slinging it over his shoulder and studying himself in the mirror. It looks casual. It looks like a boy who isn't worried about the way his date collapsed in front of him earlier (the moment when her eyes rolled back in her head and he thought it was finally over, and he felt his own heart break and he felt his own secret shame wash over him, because before she hit the grass, he felt *relief*), or the way the paramedics made him sit with them until his parents came to pick him up.

They want him to stay home tonight. The only reason he's being allowed to go to the dance is because he played the dying-girlfriend card. He checks his boutonniere and frowns. The flowers, half-open and perfect when he put them on, are blooming wildly, petals spread so wide the center rose is almost the size of his palm.

It was supposed to match Melanie's corsage, and unless there was something wrong with the nutrient packs the florist instructed him to add to their water until they were ready to be worn, it's not going to match at all. Her corsage is safely in the fridge downstairs, budding blossoms and half-furled leaves, ready to last through the night. He can't think of anything that would explain this riotous growth, unless it's the heat in his room.

Heat has never bothered Harry. He knows Mel prefers the cold, doesn't shiver when they're at the movie theater and the air conditioning is hiked way too high, even when he wishes she would, because shivering girlfriends are snuggling girlfriends, and what's the point of socially approved hanging out in the dark if you can't at least cuddle up? But he doesn't really sweat and he's never had a sunburn in his life, not even when he might as well have been courting one, with the way he runs around without sunscreen on. The sun just seems to love him. Always has.

He tans but he doesn't burn, and she chills but she doesn't freeze, and that's the way it's always been, and while he's going to ask his dad to take a look at the thermostat in his room, he doesn't really *care* if his bedroom turns into a sauna. He just wishes it hadn't spoiled his boutonniere.

Mel won't mind. Mel never minds, not when he's clearly making an effort. She minds when he's thoughtless, and when he's mean, but he does his best not to be those things, for her sake as much as for his own.

Harry March is going to wind up turning into that poor boy with the dead girlfriend, so sad, so tragic, no matter what he does, and no matter how much he wishes things could be different. The least he can do is make sure she stays happy with him until that happens.

Jacket still slung carelessly over his shoulder, he pockets his keys and leaves his room, loping down the hall.

If it weren't for the whole "my girlfriend is dying and there's nothing anyone can do about it, this is bullshit" side of things, Harry knows he'd be living a charmed life. His parents are independently wealthy: he's never known what it was to be hungry for more than a few hours, never wondered whether there will be gas for his car or a roof over his head. Mel's dad is doing it all alone, and he knows her medical bills must be a strain. She puts on a brave face, but he picks up the tab whenever they go out, out of necessity as much as chivalry.

His parents are waiting in the living room, and his mother coos and comments over how grown-up and fancy he looks, while his father stands back with his hands in his pockets. Harry gives him a nod. He nods back. He knows the gig from here: he'll go pick up Melanie, and bring her back for photographs, which his mother insists on taking whenever there's something like this to document.

He wants to mind, wants to complain about wasting time and making a fuss over nothing. He never does. He knows why this is important to them, and why it's more important to *him* than he can find the words to express. Time is short.

And maybe he dwells on that a lot, but it's becoming more and more obvious that time isn't just short, it's running out. So he retrieves Mel's corsage from the fridge, red rose and bruise-purple iris, and kisses his mother on the cheek while his father claps him on the shoulder, and he's out, heading for the car, heading for the night, heading for the future.

The future is another country, and he wishes he didn't have to go there, but they all do, in time. His passport has already been stamped. The only way not to go is Mel's way, and she'll be going too, just by a different road. A cold and terrible one down which he cannot follow.

The car's heater hasn't worked in years. There's no point, when Mel never gets cold and he owns plenty of sweaters. Still, it's sweltering in the cabin by the time he pulls up in front of her house and gets out, looking at the bright lights of the living room windows. Maybe he has a fever? But the paramedics would have caught it if he did, would have said something before they released him. It's nothing, it must be nothing.

He heads up the walkway, long legs eating distance, and for a moment it looks like a small child is standing in the shadows by the base of Mel's oak tree, watching him. He stops and blinks and the child isn't there at all. Which makes a lot more sense than a kid hanging out in Melanie's front yard in February after dark. He shakes the thought away and finishes the walk to the door, which is unlocked (as always). He still rings the bell and waits.

The doorknob turns, the door swings open, and there is Roland Cosgrove, looking at him solemnly down the slope of his nose, head tilted back ever so slightly to keep his glasses from slipping. "Mr. March," he says, in the sonorous tones of a man who was born to be a mortician and somehow became a high school chemistry teacher instead. "To what do we owe the honor?"

"I'm here to pick up Mel for the Valentine's Day dance, sir," says

Harry, holding up the box with her corsage as if it proves his good intentions somehow. "She said to get here at seven."

"She hasn't come out of her room all day," says Roland. "I think she may be too tired to go dancing with you tonight. I'm sorry."

But Harry isn't listening anymore. He heard the scuff of Mel's shoes on the stairs halfway through Roland's statement, and he can see her now, one hand on the railing, skirts swirling around her feet, and he can't stop *staring*.

He knows you can't own people, he shouldn't think of her in these terms, but in moments like this one, he looks at her and all he can think is that she's beautiful, she's so damn beautiful, and she's *his*. He's the one who gets to hold her hands, to put his arms around her and know she wants them there, to kiss those lips (painted red as blood, like she's decided to lean into the Snow White motif of her hair and skin as hard as she possibly can), to taste her lipstick.

Tonight, he'll lead her around the school gym, where they've been a thousand times before (and sometimes it feels like more than that, feels like they've been doing this over and over again for a million years, and he'd be happy to do it for a million more if only they were allowed), and all the other boys will be jealous of what he has, and all the other girls will wish their boyfriends would look at him the way he looks at her, and it will be perfect. It's always perfect when he's with Mel. She's his fairy tale. The only one he's ever wanted.

"I feel fine, Daddy," she says. "I spent the whole afternoon in bed, and I'm *fine*."

There's color in her cheeks, and even Harry can't be sure whether it's natural or painted on. She pauses to kiss the side of her father's jaw as she descends, leaving a bloody smear of lipstick behind. There's something oddly almost prophetic about that mark, and Harry can't stop himself from staring for a little bit too long before she's moving toward him, and his attention is pulled back where it belongs.

Her dress is some sort of satiny fabric that probably has a fancy six-syllable name he can't pronounce, and it shines and shimmers in the light like it wants to put shame to the very concept of sequins.

It cups the lines of her body in a way he yearns to emulate, perfectly fitted and somehow seeming not fitted at all. He loves that dress. He *envies* that dress. In his next life, he wants to *be* that dress.

The neckline is so high as to be more than appropriate and step over the line into modest, and he's confident she'll still be the hottest girl at the dance, and that will make him the hottest guy there, through the transitive property of high school hotness. He holds out her corsage in silence, relieved to see that whatever's wrong with his boutonniere hasn't spread; the buds are still tightly closed, the leaves still furled. She raises an eyebrow as she takes it, nodding toward the flowers at his lapel, and he shrugs. It's not the first time something small has gone horribly wrong when it was left for him to handle. It won't be the last.

"You look amazing," he says, unsticking his tongue from the roof of his mouth and forcing himself to remember how words are formed. "That dress is . . . It's just . . . Wow."

"You like it?" Melanie does a little twirl, still holding the boxed corsage in one hand. "I was afraid it might be too dowdy."

It stretches almost to the floor, covering the straps holding her heels to her feet, and he knows most of the other girls will be in knee-length dresses despite the weather, especially the rest of the cheer squad. They've been competing to see who can get the closest to the exact dress code cutoff for hemlines for years, and have managed to get it down to an eighth of an inch. She's so much more covered than they're going to be, and he doesn't care, because she wears that dress like it's the only style that should ever be seen at a school dance.

"You're *perfect*," he says, with fervor.

"You'll have her home by ten," says Roland. "Not ten-thirty, not ten-oh-five, ten. Do I make myself clear?"

Harry knows this part of the script. "Yes, sir," he says.

"Be careful with her tonight, Harry. She likes to put on a brave face for you, but she's not doing well." Roland's voice is serious, like he's imparting some grave and profound wisdom.

"Daddy!" protests Melanie, and smacks him on the arm.

"It's true, and Harald deserves to know if you're going to let him take you out," says Roland. "You're sick, Melanie. You have to admit that."

Harry doesn't know if other parents do things this way, constantly remind their children that they aren't well. His parents never do, but then, the worst thing he's ever had to deal with is a broken arm, and it was sort of hard for him to pretend it *wasn't* broken when it was encased in plaster and itched like it was covered in angry ants. Mel will absolutely push herself if she's allowed. He just doesn't think it's his job to stop her. He's her boyfriend, not her keeper.

"Yes, sir," he says anyway, and it's as much of a lie as it always is, and Roland nods, appearing to accept it at face value the way *he* always does, and this part of the ritual of getting out of the house is finally complete.

"Take a coat, Melanie, you know your system isn't strong enough to handle a cold right now," says Roland.

"I have a wrap, Daddy," says Melanie, with a roll of her eyes. She leaves her corsage in its box as she retrieves the wrap in question from the hook where she had it hanging, anticipating this moment.

Experience has shown them both that if she comes down in short sleeves, Roland will demand a sweater, and if she comes down in a sweater, he'll tell her to put on a jacket. Coming down as unprepared as possible is the only way they've found to get out of the house without bundling her up against an Arctic cold that doesn't exist in Portland and probably wouldn't bother her if it did.

"Ten, and not a second later," says Roland, eyes on Harry.

"Yes, sir," says Harry, who isn't going to waste time arguing; they'll already be hard-pressed to make it to the dance on time after his family finishes their pictures. He offers Mel his hand. "Ready to go?"

"Always was," says Melanie, and takes his hand, waving her corsage at her father in a farewell.

(It's far more final than any of them realizes in this moment, which marks almost as much of a divide between who they were and who they're going to be as William Monroe's death did, but understanding is so often a construct of distance, and right here, right now, they have no distance; they have no space; they have only time, which is moving, second by second, into the spring.)

"Bye, Daddy," chirps Melanie.

Roland smiles, softens, looks for a moment like the doting father Melanie has always known. "Bye, princess," he says, and watches as Harry whisks her out the door, into the cool February night. They pause on the porch to drape the wrap—a length of wine-colored fabric that matches her dress—around her shoulders, and then they're away, heading for his car at the foot of the driveway.

"Does he know?" Harry asks softly, once the door is closed and they're far enough from the house that her father shouldn't be able to hear them.

Melanie shakes her head. "No, and you're not going to tell him. He doesn't *need* to know."

(Inside the house, Roland Cosgrove's phone is ringing. He'll answer it as soon as he sees Harry pull out of the driveway, as soon as he knows his precious girl has been well and truly handed off to someone else's care. For now, he watches them go, and wishes he didn't have to let her. Wishes she was a good science experiment, obedient and biddable and willing to stay where he puts her. That's the trouble with making people, whether children or constructs. They never listen in the end.)

"Your doctors—"

"Will tell him if anything shows up on the scans," says Melanie, and opens the passenger side door of his car. She doesn't drive. Her father never approved her learning how, and given how often she blacks out, it's not safe. She can't even be the base of a pyramid for fear that she'll have one of her episodes and drop someone. Putting her behind the wheel of a car would be inviting trouble.

Harry's shown her the basics in the Target parking lot, and the experience left them both shaken enough that they mutually agreed not to do it again.

Melanie slides into the car. Harry frowns as he watches her, and waits until she's settled before he follows, positioning himself behind the wheel. The cab is much cooler than it was on the drive over, and he shivers as he fastens his belt. "My place for pictures?"

"I knew who I was going to the dance with when I said yes," said Mel, smiling. He turns on the engine and pulls out of the driveway and her smile drops away, replaced by an expression of seriousness so pronounced it makes him uneasy, makes his stomach do a slow and uncomfortable flip. She looked that way on the day she told him her illness was terminal, that without a second heart transplant, she'd be leaving him before they could go off to college, much less get married and live together in Castleview like he'd been saying. She looked that way the day she came home and said she'd been put on reserve by the cheer team, still allowed to wear the uniform and show up for game days, no longer allowed to compete.

If there's a scholar of the expressions of Melanie Cosgrove, it's Harald March. He's been making note of her face for his entire life, has grown up so familiar with her smile that he might as well wear it himself, and he knows nothing good ever comes from that degree of gravity. He wants to make a joke, wants to break the tension before she can say whatever terrible thing she's about to say, and he doesn't know how. Doesn't know what would work. Not when she looks so serious, not when her eyes are so sad.

"Harry . . ." she begins.

He punches the steering wheel, and Mel jerks away, eyes widening in surprise. "Sorry," he manages. "I'm sorry. I just couldn't . . . No. You can't, Mel. You *can't*. Not tonight. I know you're going to sooner or later, but it's almost Valentine's Day, and you're supposed to be my Valentine. We're going to the Valentine's Day dance, *together,* and if you're going to break up with me, you can do it tomorrow like a normal person, not in my car after you've already taken the corsage I brought for you. I'm sorry, but you can't. I won't accept it."

"I can break up with you?" asks Mel wonderingly, like those are words she's never envisioned in that order, like Harry has just provided her with groundbreaking new information.

"I have to drive," says Harry, gripping the wheel so tightly that his knuckles stand out white and angry. It almost hurts, he's holding on so tight. He's never really learned how to let go.

"I don't think so," says Mel, tone still a little distant, like she's considering an entirely new concept. "I mean, I think about dying on you. I think about dying on you a *lot*, and what that's going to look like, and I'm pretty sure I've listened to you giving my eulogy in my imagination so many times that I could recite it in my sleep—"

"Could we *not*? Do you think it might be possible for us to have one normal date where you don't talk about making me bury you? Especially when I've just watched you collapse on the football field? I was afraid you'd *died*, Melanie. I thought you were *dead*."

"Well, yeah," she says. "You're pretty smart. But about this 'breaking up with you' idea, what even *is* that?"

Harry hits the brakes and twists around to face her, frowning. "What do you mean, 'I'm pretty smart'? What's that about?"

"I asked my question first. I'm not breaking up with you, Harald. I told you in second grade that I was going to marry you, and as far as I'm concerned, that still stands, or would, if I hadn't spent the last couple of years waiting to die. I'm *never* breaking up with you."

"No, just leaving me."

"Only if I don't have any other choice."

Harry doesn't understand any of this. He returns his attention to the road, scowling, the temperature in the car beginning to creep upward again. "You still haven't answered my question."

"You said you thought I'd died," says Melanie. "What did you see?"

"You were waving, and then you went pale—even for you—and all the light went out of your eyes. They rolled back in your head, and I woke up on the ground, with you leaning over me," says Harry. "Trevor said you fell. That you weren't moving and they couldn't . . . they couldn't . . ." He can't even say it. He punches the steering wheel again.

He's never been the sort of guy who hits things that can't hit back, but right now, it feels like his confusion is too big for his body, and anything he can do to shake it loose, just a little, just enough for him to breathe, is a good idea.

"They couldn't find my heartbeat," says Melanie. It doesn't sound like a guess.

"Yeah."

"I want you to stay calm and keep driving," says Melanie.

"What are you—"

"If you can't, you need to stop the car and let me get out right now."

"Melanie, we're still more than a mile from the school. It's dark and cold out there."

"And when have you ever known me to care about the cold, huh?" Melanie looks at him challengingly. She's so pale that her face stands out even against the shadows. She might as well be a ghost.

He hates the thought. He shoves it aside.

For her part, Melanie doesn't point out that she ran the full distance between her house and the school today, ran it like she was still thirteen and strong and immortal, still a full year away from the horrifying comprehension that she was a limited-time offer, that she was going to end. One day the world would wake up and Melanie Cosgrove wouldn't wake up with it, the same way it had woken up without her mother and her twin sister. All of them are here to go.

Maybe that's why she was willing to listen to the child who broke into her room while she was sleeping, even if she doesn't believe a single word they said. But she still can't feel her heartbeat, and the temperature in the car is smothering. She wants out. She wants out and she wants to *run*, not lock herself immediately away in the high school gym, away from the cold winter moon above them.

It's almost spring, and part of her knows that when the spring comes, her strength will go. She doesn't understand the knowledge yet. She will. She just needs time.

"Okay," says Harry. "I'm driving. You see? I'm driving."

"And you're going to keep driving, right? Not turn the wheel too hard and run us into a tree because you don't like what I have to say?"

"Melanie," says Harry, offended. She can hear it in every syllable of her name, which only gets pronounced beyond the first three letters when he's unhappy with her, or her father is in the room. "When have I *ever* run us into a tree? Honestly, you'd think you'd have more faith in my driving by this point."

"They couldn't find my heartbeat because I didn't have one," says Melanie. "I still don't."

The car lurches a little as Harry nearly loses control—but there are no trees nearby for him to have slammed into, so she supposes he's managed to keep his word—and then he gets the car back on the level, and laughs.

"Very funny, Mel. You have to have a heartbeat. If you didn't have a heartbeat, you'd be dead."

"Yeah. Very funny." Her phone is ringing, tucked away inside the little clutch purse she bought to match her dress. She busies herself with opening it and pushing past the welter of pill bottles and emergency medications to answer. "It's my dad. I have to take this."

"Already?" Her father is notorious for checking up on her during their dates, like he doesn't trust Harry to keep himself from ripping her clothes off if he leaves them alone for more than fifteen minutes. Still, he normally waits until they at least have time to get where they're going.

Melanie lifts the phone to her ear, forcing herself to smile. Her father will hear it if she doesn't. "Hi, Daddy! What's going . . . Really? Right *now*? Are you sure?" She pauses, and Harry hears a whole story in that silence. He's heard it before.

But what he hasn't heard is the pager in her purse going off. That would mean her name had finally come up on the transplant list. He'd run out on his own birthday party if her name had come up on the transplant list.

"All right, Daddy," says Melanie, and drops the phone back into her purse.

"Should I turn around?"

She doesn't reply.

"Mel, am I supposed to be taking you home?"

She turns her head, so that she's looking out the window at the moon-drenched streets outside the car. The silence stretches like taffy, and when it finally snaps, she appears to come to a decision of some kind. He just doesn't know what kind it *is*.

"Pull over," she says.

"Melanie, what are you—"

"Pull over, and I'll tell you everything I know. Everything I can. Or take me home, and I don't think you'll ever see me again." She turns back to him. "It's up to you."

Where the Sidewalk Begins

Harry doesn't hesitate before he pulls over, easing the car up to a stretch of curb he's never stopped at before. They're in a residential neighborhood, too close to several houses for this to be a good make-out spot, too far from home for it to be a good place for him to drop her off. He'd never tell her this, but he doesn't like to let her walk home alone when he can help it. Maybe it's presumptive and chauvinistic of him, since he knows she can take care of herself, but he's the kid with the dying girlfriend. He's allowed to be a little overprotective.

Melanie waits until he kills the engine before she twists and thrusts her arm toward him, still-bare wrist tilted upward. "Take my pulse," she commands.

"I have a pulse oximeter in the glove compartment," he says. Her father insisted he get one when he started driving her around, said they needed to be able to check her heart rate and oxygen saturation levels accurately no matter what the situation was. They've only used it a handful of times, and she carries one of her own in her purse.

Melanie's expression, what he can see of it in the shadows, is relieved. "And you trust that no one's tampered with it?"

"What are you talking about?"

"Yes or no, Harald?"

"Yes, Mel, I trust that no one has broken into my car solely to tamper with my pulse oximeter. You're being really weird tonight."

"I know." She smiles, shadows rendering her painted lips black against the white of her skin. "Get it out and put it on me."

It's one of the finger-clip models, designed to slip over her index finger and turn on with the press of a button. It's not exact enough to be a true diagnostic tool, but it can put them close enough to the ballpark to keep everyone calm and get her to help if she needs it. Harry places it on her hand and presses the button.

Melanie says nothing, just keeps breathing normally, letting the little machine work its magic. After about thirty seconds it beeps, and she turns her hand, holding it up to show him.

Her blood oxygenation is 100%, which is high for her—she normally averages around 95% when she's having a good day, and dips a little lower on a bad one. 90% means he's supposed to take her straight home. Anything lower than 90% means he's supposed to call her father immediately. He's had to do that twice, and he hated it both times. So seeing that 100% is pleasantly reassuring. He likes it.

He doesn't like the number on her heartrate line. If this were one of the fancier models, like the one in her purse, it would probably be sounding some sort of an alarm right about now, telling them both that something was seriously wrong. It has to be, for her to be showing an impossible result. "Your heartrate can't be zero," he says, crossly. "You'd have to not have a heartbeat for it to be zero."

"Because right now, I don't have a heartbeat," says Melanie. She takes the pulse oximeter off, hands it back to him. "Try it on yourself."

Harry frowns and attaches the small machine to his hand. Another thirty seconds pass before he gets his answer: 98% pulse oxygen, heartrate 62 beats per minute. That's a little lower than it usually is, which doesn't make much sense, since his girlfriend is telling him she's some sort of zombie. But then, nothing about this night makes sense.

"This is weird," he mutters.

"It gets weirder," says Melanie, almost cheerfully. She opens the car door and steps into the night, letting a gust of cold air in. Has it always been this cold in February? Harry shivers.

It has. He knows it has. He's just never felt it like this before.

Melanie doesn't walk away from the car, doesn't leave him. Just shuts the door, puts her hands on her hips, and says, in a perfectly conversational tone, "All right. I'm ready to listen now, if you've been following us the way I think you have."

"You can feel me," says the little girl he thought he saw before in her front yard, melting out of the shadows of the nearest hedge. She's short and slight and almost disappears in the dark, but when she smiles, it's impossibly visible. "That's a good sign."

"I couldn't feel you, I just figured anyone who was willing to break into my house to tell me a fairy tale would probably be planning to ambush us at the school."

"So I guess if I tell you I wasn't here until you called me, you'll call me a liar."

"Yup," says Melanie, almost jovially.

Harry gets out of the car and leans against it, watching the two of them warily. "One of you want to tell me what's going on?"

"You have your own guide, Summer boy," says the child. "I wouldn't want to interfere."

"I promise you, no one has come to guide me to anything," says Harry.

"If you can help me, you can help him," says Melanie. "We're a package deal. He fell down the same time I did."

"But he still has a heartbeat, right?" asks the kid. "That's because he's summer-tied, not winter-bound. He's not dead yet, and I'm the spirit of the *Winter* Ascendant. I can't help him."

"Then you can't help me," says Melanie, and moves to get back in the car. Her back is stiff, her shoulders straight. Harry recognizes her posture. It's the stance she takes when she's about to demonstrate the depth and breadth of her rather impressive stubbornness, which has been dazzling him since they were kids and he watched her successfully argue her father into taking them to Disneyland, even though he'd said it wasn't possible, that her heart couldn't take the strain. She got to meet Mickey then. She's going to convince this kid now. He knows it.

Apparently the kid does too, because she sighs and speaks before Melanie can open the car door. "Wait." She sounds faintly distraught, like this isn't the way she expected her evening to go, and that's reasonable enough, since this isn't the way he expected *his* evening to go, either. He was supposed to be at the school by now, getting Mel a glass of punch, maybe, or walking her onto the dance floor while some song he only vaguely recognized played over the sound system. Apparently, none of them are getting what they want tonight.

Not even Mel's father. He's never seen her blatantly ignore a summons like this before. It makes him uncomfortable in a way he doesn't know how to articulate, like the world is tilting on its axis.

"I thought you didn't believe me," says the kid, a mulish note in her voice. She's not as stubborn as Mel, he can tell that at a glance— he's never met anyone as stubborn as Mel, and he's met a lot of people—but she's up there.

Harry has never quite seen the point of stubbornness. He's willing to dig in his heels when he needs to, when it's important, like he's done all the times Mel's father has tried to dissuade him from getting her too worked up, talking like their relationship is somehow the thing that's going to take her *out* of the world and not one of the things that makes her willing to stay *in* it. He's always known he won't be enough to keep her here, no matter how tightly he holds on to her, and if sometimes that holding on has become a bit all-consuming, who can blame him? He hasn't dissolved his own desires in the need to keep her anchored, but he's buried them from time to time, sublimating who he might have become under the need to be the perfect boyfriend. So perfect that she'll never die and leave him on his own to figure out who he's meant to be without her.

Is that what love's supposed to look like? He doesn't know. It's the love he's always had.

"I didn't," says Mel, slowly turning to face the child again. "What you're saying sounds like a first-class ticket on the train to crazytown, and I'm pretty sure you're the mayor. But nothing has made sense since I fell down on the football field, and when I got up to get dressed for the dance . . ." Her voice falters.

For a moment, a long, terrible moment, Melanie is completely silent. Harry, as he's always done, hurries to fill the gap.

"I don't think we've been introduced, which is funny, since I usually know all Mel's friends, and I think I'd have noticed if her father decided to let her start babysitting again. He's always been really opposed to the idea. Something about it being bad for the kids if they have to watch their sitter stop breathing before Mom and Dad get home. I'm—"

"You're Harry March," says the girl. "You're lucky, you know. Not all the Summers start out this close to their Winter. Not all of them even get along. The last Summer *hated* her Winter. I wasn't around when they were crowned, but everyone says they hated each other from the start, and the longer things went on, the worse they got. You're not going to be like that, I can already tell. You're going to be a proper sitting court, and you're going to do your jobs."

Harry frowns. "So you know who I am, and you don't make any sense, and I support not making sense—sometimes, making sense is a waste of both time and wit on an inferior partner, although I'm a little stung to already be dismissed so fast—but I'd like to know who *you* are if we're going to be standing about on dark streets, chatting with one another. It seems polite to make our introductions, don't you think?"

"You know, when they told me I was the nearest and I'd be making this little speech, they didn't tell me you'd be hung up on manners," says the girl, sounding amused beyond her years. "You can call me Jack."

"Is that your name, or just what you want to be called? I'm happy with it either way, you understand, since 'Harry's' not technically my name—'Harald' is what they put on my birth certificate—but I can't say I've ever met a girl named Jack before."

The girl looks distinctly amused, turning her face toward Melanie. "Is he always like this?" she asks. "He talks a lot more than I expected."

Melanie shoots him a fond look, lips curled upward at the edges in that way he's always loved, the way that means she's really and truly happy. "He's not *always* like this," she says. "Sometimes he's asleep."

Harry wants to argue. He doesn't, because she has him dead to rights, and arguing with Mel currently feels a lot less important than whatever the hell is going on with this weird kid in this strange neighborhood. He can almost feel the eyes watching them through the nearby windows. He clears his throat, and both girls turn toward him in silent inquiry.

"We're going to be late to the dance if we don't get moving now," he says.

For the first time, the little girl looks alarmed. "You can't go to the dance," she says.

"Well, not directly," he says. "We have to go to my house first. My parents are waiting to take our pictures."

"If she's willing to listen to me"—Jack hooks a finger toward Melanie, indicating her—"something must have changed. Something big enough to get her attention."

"It's my father," says Melanie. "He called and asked me to have Harry take me home. Said his pager went off. But I carry a pager too, and if they were only planning to call one of us, they would have called me."

"He's heard about William, then," says Jack. "Damn. I'd hoped that with the Alchemical Congress in shambles, it would take longer for the news . . . Well, it can't be helped, and what can't be helped shouldn't be dwelt on any more than absolutely necessary. I hope you like those shoes, because they're the only ones you've got now."

Melanie blinks. "What?"

"You can't go back there, and you can't go to the dance. He's supposed to have his own guide, but I don't feel any other unclaimed Jacks or Jennys in this area, so I guess I'm filling in until we can get things a little more nailed down. Lucky me."

"Mel, get in the car," says Harry.

Jack looks even more alarmed. "Where are you going?"

"To my house, to get pictures with my parents, and then to the dance," says Harry. He gets back into the car, slamming the door with a decisive bang, and waits.

Mel looks from the car to Jack, hesitating. Then she shrugs, says something he can't hear, and gets back into the passenger seat. Harry waits for her to fasten her belt before he starts the engine and pulls away from the curb.

"What was all that about?" he asks.

"She came to my room before," says Mel. "When I ran home from the school."

"You mean when you ran off and left me for the paramedics?" Harry shakes his head. "My folks almost didn't let me come get you, they were so worried there might be something wrong with me. I managed to convince them it was just dehydration, and they bought it, even though it's February." He's never gotten dehydrated, not even in the dead of summer, but every coach he's ever had has worried about it, like it was some terrible specter hovering above all blond boys everywhere. It became a running joke a couple of years ago, one of those things that can't be avoided and hence needs to be laughed at whenever possible. Out of Gatorade? That's fine, steal Harry's, he'll never notice.

"Really?" asks Mel, voice flat with disbelief.

"Yeah, well, the paramedics said I was fine and I didn't want to tell them you'd been there, and even if I had, I don't think 'sympathetic fainting' would have come off as all that believable." Melanie's phone is buzzing—she must have turned the ringer off—over and over, like it's demanding her attention. Somehow it manages to sound ominous, like the rattling of a snake or the droning of a wasp.

Harry gives her purse a wary look. "You going to answer that?"

"No, and you're not going to answer yours, either." As if she's become some sort of oracle, her phone stops buzzing and his begins to ring. Harry doesn't want to take his eyes off the road, but he does, pulling the phone out of his pocket, and the name displayed is MR. MELANIE'S DAD, SIR, a joke Roland has never appreciated but

Harry considers a useful reminder that it's important to be polite when he's speaking to his girlfriend's father, and not try to talk the man in circles the way he usually does when he has to deal with an unwanted adult.

He drops the phone on the seat like it's bitten him. He's never seen Mel dodging her father's calls before. That's been one of the cardinal rules of her life as long as she's been carrying a phone, and she was the first person his own age who got one and was allowed to have it at a school, since in her case it's considered a medical necessity. If she wants to be allowed to leave the house unsupervised, ever, she answers when her father calls. It doesn't matter what she's doing. He's seen her answer the phone during tests and during cheer practice and during dates and when he's known for an absolute fact that she doesn't want to talk to her father. When he calls, she answers.

Dr. Cosgrove never calls Harry, because he never needs to. Melanie always gets there first.

"What's going on?"

Mel doesn't answer.

"You're telling me you don't have a heartbeat and weird kids are appearing out of the shadows, and now you're dodging calls from your dad? Mel, this isn't like you, and this is all way weirder than I thought the night was going to be."

"You told him you don't have a heartbeat?" Jack's question is mild but interested, and it comes from the backseat.

Melanie yelps. Harry outright yells, slamming his foot down on the brake and bringing them skidding to a halt. However that kid got into the car, she didn't bother putting her seatbelt on, and the momentum of their stop slings her forward into the front seat, where only the iron bar of his outstretched arm pulls her to a stop before she can go crashing through the windshield.

Touching her, even glancingly, is like shoving his arm into a bucket of cold slush, the stuff that forms in puddles at the bottom of the driveway during the middle of the winter, the stuff that makes goosebumps break out across his entire body. He turns to stare at her, and she looks shamefacedly back, visibly embarrassed by her abortive flight.

"Um, sorry," she says, peeling herself off his arm and using her hands to shove herself back into the backseat. "Should have done up my belt, I know. Didn't mean to startle you."

"Oh, that makes it all okay," says Harry, a bubble of hysterical laughter forcing its way up his throat. "The weird kid who can't possibly be in my car says she's sorry for startling me, and my girlfriend doesn't have a heartbeat! This is such a good, normal night! I'm having a wonderful time!"

"I said *sorry*," says Jack, more peevishly. "And I can be in your car because *she's* in your car, and anywhere she can be, I can be too. So I'm here."

"Fuck this," mutters Harry. He hits the gas, and they start moving again.

"Where are we going?" asks Jack.

"*We* are not going anywhere," he snaps. "Melanie and I are going to my house so my parents can take pictures of us before we head for the dance. I bought our tickets almost two months ago. I bought these flowers special. We're going to the dance, and we're going to *dance,* and we're not going to deal with whatever weird-ass thing you're trying to sell. We're not interested."

"I think you're going to be," says Jack. "I think you're going to be a lot more interested than you think you are."

"Well, one of us is wrong," says Harry. "Let's find out who, shall we?" He keeps driving. The road still makes sense. The road isn't speaking in riddles or materializing in his car or ignoring calls from its father. The road is normal.

"Harry," says Melanie.

"No," he says, almost cheerfully.

"Harry, I just need to—"

"Nope. We're going to my house." It's getting easier to sound cheerful about everything that's happening. Maybe this is what it feels like to go mad. Wouldn't that be nice? If mental illness worked the way it does in books and movies, and just happened all at once and perfectly cleanly, no psychologists or arguments over whether his tendency to answer everything with a joke signaled some deeper childhood disorder. He's tried telling the concerned adults who insert themselves into his life from time to time and refuse to go away, that he has dying girlfriend disorder, a rare condition signified by sometimes waking up feeling like he's fallen into an episode of *Grey's Anatomy*, like his whole life is being dictated for the ratings by some asshole author who doesn't fully believe in his existence or autonomy or right to make his own decisions. He's tried to tell them, and they've made little notes in their computers about him having issues with reality, or not understanding the difference between fiction and things that actually exist, and he's pretty much done with the whole concept of "sanity." So if this is madness, finally showing up to take him home, he's happy to go.

"Harry." Mel sounds exasperated. He hears that from her a lot. "I need you to stop driving and *listen*."

"Nope. Had your chance to explain things in small words that weren't confusing and didn't involve teleporting preteens, didn't take it, so I'm going to need you to not talk for a while, so I can focus on the road." The kid in the backseat is still there, he can hear her breathing, and that means this is really happening, this isn't just something he can wish away by refusing to see it, and he hates that. He *hates* it with a brightness that's almost surprising, because this isn't how the world is supposed to work.

Melanie sighs and places a hand on his arm, and he barely suppresses the urge to jerk away. Like the kid, her skin is bracingly cold. She's always run a little toward the chilly side, but this is like she's just taken her hand out of the freezer, like she's been juggling ice cubes when he wasn't watching. Unlike the kid, it doesn't feel like shoving his arm into a puddle of slush. It feels like . . .

It feels like the first thaw, when winter starts to break and the spring starts pushing through. Like snowdrops breaking ice, like icicles melting in the eaves. It feels *right,* and while Melanie has always been perfectly fitted to his arms, she's never felt this *right* before.

It makes him want to stop the car and take her in his arms.

It makes him want to never touch her again.

Something people often overlook about Harry March, easygoing and laughing as he is, and something he's never even admitted to himself, would be surprised to hear anyone say about him: the boy—almost man—has a streak of stubborn in him wider than a four-lane highway, same as Mel. It takes a lot of hardheadedness to stand up to every adult in your life saying—some openly and some in little, brutally considerate hints—that you'd be better off leaving the girl you love before she can die on you. It takes a remarkable amount of self-possessedness to be so sure of who you are and what you want that you're willing to fight the world, fight death itself if necessary, and all by the age of seventeen.

Harry doesn't like to be told what to do, not even by his own feelings, and it's only the fact that he's loved Mel for so long that the thought of not loving her is almost alien that keeps him from shaking her hand off his arm. He settles for shooting her a quick, sharp look across the darkness of the cab.

She either doesn't take the hint or doesn't see it, because she leaves her hand where it is. Her fingers aren't warming up, not at all. "Why aren't you answering your phone?" he asks. "Why don't you want me to answer mine?"

"Daddy wants me to come home right now," she says, and finally, blessedly, takes her hand away. "He says it's an emergency."

"So maybe it's an emergency. Emergencies can happen any time. That's what makes them emergent."

"He didn't sound like it was an emergency. He sounded like he was sad, like he didn't want to be saying that to me, but he felt like he had to, and I know if you take me home now, you're never going to see me again, and I'm never going to see you again, and I don't know which is worse."

They're the same thing and they're not the same thing and Harry doesn't say anything, because whatever she's trying to wrestle with, he's not going to help by making a crack about it. Not right now.

"I don't know how I know that. I just do." Her voice is small and miserable, and for a moment he's furious with whoever made her sound like that, until he remembers it was him. She's not making any sense, and so he's not doing what she asked, and she's upset about it.

They've never manipulated each other, never used tears or tricks to get their way. It's like they both understood instinctively long before they knew how to articulate it that their relationship has to be built on honesty or it won't work. (In some ways, Harry March and Melanie Cosgrove are both older than they ought to be, growing up too fast in the face of overwhelming pressure. In other ways, both of them are younger than they ought to be, sheltered in her case by medical necessity and in his case by wealth and confidence. They're both aware of the ways in which they've been lucky, although the ways in which they've been unlucky sometimes seem to loom much larger.)

"She's at the tail end of her season, but it still knows how to speak to her," says Jack. Harry, who had almost managed to forget the impossible child in his backseat, jerks upright. "She's been lurching into it for longer. Yours will start speaking to you soon enough. I just hope we can find your guide before then. I hope whoever it is will be someone I like. Maybe we could get the Corn Jenny who coached me. Probably not, though. I'm sure she'd already be here if she'd been chosen for you."

"Kid, you don't make any sense at all," says Harry tightly. "I need you to start making sense and I need you to start making sense right now."

"Or what, you're going to put me out of the car?" Jack laughs derisively. "Good luck with that."

Harry takes a gamble. It hurts a little, because it goes against so much of what's become instinct over the last decade, but it's what he has. "I'll call Mel's father and tell him where we are," he says. Mel gasps, wounded. He doesn't allow himself to look at her. This is all too weird, and he needs it to start making sense before he can decide what happens next.

"You wouldn't."

"You really want to test me on that?"

Jack is quiet for a long, sullen moment before she asks, "If I tell you what's going on and you still don't think it makes sense, will you call him anyway? Because there's not much point to this if you're going to call him anyway."

"If I believe you're telling me everything you know, I won't call him," says Harry, with the solemnity of a promise.

Jack takes a deep breath. "Keep driving," she says. "I'll tell you what I can."

Harry hits the gas a little harder.

Three hundred years ago, a man named William Monroe was crowned Winter King," says Jack. "You have to understand two things first off: it wasn't an accident, and he didn't have a choice. Once the candidates for a coronation are identified, they either take the throne or they die. Depending on the time of year when the coronation is called, half of them are already dead."

"Okay, stop," says Harry. "You said you'd explain. There's a lot of assumption in that sentence, and I need you to back up and try again."

Jack inhales. "Melanie's dead," she says.

Harry doesn't hit the brakes this time. It's not easy, but he keeps driving. "Hence her insisting she doesn't have a heartbeat," he guesses. "Is that what you're saying?"

"Yes," says Jack. "Her heart stopped at the exact moment that William Monroe's did, as did the hearts of roughly two dozen others across the North American continent. He died immediately after his plane took out a woman named Diana Cartwright on the runaway in Ohio. Diana had been crowned alongside him, named the Summer Queen, meant to maintain the balance of the seasons between the two of them."

Harry scoffs. "This has nothing to do with us."

"This has everything to do with you," says Jack sourly. "You and Melanie are candidates for the crown."

"Meaning what, exactly?"

"Meaning you have between now and the hare moon to find and claim the crowns, or Melanie dies again, this time for good, and you get to shuffle along without her until the long night moon, and then you die too. There's nothing in this world that can save either one of you without your crowns."

Harry is momentarily speechless. Then, to his immense relief and vague surprise, he starts laughing.

"Oh, man, the two of you must have worked on this all week! It's a prank, right, Mel? You swapped out the pulse oximeter and hired this kid off of some pranking blog or something. My Valentine's Day present is my girlfriend trying to make a joke. Good one, hon. If you'd been a little bit less ridiculous, you might have sold me on it."

But Melanie isn't laughing. Melanie is watching him with large, liquid eyes, looking for all the world like his laughter is some sort of personal offense. He stops laughing.

"You think I'd lie to you about my heart?" she asks, voice barely above a whisper.

"What—No, of course not! I know how seriously you have to take your heart, I do, I just . . . You *have* to have a heartbeat, you can't be dead. Dead girls don't get dressed up for the Valentine's Day dance. They don't drink punch or kiss their boyfriends before curfew. They don't do anything. You've been trying to get me used to the idea that you're going to die and leave me soon, and I know that, I *know* that, but that doesn't mean I'm going to be okay with it! It doesn't mean I'm *ever* going to be okay with it! You can't be dead, and that means none of this can be happening, because I won't *let* it. This is all a big joke, and it's not as funny as you think it is."

He can see the lights of his house up ahead of them, bright and familiar and welcoming as they've always been. Brighter than they ought to be, maybe, because the front door is open, flooding the front yard with light, and that doesn't make any sense; his family turns the heater on as soon as the first real signs of autumn start to show, and they don't turn it off again until summer arrives. His mom always says they can't heat the entire outdoors, and then his dad laughs and says there's no reason why not, since they can certainly afford it, and they go round and round like that any time someone opens a window rather than turning down the thermostat.

The reason for the open door becomes clear a moment later: Dr. Cosgrove is standing on the front porch, apparently arguing with Harry's father, from the way both men are gesturing. Dr. Cosgrove's car blocks the bottom of the driveway. They're still too far away to see details, but Harry doesn't need to get any closer to see that his father is agitated; he can read it in the lines of the man's body, tight and somehow offended, even at this distance.

Harry hits the brakes. Softer this time, not wanting to throw anyone through the window, and maybe it's that and maybe it's learning from experience, but Jack stays in the backseat. "Whoa," she says. "He got here *fast*."

"We don't live that far apart," says Harry, lips gone inexplicably numb. "I used to ride my bike between our houses, before I was old enough to drive. Mel, what's your dad doing here?"

"I don't know. I expected him to be mad when I didn't pick up, but I didn't think he'd come to Harry's house." Her phone buzzes again. This time she knows it can't be her father, because he's right in front of her and doesn't have his phone, so she picks it up and swipes her thumb across the screen. Her eyes go wide. The question of whether she's wearing foundation is answered as her cheeks get just a shade paler—not enough for a true pallor, enough to confirm to Harry that the blood has just drained out of her face. "Oh," she says, voice soft.

"What?" asks Harry.

"Today when we both collapsed on the field? Christine filmed the whole thing, and she posted it on Instagram, and someone saw it and got her footage on the local news. It's all over. Everyone's seen it now." She drops the phone into her lap, staring blankly out through the windshield. "My dad's seen it. He knows I snuck out."

"He knows you died," says Jack. Her voice is low, urgent, on the verge of panicking. "We have to go."

Melanie twists to look at her, blinking. "But that's my *dad*," she says, like she's afraid Jack has somehow managed to miss that essential fact of the situation. "He's probably freaked out and worried about me. That's why he's being all weird."

"I'm not the first Jack Frost who's tried to come for you," says Jack hurriedly. "I'm the tenth, actually."

Melanie blinks again. "What?"

"Jack *Frost*?" asks Harry, much more interested in that bit of nonsense than the rest of what's going on. "What do you mean, Jack *Frost*?"

"Oh my gods above, below, and slightly off to the side, if I find out why your Corn Jenny isn't here yet and it's anything short of getting jammed into a movie-theater popcorn maker, I'm going to stuff her in there my own damn self," moans Jack. "We don't have time for this. We need to get away from here. Can you just get over yourself and *drive* already?"

Harry hesitates. He doesn't want to leave when his father is clearly fighting with Melanie's, wants to go over there and make a joke, to keep the peace the way he always does, the way he always has. But Melanie is looking at him with such anxiety in her eyes, and he's not sure how she's having such an easy time handling all of this (unless her heart really has stopped beating, says a small, traitorous part of him, a little voice he doesn't want to listen to; all this would be easy to believe with irrefutable proof at hand), but he's sure he needs to wipe that look off her face, whatever it means.

So Harry puts the car in reverse and backs away, and in an instant's time, he's driving away.

Somehow it feels like nothing so much as running away from home.

Sleeping Beauty

At the exact moment William Monroe's heart stops, so does Melanie Cosgrove's. It's like flipping a switch, one thing resulting in another, without any gap between them. But that isn't the only thing that happens in that instant. This would be a much shorter, much kinder story if it were.

When Melanie's heart stops beating, another heart starts.

The rhythm of its motion is slow at first, each muscular contraction followed by the smallest of pauses, but they gather speed quickly, becoming something steady, becoming something new. After a few minutes have passed (*Melanie lying dead and growing cool on the football field*), the heart's owner takes her first shuddering breath in seventeen years.

A moment after that, Melanie opens her eyes, unmoving heart still silent in her chest, and the newly wakened girl does the same. She blinks up at the darkness above her, the cobwebs tangled in the eaves of a room that can't truly be called a basement but serves much the same purpose: it is underground, accessible via a single narrow door, and intended for the storage of things that were meant to be forgotten. She has been stored here. She has been stored here for a very long time.

With the understanding that time has passed comes a slowly dawning understanding that her breath is pushing air into her body. She *has* a body, hers, no one else's, hers alone, and she commands that body to sit up, to let her get a better look at her surroundings.

Her muscles are slow and reluctant to respond to her commands, accustomed as they are to untroubled motionlessness, and the fact that they respond at all would seem like some sort of a miracle if she had more of an understanding of her own limitations.

As she sits up, she becomes aware that she has risen from a shallow pool of warm, brackish liquid, the color of the scum that gathers in the bottom of a fountain. It is green-brown with algae; it smells of yeast and nutrients. It runs down her arms and drips from her hair as she looks around, still not fully understanding what she sees, still not equipped to understand.

The basement that isn't a basement is lined with shelves, and the shelves are lined with strange equipment, things she doesn't have names for and can't identify. Beakers and bottles of inexplicable liquids; jars and packets of strange herbs and powders; boxes of rocks, even—some of them broken down with hammers, others waiting for their turn in the vast mortar and pestle that dominates one of the work tables.

There is a mirror against one wall. The girl sitting in the shallow liquid bath yearns for it as soon as she sees it, yearns for it the way a flower yearns for the sun. She attempts to stand, and her legs, which have never been used for this purpose before, respond to the indignity by dumping her to the floor in an ungainly heap of angles and limbs.

She sprawls there for a moment, struggling to catch her breath, hating the inexplicable force that has done this to her. The idea that perhaps resenting gravity is not the most sensible course of action will take some time to come to her; when it arrives, she will hold fast to her hatred, having nothing else to take its place.

The fall jerks several tubes out of her arms and back, leaving her dripping more than just the brackish liquid on the floor. There is no pain, either from the disconnection or the impact. Pain will come later, when she has a better understanding of her own outline. Many things will come later. In the here and now, she is pushing herself up with hands flattened against the concrete floor, smearing lines of chalk and charcoal that have been sketched there (but not smearing the paint beneath them; they are temporary accents for a much larger, more permanent working, and they were never meant to last through a trauma such as this), pushing herself up and finally to her feet, standing on legs that quiver and shake and threaten to dump her to the floor again.

She does not allow them to. She stands for the first time in her life, and she stands straight and true, and she is a testament to the alchemist's art. Not all testimonials are positive things. Not all monuments were meant to stand.

Step by shaking step, she makes her way across the room to the mirror, and sees herself for the first time in her life.

She is tall and she is lovely, and only her hair, wet and streaked with green algae as it sticks to her back and shoulders, makes it apparent that her skin has any color to it at all, for her hair is white. Bone-white, bleach-white, white as the driven snow. Her lips seem terribly red against the pallor of her skin, and her eyes are very blue, and she would be beautiful if she weren't so entirely terrible. She is the ghost of a girl, and not a girl at all.

She is seventeen years old and she has been dead since the day she was born and as she looks at herself in the mirror, she understands two things:

First, that to be alive is a wonderful thing, and something she very much desires. Something she has always very much desired, for all that before this moment she was unaware that she desired anything at all.

Second, that she once had a sister, a girl with whom she shared the waters of the womb, floating in peaceful silence before there was anything else in the world. And somehow that sister was able, through accident of birth or timing or something far more sinister, to break free and walk the world as if she were a real person. As if she somehow had the *right* to be the one who lived while her sister, her *sister*, died.

In that moment, the girl in the basement finds the second thing she has to hate. Gravity, and the girl whose name she does not know, the girl she can conceptualize only through her absence.

She doesn't know where she is, doesn't know her own name or how she's intended to get out of this room, but she knows how to stand, and she knows how to hate, and she knows that in this instant, those two things are enough.

She's going to have a life. Even if she has to take it away from someone else.

She turns a circle, looking at her surroundings, trying to understand the things that make no sense, that she was never meant to know. She's still turning when there is a click and something she didn't have the context to recognize until this moment as a door swings open, revealing the young man on the other side.

He looks to be a few years older than she is, tall and gaunt, but tan. He's seen the sun, this man, this *boy,* and she hates him for it. Hate is coming more and more easily to her, the only emotion she fully understands at this point in her slow climb toward fully realizing who and what she is, the scape and the scope of herself. She has her edges, she knows that, she has her limits; but she also has a child's innocent solipsism, the gentlest inability to stop viewing absolutely everything in reference to herself.

It would make her a monster, if she knew what a monster was. Right here and now, she barely even knows what *she* is, and knows only that she hates.

"Hello," says the boy. "You must be Aven."

The name isn't familiar in the sense of her ever having heard it before, but she knows it all the same, knows it down to the bones of her, because as soon as he speaks it, she understands that he's correct: she *is* Aven, and so she must be Aven, must be the person that she is. There's no other option. She hates him even more for that, for taking the moment when she could have been absolutely anyone and turning her into a specific someone, a person with rules and limitations. She is more concrete now than she was an instant before, and it isn't fair. It isn't fair at all.

"I'm Trevor," he says, and takes a few more steps toward her, not seeming to realize how much danger he's in. His hands are empty. She doesn't know why that should matter, but it does. "I'm your

Corn Jenny. It's a stupid name, I know, but I didn't pick it. I don't understand why the other three seasons get to be 'Jack,' and I get stuck with the only girl's name in the bunch, but whatever. I'm going to help you navigate this labyrinth. I'm going to help you *win*."

Aven likes the sound of that. She likes the idea of winning. Every word he says seems to unlock another cascade of things she already knows and understands. She doesn't attack him. For now.

"And once you win, I'll sit at your right hand forever, the Summer Ascendant, and we'll keep anyone else who wants to walk the fields from challenging either one of us." He smiles without humor. "If we play our cards right, you can even rule alongside your sister."

Sister . . . yes. She remembers a sister, hair as black as the corners of this room, and a heartbeat like the rhythm of the universe, filling and defining everything, until the moment it had been terribly and traumatically taken away.

Aven would like to see her sister.

Would like to make her understand why she shouldn't have gone away like that.

Slowly, she smiles at the tan boy who she still hates with all her heart but will listen to, for now. And Trevor, not recognizing the danger—or maybe simply not caring—smiles back.

Explanation

They're almost to Melanie's house before Harry realizes where he's going, following a pattern of behavior that's been with him for so long that he doesn't even have to think about it anymore. He glances at Mel, alarmed.

"Sorry," he says. "We can go somewhere else if we need to . . . Sorry."

"No," says Jack. "No, this is good. We know where her father is. This may be the only time it's safe for us to go to their house."

"What do you mean, 'safe'?" asks Melanie. "It's my *house*. He's my *father*. Of course it's safe for me to go there."

"Then why is he at Harry's house right now, yelling at his parents?" asks Jack. "Think for a second, Melanie. I know you can. You're a smart girl, when you're not drugging yourself to keep your heart-rate down."

Melanie says nothing, and Harry knows the barb hit home. Some of the drugs Mel takes to keep herself alive slow down her thinking, make him worry about taking advantage of her by mistake when he asks a question that would have been fine the day before but has somehow become dangerous ground. She hates them. She hates feeling like she can't understand her own life, and he hates the way they steal the light from her eyes. He loves the way they keep her with him.

For the first time tonight, he realizes how sharp and present she's been since he picked her up. Everything she's been saying is absolutely ridiculous, this whole situation makes no sense at all, but she's a part of it in a way that she so rarely is. She's *here*. Whatever else is happening, he has to be grateful for that much.

"He's just worried about me because he saw the news," says Mel, and her voice is unconvincing, and Harry can tell she doesn't quite believe what she's saying. It's not the truth, not even to herself.

"Yeah, sure," says Jack. "That's why he's been stopping us from getting to you for the last ten years. You didn't think I was the first one, did you? We've been trying to make contact for a decade, since the first time you made contact with your season. Every Jack Frost before me who's gotten near you has disappeared. I wouldn't have come if I'd been able to fight the pull of Winter trying to manifest."

"You keep using words and terms like we're supposed to understand them, and that doesn't mean we do," says Harry. He pulls up in front of Melanie's house, the car perfectly visible to anyone who happens to drive by. If they're really avoiding her father—if it's really as important as this weird kid seems to think it is—they're not going to have much time. "Mel, if you're doing this, you'd better do it."

"I'll be right back; keep the engine running," she says, and kisses his cheek before she slides out of the car and runs for the front door, surprisingly agile in her low heels.

Harry waits until he sees her unlock the front door and vanish into the house before he lifts his chin and looks at Jack in the rearview mirror.

"All right," he says. "Stop being weird, stop being vague, and stop trying to talk me in circles. You're going to tell me what's going on, and you're going to tell me right now, or else."

"Or else what?" The girl folds her arms defiantly. He doesn't get the sense she likes him very much, and that's fine by him, because the feeling, such as it is, is more than mutual.

"Or else I kick you out of my car and lock the doors so you can't weasel your way back in," he says. "And then I take Mel back to my house so her father can make sure she's okay. I don't know what's going on with her heart, but I do know that if the pulse oximeter can't pick up her heartbeat, something's probably bigtime wrong." He's not sure why he's been humoring her as long as he has, really.

Probably because it's getting warmer in the car by the second now that Mel's gone, and because his boutonniere is continuing to bloom, putting out what look almost like new leaves, although they must have just been hidden behind the flowers before. Cut flowers don't grow.

"Right," says Jack. "You're not primed to believe me the way she is, because I'm not yours the way I'm hers. I wish to hell I knew where Jenny was. She should be here by now."

Harry says nothing, just frowns at her reflection and waits.

Jack, apparently seeing that she's not going to win him over by complaining, takes a deep breath. "My name is Jack," she says. "You already picked up on that part."

"Never met a girl named Jack before."

"Neither have my parents. They named me something else, and when I was tapped for this position, one of the things it cost was my name. I am the spirit of Winter Ascendant. I don't necessarily exist the way normal human people do, not anymore, and I gave up all the things I was in order to become the thing I was meant to be."

Harry manages, barely, not to twist in his seat and stare at her. "What the fuck are you talking about?"

"Haven't you ever felt like some things were bigger and smaller than they seemed from the outside, and both at the same time? Ideas that felt like people. People that felt like ideas. Humans are very fond of anthropomorphic thinking, and there's a reason for that, because the way the universe works, if enough people think hard enough, for long enough, that something works in a certain way, reality will change to make that possible." She sounds so earnest, so utterly convinced that what she's saying is true, that he can almost overlook the fact that it's completely and utterly ridiculous. "A long, long time ago, people thought the seasons had faces. They thought the seasons were people just like they were, and if they asked the Summer nicely enough, they could get a better harvest, and if they asked the Winter nicely enough, they wouldn't all freeze in their beds."

"Tell it to global warming," he scoffs.

In the mirror, Jack's expression grows even graver. "Well, that's part of the problem. But see, those people a long time ago, they thought so hard that the seasons were just like them that they started electing people to represent the seasons. They called them temporary kings and queens, and gave them everything they could possibly want, right up until they killed them for the sake of the community. Blood on the snow and blood on the barley and all that good shit."

Harry blinks. "That's barbaric."

Jack shrugs. "Those were barbarous times. And anyway, they stopped killing people eventually, turned the idea of standing in for a season into something symbolic and fun for the kiddies. That's when people like me started showing up, the seasons Ascendant. I'm *not* the living Winter, never could have been, even if I'd wanted the gig, which, hello, no one sensible wants the gig. It's a shit job. But I'm tied to the living Winter. If your pretty poison apple girl manages to win her crown, I'll be part of her household, along with every other Jack Frost in the world—and we outnumber you lot by quite a bit. There are hundreds of us, maybe thousands, because the seasons are different everywhere you go."

Living in Portland, Oregon, where the coastal winds shape the weather and the mountains loom like walls against the sky, Harry is well acquainted with how an hour's drive can change the weather. Still, he frowns. "So you're saying Melanie—*my* Melanie—is some-how one of you people?"

"Not quite," says Jack. "Melanie is one of the candidates to become the living Winter for this continent. The Incarnate seasons are a lot less common than the Ascendant seasons. There are only seven crowns, and each of them can only be worn by one person at a time. The Winter King of this region just died, and Melanie's one of his potential replacements."

"You *do* realize how ridiculous this all sounds."

"Sadly, yeah, and that's part of why I was the one sent to try to make her understand what was going on. Still don't know where your damn Jenny is."

"I know a bunch of Jennies, but they're all at the dance, where we're not." The front door of Mel's house opens and Mel emerges.

Her dress is gone, and he mourns it a little, even as he can see the sense in her change of clothes. Jeans and a simple shirt under his school jacket make a lot more sense if they're running away from home (and this is ridiculous, they're not *running away from home* on the word of a weird kid who still isn't making half as much sense as he wants her to; that would be ridiculous, and while they're teenagers and hence allowed to sometimes do stupid things, they try not to be ridiculous, Melanie because she's watching her health, Harry because he doesn't want to worry his parents), and he knows her well enough to know that the backpack slung over her shoulder will be full of medical supplies, snacks, and other necessities.

"Not *a* Jenny, *your* Jenny," says Jack, with new urgency. It's like seeing Melanie again has her concerned about running out of time. "I'm a Jack Frost, I belong to Winter. You were supposed to get a Corn Jenny by now. The one for this region is an older lady who's been doing her job for absolutely ages. She'd be doing so much better of a job explaining things than I am, and she speaks Summer—I don't. She could probably put this whole thing into, I don't know, football terms or something so it would make sense to you. The best I can hope is that you're infatuated enough with my dead boss to keep listening."

"She's not dead," says Harry.

"She is right now, but she doesn't have to be," says Jack. "Neither of you does, not all the time. If you just listen, and do your best to make more progress than the other pairs—if you can get to the crowns first, she doesn't have to be. Not for keeps."

Harry tightens his hands on the wheel, watching Mel cross the lawn. "Keep talking."

Jack leans forward, resting her elbows on the gap between the two front seats. "Seasonal monarchs are exactly that—seasonal. For three months out of the year, they die. We measure the terms of waking and dying by moons, since the calendar isn't always in synch with the seasons. For her, that means when the flower moon shines in the sky, she dies, and sleeps through the rose moon and the hay moon. And then, when the green corn moon shines, she wakes up. Weak after her long sleep, but alive, and here. With you."

Jack knows what he's afraid of; he can tell by the way she stresses those last two words, the way she pauses to let what she's just said sink in.

Melanie is almost to the car when Jack continues: "It works both ways, of course. You'll have three moons together, and then, come the cold moon, you'll die, and you'll sleep through the deeps of winter. She'll keep her crown and her counsel alone, and you'll wake up at the start of spring."

"Six months out of the year," he says numbly. "That's what you're offering us. That's not a life. That's a long vacation."

Melanie opens the car door and slides back into the passenger seat, a worried expression on her face. Harry frowns over at her.

"Mel? What's wrong?"

"Apart from feeling like I just robbed my own house?" She hugs her backpack to her chest. "The phone rang the whole time I was inside. The house line, not my phone. It would go until the answering machine picked up, and then whoever was on the other line would hang up, and then they'd go again, and again, and I don't know if it was the same person every time, but it scared me. Dad's colleagues are the only ones who use that line, and I don't like it when they call the house."

"Why not?" asks Harry.

"I don't know. When they call, they sometimes come to the house after they talk to him, and . . . and they just make me uncomfortable." Melanie shrugs awkwardly. "There was this one woman, Dr. Barrow, but she only came around a couple of times, and we haven't seen her in almost a year. She used to look at me like I was a science project. I didn't like it."

"Have you tried telling your father this?" asks Harry.

Melanie's phone buzzes again, another call to be ignored. She glances at the screen regardless, grimacing at the name displayed there. "It's my father," she says. "*He's* my father. How am I supposed to tell him I don't want him to meet with his colleagues because they give me the heebie-jeebies?"

She's a teenage girl, occasionally rendered frail by her ailments, aware that she's beautiful. It's not arrogant, although she's fully capable of being arrogant about things she's actually *done*, things she's worked for and accomplished: she's never wanted or needed to weaponize her prettiness, because she's had Harry for as long as she could remember, and while her looks have something to do with it, she hasn't always been pretty while they've been together. It's just factual, something she needs to know if she's going to walk in the world.

People who think a pretty girl is prettier when she doesn't know it are people looking to take advantage of a pretty girl who doesn't understand the danger she's in, and Melanie doesn't have the time for that. She never has. So she knows she's beautiful, and she knows her father's colleagues look at her like she's a science experiment, and she knows it makes her profoundly uncomfortable in a way she has difficulty articulating, in part because it *isn't* connected to her looks. If they looked at her the way the boys look at her in the school halls, or the way her freshman-year math teacher looked at her, she'd understand it. She wouldn't *like* it, but she would *understand* it, and that might lessen her discomfort in some genuine and measurable way.

These people look at her like something they want to own, to possess and take apart, like she's a toy that someone else has and doesn't deserve, and it makes her skin crawl, and it's so far beyond her experience in all other things that she can't articulate it so that it can be understood. Not by her father, not by Harry, not by anyone. Until she grasps it for herself, she can't possibly show it to someone else, and that aches.

"I have everything I need," she says. "Harry, should we go back to your place and get whatever it is you're going to need?"

"Need for what?" he asks.

"You're not this stupid," says Jack. She leans forward, head between the seats, and looks at him. "I know you like to play the fool, class clown, that whole routine, but you're *not* stupid. You never have been. Melanie *died* today. If her father gets his hands on her, it's game over, and we're not going to take the season, and you won't be coronated, and if you don't get coronated, you die too."

"How does that work, exactly? I want you to break this down like a football play. Use the simplest words you can. And no, Mel, we're not going back to my place. There's stuff there I could use, but if we're running away from home like assholes, I'm not putting my folks into the position of being the last people who see us alive. That's the sort of thing that gets you on the evening news, and not in the good way."

In the backseat, Jack puts her hand over her face and sighs. This would be so much easier if Harry's Corn Jenny had shown up when she was supposed to. He needs a guide. She's not equipped to talk to him. Melanie is naturally inclined to listen to her, to trust her as a friend or at least as not an enemy. Jack could no more betray the incarnate Winter than she could cut off her own hand without flinching. She could betray Harry, though. She's heard stories of ascendants who've done just that, decided their incarnate was yoked to the wrong partner and arranged to have someone removed from the competition in order to get them a better one.

But all those stories are from other lands, or from centuries ago, when North America still understood how to conduct a coronation. She's the latest in a three-hundred-year line of ascendants desperate to see things change, and some of the rules have been muddled or forgotten in the interim.

Jack is the only person in this car who understands what's happening, and she has no idea what she's doing.

"You play football, right?" she asks, a little desperately. Harry nods. Keeping tabs on him has never been her job: her last year has been spent learning her own new role in the cosmos and studying one Melanie Cosgrove, in the hopes that maybe a coronation would happen during her lifetime. She never expected it to be this soon. None of them did.

For the last three hundred years, William Monroe has maintained an iron grip on the continent, forcing his counterpart into sleep and ignoring the damage this has done to the world. This was never going to happen. This was never going to be her job. Everyone who understands the system has known Melanie, while an ideal candidate from the outside, wasn't going to live long enough for a coronation to be called. It simply wasn't possible.

And now here she is, and here they are, and this is happening. Jack has to deal with it.

"In football, every player has a role to play, right?" Harry nods again, and Jack begins relaxing into the metaphor, just a little. "Imagine if you played football with one big team that you split down the middle to represent the opposing sides, and that was how a normal game happened. That's you and Melanie now."

"What?" asks Harry, sounding almost alarmed. "We're not on different teams. Melanie's on my team."

"Yes, it's one big team that plays against itself sometimes. You and Melanie are trying out for the position of quarterback on the two halves of the same team. The team will do a better job if the two of you get along with each other, but it will work if you don't. Just not smoothly or as well. You won't win as much when you *do* play against other teams. You with me so far?"

"Not really, but sure," says Harry sullenly. Melanie's phone buzzes again. She looks at the screen, and makes a face.

Leaning across the car, she puts a hand on his arm. "Maybe drive," she suggests gently, and Harry turns the engine on, pulls away from the curb, and starts to drive.

"Where are we going?" he asks.

"I don't know," she says, somewhat reluctantly. "If we can't go back to your place and we can't go to the school without my dad catching us, I don't know."

Harry has dreamt of this night since the day they handed him his learner's permit and his father tossed him the keys to the car that was his birthday present. All he's wanted to do that whole time, the quiet chanting need behind every action and every hour, has been to put Mel in his passenger seat and drive. Just drive, as far from parents and teachers and doctors and hospitals as he can, take her someplace where they can be happy and she can be healthy and they can have the life they've never been quite willing to risk planning together. It's all he's wanted, and he's always known it wasn't possible, that it wasn't fair to even want it as much as he does. And now he's doing it, on the word of a kid he doesn't know and the evidence of a broken pulse oximeter.

Mel looks better than she has in ages, though, cheeks flushed under her foundation, which seems to stand out more now that there's some actual color in her face, some sign that she's actually alive under there. Her eyes are bright and she's breathing easily, and while this could be one of those instances of someone who's really unwell having a brief surge of apparent good health before they collapse, he's been her best friend for most of their lives, and he knows what it looks like when she's fighting off an episode. He doesn't think she's going to crash anytime soon.

It's almost like he has her all the way, maybe for the first time. It's almost like they're normal people.

"To become one of the two quarterbacks, you had to try out though, right? You had to go through some sort of an audition process, to prove you were strong enough and fast enough and whatever else a quarterback needs to be enough to do the job. So you and Melanie, if you want to play those positions, you have to go through the trials. And then if you're the best, you both get the place. But if either of you fails, since you went in together, neither of you gets to play." Jack pauses. "I feel like this should be more formalized, somehow."

"Ya think?" Harry shakes his head. "This is all deeply weird, and if I could find my girlfriend's pulse, I'd put you out of the car."

"Thank you," says Melanie. "For *not* putting her out of the car. We need to understand what's going on." Then she grimaces. "And I need to maybe beat my phone to death with a brick. Do you have a brick in the car?"

"There's a tire iron in the trunk, but until I know where we're going, I don't particularly want to stop driving," says Harry.

"It might be easier to decide where we were going if we weren't in the process of actively going there," says Melanie.

"Yeah, but we'll lose momentum and pick something that makes sense, and then our parents will find us," says Harry.

Jack makes a small, amused noise. Melanie twists to look at her.

"Sorry," she says. "The idea that the biggest thing you have to worry about right now is your parents finding you is just hilarious. It's also not completely wrong. *His* parents are pretty harmless. Nice people, and it's not their fault they got wrapped up in this. *Your* parents, on the other hand . . . hoo, boy."

"My mother died when I was born," says Melanie. "She had the same heart condition I do. Giving birth to me and my sister killed her."

"I bet you hate the *Star Wars* prequel," says Jack. "Didn't you ever ask yourself how you can have a condition that hospitalizes you six times a year and requires you to take more drugs than a pharmacy, *and* have inherited it from your mother? Your heart is basically made of tape and twine. It should have stopped beating years before it did, but you had so much of the Winter stuffed in there that it kept going, because it didn't know how to stop. How did your mother have the same condition and live long enough to get pregnant, much less carry twins to term?"

Melanie doesn't answer. Harry knows she's asked herself the same question, because she's asked it of him, usually right after he's said something about the future, when she's fallen into the pit of blaming herself for her own impending death, and for not being strong enough to break up with him.

"The story he's been telling you for your whole life hasn't been true," says Jack darkly. There's a bitter viciousness in her tone that Harry appreciates, even shares. There have been times when he hated the man.

"Are you trying to say my mother's alive?" asks Melanie.

"No. I'm sorry. Except for the part where even if she were alive, she'd still be the kind of person who married your father and agreed to his wild experimentation, and that means you're better off without her in your life. But no, she's not alive. She died when you were born."

"So what was the point of—"

"She died because your father killed her. Between your birth and your sister's, he drove a stake through her heart."

Melanie doesn't say anything. The silence grows, deepens, becomes so profound it fills the entire car, and Harry, who has made a life out of shattering uncomfortable silences, can't take it anymore. "Mel's mom was a vampire?" he asks.

"No," scoffs Jack. "She was an alchemist. Which means she might as well have been a vampire—vampires are more honest. They at least tell people they've come to suck their blood and drain them dry. Alchemists pretend they're doing the things they do because they want to make humanity better, but they mostly just make things better for alchemists and mess up the universe for everybody else. Sometimes they break it in ways we can't even comprehend until they're over. Like creating a thirty-year time loop that keeps rewinding and replaying the entire planet for centuries."

Harry stares at her in the rearview mirror, mouth hanging open. "You're serious."

"Yes."

"Mel's mother was an . . . alchemist? Those aren't real."

"Neither are people so tied to the seasons that they stop qualifying as entirely human, and yet here we are, in a whole car full of them." Jack shrugs. "We have to deal with what the world hands us, and not argue too much about whether or not it's logical, or reasonable, or real. 'Real' is just a word people use to dismiss things they don't want to work to understand."

Harry resists the urge to take his hand off the wheel and rub his temples. He recognizes the road around them now, at least, and knows roughly where they're heading: if he doesn't turn the car around, they're going to wind up at the botanical gardens. The gardens are technically closed at night, but really that just means they won't have to pay to get inside: the visitor's center and gift shop lock up, and any staffers still in the area to check on the center's rehabbed birds will yell if they see people there when they aren't supposed to be, but Harry grew up in this area. He knows how to avoid being seen. More, his parents are huge donors to the gardens, and if he identifies himself, he'll be forgiven as being overly excited to spend a little private time with his girlfriend.

He's not sure how anyone who sees them will justify Jack to themselves. Maybe they'll assume Melanie's babysitting and had to bring her charge along with her, and that will explain why he's in a tuxedo and she's in a sweatshirt. Or maybe he's worrying too much. They're kids. Adults never pay as much attention to what's actually happening as they do to the fact that kids are doing things, kids are where they aren't supposed to be, kids are *disobeying*. They could probably have a literal Frankenstein monster chasing them and the adults wouldn't notice, if they were on the wrong side of a gate.

Yes, the botanical gardens will do nicely, he decides, and if the world shifts a little around them once a clear destination has been settled upon, well, he doesn't know how to notice that yet. Eventually it will come as easy as breathing, but right here, right now, he can be forgiven for not paying full attention, for not understanding the consequences of his choices. He's always been insulated from consequences by the reality of who his parents are—he isn't as spoiled as he could have been, thanks to his utter devotion to a girl who money could never have been enough to save, but he's still used to being able to buy his way out of almost anything—and this will be a learning experience for him.

He doesn't particularly want a learning experience, but then, who ever does?

"So you're saying Mel's dad murdered her mother," says Harry.

"I mean, yes, but that word isn't sufficient for what he did," says Jack. "He sacrificed her, and she was a willing sacrifice. They both worked for a man named James Reed, who was maybe the oldest alchemist in North America, and was made in a lab by a woman named Asphodel Baker."

"This is ridiculous," says Melanie.

"She wanted someone who could be her hands while she did something really big and really stupid for a while, and so she made herself a proxy. He was her son and her student and her lover, and as far as the American Alchemical Congress was concerned—as far as he was concerned—he was her killer. Now, that's a long story and we don't have time for it right now."

Harry, who is pretty sure you know when you kill someone, frowns and doesn't say anything. Melanie is not so sanguine.

"If we don't have a lot of time, you're wasting it," she snaps. "I need you to explain what's happening."

"I'm trying," says Jack. "I'm trying. This isn't easy, it's complicated and it's contradictory and sometimes it's all piled up, one thing on top of another like a game of pick-up-sticks, only half the sticks are venomous snakes, and they haven't been fed in a while. I can't tell you everything in a single, linear order, because everything is connected to everything else. What I *can* say is that I won't lie to either one of you. Melanie, I *can't* lie to you, even if I wanted to, and Harry, I *could* lie to you, because I'm not your servant, but I won't, because it would hurt my lady, and hurting her is anathema to who and what I am. The idea of being dismissed from my role is the worst one in the world, and I sort of wish I hadn't been tapped to be a guide, because if you lose, I'm fucked. If you go directly up against whoever eventually wins and they hold it against me, I can be stripped and sent down to humanity, and that's the worst thing I can think of."

"You said we don't qualify as entirely human anymore," says Harry. "And that Mel's mom was a vampire."

"Alchemist," says Jack.

"Neither of those things exists, so I'm going to say same difference," says Harry. He pulls into the gravel lot set aside for the botanical gardens and gets out of the car, slamming the door behind himself as he shoves his keys into his pocket.

Melanie gets out more decorously. She seems more dazed than angry, which he supposes makes sense, since most of the ridiculous claims Jack is slinging are aimed at her; she's overwhelmed in a way that he isn't, and probably will be for a while. He'll just have to work harder to keep her safe, until whatever-this-is is over.

She glances at her phone, and sighs in obvious relief. "No service out here," she says, shoving it into the back pocket of her jeans. "I don't have to keep ignoring his messages if I can't see them."

"And they won't be able to track your phones if you're not on the grid," says Jack approvingly, as she climbs out of the car. She glances at Harry. "Smart," she says, in a snidely judgmental tone that makes him bristle, because he's heard it before.

He gets it from teachers who've decided his goofy affability is a shield for a lack of intellectual acuity, even though his grades have always been excellent, and from classmates who don't have access to his scores and schoolwork, but who assume any progress he makes is a consequence of his parents' money and not any work he's actually done for himself. The only person who's never written him off as stupid, even for a moment, is Mel, and that's just because he's never been able to play the fool hard enough to fool her.

If he's being honest, he's never really tried.

"All right," he says, once they're all out of the car. "Follow me."

He leads them across the street and down the shallow slope to the edge of the woods. Portland, Oregon, has a famously great climate for growing roses and other flowers, to the point where they host one of the world's test gardens for new varieties, where the horticulturists who develop new flowers bring them to have their first and most impressive show crops. So it makes sense that the botanical gardens decided to pivot in a different direction, specializing in native plants and thriving scrubby shrubs. It's not terribly impressive to the eye, but it's a gorgeous show of conservation and concern for what Oregon was before it became Oregon, when it was part of a continent and not a country.

Harry has always liked the botanical gardens: He likes how *real* they feel, how unassuming, like they don't care about how many tourist dollars they can attract as long as they can keep feeding lightning-struck owls and ravens with the bad luck to survive losing fights with trucks. The wildlife-conservation angle of the place is small and mostly for show, a sort of glorified roadside zoo, but the birds are happy, healthy, and unsuited for release, and so he doesn't feel bad about adoring them the way he does.

They remind him of Mel. Caged but defiant, broken and beautiful and completely prepared to take someone's eye out if challenged.

Halfway down the slope, the path branches, and he leads them left, toward the stream and the memorial bench someone paid to put there. It seems like a good place to have a life-altering conversation, if that's something that actually has to happen.

Once there, he boosts himself onto the back of the bench, balancing on the narrow strip of wood, and looks levelly at Jack. "Okay. You're going to talk now. No more backtracking, no more trying to tell us what *you* think we need to know, just as linear a story as you can manage. Got it?"

"Got it," says Jack, and she sounds vaguely amused, but she doesn't argue as she walks a few feet away and leans up against a tree, folding her arms over her chest.

"All right," she says. "The first thing you need to understand is that alchemists are how the old magicians and philosopher-wizards reconciled the world as *they* knew it with the rise of scientific thought. Science didn't destroy magic. Both have always existed. Combustion and electricity and the lever didn't all start working the day people stopped chucking fireballs at each other. That's silly. Magic is what magic is, and it doesn't give a damn what people think of it. But *people* give a damn. *People* learn to think one way and not another, and then they think their way is the only way there is, and all other ways of thinking are wrong, or primitive, or misguided. So there were wizards, and then people figured out science was easier on the mind and body than magic, and they started doing science instead, and the people who still wanted the kind of things you really need magic for started doing alchemy, so they didn't lose it all."

"If this is some kind of fucked-up LARP bullshit, I'm out," says Harry, throwing up his hands. "I am not going to pretend to be an elf just so we can run around in the woods being elves together."

"It is not some kind of 'fucked-up LARP bullshit,'" says Jack, sounding amused. "I mean, it *is* fucked up, and it *is* bullshit, no question about that, but it's also real. It's happening. Magic never went away the way people want to say it did, it just evolved. Everything evolves. Alchemists use science and philosophy and really, really rigid ways of thinking to influence the world. And Melanie's parents met when they were both apprenticed to Dr. James Reed."

"Who you said before was Frankenstein's monster," says Harry. "Right?"

"Not quite, but good enough for shared concept," says Jack. "His maker put him together from the things she thought were best about a man, and he was handsome and charming and clever, all the things Shelley said about her own mad scientist's monster. Shelley was an alchemist too, by the way."

"Mary Shelley?" asks Mel, who has been quiet since they reached the clearing, listening in wide-eyed silence that Harry supposes makes sense, since it's her parents they're talking about.

"A surprising number of alchemists hide as authors," says Jack. "If they get lucky enough to write a book that sinks into the way people think, they can amass an amazing amount of power in a very short amount of time. I won't say there's no effort involved—they have to write a book to start the process—but it's easier than lassoing storms or bringing corpses to life, so it remains a popular career path. Professors and doctors, also common."

"Huh," says Harry. "Okay, keep talking, weird kid."

"Roland and Ariadne Cosgrove both showed promise in the alchemical arts, and found themselves bound to James Reed, whose goals have always been somewhat . . . abnormal, even for an alchemist. He was obsessed with the idea that a force called the Doctrine of Ethos could be cajoled into becoming Incarnate if he could just make it an attractive-enough vessel to inhabit."

"You are officially speaking gibberish," says Harry.

"I already told Melanie most of this, but here goes: there are certain natural forces and phenomena that have been convinced, by centuries of human belief, to turn themselves into people."

"People," says Harry blankly.

"Yes."

"So that's what you've been doing a piss-poor job of explaining this whole time. You're trying to say winter somehow turned itself into a person, and Melanie *is* the winter."

"No."

"No?"

"No, Melanie *isn't* the winter, and you're not the summer." Harry starts to relax, and he shouldn't, because it means he's caught just a little bit off-guard when Jack adds, firmly, "Yet."

His head snaps up, and he looks from the girl to Mel and back again, both of them washed out by the moonlight, both of them shadowed enough to make it difficult to read their expressions. He can't believe he's listening to this. He can't believe *Mel*, who normally has no patience for fairy stories, is listening to this. She should be laughing her head off and demanding they get out of here, head to the Roxy for pancakes if they're going to skip the dance.

And her father shouldn't be going to his house to yell at his parents, or blowing up her phone with calls and texts just because he saw her on the news. Yes, the scene on the football field looked bad, but Mel was fine, and she's fallen down before, when her blood pressure dropped too abruptly. Nothing about that scene should have frightened her father enough to make him react this way. Nothing, unless the upsetting part was seeing Harry fall down, too.

And Mel doesn't have a heartbeat. Harry doesn't want that to be true, but he's had a lot of experience feeling for the particular, not entirely even, rhythm of her heart. He can say it's the pulse oximeter as much as he wants to, and if this all went away right now, he might be able to eventually convince himself he believes it, but he knows what's true and he knows what's real, and what's true is that Mel's skin is cold to the touch, and she doesn't have a heartbeat, and something is very wrong. Something has changed.

So he's willing to keep listening, no matter how ridiculous this is, because there's no other explanation being offered. This is what he can do.

"What do you mean, 'yet,' and what does this have to do with Mel's parents being alchemists?" he asks.

Jack takes a deep breath. "Will you both agree to accept, for the purposes of this conversation, that sometimes, natural forces embody themselves as humans for reasons of their own?"

"Yes," says Melanie.

"I guess," says Harry. "If I have to."

"Earlier you said that once a force embodies itself, it keeps doing it," says Melanie. "What does that mean, exactly?"

"It means the first time the living Winter became a person, that person was *perfect* for the Winter, somehow. They were the platonic ideal of the idea, and they lived the season like they had never been anything else and never could have been anything else. They may even have forgotten what it meant to be human—although it's a lot more likely that the first Winter, and the first Summer, were never people at all. They were probably sculpted, from ice or wildflowers, snowflakes and fresh fruit. Alchemy is all about transmutation. Turning something shaped like a person into an actual person is easy, and if the conditions were right, the natural forces we're talking about could have done the transmutation without an alchemist to help. And then the season got to walk around and be a person for a while, and that was very fun for them."

"But?" asks Harry. When Melanie turns to look at him, he shrugs. "There's always a 'but' in a story like this."

"But once the season had been a person, it got addicted to being a person. When something turns human, humanity changes it, even if only a little. So now there's always a Summer, and always a Winter. Multiple, actually, of each, seasonal monarchs scattered around the world, manifesting entirely on their own, people who hold the power and potential of a season in their hands. Some people are born naturally inclined toward one season or another—the people who go out barefoot on frost-covered grass because their feet aren't cold, or who run marathons in the middle of July and don't worry about heat exhaustion. The people who are *inclined*. Most of them will never be called to serve their season. They grow up and grow old and become more complicated, and the more complicated they are, the less room they have inside them for something as simple as a seasonal orientation. The timing has to be right. But if it happens that a crown is to be passed, all those who are near enough—and that usually means 'on the same continent,' since there's no point in activating the potential candidates in Europe for a coronation in Australia—will be called to compete, and the two who win will take the crowns. Summer and Winter, born again, out of blood on the barley and blood on the snow."

"This is making my head hurt," complains Harry. Mel leans over and puts her hand on his knee, and he covers it with his own, holding on to her. He still can't feel her pulse, not in her fingers and not, when he shifts his grip a little further down, in her wrist.

This is happening.

"It made my head hurt, too," says Jack. "All the candidates in an area will be called, but they tend to arrive in pairs, because they naturally cleave to each other when they find one another. It's not a soulmates thing or any of those weird-ass romantic tropes. It's more 'we make a wheel when we're together, let's roll,' and then they enjoy one another's company too much to stop. So they come to the challenge in pairs, and sometimes—not often, but sometimes—both halves of the same pair will win. Other times, one of them falls and the other hooks up with someone unpartnered, and they continue that way. In the end, the last two standing take the crowns, and they keep them until they either die or set those crowns aside."

"You said before that the dead guy, William Morris, was crowned three hundred years ago," says Harry. "Talk more about that."

"William *Monroe*. Not the talent agency. Once you're crowned, you're dead for three months out of the year. Like, dead-dead, glass box or pine box or whatever makes you comfortable. And during that time, if someone destroys your body, they can claim your crown—not that I can understand why anyone would want to, since taking the winter crown in the middle of July would mean committing suicide in the weirdest way I've ever heard of. But the rest of the year, you're healthy and functional and not dead, like, ever. Old

William liked being the living Winter, liked the power it gave him, and the control. He didn't like being dead, though."

"Who would?" asks Harry.

"I mean, most of the monarchs are cool with it, because the three months of deadness might suck, but the other nine months of the year are pretty slammin'," says Jack. "Health, prosperity, usually wealth, since the world literally provides for all their needs—it's one of the better gigs, and has been since humans stopped symbolically massacring the living seasons to bring about a better harvest. Most continental monarchs do their jobs for at least a hundred years before they decide to hand off their divinity and call a crowning."

"So what happened here?" asks Melanie.

"William disliked being dead so much that he bargained with the alchemists to keep himself from dying. And the solution they hit on was exploiting the fact that multiple crowns exist in parallel and keeping him in motion. As long as he was never in a place where summer was happening, his own personal winter remained in effect." Jack shudders. "That's the only thing I didn't like about being called to become the Winter Ascendant. It meant working for that asshole. Because each region's crowns turn out to be pretty tightly linked, when he didn't die at the start of summer, the North American Summer Queen never woke up. She came back to life, but not enough to actually open her eyes. And he kept her like that for almost the entire three hundred years they served together."

"What an asshole," says Harry. "So that's how this Reed guy got involved."

"Yes. Asphodel Baker was obsessed with the incarnate natural forces. She thought the existence of the living seasons proved that anything could be forced to manifest in a human form if the right preparations were made, and that controlling that human form would mean she controlled whatever natural force that person represented. She couldn't take the seasons, because there are too many of us—"

"Wait," interjects Harry. "How many of you *are* there?"

"The Incarnates represent the two big seasons, and then the Ascendants either serve them directly, as I do, or they represent the transitional seasons. So Winter has Jack Frost, and Summer has Corn Jenny. And then you have Jack in the Green for spring and Stingy Jack for fall."

"Someone really liked the name 'Jack,'" comments Harry. "I'm sure that's not going to be confusing at *all*."

"I'm Winter enough to have been called when there was an opportunity for the season to manifest in my area, but not Winter enough to have been held back for a coronation," says Jack, sounding amused. "I serve the Winter Incarnate, whoever that may be, meaning that for the last year, I served William Monroe, even though I didn't want to. There are dozens of Ascendants. Sometimes we live only miles apart. And that's how things are meant to work, but because the system needs such a volume of people to function properly, Asphodel knew she couldn't claim us, and so she started setting her eyes on new systems."

"Hence the whole 'Doctrine of Ethics' thing," says Harry.

"Ethos, and yes," says Jack. "She passed her obsession down to her student before she convinced him he had to kill her in order for her to progress to the next stage in her enlightenment. He was an obedient creation, if he was nothing else. While she took her rest, he continued with the work."

Melanie is starting to get the feeling that these people have a different definition of "death" than the one she's always known, and she frowns. She's spent most of her life afraid of dying, of leaving her father and Harry alone. If her father really is an alchemist, he must have known death didn't necessarily mean going away, and so many of the things he's said and done to her are taking on a new light. She doesn't like it.

"Did he succeed?" she asks. "In making the Doctrine of Ethos ascendant, or whatever?"

"Incarnate," says Jack. "I know it's confusing now, but it's like learning any new language. It all starts making sense once you have the pieces. If you force a natural concept to become a person, you incarnate it. If someone is tied to a natural concept but doesn't fully represent it on their own, they're ascendant. And if someone embodies a natural concept so completely that they take ownership, they control it and how it works on the world, they manifest and become that concept incarnate. Right now, you're potential incarnates. If you get the crown, you'll manifest as the Winter Incarnate, and you will *be* the living Winter, not just linked to it. You'll be able to call down storms and walk the winter ways that currently don't exist for you. All you have to do is win."

"You make that sound easy," says Harry.

"Oh, it won't be," says Jack. "Because every single person who's eligible has someone like me, or like Corn Jenny, who's *supposed* to be here to help walk you through this, telling them how it works. And maybe some of them will be better at explanations than others, and maybe some of the candidates will be better at listening than others, but every candidate gets a guide. That's why there are so many ascendants. The winners catch the crowns. The losers die for keeps. Can I get back to explaining what Melanie's father has to do with all this?"

"Sure," says Harry, and frowns. He doesn't like any part of this. But he likes Mel's hand on his knee. He likes the fact that even if he can't find her pulse, he can find *her,* and if there's anything he's taking away from this Jack kid's fumbling attempts to explain herself, it's that if they get these crown things, Mel won't have to leave him. Not now, not tomorrow, not ever.

They'll get to stay together, and all they have to do is embody two natural concepts that have no business being people in the first place.

"Melanie's parents," says Jack, in a tone that implies *this* time she's going to be allowed to finish her thought; *this* time she's going to get to the ending, "were recruited by Reed at the beginning of their apprenticeships, and he became their master of record. Formal alchemy is a lot like formal academia. They like their rules and rituals and ways of doing things. He infected them with Asphodel's obsession, and Ariadne became convinced he was going about things from the wrong angle. She thought manifesting the Doctrine would destroy the vessels—it was too big, it was too complicated, it was never meant to be a person—but if he could learn to shape and refine the perfect vessels with something smaller, he'd be able to do it. She and Roland drew up one of the most ambitious private plans anyone had seen. They would craft their own vessels to contain something that was supposed to be impossible to catch or control, they would give of their own blood and their own power to craft those vessels properly, and in the course of time, despite never having known the touch of one another's flesh, she became pregnant with their greatest creation."

Harry shoots a nervous glance at Melanie. "Is that why your dad was so worked up about the idea that we might be sleeping together?" he asks, swallowing hard.

"No, he was so worked up because we were sixteen and he wasn't sure I wouldn't have a heart attack in the backseat of your car, and if we didn't use birth control, he might wind up a grandparent with a dead daughter trying to raise a baby all by himself," says Melanie, with the sort of ridiculously perky cheer she's always brought to saying terrible things. "I don't think he cared much about my virginity as a social construct, just as a medical one."

"Well, this is charmingly horrific and apparently I've said enough smart shit that you've both forgotten that I'm *thirteen* and would like you to not," says Jack, as if she hadn't been the one to introduce sex into the conversation. "Anyway, they got married to guarantee chains of custody, and continued their efforts. Ariadne confirmed she was carrying twins, and they decided this was a sign that they would ensnare both seasons at the same time. But that wasn't possible."

"Why not?" asks Melanie.

"Seasons Incarnate are always born at the appropriate time of year. She went into labor on the winter solstice, which would have made you both perfect vessels for the winter but left neither of you suited for the summer. So she proposed a solution while she was in her hospital bed. When their first daughter was born, Roland drove a stake of polished mistletoe into Ariadne's heart, killing her where she labored and stopping her birthing before the second girl could be delivered. It would have played perfectly to their plans, if he'd been a little more aware of the mysteries of the female body."

"The fuck?" asks Harry.

"He didn't wait until she had expelled the placenta. Melanie was still connected to her mother when she died, and the symbolic nature of Ariadne's sacrifice broke her Winter-primed heart before the connection was severed. As the doctors fought to save the suddenly struggling infant, Roland removed his wife from the hospital with the second babe still in her belly, suffocated by the weight of her own mother's flesh."

Melanie has heard this story before, but in a very different form. She heard her mother's heart gave out from the strain of birth, that her twin sister had been stillborn, not suffocated in the womb. She says nothing, only stares as her hand clenches tight on Harry's knee, fingers digging in until he winces. He doesn't pull away, choosing instead to bear up under the pain and lend her what support he can.

Jack doesn't appear to notice the distress she's causing, and continues blithely on: "His wife and research partner was dead, and his perfect vessel was flawed. Reed's suggestion was to harvest Melanie for parts, repurpose her to serve the greater alchemical goals of their organization. Roland refused, choosing instead to extract the second babe from Ariadne on his own and put her into a state of unborn stasis until the summer solstice."

Melanie stares at her in silent horror.

"Your sister lives," says Jack. "She has lived this entire time. She never wakes, she never walks, but she lives, by the cleverness of your father's art and the horror of your mother's sacrifice. She was intended to embody the Summer Incarnate, and she still carries that potential. She's one of those who will be set against you as you continue." She nods toward Harry. "Your father, once he becomes aware that a crowning is at hand—if he doesn't know already—will be looking to remove your boyfriend from consideration. His intention was always to own both sides of the season."

Melanie stares at her. Harry does the same. Neither of them says a word.

Jack shrugs. "So that's where we are right now. It's time to start running for your lives, because if you don't win this race, you're finished."

Into the Woods

Roland Cosgrove was not expecting this.

He knew when the aftershock of William's death hit the remains of the Alchemical Congress, setting off a hundred sensors and monitoring devices, that there would be consequences. He knew the reaction from the Congress would be immediate, teams being dispatched to collect as many of the candidates as could be found and identified, whisking them away before the challenge could begin. Not all of them had been located over the years since he and Ariadne began their work; the techniques they developed together were still in their early days when she died and left him alone with a broken babe and no real idea of what he was doing as a father.

(If only he had realized the placenta had yet to be expelled, he might have saved himself so damn much trouble. But then, keeping a damaged, disabled daughter under his thumb had been difficult enough to seem impossible some days; he can't really imagine what it would have been like trying to manage a fully healthy one.)

Without Ariadne to assist him, with Aven sleeping in what was once their shared lab, and Melanie taking up the majority of his leisure time, Roland has neglected his duties to the Congress for the past seventeen years, spending most of his time on his daughters, both the known and the unknown. The techniques for finding the potential avatars for summer and winter have never been sufficiently refined; they'll have missed some, no matter how closely they hewed to his notes.

Their attendants, the seasonal Ascendants, are easier to find, for all that they're less powerful. They come and go more quickly, for one thing, and William has always been happy to throw the ones who displease him out of his good graces. Roland is sure that by now, more than half of those ridiculous constructs have been caught, and while some will have died in the process, there will still be more than enough remaining to guarantee the outcome.

He damns William and Diana both as he drives toward his house, gas pedal pressed hard against the floorboard, hands locked on the wheel. If she had only managed to shake herself to early consciousness last year, Reed would have been alive, and the Congress would have been in full strength, not damaged and decimated by Reed's attack against his own. The fact that he's blaming a woman who spent the better part of three hundred years asleep for the actions of his own master doesn't strike him as unreasonable in the slightest.

Roland is an expert at blaming anyone for his troubles but himself. He blames Ariadne for going into labor too early, blames the doctor for not realizing he was about to kill his wife and asking him to wait long enough to clear the detritus of her firstborn out of the way. He blames Melanie for being imperfect and Aven for being unable to walk in the world while her sister's heart was beating.

But right here, right now, he blames the March boy most of all. Oh, he always suspected Harry of being Summer-called, has seen the signs in the boy almost from the beginning, but he never saw him as a danger. Harry wasn't strong enough to challenge Aven for the season if and when she woke and went to claim her birthright, and it was the season in his soul that caused him to cleave so closely to Melanie, to recognize her as the other half of himself and worry as much as he did about keeping her safe and whole.

A non-seasonal boy would have behaved more like a, well, boy, and might have broken her heart, which was already too broken to withstand the strain. A non-seasonal boy (and Roland still thinks of that as, obliquely, a "real" boy, even though he's never heard of any other artificial vessels for the seasons) would have been equipped to leave her, not to fight like a lion to keep her safe. Harry was never the enemy.

But Harry gave her the confidence to run, to jump, to fight for a life outside the walls of the garden her father had so carefully planted for her. Melanie might have been willing to be kept smaller than she was if only she'd been alone. Roland doesn't know.

And now she does, somehow. When he'd seen her off for the dance, he'd done so believing there was still time to get things in order before he had to explain the situation. He'd expected to be able to prepare. He's *been* preparing for eighteen years, since the day Ariadne announced she was pregnant and they were moving into the practical stage of their experiment. Theory was all well and good, but it was only in the field that anything could truly be tested.

They had believed they could raise the seasons in harmony, Summer and Winter side by side and devoted to one another, contained and controlled and too prepared for the coming challenge to risk defeat in any form. Ariadne had been working on ways to kill William and Diana even before they finished designing the girls; she had proposed, more than once, that they give the girls the hearts of their predecessors for their eighteenth birthday, making them Queens of Creation as they became adults.

Roland never expounded on that part to Reed. James Reed was many things. Teacher, student, scholar, master. Brilliant alchemist, and even more brilliant scientist and showman. But he was not, and never had been, generous of spirit. Roland and Ariadne were able to get their "little project" approved solely because it fed into the work Reed was already doing as regarded the Doctrine of Ethos, and any progress they enjoyed would be suitable for immediately repurposing and incorporating into his own research.

But for Reed, the idea of any other individual controlling any aspect of the universe was and always had been unacceptable. His intention was that his Doctrine should mature—which Roland assumes it has, assumes some of Reed's little cuckoos flew home to roost, killing their creator in the process—and seize the reins of creation, rendering the rest of the manifest forces irrelevant.

Roland believes that somewhere in the world, the Moon walks on human legs, watches with human eyes, and since the Moon will always shine in the night sky, he assumes that even with the Doctrine awake and ascendant, the rest of the manifest forces do and will and must remain very relevant indeed.

So he's always suspected Harry was seasonally inclined, but he didn't expect the boy to announce his candidacy with such spectacular vehemence. The video showed both of them falling at the same time, and no matter how many times he rewound and resumed, it never showed Harry breathing before Melanie's own breath resumed. He's seasonally tied, all right. And he's going to be Melanie's partner in the challenge to come.

Unless Roland can find them, and dispose of the boy, and introduce Melanie to her sister, who was supposed to be her second all along. He would have introduced them already if Aven had been awake, and if he'd been given any indication a coronation was approaching. This is all happening too fast, and he didn't consent to it, he didn't ask for it, he didn't agree to it in the slightest . . .

He pulls up in front of his house and frowns when he sees the living room light. He turned it off before he left, he knows he did, and while that might be a small thing to worry about on this night of gods and monsters, a home invasion is the last thing he needs right now. He's been robbed before, hungry locals desperate for a hot meal, or money for drugs, or the narcotics they're sure he keeps on hand for Melanie's care. Some of those opportunistic souls have even survived the experience, although none of them will come anywhere near him if they have a choice in the matter. He ran into one of them at the supermarket a few years back, and the man actually pissed himself before fleeing out the back door, his purchases and his new wife discarded. According to the papers, he had been a small-time criminal who'd turned his life around over the course of three years following a "rock-bottom experience" that even the pretty new wife had been unable to explain in more detail.

Seeing Roland, even for a moment, had been enough to shatter that fragile new equilibrium and send the man back into the arms of his old demons. His body had been found in one of the local motels not three months later, a needle in his arm and a smile on his thinned-out face. Roland had read the report in the paper with a smile on his face and a song in his heart. Such was the only fair punishment for someone who would enter his home without permission.

Only now it looks as if someone has done precisely that. Whoever it is, they'll pay for this insolence. Unless it was Melanie, little broken bird too afraid of freedom to flee her cage for long. Yes. He'll hope that it was Melanie, coming home where she belongs.

He pulls into the driveway and stops the car, rage and hope roiling in his chest and clouding his mind. He would have been more careful a year ago, he knows, when Leigh Barrow was still alive; she had been an experiment of the worst kind, stitched together from a dozen women, some of them alchemists in their own right, all of them too clever for their own good. Her creator would have been considered a serial predator if he hadn't been doing it for science. Roland isn't sure the man shouldn't be thought of that way anyway, although he supposes being remembered as the creator of Leigh Barrow, the Butcher of North America, is probably a worse punishment than being remembered for his own actions. In such moments, with such choices, are monsters erased and remade into something more palatable.

There are men for whom being forgotten has always been, will always be, a much direr punishment than any form of memory. To be erased is to be unmade by the alkahest of time, and they deserve nothing more. He doesn't clutter his memory with their names.

But he would have been more careful if there had been any chance it was Leigh inside his house, Leigh turning on the lights and moving through his private spaces. She'd done it a few times, letting herself in with Reed's key, or simply popping the locks and opening the doors. As far as Leigh had been concerned, anything her master claimed belonged to her in equal measure, and Reed had been more than willing to indulge her, the way a hunter will indulge a favorite dog with a prime piece of the kill and a choice spot by the fire. Only, he had indulged Leigh with freedom and with murder.

Roland misses his master very much, wishes Reed were here to work with him as they navigate the unexpected gift that is this well-timed coronation. At the same time, the loss of Reed is balanced by the loss of Leigh, who had been nothing but a scourge upon the alchemists of North America, who should never have been given the freedom to walk and run and terrorize as she had for so long.

He walks toward the front door, keys in his hand, ready to confront this invader. If it's Melanie, he can welcome her home. If it's an intruder, well . . . perhaps a good harvesting will settle his nerves. Like most alchemists outside the Congress, Roland is well skilled in the art of dismantling a human body; he can have the fool who dared violate his sanctuary in pieces in a few minutes' time, and won't even have to clean blood off the walls. Yes. It will be a good exercise before he goes looking for his wayward daughter, who should never have dared to run from him as she has, who should never have been so bold as to disappear.

He's even looking forward to it by the time he reaches the porch and the door swings open, ready to welcome him inside. He frowns at the boy in the doorway, not quite his daughters' age, still gangly and unfinished in the way of teens with growth yet buried in their bones. He has dark hair and dark eyes and a lovely tan, and he's a stranger, which is strange. Roland is viewed by many in Portland as something of a recluse, and yet he knows everyone who comes anywhere near him on any sort of regular basis. If this boy is an opportunistic burglar, choosing the first house with no cars in the driveway, he's made a dire mistake, and will not survive to make another.

"We've been waiting for you, Dr. Cosgrove," says the boy, and steps aside, clearing the way for Roland to enter. He does, blinking in bemusement, and stops as soon as he's past the door.

The house is warm as July, and the air is as fresh and sweet as any summer's afternoon. He can smell wildflowers, and pavement that's been baking in the sun for hours, letting off bursts of strange chemical signatures that make sense only in a specific context. He spins to face the boy who has invaded his home, eyes narrowing.

"Who are you?" he demands.

The boy's smile stops barely shy of mockery. "You can call me Corn Jenny, if you have to call me anything," he says.

Roland's eyes narrow further, leaving him to watch the world through little more than slits. "What are you doing here?"

"That's a funny way to talk to the person who saved your daughter from a creepy murder basement," says the boy, and the heat of the room is explained, the radiant warmth of it all. Roland has been living in a house with the living avatar of the coming winter for seventeen years, aware all along that the summer slept below them, far under the earth, contained in a cage of silver and mercury, lead and charcoal, sustained by his alchemic art. But with the summer burning in her veins, Aven doesn't need him anymore, if she's ever truly needed him; if she's ever needed anything beyond her season and her sister.

"I was always the weakest of the local Ascendants, and it's reasonable that you wouldn't have noticed me," says the boy, says the Corn Jenny, slipping his hands into his pockets and stepping backward, out of reach, out of range. He seems to be looking at a point behind Roland, and the older man goes still, settling into position, heels sinking into the floor as he slowly accepts the fact that he's not going anywhere. Ever again.

He's going to die here, tonight, and the only thing he can do for his master, for his partner, for his daughters, is to accept the fate he's earned with equanimity.

"What are you doing here?" he asks, voice gone soft.

"I was on the field when Harald March collapsed," says the boy. "The summer surged into him and overloaded his buffers, and he fell down, just a split second after that vacuous cheerleader he's been dating fell down. I knew what it was as soon as I felt it happen, but I didn't feel him link up to me. He wasn't mine to shepherd. There was another Summer in potential somewhere nearby. That's why there are always so many more of us, you see. One Ascendant for every possible Incarnate, so they don't have to share guides. We just got lucky. We aren't expected to kill each other during the coronation."

He smiles, and Roland has no doubt that this boy will kill anyone he feels he needs to in order to see his candidate to the throne. He'll reap a harvest of Corn Jennies, fill his basket with bushels of their heads, and not see for a moment that he might have done something wrong. That's good. Aven is going to need a strong right hand if she's going to win this. She knows so little about the world. She's not prepared for this fight.

Roland has done his best to teach her, has spent nights in the lab reading to her, has liquified what knowledge he could and fed it into her IVs, but as she's been little more than an unrotting corpse for most of her existence, she hasn't really been able to integrate or understand the things she knows. If not for the tinctures that impart understanding to those who drink them, and the long alchemical tradition of compressing knowledge to make it easier to bring a new apprentice up to a minimum necessary level of functionality, she wouldn't even have the understanding she does. She can talk. She can think. She can do so much more than anyone else her age who's spent her life in a form of suspended animation would be able to do.

It's not going to be enough. A good Corn Jenny will make the difference between success and failure, at least until she can be united with her sister. Together, they'll make an unstoppable force. Reed's own work has already proven that. Incarnate two forces in the same blood, give them a connection as physical as it is theoretical, and the world belongs to you.

And like Reed before him, he's going to die at the hands of his own creation, undone by his own effort to understand the universe a little more intimately. But unlike Reed, he's going to go without a fight. This has never been his story. He was a motivating force, not a narrative necessity. He accepted that the night his wife died.

The boy steps closer, apparently taking Roland's expression of calm acceptance as a lack of fear or, worse, a lack of respect.

"He doesn't have a guide now," says the boy. "Harald, I mean. I found her as soon as I felt our Lady wake, found her before *she* could find *him*, and I made sure she won't be telling him anything I don't want him to know. He'll burn from the inside out as the Summer starts to claim its own, and when the heat's too much for him to handle, I'll be there to douse the fires. I'll be the trusted friend who saves him, and he'll never realize I was the one who damned him in the first place. Unless I tell him so." The boy pauses, blinking, and a smile spreads across his face, like he's just had the best and most clever idea had by anyone, ever. "I think I'll tell him he was supposed to have his own attendant before he dies, and that I removed her from the court before she could tell him how to handle what he's becoming. Aven won't have any of those problems. Aven will have me every minute of her journey, and I'm going to make sure she becomes a queen. You don't have to thank me for taking care of your daughter."

"I wasn't going to," says Roland.

"No, you weren't, were you? Because you've never cared much about taking care of her. She's just been a burden to you."

The urge to argue with that assessment is surprisingly strong. Roland has attended countless support group sessions at the hospital, rooms packed with loving, panicked parents whose children have walked right up to the border of death's country and turned back at the last second, or not turned back at all but crossed over and been lost forever. He's been through grief counseling and miraculous recoveries, and he's stayed because he recognized himself in their struggles. He may not have been grieving in the same ways they are, may never have hit the same plateau of hopeless resignation, but he's grieved.

And the whole time he's been grieving, he's also been returning home to kiss his officially surviving daughter on the forehead before shooing her off to sleep, aided by the drugs he slips into her evening tea, the ones he makes to complement the ones he substitutes for the capsules containing her officially prescribed medications, and then slipping away downstairs to the daughter no one knows he has.

He's known for years that if the mundane authorities ever had cause to search his basement, he'd be unable to explain the girl sleeping there, bone-white and cold as the grave. For the first year or so, when the girls had been infants and Melanie had slept almost all the time, when not waking to cry fitfully or require hospitalization, he would have been accused of nothing worse than grave-robbing, and maybe necrophilia, depending on how perverse the minds of the arresting officers turned. The fact that a premature newborn looked nothing like a child of even a month wouldn't have stopped them from going "his daughter died at birth, he has a dead baby in his basement, clearly he stole her body," and their tools weren't remotely sophisticated enough to detect the signs that Aven was not, in fact, dead.

But things that aren't dead don't stop growing, and Aven has been no different. Her growth kept pace with and sometimes exceeded Melanie's. She shares her sister's heart condition, having been even more connected to their mother at the moment of Ariadne's death; if anything, her condition is worse, and he's not sure her heart will ever be capable of beating on its own. But if she wins the Summer, it won't need to. If she wins the Summer, the laws of life and death will apply to her differently, and she'll be free of the limitations of her anatomy. Both his girls will.

He didn't expect to love them when he helped his wife to make them, and his love is, perhaps, not the clean, uncomplicated love he sees from other parents, is more proprietary than parental, but they're his girls, his creations and greatest achievements, and he loves them, no matter what it may look like from the outside. He's proud of them for living long enough to reach the coronation, and he's proud of Aven, functionally newborn as she is, for already figuring out the best way to betray him.

Fingers curl over his shoulder and grip him tight. It's not the tightness of someone trying to show their strength, causing pain on purpose: it's the tightness of someone who doesn't understand their own strength, doesn't know yet what it means to *have* strength. The worm moon hangs in the sky above them. Winter is waning, all those Jack Frosts preparing to lay their mantles down and go about their ordinary lives until it comes around again, all those potential Incarnates growing weaker by the moment, with no means of understanding the why or the how of it. Their attendants will do what they can to educate them, but even Roland, alchemist and scholar, finds their self-regulating structure difficult to follow. He doesn't understand what form those preparations will take, or what lessons she has to learn. This is all a mystery to him, one of the last in the world, which has been picked apart and rebuilt so many times for the pleasure and convenience of men like him.

The fingers dig in deeper, tug him back. He keeps his feet planted even as his chest tilts, pulled inexorably toward the person behind him. He wants to turn. He wants to see her, see her awake and in motion, see whether she has Ariadne's eyes. Melanie does. Melanie looks so much like her mother that it hurts sometimes, even if Ariadne was never that pale. Ariadne was a real woman, human, flesh and bone where his Mel is stone and snow. Aven, for all that they floated together in the womb, was woven from different materials, corn husks and roses. Both of them have hearts of thorn and briar. They'll know each other when they come together.

Trevor looks past him, frowns a little. "I think I have to go now," he says, almost deferentially. "This isn't a place for outsiders. This is a family matter. It was nice to meet you, Mr. Cosgrove. I promise, I'm going to take excellent care of your daughter."

Then he turns and walks away, and Roland is alone with his creation.

He's been alone with his creations, either singular or in unwitting tandem, for the better part of seventeen years, and there is no fear as Aven turns him to face her. She's raided Melanie's closet, is dressed in one of Melanie's favorite sweaters, and they might as well be the same girl save for the hair. No matter how often they tried, he and Ariadne had never been able to convince their models to match. The seasons always came through, one way or another.

Summer is for sun-bleached bones drying at the bottom of a canyon, for color stolen by the heat and not yet replaced by char. Winter is for nights as black as the feathers of a raven's wing, for color dampened and overwhelmed by the cold and not yet brought back to blossom. He looks at Aven and he understands two things:

That she has her mother's eyes, deep and drowning blue, beautiful as anything, and exactly like Melanie's. In their eyes and their features, the two girls are perfectly alike. Dip one in bleach and the other in ink and they could trade places with no one in the world the wiser. Not even him, and for a moment, it's hard to convince his horrified and hammering heart that he's truly looking at his younger child, that Aven has been awakened by the coming of the crown and risen from her bier.

She is shaped exactly like her sister. Melanie has had the advantages of a life outside the lab, of running and climbing and seeing the world through her own eyes. Aven has had the advantages of focused alchemy, of electrical currents to keep her muscles from atrophy and machines to move her according to the proper design. Of the two of them, she is his Galatea, but he is not her sculptor, for every choice he made with her form was based on Melanie, on the things she did and chose to do. He has made her in the image of her sister, bright mirror, now looking at him with gravity and consideration, but not a hint of compassion or care. She doesn't love him, and that's a good thing, because this is the second thing he understands:

He's going to die tonight. He will never see the coronation, never know who claims the crown, and somehow that's the only part of this that pains him, the only part that gives him pause. He started this story: he picked up his pen and wrote the opening lines of his own volition. There would be only one potential Incarnate in this shitty little city with its shitty little slogans—"Keep Portland Weird," as if these people have ever been half so strange, half so counterculture as their own imaginations—if he had chosen a different path of research, or if Ariadne had suggested another way. He did this. He *made* this. It seems only fair that he should be allowed to see it through.

But then, Ariadne made it as well, did as much of the math as he did, worked out as many of the calculations, and when the time came, when their incubators and eggs had failed, she was the one who had proposed a more traditional methodology, who had willingly nestled their two greatest works beneath her breastbone and fed them on her own body as much as on mercury and mistletoe. Ariadne carries as much of the praise and as much of the blame as he does, and she didn't get to see it through. So maybe this is just a way of evening the scales, of putting things the way they should have been all along.

Maybe he never had a chance.

"Hello, Daddy," says Aven, voice raspy with disuse and slightly deeper than her sister's, unshaped by a lifetime of pitching her words higher than necessary, trying to make herself seem feminine and harmless. He's never understood the need of women in this culture to seem smaller than they are, but he knows it comes from the outside: everything around them is telling them, every hour of every day, that whatever space they occupy is stolen from someone who could use it better, spend it more wisely, benefit it more. Even his Ariadne hadn't been immune, and she could have been a queen of the alchemical paths, if only their master's work had progressed a little more quickly, if only she'd had access to the wonders of the Impossible City. Hearing Aven speak is like hearing Melanie with none of that nonsense and cultural baggage piled upon her head, and he glories in it, even as he hears his ending in her tone.

"Hello, Aven," he says.

She cocks her head to the side, almost insectile as she studies him. "Why did you name me that?" she asks. "My attendant tells me that my twin's name is Melanie. Greek. Means 'darkness.' Aven is Irish. They don't match. They don't go together. They should go together."

"But they do," he says, as carefully as he can. She's going to kill him. There's no reason to antagonize her and speed the process along. "'Aven' means 'radiance.' You were always going to be the sun to her moon, and we chose your names accordingly."

"We?"

"Your mother did much of the work. She was more interested in the symbolism of words and names, had a better eye for it. We were still trying to decide on your middle names when she died, which is why you don't have any. It seemed unreasonable to give you something without consulting her, and well." He shrugs. "She wasn't available to be consulted. I did the best I could with what I had."

What he'd had was an unprecedented situation, a dead wife and a dead baby who nonetheless needed his full attention, while his living daughter also needed his full focus if he wanted to keep her alive. And he *had* wanted that, very badly, still wanted that more than almost anything. Keeping the girls from dying has been an intense amount of work, and if he'd been happy to see either one of them dead, he wouldn't have been at the March house, demanding the return of his daughter after he'd seen that video.

(Where, exactly, had he gone wrong? He's always done his best to take care of Melanie, to make sure she felt like she had as much freedom as her broken, breaking heart allowed, has been very careful to draw the lines between parental restrictions and the restrictions imposed by her condition. He started letting her go out on dates with Harry when they were only fourteen, almost a full year before any of the other parents were allowing their girls to go out unchaperoned. And yes, part of that had been knowing that her body wouldn't allow her to cross certain arbitrary lines, that her virtue, such as it was, would remain intact until the coronation, if she lived to see one, but he still let her go. She was supposed to trust him, to believe he had her best interests at heart, to come to him when she had a problem or a concern or when something happened, like *her heart ceasing to beat in her chest,* not run away with the boy who looked at her the way a puppy looks at a biscuit.)

Aven makes a small, inquiring sound that he can't help reading as displeasure, and Roland stands a little straighter. He never wanted to be the villain of the piece, not where his girls were concerned, not where the world was concerned. He wanted only what any true alchemist wants, to push the limitations of human knowledge forward to a better, brighter place, to *understand* the inner workings of the universe and, perhaps, to claim some of those inner workings for his own. So he wanted power. So what? Ariadne wanted that as well, died wanting that, died with the demand that he finish what they'd started on her lips. He can't be blamed for being what the world made of him, any more, he supposes, than they can be blamed for being what he sculpted them to be.

His girls. His masterpieces. His children. Reed's cuckoos may have been more powerful than his girls, designed to embody a universe while his stood only for the seasons it contained, but he has known them as father and creator both: has kept them close and watched them grow, and he believes, truly believes, that they will be stronger for that.

"You let her wake and walk," says Aven, and she either makes no effort to conceal or doesn't yet recognize the venom in her own voice. Oh, she's angry with him, this spun-sugar sunshine girl of his own creation; she's furious.

She'll figure it out soon, if she doesn't already know.

"Why her and not me?" She leans closer, her eyes fixed on his, and he can't keep himself from cataloging the little differences. Melanie, pale as she is from both her confinement and her natural connection to the washed-out winter, has at least seen the sun in her lifetime: she has a few faint freckles on the crests of her cheeks, the bridge of her nose. She has a small scar just above her lip on the right-hand side, as faded out as a sanded mark on a piece of beechwood, from where she fell off the swings and busted her lip against the blacktop in first grade.

She's walked in the world and the world has walked in her, and Aven has never had that, and he understands her anger, he truly does, even as he wishes he'd arrived home before that Corn Jenny boy, before her ears had been filled with a terrible, unforgiving poison that painted the situation as simple and him as the villain. If he'd only thought a moment more about what Melanie's collapse might mean for Aven before rushing off after the teens, he might have been able to shift this story along entirely different lines.

Too late now. Aven cocks her head to the side, watching him

intently, and he knows that if he doesn't answer now, he won't be given the opportunity.

"She was born first, and damaged by my own carelessness," he says. "The doctors already knew she had survived. You were still inside your mother. Your suffocation was guaranteed, and so when she was removed for burial, they allowed me to take you as well."

So many charms and small revisions had gone into that night, so many exhausting attempts to remove all traces of strangeness from the memories of the medical team attending the birth. One of the nurses had lost the ability to perceive wood due to the workings he'd laid on her mind, amplified by his panic and his grief. Her death had been front-page news, involving as it did a respected member of the community crashing her car into a fallen tree without hesitation or slowing down in the slightest. The clipping is in his file upstairs, a curiosity and a reminder that alchemy should not be used carelessly, but he didn't grieve. Why should he have? He met her once, and she hadn't been able to stop the labor and summarily give him the opportunity to save his wife.

Their original plan had been ambitious but workable: make the infants alchemically, using a mixture of techniques provided by Reed's research and others documented by Shelley and Frazer, whose own attempts at creating life had borne unique and terrible fruit. Allow them to age normally, yoke them to the calendar in all proper truth, and stop the progress of Ariadne's womb on the solstice. He still has the remaining doses of the tinctures they brewed in his office, locked in a small, secure safe, a keepsake and a condemnation. The infants should have been able to sleep in their suspended animation until the equinox arrived, eight months gestated and ready to draw their first breaths before and after the stroke of midnight, Melanie on the winter side of the equation and Aven in the spring.

The only risk they anticipated at the time was that Aven might, *might,* be more tightly tied to the spring than to the summer, but there was no way to deliver both girls solidly in the grips of their native season, not without the chance of losing them both. It was a good plan. It worked in tests, wrote out beautifully, and made logical sense.

But when they delivered the first tincture to Ariadne, she gasped and staggered and said she could feel the winter howling in her bones, that the season didn't want to let go. They had no way of explaining to the universe that they were trying to make things perfect; it saw only that they were trying to take a perfect vessel for the living Winter away, and it reacted accordingly. Ariadne's body, rather than stopping the process of gestation, had immediately accelerated it, and her labor had begun.

Aven purses her lips.

"I don't believe you," she says. "Trevor tells me you're an alchemist, one of the best, and you should have been able to save us both."

"I did save you both," he protests, a little desperately. She's his daughter. He wants her to love him. He wants her to *understand* that everything he did, he did out of love for her and for her sister. "The doctors would have taken you away. They might have put you in an incubator, but they wouldn't have been able to support your connection to the summer. You would have wasted and withered and died before you even had a chance. At least this way, you were able to grow up. And look at you! Just look at you. You're perfect—"

He's said the wrong thing. He knows it as soon as her face hardens and her lips thin, and she takes a step backward, away from him. "If I'm so perfect, why didn't you wake me as soon as summer started? Why didn't you raise us both?"

"Oh, Aven . . ." So many reasons. So many good, terrible, uncountable reasons. He could never have explained where the second baby came from, for one thing, and with their hair being so different, he couldn't have passed them off as the twins they were until they were at least three or four years old; he would have been accused of kidnapping his own child, forced to submit to blood and paternity tests that might have revealed things the world wasn't ready to confront. Yes, he *was* their father, absolutely, on a genetic level, and he wasn't at the same time, just like they were twins and weren't, were sculptures built to follow the same design, mirror images of the lost Ariadne, but were made of such different base materials that he couldn't be sure even now, even after all Melanie's invasive medical interventions, what doctors would find if they compared the two girls under a microscope.

"Your heart never started beating," he says. "You were pulled from your mother's body already dead. That part is true. The tincture we had given her before her labor began meant when you died, you stopped changing, and so you hadn't yet started to decay. I was able to resurrect you, but not repair the damage. I've been stimulating your body to grow, keeping it in a state of suspended animation, refusing to let go until a coronation could be called. I never knew if it was going to happen in your lifetime. I didn't know whether Melanie's heart would be able to last long enough to give you the chance."

"And Melanie's heart mattered more than mine?" Her eyes narrow, snake preparing to strike.

Roland, still laboring under the delusion that he can somehow talk his way through this maze of his own making, quickly shakes his head. "No, not at all. But you were made twins for a reason. We wanted you to embody your specific seasons, and we wanted you to reflect each other, to be a bonded pair. To depend on one another."

To control one another, he adds, silently. If all had gone according to plan, they would have been able to compel the good behavior of either girl by hurting the other. Reflected pain could sometimes be worse than the original.

But Melanie is bonded to the March boy now, if the video is anything to go on. The start of the coronation had knocked her down, as only befits one whose seasonal monarch had died while their season was in even technical ascension, and Harry at virtually the same time, when the approach of the spring should have been enough to keep him standing, at least for the time being. He'd die in truth on the winter solstice, along with any other summer candidates who somehow survived their season, and then only the one bound to the winning Winter would wake up at season's end.

Kill Harry, and Aven would be able to reclaim Melanie. It was so simple, so obvious. So complicated. People made everything complicated.

"Well, Daddy, I guess I don't depend on anyone now." She leans closer again, eyes now fully open, and she smiles. His heart lurches in his chest. She is a monster of his own making, this sweet summer girl who dreamed her life away while her frozen sister danced through her days, through birthday parties and cheer practices and all the complicated dangers of living. "I certainly don't depend on you."

"What are you going to do with me?" The question is a mistake, he knows that as soon as he asks it, because once she answers, she'll be committed to whatever course she's chosen.

"Nothing bad, Daddy," she says, and her eyes are wide and round and so innocent that for a moment he can almost make himself believe her; can almost accept that she means it. But she does everything innocently, everything on the basis of wanting it to happen right now and to suit her still unfinished, unformed desires. She was born seventeen years ago. She was born today.

"You killed Mom, after all," she says, and that's it, then: there's no walking away from this. Roland Cosgrove closes his eyes. Whatever comes next, he won't honor it by watching it happen.

He does, of course, after she cuts his eyelids away. The only lessons she has are the ones he gave her, and he was preparing her to fight and win a war against unknown enemies with unknown training and unknown capabilities. When pressed, she is joyously prepared to prove that she is her mother's daughter, for all that she's been asleep for most of her life.

The sun is rising by the time she finally lets him go, and by then, Harry and Melanie are far away, crossing into California, not looking back.

California Coastal

Dibs on the shower!" Melanie yells, excitement and delight in her voice as she sprints across the motel room for the narrow rectangle of the bathroom door. Harry steps out of her way, to let her charge through. Jack, who is smaller but in some ways savvier, doesn't even bother stepping into the room until Melanie is safely through the door.

The door slams behind Melanie, and Jack begins counting on her fingers, holding her hands up to exaggerate the gesture as much as possible. "Ten," she says. "Nine, eight, seven . . ."

The door slams open again, Melanie sticking her head out into the room. "The biggest spider I have *ever* seen has already called dibs on the shower," she reports.

"Need me to come and get it?" asks Harry.

"Since when have I needed you to deal with a spider? I just wanted you to know, in case the spider comes out and wants a bed." She withdraws back into the bathroom.

Jack, who has stopped counting, finally pushes into the room and throws herself on the bed nearer to the window. "Mine," she announces.

"Someone has to take the floor," says Harry dubiously.

"Or you and Elsa could stop pretending you'd rather not be sharing a bed and give up waiting for me to be asleep before you get out of your sleeping bag."

Harry frowns at her. "Her name's Mel, and we're being considerate. You're like twelve."

"Technically thirteen. I chose to stop aging when I hit my ascendancy, which most of us do, and I won't get any older until I let go of the choice."

"When's that going to be?"

"I dunno." Jack stretches languidly, arms above her head. "What's the statute of limitations on parental reclamation? If a missing twelve-year-old shows up ten years later, and they're still twelve, will the state try to give them back to their folks, or will they just look confused and say 'Well, guess she's a freak of nature and might as well be emancipated'?"

Harry blinks. "I genuinely have no idea."

The water turns on, the sound echoing through the cheap motel room. Harry's expression of confusion becomes a frown.

"This place needs a lot of work."

"Yeah, but it's cheap, and as long as you can provide photo ID and pay for your room, they'll let you sleep here. Can't say the same about the kind of place you're used to. If we don't want your parents to find us . . ."

And they don't want his parents to find them, want it less than almost anything (except the still-looming threat of Melanie's father, which seems like a much more immediate and concrete danger; the thought of fearing Melanie's sister hasn't occurred to any of them, not even Jack, who's fully aware the girl survived). They stopped at each ATM they passed on the way out of Portland, regardless of what bank they belonged to, Harry pulling out every penny he could manage before his folks realized what was going on and stopped his cards. They haven't turned his credit card off yet; he's hoping that, combined with the way Mel's father yelled at them, and the fact that Mel is also missing, will mean they assume, correctly, that they've run away and not been abducted. His parents won't be thrilled by the idea that he's run away with his high school girlfriend—his mother will probably make the face that means she's silently judging his life choices, and finding them universally wanting—but they'll understand the reasons, especially if Dr. Cosgrove threatened to keep them from seeing each other anymore.

They know how much Melanie means to him, how much of his own teenage experience has been shaped and formed by her illness, by trying to keep her with him as long as possible. His father will probably think this is romantic, that Mel is finally, officially dying and she and Harry have run off together to make sure they can spend her last moments with each other, probably against some beautiful beach backdrop or the like. He'll fight any attempt to freeze Harry's cards, but he won't check in on him directly. If he did that, if he knew for sure where the missing teens were, he'd feel obligated to alert the authorities. This way, if he stays ignorant, he doesn't have to tell anyone what he doesn't know.

That's how Harry's father has always operated, so the fact that Harry's credit card still works isn't that much of a surprise. What's more surprising is that he's only received one text from his mother, shortly after midnight on the night they disappeared, consisting of only two words:

"Keep going."

Does she know what he's done? What he is now, what Melanie is, what they've apparently always been? Why they were pulled together so magnetically as children, unable to resist the pull of one another's presence? Even during the time when he should have been running away from her, shrieking about girls and cooties, he had chosen sitting quietly with Mel over almost everything else in the world. If she'd been less willing to sit by the field and cheer while he played football with the rest of the neighborhood, he might never have found his way to football, because he would have been too willing to stay by Melanie. Does she know?

Or does she just think they're one of those rare but naturally occurring relationships, the ones that sometimes form between children who meet at the exact right moment in their lives, the ones country singers write songs about and romance writers build careers on? He always thought that was the case. He thought he loved her because she was *Mel,* not because she was some metaphysical vessel for the winter, while he was the same for the summer.

According to Jack, he's always been at least a little right: she says seasonal avatars in potential always feel strongly about one another, they can't help it, but most are hostile on their first meeting. "Ever met somebody and wanted nothing more than to punch their stupid asshole face in, even when they haven't done anything wrong?" she asked, last night as they were settling into the first of what he's sure will be a string of nowhere motels. "Like, immediate and absolutely *loathing,* theatrical-level dislike."

Harry was quiet for a few minutes before haltingly admitting it had happened a few times. Jack, looking smug, settled back against the dresser she was using to prop herself up, and smirked.

"Those were probably other potential incarnate seasons," she said. "Maybe yours, maybe hers, doesn't really matter. You hate them instinctively, because you already know it's going to come down to one of you. One head, one crown."

"But I don't hate *Mel,*" he objected. "I get mad sometimes, when she doesn't want to do something I really, really want to do, or when she wants me to do something I don't want to do, or when she has to go to the hospital and we were supposed to be doing something together, but I never *hate* her."

"Nope. You wouldn't. She's your parallel."

Harry didn't like that when Jack said it, and he doesn't like it now. Mel always takes at least fifteen minutes in the shower, usually longer when she thinks she can get away with it and the hot water doesn't run out. This place is exactly as nice as he'd expect from a motel that only costs eighty dollars a night and isn't close enough to the highway to get a lot of tourist trade, which makes the hot water anybody's guess. Maybe it'll last five minutes, maybe it'll last all night. Either way, it's worth the risk.

"What you were saying before," he says. Jack gives him the politely interested look of a teacher trying to deal with a particularly slow pupil, one they're sure could grasp the material just fine if only they'd take a moment to really think about what they're being told. "About Melanie being my parallel."

"Ah, yeah," says Jack. "Everyone competes for their crown alone, in the end. You could win and she could lose, or vice versa. But you'll be stronger if you go in with your opposite number already linked, and that's what you and Melanie have done. Together, you form a solid base from which to make a play for both seasons. It's like lacing your fingers." She holds up her hands and twines her fingers to illustrate her point. "I can hit a lot harder this way."

"But you can only hit once," says Harry.

"So it's not a perfect metaphor. What metaphor is?" Jack shrugs, then groans and lets her head flop backward, against the bed. "I'm not supposed to be explaining all this. I've only been ascendant for a *year*. That's barely enough time to *sample* the seasons, much less understand them! If I ever see your attendant again, I'm going to kick her teeth in, I swear to God I am."

"My attendant being this corn Jenny lady you keep saying will show up any time now?"

"Yes," says Jack, nodding vigorously. "Every potential incarnate has an ascendant attendant, and I bet you can't say that five times fast. So there should have been a Corn Jenny already attached to you when the coronation began." The way she says the name is subtly different; he can hear the capital letter on the "C," the change from noun to proper name. He's not sure he can replicate it, but he can hear it, and that's a start. "She should have shown up to explain everything I'm trying to explain to both of you, and that way your questions would always have taken priority, and she would have known how to approach things from the summer side. I can't. I'll always speak from a world where winter reigns supreme, because that's what I know."

"Are all corn—sorry, Corn—Jennies female?"

"No, just both the ones I've met," says Jack, with a lazy wave of her hand. "It's sloppy of me to give the impression that boys or girls have anything to do with any of this. They're always people, though, since that's what it means to be an anthropomorphic manifestation of a natural force. Not much point to it if you're not going to actually, you know, anthropomorphize."

"Okay, so they're called 'Jenny' because—?"

"Because I refuse to be a 'Jill Frost' or whatever bullshit gendered name they'd slap on my position if they tried to divide things into boys and girls, and as far as I'm concerned, all names are gender-neutral. Ever notice how no one bats an eye when you call your girlfriend 'Mel,' even though that's usually a man's name, but no one calls you 'Harriet'?"

"I'd knock the block off of anyone who tried it," he growls, then stops, startled by his own vehemence.

"There, you see?" asks Jack. "You call me 'Jack' and her 'Mel' without batting an eye, and you never wonder if you're insulting our femininity, but if someone trod too close to insulting your masculinity, you'd be on them in a second. So we stick with 'Corn Jenny' in part because it's tradition, and in part because it makes us happy to call the guys who get called to serve the summer by a name that makes them wince. It's a man's world, little buddy. Leave us the small pleasures we can salvage from the ruins."

Harry feels like he ought to be offended somehow, and then he feels like he's being silly even considering getting offended by something said by a twelve-year-old who may or may not actually be thirteen. Either way, she's not even in high school yet. "Got it. sorry."

"It's fine. This is a lot, and it doesn't all make sense from the outside, and you're way, way on the inside while still looking at the outside of things, trying to figure it all out. Anyway, blame the French."

"What? Why?"

"I mean, blaming the French is always a good idea, but in this case, we're doing it because a lot of these concepts made their way into English by way of French, and French is a heavily gendered language. So everything got a 'girl' or 'boy' label slapped on it, and the seasonal ascendants all got common names in whatever language worked best for the area. Honestly, if we're really getting into the semantics of it all, it's sort of weird that it's 'Corn Jenny' and not 'Harvest Jack' or something else like that. All the rest of us are Jacks."

"Huh," says Harry. This is interesting, it really is, but he could have this conversation with Melanie in the room. He glances at the bathroom door, confirming that it's still closed, then looks back to Jack. "So I don't like Melanie because she's my parallel?"

"No. If anything, you should have been more inclined to avoid her. Not hate her, but keep her at a decent remove. She's the opposition, after all. The fact that the two of you decided to bond instead of battling each other just means you're going to be stronger going into the coronation that's coming."

"I thought a coronation was an event. Like a wedding or a graduation. Not a competition."

"I mean, it is, at the end. This is sort of like . . . sort of like the reception before an art opening, or the part of the birthday party where everyone's still milling around talking about things other than presents and cake. This is the floor show. The disaster movie already in progress." Jack sits up, looking at him gravely. "There will *be* an event. When the two still standing claim their crowns, there will be an event. The coronation started as soon as the old Incarnates died, and the new ones began the process of competing for their place."

"I'm not competing for anything," says Harry.

"Sure you are. At this stage, you compete just by staying in the running. That's part of what makes you stronger when you've bound to your parallel. You can do all sorts of things that would normally disqualify you for being too connected to another season."

"What, like, Melanie eats ice cream and she can't be the winter anymore?"

"Not quite, but right neighborhood. More like Melanie buys some flower seeds and puts them in a pot, and she's disqualified because she's engaging in summer activities. And then she's dead, because the only thing that's keeping her moving is the sheer volume of winter she has crammed into that ruined honeycomb she calls a heart."

"Seasons don't need anything as plebian as organs," murmurs Harry, and Jack casts him an approving look, like a teacher who's relieved to see one of her pupils finally catching on.

"It's all about the symbolism from here on out, buddy," she says. "Symbolism and murder."

Harry looks alarmed. "I don't actually plan to kill anyone."

"If you're lucky, you won't have to. The other candidates will already be eliminating each other, all across the continent, and then hunting each other down so they can eliminate some more. If we're lucky and you keep moving—and moving doesn't lead you smack into the path of one of the other candidates, silver sickle in hand and harvest on their mind—you might make it to the labyrinth without spilling any blood at all." She looks at her hand then, studying her nails with casual nonchalance. "It's a lot more likely that there's going to be killing, of course. It didn't used to work that way."

"So why does it have to work that way now?"

She lowers her hand. "Because the only way to eliminate the competition is to either kill them or convince them to renounce their claim on the crown, in so many words, and really *mean* it. This isn't something you can trick someone into doing, or do by accident. You have to understand that you're severing yourself from your season."

"Then we do that!" says Harry, suddenly excited. He sits up straighter. "We give up the crown and we go home and everything's normal again."

Jack looks at him with pity. "I know you're smarter than this. What part of 'your girlfriend's heart gave out and she's been dead for two days' isn't getting through your head? Mel claims her crown or she's done. Finished, *finite*, no more Melanie. There's no other way for her."

"A transplant . . ."

"Wouldn't save her, because she's already gone." Jack shakes her head. "She's been gone since she fell down, since the winter in her bones started to uncurl and assert itself. All she can do now is win. You can sever if you want to. We'll miss you. And you'll die too, of course. Now that the summer has you, you win it all or you die."

Harry looks at her blankly, and she manages, barely, not to laugh.

"I've had to explain the same things to you four or five times now, while Mel hears it once and starts asking new questions," says Jack. "It's not because she's paying more attention than you are. It's because she's closer to coronation than you are. All her veils got torn away when her heart stopped beating."

"I don't . . . I can't . . ."

"Harry." Jack looks at him and sighs. "We had this conversation last night. I swear we did. I explained everything to you, even though I'd already done it at the diner, and in the car, and at the botanical gardens. Melanie's father was an alchemist, and she lived with him for seventeen years. Even with him trying to hide the true nature of his work and her origins from her, the background radiation of that house was priming her to accept all of this as the real world, and not some sort of delusion. You, though. You lived in the 'real' world that whole time. Alchemy, sorcery, seasonal monarchs, they're all the same thing to you. They're fairy tales. All this stuff sounds like nonsense, because in the life you were living, it *was* nonsense. You're acclimating, but you're acclimating slowly. That makes sense. You're a real person. Melanie adapted more quickly because she's not."

"Not a person?"

"Not *real*. I mean, she exists, she's here, she became the person she was going to be as much despite her father as because of him, and now that she *is*, it's going to take work to make her *not*, the same as it would for anyone. But she didn't start out real. She's a skin horse, and you've loved her into being something bigger and more concrete than she would have been entirely on her own."

"Skin horse . . . ?" Harry's head is spinning. Jack says these things like they make sense, and then she moves along, heading for the next thing she wants to say, not pausing long enough to see if he's following her. It makes him feel like he's the kid in this conversation, and she's the almost-adult. It makes his brain hurt. He wants her to stop.

"Did you ever read *The Velveteen Rabbit*?" asks Jack. When Harry shakes his head, she sighs. "Terrible book, absolutely awful for kids, never let kids anywhere near it, it just scrambles them up inside. Anyway, it says toys are alive, and they do stuff when their children aren't around."

"Like *Toy Story*," says Harry, pleased to finally be following something she's trying to say.

"That's probably where the idea for those movies came from, yeah," says Jack. "Anyway, in the book, when the velveteen rabbit is all new and perfect and shiny as anything, the boy who owns him also has a rocking horse covered in real horse skin. That's how you know it's classic children's literature. When there's just straight-up taxidermy in the nursery. Anyway, they call the rocking horse 'the Skin Horse,' because that's not fucked-up and creepy or anything."

"And because the Skin Horse has been in the nursery for so very, very long, he knows things none of the other toys know," says Mel. Harry looks over his shoulder and sees her in the bathroom doorway, damp and dripping and flushed red from the heat of the shower, a towel wrapped around her body and her hair pulled over one shoulder. Now that he's paying attention, he can smell the steam and the cheap hotel soap hanging in the air. He doesn't know how long she's been listening. "Things like the fact that children grow up and put their toys aside, and more children always come. And he knows about being real. He teaches the velveteen rabbit, because even though they're just toys, toys can love as well as real things can. He says 'Real isn't how you're made, it's a thing that happens to you. When a child loves you for a long, long time, not just to play with, but *really* loves you, then you become Real.'" She shakes her head. "I always thought that was one of the most beautiful things in any book, and one of the most dangerous ones, too. I tried to love my dolls so much they'd be Real and never leave me, and it never worked, so what did that say about me? Was I not good enough to love something into Realness?"

Harry blinks. This isn't a secret, not exactly, because he doesn't think they have any secrets left from one another, but it's still something he's never heard before, and he also thought they didn't have anything new to say to each other. They're not boring and he's never been bored, but they're in that long, comfortable middle that comes to any good relationship, whether romantic or platonic, where they know each other completely enough that there are very few surprises.

Or that's where he thought they were, at least. Maybe there are more surprises here than he knew.

"Reality doesn't work that way," says Jack, with apparently sincere apology in her tone. "The person who wrote that book was—"

"Another alchemist?" asks Melanie sharply. She hasn't been taking her pills since they fled Portland, Harry realizes; he knows she got them when she raided her bedroom, has seen them in her bag when she opened it to get out fresh clothes, snacks, or a hairbrush, but he hasn't seen her swallow a single one. Her mood, normally stabilized and smoothed out by the sedatives that keep her heart from racing, is returning to its natural state.

"Yes," admits Jack. "She was speaking of the creation of alchemical servants, the same way Shelley was, just less . . . fleshily."

"Has *anyone* ever written a damn book for reasons other than encoding secret alchemical knowledge for future students?" demands Harry. "Because this seems like a really inefficient way to run a school. 'No textbooks, kids, but here are nineteen children's novels and a couple of classic works of science fiction that might teach you some basic principles if you squint hard enough.'"

Jack actually cracks a smile at that. "Most books weren't written by alchemists," she says, in what she probably intends as a reassuring tone. She doesn't quite get what she's aiming for, but at least she's trying. "All literature is a form of alchemy, turning letters into words into messages from the past, like chucking bottles into the tide. So by that definition, all authors are alchemists, and ought to change their titles."

Harry huffs. Jack holds up a hand to quiet him.

"But in the sense you're talking about, no, not all authors are alchemists. Most alchemists these days go into either academia or medicine, as places where they'll have access to the resources their work requires. But they used to be better able to keep labs in their basements and do something else with their evenings, and they wrote books because it was a way to keep knowledge circulating without getting stoned to death in the village square. Also because it let them influence the way non-alchemists saw the world. And non-alchemists will always outnumber alchemists."

"Okay, and?" asks Harry.

"And convincing another alchemist that you're right about the way things work and he's wrong about it is borderline impossible," says Jack. "Alchemists are stubborn. You sort of have to be when you're trying to distill moonlight into a liquid that you can pour into a river to light it up at night, instead of just buying a bunch of glowsticks like a normal person. They don't do 'practical' when they can do 'ridiculous but impressive' instead. And since the universe runs at least partially due to the way people think it runs . . ."

Mel walks over to the beds, still wrapped in her cheap white motel towel. The smell of cheap soap gets stronger, but Harry doesn't mind; not when it's mixed with the smell of hot skin and clean water. She hasn't stopped to gasp for breath and clutch the walls in two days, and she just took a shower without leaving the door open in case she fell down and needed help. That's a precious enough thing to be worth a little soap in the air.

"That's why forces get stuck embodying over and over again after it happens for the first time, right?" asks Mel. "Because people believe they do."

"Exactly," says Jack, sounding a little smug. She likes it when they follow where she's trying, in her own abstracted way, to lead them. "The moon turns into a person because the alchemists demand it, they write a bunch of books where the moon's a person, and then all the people in the world who *aren't* alchemists believe that sometimes, the moon's a person. And the weight of all that belief, the conviction, actually changes the universe."

Harry flops backward on the bed. "This is making my head hurt," he complains.

"So stop asking questions," says Jack.

He pushes himself up onto his elbows and frowns at her. "I thought you wanted us to understand all this."

"Not really," she says, with a shrug. "If you can accept that Melanie's heart has stopped beating and won't start again unless she claims the crown of winter, and you need to do the same with the crown of summer if you want to stay with her, then my job is done. If you'll fight the other candidates when they present themselves to you, and you'll avoid them when you don't think you can defeat them, then you know everything I need you to."

"I don't think I can kill someone," says Harry. "I just don't . . . No. I don't think I can."

"Some of them won't be looking to kill you," says Jack. "The last coronation in Europe, the girl who won the summer did it with six kills at the very end, and seventeen Pokémon battles. She carried a big binder of cards with her everywhere she went and she challenged her competition to fight her for the crown. None of them wanted to kill an eleven-year-old girl, so they went along with it, and she didn't tell them until they were renouncing their crowns that she'd gone to the Pokémon world championships the year before. Didn't win, but came in second. She's a badass, and if I were a Summer Ascendant, I would have booked it for Europe the minute I heard about her. Serving that Summer Queen would have been way better than serving the sleeping one."

"Hey," says Harry, feeling obscurely stung by the idea that Jack, who isn't Summer-tied at all, would have fled the continent rather than stay and work with the monarchy she had. Somewhere along the way, he's started believing this is actually happening. It's too ridiculous for him to have come up with on his own, and too elaborate to be some sort of fever-induced fantasy, and too imperfect to be wish fulfillment. A Melanie who isn't going to drop dead on him at any moment is basically his dream. A Melanie who dies every summer and doesn't wake up until the fall is a bit too cruel for him to have imagined.

"It didn't happen. You can't change a season after it's been set, and no, I don't know how normal Incarnates and Ascendants are chosen. Your ice-girl there was made to play her part, but that's about as far as it goes. You happened all on your own."

"I always knew you were a natural wonder," says Mel, and leans over to kiss his cheek. Her lips are cold. Her lips are always cold these days, even when she's fresh out of the shower and gently steaming in the open air. She rests her damp head against his shoulder and looks to Jack. "So we don't need to get anything that's happening to us, we just need to deal with it, is that what you're saying?"

"Pretty much." Jack stands, stretching again. "And I need to get some McDonald's. I'm feeling a distinct lack of processed potato product in my system. If I leave you two alone in here, do you promise to stay put and not go wandering around, trying to get yourselves killed?"

"They're not really going to be trying to kill us," says Harry.

"Okay, then, try not to get yourselves challenged to any Pokémon battles before I come back with fries. Stay here and watch television or make out or something. I'll only be a few minutes." Jack pauses to take a twenty from Harry's wallet and then she's out the door, vanishing into the night.

Melanie and Harry, alone for the first time since the football field, exchange a look that ends when Mel ducks her head and looks away, suddenly shy. "I'm sorry about all this," she says. "It feels like my fault."

"Hey." He grabs her cold hand in his, squeezing her fingers as he pulls it to her chest. In the process, he stops her from pulling any further away from him, and he can't say he feels bad about that. "This isn't your fault."

Her fingers are like ice. But it doesn't feel wrong, not the way it feels when he touches Jack, whose cold is just as deep and just as immutable but burns, still carries that awful "sticking your hand into slush" feeling. Touching Melanie is crisp and refreshing and right, and she's supposed to be here, and so is he and this is the way the universe works. This is the way it fits together.

"You heard her, any one of the eight times she tried to talk her way to a straight answer," he says. "I was born to be tied to the summer. Whatever that actually means, and I guess I'm going to find out the hard way, you had nothing to do with it. If your dad hadn't messed with you and tied you to the winter the way he did, I'd be someone else's parallel, and there's no way of knowing whose. Maybe Chloe's."

He knows he's said the right wrong thing by the way Melanie's expression darkens. It's not that she hates Chloe—he's never known Mel to muster the energy to hate *anyone*, although that could change now that she's not spending most of her time trying to will herself not to die—it's that she's never appreciated the way their classmate has devoted herself to trying to woo Harry away from his "living dead girl" of a childhood sweetheart.

Invoking Chloe is low, but it's always worked when he's needed to snap her out of a funk before this, and he doesn't want her going down a hole if he can help it.

"So see, summer was always going to come for me. I guess if anyone should be apologizing here, it's your dad, for messing around with you before you were born. But I'm not going to call him up and ask him to, because wow am I glad that if I have to be part of some ridiculous scavenger hunt for the seasons, I'm doing it with you."

"You really believe her, then?"

Harry hesitates for a moment, considering, before he nods. "I do. I mean, I probably wouldn't if you had a heartbeat, but you don't, and you're already cold. And I'm so hot all the time that I'm pretty sure I don't get to eat ice cream anymore, unless what I want is ice cream soup."

He feels like he has a fever right now, like his skin's so hot it would sizzle if she touched him. It's not the nicest feeling. Most of the time, he doesn't even notice how warm he is, but right now, it's almost all he can think about. But Melanie is looking at him with the mock-serious expression she always wears when she's about to say something absolutely terrible, and so he pushes the thought aside, focusing on her instead.

"Milkshakes will still work, as long as you don't use a metal straw," says Melanie helpfully.

"That was definitely my first concern," he says. "Even if Jack's not telling the truth and we've just been tricked into helping some kid run away from home, I was worried about the fact that I now have a permanent fever and can't drink milkshakes through a metal straw."

Melanie laughs. It's one of his favorite sounds in the world, and hearing it reminds him of how rare it's become over the last year. He's still enjoying the sound of her laughter when the window crashes inward, showering the small room in shards of glass, and what looks like the engine of a small car slides across the floor.

Melanie's laughter turns to shrill, startled screaming.

Jack steps out of the room and into the cool air of the February night. She breathes in deeply, cleansing the warm interior air from her lungs. She's not the Winter Incarnate, to drop dead the day spring starts, but she has a little more than a month before her Ascendency ends and she's busted back down to ordinary girl for the growing months. Spring and summer will find her powerless, and if the coronation is still happening when they arrive, she won't be able to help her charges, either the one she's attendant to or the one she's picked up on the way.

Where the hell is Pamela? She was supposed to have the summer side of the story. She was supposed to tell the March boy exactly what he needed to know to win, and put it all in terms he could understand. And she knew her charge was a natural occurrence, that he wouldn't be as easy to convince as Melanie, wouldn't have the physical signs to go by.

This would all have been easier if it had happened in the summer side of the year. He'd be sprouting grass and toadstools everywhere he went, and he'd have to come to terms a lot faster. He'd definitely stop asking her to repeat herself. That would be so nice, and she wants that for herself, and she's not going to get it. She also wants Pamela to suddenly make an appearance, late and apologetic but present and ready to do her damn job.

Jack sighs. The golden arches of McDonald's are only about a block away, easy walking distance, especially for someone like her who doesn't mind the cold. She shoves her hands (one still clutching the pilfered twenty) into her pockets and heads down the motel steps, glad they've stopped for the night at the crest of California, far from the bustling, poisonous prosperity of the Bay Area, where two teens traveling with an obviously unrelated child might have attracted unwanted attention.

They'll wind up there eventually, she knows; she can feel it in the pit of her stomach, a ball of nausea and knowledge swirled together in equal measure, almost choking her. That's not where the coronation will be held, of course. That understanding will come later, after they've faced and survived their first few challenges. Assuming that they do.

She believes both of them have some steel in their souls, some potential to win this thing. Parallels always start out at an advantage, as far as she understands; they have something to fight for. Each other.

She can't imagine what coronations must have been like a hundred years ago, before the internet, when none of the attendants would have had any way to reach each other or to compare notes. This is North America's first coronation in three hundred years. They'd all be completely lost if they couldn't email their counterparts.

Not that any of them are giving away their locations. Not intentionally, anyway.

Cars litter the parking lot. These little tourist motels are the same no matter where you're starting out in the country; they're a miracle of North American architecture, balconies cupping the body of the parking lot, tiny rooms stacked like cells in a honeycomb. She's seen more than her share of them since closing the door to her childhood home in Evanston, Chicago. Running away from home became a lot easier once she didn't have to be afraid of freezing to death, always her father's favorite threat. ("Be good, girl, or I'll let you sleep outside in the snow, see how you like it when your hair freezes into icicles and your skin goes blue.") Well, she's slept outside in the snow plenty of times since then, and her hair's never frozen into icicles, and she's never even cracked the ice she stretches out atop.

Being tied to the winter has its benefits. Summer's a monster, but she never liked the summer anyway. Hot and nasty and full of midges. She has to be more careful in the summer, when she's as vulnerable as any ordinary girl, when she sweats and ages and risks heat stroke every time she goes out in the sun. But in the winter, she's as close as she can be to invulnerable.

Until they take their crowns, Harry and Mel are a little sturdier than the ordinary people they've always believed themselves to be. He won't feel hot, she won't feel cold, and the weapons of their seasons will be reluctant to do them harm. That may seem like a small thing, but she's heard stories of potential Winters shoved into fireplaces and potential Summers locked in freezers, and it wouldn't work in the reverse. Their connection makes them stronger than they might otherwise be at this stage in the coronation, but their lack of preparation makes them weaker, and she's not sure which aspect will dominate.

The night air is sweet with diesel fuel and mountain air. Jack breathes easy as she walks onward to the McDonald's, where the smell of grease and fried potatoes greets her before she steps into the parking lot. The lights glow steady and even, the same way they do everywhere she's ever been, all across the continent. It's one of life's little certainties. The seasons change, the moon beams, and McDonald's will sell you hot, fresh, calorically dense food at a price that's unsustainable unless you control supply chains and buy everything you need in bulk.

She's a semi-mortal manifestation of the spirit of winter, she only ages when she wants to or the summer is in ascendancy, meaning she'll get three months older every year for the rest of her life, and that life is likely to be very, very long, but she's also a thirteen-year-old girl in the body of a twelve-year-old, and she's about to get *McDonald's*. She's practically skipping by the time she reaches the door and pulls it open, releasing that smell unique to fast food lobbies and somehow universal across them all. Pizza, hamburgers, chicken or fish and chips, it doesn't matter, because the air inside will smell exactly the same regardless.

The air conditioning is running so high that even she can feel it, like an ice cube dropped down the back of her shirt, and for a moment, she shivers. There are four people already there: the man behind the counter, a woman clearing tables, both of them wearing the familiar polyester uniforms of the chain, and a pair of teens a few years older than her, probably a year or so younger than Harry and Mel, lounging in a corner booth like bored cats, all long limbs and arrogant expressions. Jack envies them, a little.

She didn't know how profoundly she was stopping her own clock when she agreed to carry the winter (and it's more of a choice for the ascendants than it is for the incarnates, although she knows better than to tell them how long they're going to be teenagers); she only knew that if she had to stay where she was, she would explode, she would light a match and burn the whole place to the ground with her entire family still inside, she would kill or she would die or she would do both at the same time. And so when the woman with the snowflake pattern in her irises came to her and said that she had a way to get her out, she didn't hesitate, not even for a second, not even when the woman told her she'd have to give away her name, the only thing she had remaining from her grandmother. Understanding came later, in long sessions at the kitchen table, her tutor trying to impart every scrap of wisdom she was going to need.

Ascendants know when they're approaching a natural end. It can be put off for a long time, but not forever, and in the end, Irene went into the long winter that waits for them all at the end of their service.

Jack has no intention of seeing it for a long, long time. She's happy to stay where she is, to let the missing-child posters fall further and further out of synch. But she looks at teens old enough to walk the world without arousing suspicion and she can't help but wish the call had waited just a little longer before it came to fetch her home.

She sidles up to the counter and waits for the bored man behind the register to acknowledge her. That's one more mark in favor of

McDonald's and other chains like it: there's nothing the people who work there haven't seen, nothing that impresses them anymore. She could walk in with a live gorilla and they'd just tell her there were no pets allowed.

If the man thinks anything of her age and apparent lack of adult supervision, it'll be that her parents are in the car, or that they've dropped her off to treat the McDonald's like a daycare while she does neglected homework. "Welcome to McDonald's may I take your order," he finally drones, all without taking a breath or fully registering her as a unique individual. (When the police speak to him in an hour, he won't be able to describe her beyond "Young kid, pigtails, I think, ordered chicken nuggets and a strawberry milkshake." He won't even remember the fries, unremarkable as they are.)

Jack smiles, places her order—extra fries to take back to the motel with her, after she's had her nuggets hot and crisp from the fryer— and waits politely to receive her tray before she heads for one of the many open booths. She chooses one that's well away from the lounging teens, preferring a little privacy while she eats.

She doesn't get it. She's barely pulled the skin off her first container of honey mustard when one of the teens slides in next to her. The other settles directly across from her, and that's that: she's boxed in.

Not only boxed in, but in the company of her own kind. They radiate summer and winter, not like the Incarnates do, but the same way she does, captive and chained and unwelcome here. She should have felt them sooner. She should have been paying *attention*. The ice cube down her back had been a warning, and she ignored it in favor of her stomach.

Foolish Jack. Bad Jack. And maybe doomed Jack, depending on how this plays out.

"Alone?" asks the one beside her. "That's a sad story. Little girl all by herself at nine o'clock at night, something's gone really wrong."

"Someone should call your parents," says the other teen, voice dripping faux concern.

"Maybe someone already has."

Jack looks between them, a small frown on her lips and as much casual disdain as she can summon in her eyes. "I don't recall asking you to join me," she says.

"Oh, but you did."

"When you stopped in our town during coronation, you did."

The teen next to her steals a nugget from her box and dips it in the honey mustard. "Where's your Jenny?"

That confirms the boy's identity. He's all long, lean power and hostile grace, bubbling with the kind of resentment that burns anyone who gets too close. She would have felt them sooner if she hadn't been flush with the presence of her own Incarnate, half-drunk on her season. He's her opposite number, and he'd destroy her if she let him.

"I don't have one," she says curtly, pulling her tray away from him. "I don't know anyone by that name."

"Least believable lie *ever*," says his counterpart, snapping the words like chewing gum. "It's not where it was, but 'Jennifer' is still one of the most popular names in the United States. You can play at being ignorant, but for the love of the laboring wheel, don't pretend to be *stupid*. You know someone named Jenny. You know a dozen people named Jenny."

"Jack," says Jack, meeting the other girl's eyes for the first time. They're wide and round and hazel brown, the irises patterned with snowflakes. She's been ascendant for a few years at least, then; it takes time for the eyes to frost over. Jack's own eyes haven't started yet, and probably won't until she's seventeen by the calendar and fourteen by the clock. "What are you doing here with this loser? He your boyfriend or something?"

The Corn Jenny by her side flushes red, offense and indignation in his face. The Jack Frost across from her sighs, looking put-upon. "Please. I have standards, and he doesn't suit them. I like my dates hot, happy, and human, not pasty, petulant, and . . ." She stops there, seemingly at a loss for how to finish her own sentence.

Jack takes pity. "Perennial?" she suggests.

The other Jack nods, expression going smug. "That works good. No, we're not dating. Met this morning, in fact. My Winter and his Summer both hit town about the same time, following a rumor that a parallel pair was heading down the coast from Portland. You know anything about that?"

"Parallels? Really?" asks Jack, making her eyes huge, trying to play on the teenage sense of superiority when talking to anyone younger than themselves. Maybe she can convince these people she doesn't know anything. They already know she's an Ascendant, but that was unavoidable once they got close enough to start eating her food.

"As if you didn't know," scoffs the Corn Jenny. "How'd they get this far with only you? You're just a kid. How young are they hiring these days?"

"I'm fourteen," says Jack. Age is a function of the calendar, and the calendar is what calls them. It tries not to call them too young when there's a coronation on the horizon, but this one was unexpected, and so she'd been called as soon as the winter blossomed in her bones. Everyone incubates at their own speed and in their own time. The youngest she's heard of had been seven when the summer called him to service, and had been one of the best Corn Jennies in the world for the time he spent with the season.

Age is just a number on a chalkboard somewhere, and it doesn't matter nearly as much as these two overly arrogant examples of the Ascendancy want it to.

"Fourteen," scoffs the Jack Frost. "I've been sixteen for fifty years."

That doesn't make sense with the rate at which they age. They're still mortal, after all. Jack doesn't reply, just makes a politely noncommittal sound before taking an entirely impolite slurp of her milkshake.

"I can't imagine having actual parallels in my care during a coronation and being careless enough to leave them alone," drawls the Corn Jenny, stealing one of Jack's fries and ignoring the way she glares at him. He turns it over between his fingers, trying to make the gesture seem casual and cool. He's an older teen tormenting a young one, and nothing about him is cool. Nothing about this situation is cool.

Especially not Jack, who is getting colder by the second as the situation sinks in. "What are you doing here?"

"Having a burger," says the Jack Frost.

"Seeing the sights," says the Corn Jenny.

"Waiting."

"Shouldn't have to wait much longer, though. Shouldn't take too long."

Jack looks between the two of them, following the conversation like a tennis ball lobbed gently back and forth. "What shouldn't take long?" she demands.

The other Jack Frost looks at her, seeming to really see her for the first time, and smiles the slow, languid smile of a predator seeing their prey cornered and unable to run away. "Resolving the challenge to the crown, of course," she says.

Jack vaults over the back of the booth, leaving her food behind, no thoughts in her head except for getting to the motel before something truly terrible can happen. She's not sure what good she'd do; depending on how far along their Incarnates are, she might be throwing herself into the face of certain doom, changing nothing, only leaving herself dead and broken on the ground. But she's sure of one thing: that she was summoned by the season to attend on Melanie Cosgrove, and if she fails in that duty, she won't deserve her place. She can't have that.

It's not loyalty. It's self-interest that makes her run.

A hand grabs her collar, jerking her to a stop through the simple expedient of holding her jacket in place. Jack snarls and thrashes.

Behind her, the Corn Jenny laughs. "Little *girl*," he jeers. "I don't know what the winter was thinking. Is your Incarnate one of your slumber-party buddies? Are you worried about them?"

Jack keeps snarling as she pulls her arms out of her sleeves and shrugs out of the jacket, shedding her denim skin as she runs for the door.

There's a clatter as both her fellow attendants abandon the booth and chase after her. The man at the register looks up, eyes narrowed at the commotion. "Hey, you kids!" he shouts. "Get out of here! This is not a playground!"

(When the police attempt to review the camera footage of the altercation, they'll find nothing but the McDonald's dining room, empty of people, the edges of the film speckled with grainy snow-flake static. If not for the discarded tray, there would be no sign that anyone was ever here, certainly not three teenagers running out the door just before the explosion at the motel.)

In a matter of seconds, they're gone, running out into the chilly February night, not looking back.

First Confrontation

Melanie is still screaming when the people follow the engine through the window, crashing into the room.

Both are male, one in a tank top despite the time of year, the other in a heavy cable-knit sweater that looks like it was intended more for the Maritimes than the California coast. The taller, the one without sleeves, settles into a fighting stance, hands raised. The one in the sweater has a knife.

It looks very sharp in the motel-room light. Melanie stops screaming. Harry pushes in front of her, and the air is far warmer than it was only a few moments before, sizzling like a summer's day. Melanie molds herself against his back, biting her lip at the heat radiating from his skin. It should hurt, like grabbing a hardboiled egg that hasn't had time to cool after being taken off the stove, like trying to handle a chunk of sun-scorched metal. It *would* hurt, she somehow knows, if she were touching anything else this hot. But it's Harry, and Harry would never hurt her, and her certainty about that simple fact of the universe is greater than the laws of thermodynamics—which are, after all, just another fact of the universe, and one that might one day be born in the body of a puzzled runaway trying to figure out what their life is becoming—and keeps her safe and shielded.

"They're parallel," says the boy in the wool sweater. "They have to be. Look at the way she's clinging to him. Timid little thing. I almost feel bad about this."

"Don't," says the boy in the tank top. "He's further along than you are. You don't want to face him when the season turns."

"Who the *fuck* are you, and what are you doing in our room?" demands Harry. He's waiting for an alarm, for a ruckus from outside, for something to tell him the adults are on their way to take care of whatever the hell is going on. He's always been sheltered from the world by his parents' money and his own relative good behavior; he has no frame of reference for what's happening right now.

But then, how many teens, sheltered or not, would have a frame of reference for this? This is beyond the pale, and even the two boys look like they realize it. It's the only reason he can see for them to have broken into the room to find him sitting on the bed and Mel wearing nothing but a towel, for God's sake, with a knife already drawn, and hesitate before finishing their attack.

"Do we really have to kill them?" asks the boy in the sweater. He sounds like he's on the verge of panic, and Harry realizes he's about the same age as himself and Melanie, a teenager dragged into a situation he doesn't fully understand. The one in the tank top is older, mid-twenties at least, and he scowls at his companion.

"No," he says. "*We* don't have to do anything. *You* have to kill *him*. After you do that, maybe the timid one renounces her crown. Maybe we let her live when she's not a threat anymore."

Harry stops listening when he realizes he's not the only one they came here intending to slaughter. He wasn't sure he could hurt someone to protect himself. He's absolutely certain he can hurt someone for Melanie's sake. It's not even a question, not really. He grabs the lamp off the nightstand between the two beds, barely registering how hot it is against his hand, and hurls it as hard as he can at the man in the tank top.

It shatters against his chest, sending shards of ceramic to join the glass already dusting the floor. The man winces, then looks to Harry, eyes narrowing.

"You don't get to attack *me*," he says sourly. "I'm not your target."

"Fuck you," says Harry. "You break into my motel room in the middle of the night, you break my window—we're going to need a new room, and I'm *not* paying for that—and you start making weird-ass threats against me and my girlfriend, and now you want to say you're not my target? You're lucky all I did was throw a lamp."

"Your *girlfriend*?" says the boy in the sweater. He sounds disgusted. He moves the knife more obviously into a stabbing position, some of his reluctance melting away. "That's vile, man. Has no one told you what's going on?"

"Fuck you, too," says Harry. "No one gets to talk about Mel like that."

"I'm not calling *her* vile, I'm calling the idea of the two of you . . . Do you not understand what's happening?"

There's a sudden absence at his back as Melanie pulls away and slides off the bed, moving toward the bathroom door with quick but unconcerned steps. The boy with the knife snarls something incoherent and swings his knife around, now aiming at her.

"We're willing to let you walk away from this, if you'll just renounce your crown," says the man in the tank top. He seems less concerned about the situation than anyone else in the room. Maybe that's because, based on the way he's dressed, he shares his season with Melanie. He lives where the winter lives. And right now, he thinks he can't die.

That would make the boy with him the potentially incarnate Summer, in direct competition with Harry. Not cool. It means he's vulnerable right now, which explains why he's so nervous; it's probably a lot harder to burst in on strangers and start threatening to do them material harm when you know that it could come with actual consequences.

"Neither of us is renouncing anything," says Melanie calmly, stopping at the bathroom door and turning to face the intruders. "You might want to consider it, if you're really all that interested in walking away from this."

The man Harry is assuming wants to claim the Winter laughs at that. Actually laughs, like there's anything funny about this situation, like there could *be* anything funny about it. And he starts to walk across the room, heading for the bathroom, and Melanie, who he's clearly identified as an easy target.

"You could renounce, you know," says Harry, scrambling to get off the bed, to put himself between the man and Mel. She's opened the bathroom door and is slipping inside, towel still firmly in place, and he doesn't want her getting hurt, and he doesn't want her hurting anyone.

And then the boy with the knife is upon him, putting on a sudden burst of speed and hitting Harry on the shoulder, using his momentum and slightly superior size to drive Harry back and slam him against the wall. He raises the knife like he thinks he's a character from a slasher movie, something with blood in the title and half a dozen sequels already in development, and he hesitates, clearly unsure as to how he's actually meant to bring it down on someone alive and staring at him, someone almost his own age.

He hesitates, in fact, long enough for Harry, who has shrugged off more than his fair share of tackles, to twist around and shove him away, and to bring his own knee up into the boy's crotch for good measure. It's fighting dirty, sure, but the guy has a *knife* and broke the *window* and still there are no alarms. Whatever's happening here, it doesn't play by normal rules, and it isn't going to start.

He's sure he'll remember the feeling of the boy's testicles deforming under the blow for the rest of his life. It makes him want to vomit. It clearly makes the other guy want to vomit even more.

He makes a small, pained sound as Harry pushes him away. He doesn't drop the knife. Harry really wishes he'd dropped the knife. The man in the tank top has followed Melanie into the bathroom, and Harry hears a loud clatter, followed by Mel shrieking. He can't tell whether it's with panic or rage. He really wishes he could. This whole night is suddenly full of things he really wishes for, things he'd happily request from a genie if one were to make itself available, that he never considered worth spending wishes on.

The boy staggers back two steps before raising his knife again, a snarl on his face, and it's clear from the way he surges toward Harry that he's no longer uncertain about how he's supposed to stab some-body. He's found his inner killer, and he's ready to let it out.

"Dude, back the fuck off!" shouts Harry, and lowers his torso, getting into position to deliver a proper field tackle. It'll hurt with-out proper protective gear (although that sweater's thick enough to virtually qualify entirely on its own), but it's hurt or get hurt and it's been less than thirty seconds and Melanie's still shrieking and no matter how many times he's been told not to tackle somebody without making sure they have the proper padding to take the blow safely, he can't stand here and do nothing while Melanie screams in the next room. So he charges, slamming his shoulder into the boy's chest just below the solar plexus. The air comes out of him in a great rush as he's borne backward by Harry's momentum, stopping only when his back slams into the wall.

He drops the knife. Harry can't focus on much other than panic and adrenaline right now, but he's still glad to hear it hit the floor, even as he's wrestling to get the other teen's arms pinned in place. "No," he says, when the boy tries to break free. "No," he says again, when the boy tries to repeat his own knee-to-the-nuts trick. It's not hard to block the boy's knee with his own leg; he must still be sore, and be having trouble moving quickly or thinking clearly. Pain will do that to a person.

"Why are you fighting us?" demands the boy, wheezing a little. "You're not prepared. You won't *win*."

In that moment, Harry makes the decision he's been putting off since this wild rush began: he decides to believe this is really hap-pening, and Jack has been telling them the truth since the begin-ning. There's a snap somewhere deep inside his mind, the sound of concepts clicking firmly into place, and he remembers conver-sations he had forgotten before, half-sentences murmured as they drove across Oregon and into California, explanations he'd been clinging too tightly to the world as he knew it to understand.

If these would-be assassins have done nothing else tonight, they've caused Harry to admit he's fighting for his life and, by extension, for Melanie's life, and it doesn't matter if he wants to do it, and it doesn't matter if he thinks it makes any sense at all, if he doesn't fight, Melanie dies. If he doesn't fight, *he* dies. The only way out is through.

"We *are* winning," says Harry, and brings up his other hand, shoving the boy's head back so it knocks against the wall, not hard enough to knock him out, but hard enough to disorient, to leave him momentarily reeling. Harry takes advantage of the boy's clear disorientation to step back and grab the knife off the floor. "We're going to win. Whatever the fuck the prize at the end of this whacked-out horror show is, we're going to win it."

He has the knife now. Somehow that doesn't make him feel better. Neither does the fact that Melanie, alone in the bathroom with a strange man, isn't screaming anymore.

The boy in the sweater looks at him with something close to pity in his eyes. "You have no idea what's going on," he says. "You don't understand a single damn thing."

"Maybe not," admits Harry, as he puts his free hand against the boy's shoulder and holds him to the wall. "But I understand that I don't want to kill you, and my attendant"—may as well pretend he has one, since this guy clearly does; of the four of them, Harry's the only one left unprepared—"says if you renounce your crown, you're out. You're not a threat anymore. You can't pick it back up. So renounce."

The boy doesn't say anything, just keeps looking at Harry with that same distantly pitying expression. It doesn't waver even as Harry leans forward and presses the tip of the knife to the skin under the boy's jaw, in that spot all the medical shows he's ever seen have told him people can't survive being cut.

He doesn't want to kill anyone tonight. He doesn't think he has the stomach for it.

But the silence from the bathroom is so *loud*.

"*Renounce*," spits Harry.

"You're parallel because you care about your Winter, aren't you?" asks the boy. "Me and Paul, we met yesterday morning, when our attendants brought us to the same town and said we should team up. We don't give a damn about each other. If we won, we'd walk away and keep our courts in isolation, the way you're *supposed* to, not get them all mixed together."

"You knew your attendants before this started?" Harry frowns. Jack explained that Mel's dad was keeping the Jack Frosts from getting to her—even implied that some of them might have died trying to reach her to do their jobs—but there's been no one protecting him from the cosmological forces of the universe. His own instructor should have been able to reach him long, long ago.

Things would be very different right now if he'd been prepared for this process to begin, he's sure of that.

The look of pity in the boy's eyes deepens. "I've known my attendant since I was eight years old," he says. "She came and found me on the playground, and she told me she was going to be my new babysitter, and somehow she made it stick. Jacks have tricks we don't, even when they aren't yoked to anyone who's been crowned, because they have to be able to prepare us for the next coronation, when it comes around. And it always comes around, little asshole in love with his own Winter. Which is a *terrible* idea, just so you know. She's probably already dead, and the closer you come to crowning, the more tangled up you'll get with her if you stay parallel. The boost to your manifestation isn't worth the chance of her taking you down before it's locked in, and you don't have to let her drag you out of consideration like this—"

Harry will swear if he's asked later that he didn't mean to do it. He wasn't planning to make things even worse than they already were, even worse than this horrible, brutal scene, which had no reason to happen the way it has, but has insisted on happening anyway. But the boy keeps talking, keeps insinuating that Melanie isn't worth saving, that he should let her go, and it just *happens*.

He doesn't fully understand what he's done until the blood is running down the boy's neck and covering his hand, and the boy is raising his own hands to clutch at his throat, trying to stop what both of them know to be unstoppable. Harry takes a step back, horrified by what he's done, by what he's witnessing, and the knife slips from his suddenly nerveless fingers to clatter amongst the shards of glass and ceramic on the floor.

He's killed someone. This stupid boy who smashed in their window (and why aren't there sirens? Why aren't people rushing to see what the commotion is all about? This should have attracted attention, this should have brought the whole motel down on their heads, and instead everything is silence, and Jack's still gone, and he has *blood* on his *hands*) is dead now, and it's because of something *Harry* did, because of a weapon in *Harry's* hand. His chest feels too tight and his heart feels like it's going to explode in his chest. Is this what it's like to be Mel? To have your own body constantly on the brink of betrayal?

Mel. Oh, fuck, Melanie. There's still silence from the bathroom, and Harry turns to reel toward the half-open door like a man drunk. He doesn't know what he's going to find there, but he knows Jack said he'd die if Melanie did, and his wildly beating heart is a painful reminder that he's not dead yet, however much he may almost wish he were. He wants to live, of course he wants to live, even in this wild new world of Ascendants and Incarnates and weird little girls who tell him it's his job to embody the entire summer in his skin, but he doesn't want to live in a world where he's a murderer. The moment is a contradiction. He's a killer and he's alive; he's the living Summer and he's an ordinary teen, scared and confused and far away from home without a clear way back; he's walking toward his girlfriend and he's walking toward a corpse.

"Harry?"

"Mel!" Relief floods through him like rain into an empty canyon, and he nearly sits down right where he is, unable to stay on his feet any longer. He settles for catching himself against the dresser, leaving a bloody smear behind, and holding himself up before he can topple to the floor. His heart seems to be calming down a little, at least; hearing her voice has healed a wound he hadn't even noticed opening, has made it possible for him to breathe. He can accept this as long as he's not accepting it alone.

"Are you all right? Did he hurt you?"

"I'm fine," says Harry, almost giddy now that he can hear her voice, that he hasn't had the claim that if she dies, he dies too confirmed for a lie. He can't handle another upset right now. He needs to be able to believe that what their so-called guide has been telling them is true. "Did he hurt *you*?"

"No."

"Mel, come out of the bathroom."

"No."

Harry pauses, frowns. He can't think of many reasons she wouldn't come out, and none of the ones he *can* think of are good ones, or ones he wants to linger on. "Mel, are you sure he didn't hurt you?"

"He tried." Her voice takes on a light, almost singsong quality. "He grabbed for me, pulled my towel off of me. I didn't like that. He was trying to catch my shoulder. He *did* catch my hair. I guess I lied a little, because that hurt, when he pulled on my hair. That hurt a *lot*."

"I'm sorry," says Harry. It's a useless sentiment, especially when he's standing here with blood on his hands, but maybe it's a good thing for her to stay in the bathroom for a few seconds longer. If she's really unhurt, it stretches out the length of time before she sees him as a killer.

Maybe it stretches out the time when she still loves him.

"It's what I get for leaving it long." Melanie goes quiet for a long, terrible moment before she says, in a smaller voice, so small it's almost a whisper, "I don't know if I want to come out, because you're going to look at me different after what I did."

Harry looks at his own bloody hands (how does he have blood on both of them, when he only stabbed the boy with one? *How?*) and swallows a peal of hysterical laughter. "I don't think that's something we need to worry about right now," he says. "You're going to look at me differently, too, I'd bet."

Slowly, the door inches open, and Melanie appears. The towel is gone, but at some point between the end of the commotion and now (and again, *how*? It's only been a few seconds . . .), she's managed to put her sweatshirt back on. It was originally one of his, and it hangs on her like a dress, covering her from shoulders almost to thighs. She could walk down the street like that and be decent, if not for her bare feet, and the wild look in her eyes, and the cuts on her forehead, and the blue-black bruise forming on her left cheek, almost the exact size and shape of a human fist.

He doesn't know if Jack ever told her to demand a renunciation. He doesn't know if she had time to try. But he doesn't hear anyone else moving around in there, and he doesn't think she got her assailant to renounce.

"Mel," he says, and starts to reach for her, only to flinch and freeze when he sees the blood on his own hands.

"Oh, *Harry*," she sighs, and slips out of the bathroom like a ghost moving through fog, not taking any care to avoid the glass and ceramic scattering the floor as she walks toward him. He should tell her to go back. He doesn't. He can't speak. He can only watch her, and think about how scared he was when she disappeared into the bathroom with a stranger on her tail, another prospective Winter who wanted nothing more than to steal the season she was heir to. He's been worried about Melanie for most of their lives. He's always known that one day, he's going to lose her. But he's never been scared like this before. Even when she's been in the hospital, it's never been this immediate of a threat.

Then she's in front of him, her pale, unstained fingers tracing his bloodstained hands before she looks past him to the dead boy slumped against the wall, his blood spreading across the floor and sinking into the cheap carpet, cooling and clotting and no longer capable of sustaining life. She sighs again, wordlessly this time, and then she's throwing her arms around Harry, pulling him close, resting her chin against his shoulder.

"I'm sorry," she says. "I'm so, so sorry."

Harry blinks. This isn't what he expected. "What are you sorry for?" he asks.

"We're parallel," she says, like that explains anything.

He wants to ask. He wants to ask what she means more than almost anything, because everything's so ridiculous right now, he may as well sit down for another incomprehensible tutoring session about things that didn't matter last week but can apparently mean life or death this week. He doesn't. Instead, he slides his arms around her and squeezes briefly before asking, "What happened in the bathroom?"

Melanie lets him go and steps back, and something crunches under her foot. She doesn't seem to notice. Harry does. Harry notices how she doesn't flinch, not even a little, as she turns on her almost-certainly-wounded heel to look at the bathroom door and says, "He followed me inside. I didn't want to . . . didn't want to . . ."

"I know. I saw."

"I didn't have a choice, Harry. He was going to hurt me. He was going to . . . He was going to make me leave you. I had to." Melanie's head tilts forward, her gaze falling on the floor, and she seems to notice the broken glass for the first time even as she murmurs, "I had to."

"I know you did. But Mel, I need to know how much trouble we're in here. I don't know why the police haven't shown up yet—" The whole encounter has only taken a few minutes, according to the old-fashioned digital clock on the nightstand, but it wasn't subtle. The sound of breaking glass alone should have raised a few alarms. He doesn't know what it means that it didn't.

He doesn't think it means anything good. Harry March has always been someone planted firmly in the world as it is, not in the world as he might want it to be. His mother sometimes sighs sadly and says having a dying girl as his best friend has tarnished his innocence, has made it harder for him to believe in the ineffable. Harry just thinks of it as being clear-eyed and level-headed, two traits that are surprisingly useful when trying to convince the entire world that he's soft and silly and a bit of a fool. No one expects the class clown to be considering a degree in forestry and land management, after all.

But this new world he finds himself in isn't realistic. This isn't the world as it is, or the world as he wants it to be: this is the world gone out of control and ridiculous, following rules he doesn't understand and can't reject. The window was broken; the motel management should have been called. There was a fight, which he knows will have been audible in the surrounding rooms; the police should be in the parking lot by now, sirens blaring and lights flashing. He can't quite deal with the fact that none of that is happening, and he can't deal with the fact that when Mel takes a stuttering step toward the bathroom, her feet aren't bleeding, and he can't deal with the blood on his own hands.

There's a lot he can't deal with right now. Denying it isn't making it any less true, and so he forces himself to take a deep breath and walk forward, passing Mel, pushing open the bathroom door to reveal the wreckage on the other side.

He was so wrapped up in fighting for his own life that he didn't hear the sounds from the bathroom that charted Melanie fighting for hers. The lid from the toilet is on the floor; the mirror is broken, and the crack pattern almost perfectly matches the shape of cuts on her forehead. He finds he doesn't like the image of her head being slammed into the wall any more than he likes the image of someone punching her in the face, but what he likes and what he doesn't like don't matter anymore.

The shower rail has been yanked down, and the man in the tank top is in the bathtub, or at least, his body is. The man himself is gone, as far away as the boy in the heavy sweater, both of them departed down paths that aren't open to the living. The shower curtain is wrapped halfway around him like a shroud, but that isn't what killed him. Harry might feel better, if it had been. That's a weird thought to have, since the idea of Mel wrapping a shower curtain around a man's neck and strangling him with it isn't exactly soothing, but it would be more realistic than what he's seeing.

The man's skin is covered with a fine tracery of frost, darkened at the fingers, ears, and nose until it turns almost black, like he's suffering from the worst case of frostbite ever recorded in a motel room near the highway. The skin that isn't virtually charred is still iced over, and the best phrase Harry's startled mind can provide him with is "freezer-burned." Bile rushes up his throat. He claps a hand over his mouth as he staggers back into the motel room, choking back shock and vomit at the same time.

Melanie has pulled a pair of leggings out of her bag. She's fully dressed now, leggings, sweatshirt, and even a bra she dug out of some mysterious crevasse. He has no idea how she's managed to fit so much in the one small bag she took from her father's house. That's less a "living incarnation of the Winter" thing and more a "cheerleaders have access to some weird storage dimension that the rest of us can't get to" thing, because he's seen all the girls from the squad pull similar stunts. Sometimes he's seen it a bit more clearly than he wanted to, like when Chloe "accidentally" spilled the bag containing all her undergarments in front of him. But that's not the point. Mel's sitting on the edge of the bed they were supposed to share tonight, staring at the body against the wall.

"Yours bled more than mine did," she says, voice distant, and if his response to her first kill (how he hates the word "first") was nausea and horror, it sounds like hers is total detachment from the situation around them. *This isn't happening,* her voice says, even as her body says something different; *this is a new situation, but it isn't a real one, and it isn't anything I need to worry about at all.*

"Mine had a knife," says Harry. He doesn't want to go back into the bathroom, but he knows they don't have forever. Someone *will* come looking, even if the commotion somehow mysteriously didn't attract any attention; someone will notice the broken window, which is large enough to be visible from the parking lot, and then they'll be caught.

He used his credit card to pay for this room. They're *going* to be caught. No matter how much he wants to grab their things and get out of here, they're *going* to be caught. So someone has to go back into that bathroom and retrieve Melanie's clothing, and from the way she's sitting placidly on the bed and staring at the corpse against the wall, it's not going to be her.

There is a click, a whirr; the sound of an automatic lock disengaging and a door being opened.

"What the *fuck*?!" demands a familiar voice, less than half a heartbeat later. Harry lifts his head, grateful to see Jack for the first time, less grateful to see the two unfamiliar teens who come pelting up behind her and flank her, staring in unified horror at the wreckage of the room.

Well, not Jack. She's staring, but she doesn't look horrified in the least. If anything, she looks relieved, like this is an outcome she hoped for but couldn't allow herself the luxury of imagining. It's a feeling that only grows when her eyes flick to Melanie.

"Is our Lady hurt?" she asks, with more deference than he's ever heard from her before.

Harry startles a little at that tone, but assumes it has something to do with the teens behind her, whose expressions haven't changed, but who at least aren't screaming yet—something he really, *really* wants to avoid as long as possible—and so he answers. "She got her head knocked against the mirror, but she's mostly okay," he says.

"No lasting damage done," says Melanie, and turns to face the three in the doorway, blinking languidly. The bruise on her cheek has finished spreading. It's an ugly thing, splayed out and uneven as a squashed spider, and part of him loves it anyway, because it's hers, because its presence means she's survived. "Hello, Jack. Who are your friends?"

"These fools aren't my friends," says Jack, with her familiar disdain. She steps forward, past the threshold, and she's in the room, and there's something symbolic about that, and Harry can't dwell on it, because the teens are still there, still silent, still staring. One of them is holding Jack's denim jacket, and as he watches, she reaches back and snatches it away, gathering it in her own arms. "Sorry I didn't bring your fries. Fools again. They interrupted me while I was eating."

"You . . . won?" says the taller of the two teens, and Harry knows him instantly, knows him inside and out. He was called by the Summer twenty years ago, and has been aging slowly since then, long enough to grow to resent his lasting youth and dream of a coronation that can let him hit adulthood through some mechanism he doesn't fully understand and thus can't transmit to Harry; his name was Jared, once, and has been Jenny since long before his parents took his image off the school milk cartons. He's a sharp, hostile excuse for a human being, and was even before the season found him; cruelty may not have been the reason he was selected, but it clearly didn't hurt.

He's a Corn Jenny. He's always been a Corn Jenny, but when the Summer was seeking Ascendants in his area, he got the call, and the dead man in the bathroom is the third potential Incarnate he's trained, or tried to, and he really thought he was going to have a chance at the crown this time. He really thought they were going to win.

His idea of "winning" includes Harry and Melanie both, both of them dead on the floor of this room, while his own candidate walks triumphantly closer to his inevitable victory. Harry's eyes narrow. He does wonder, briefly, if Mel can see into Jack's thoughts like this, but assumes she would have told him if she could, and so shunts the thought aside as he walks toward the door.

The strangers quail a little, but they don't run. That's good. He doesn't want to have to chase them.

"You don't . . ." says the other teen, the one he assumes must be their Jack Frost, since he can't feel her at all. "You don't have to kill us." A sharp whine comes into her voice. "We're not in the running. The season touches us but it doesn't own us, and we'd die if we tried to claim the crown."

"Did you send those assholes to break our window and murder us in our beds?" Harry asks. Neither of them says a word. He balls his still-bloody hands into fists, and bellows, "*Answer me!*"

"We didn't tell them to kill you in your *beds*," says the Corn Jenny. It's almost pathetic, how much this boy, who was willing to see him dead only minutes ago, wants Harry to like him. It bakes off him like heat off a summer sidewalk, practically visible in the air of the destroyed motel room. "We just . . . We told them . . ."

"They were supposed to make you renounce, not kill you," says the girl hurriedly. "They were supposed to remove you from the running. We told them to be careful, because we knew you were parallel. Parallels are dangerous."

"You knew?"

"Of course we knew. Everyone knows. Everyone you pass can feel you, and the longer you stay paralleled, the more dangerous you're going to get." The girl's voice hardens, turning bleak as winter ice. "You'd know all this if you had proper support. One little girl isn't going to be enough to see you to the finish." She shoots a sharply venomous look at Jack. "You could replace her, you know. Take an upgrade to people who have a better idea what they're doing, and can actually get you to where you need to be."

Harry hears a rustle from behind him. Melanie has left the bed. Her approach is silent, until she's right behind him and sets a hand against his shoulder, fingers cold as ever.

"No, thank you," she says. The distance is gone from her voice. "Jack got us this far, didn't she? And Jack was enough for us to take out your candidates. I don't think we're in the market for a replacement."

"Fuck you," says Jack, more succinctly, as she turns and flips off the pair. She walks backward across the room until she's just in front of Harry, but stops shy of brushing against him.

"Do we need to worry about them?" asks Harry.

"No," says Jack dismissively. "They're just Ascendants. If they don't find a new Incarnate to attach themselves to, they're done—and they know better than to hurt me, because you've seen them and you wouldn't accept their service." Her smile is more of a snarl, a baring of her teeth to the intruders who would dare approach her territory with ill intentions. "They're out, they've failed."

"What do you get if we win?" asks Harry.

"Oh, I get a healthy serving of what the fuck is wrong with you? The seasons can only keep the rest of this motel from noticing us for so long, and once they do, it's going to be time for cops and questions. Get your shit, we're leaving."

"I paid with a credit card," says Harry.

"Won't matter." Jack waves his concern away. "You're still a part of the world—you have to be, when you stand for something so big and so integral to the world itself—but you're a little bit apart from it as long as you're in contention. No one's going to think to check the receipts or come looking for you, unless you lose."

"What happens then?"

"Well, you die, for one thing," says Jack, ignoring the teens still standing in the doorway as she moves to get her things. "So there's that. Mel takes the Winter or you both go down."

"Does that mean I *have* to take the Summer if she takes the Winter?"

Jack pauses. "You know, that may be the first good question you've asked me. No. She's required, but you're not; you can refuse, you can step aside, and you can abdicate, all without dropping dead on the spot."

"What the hell?" asks the boy in the doorway, and Harry is reminded that they have an audience, that this might be a conversation best saved for the car.

"None of your damn business," snaps Jack. She grabs her backpack, slings it over her shoulder, looks to Melanie as if for permission. When Melanie nods, she strides across the room and vanishes into the bathroom. She doesn't exclaim or shout, only rummages around for a moment before emerging with Mel's clothes and toiletries in a roll under her arm and an unfamiliar wallet in her hand.

For a moment, the girl in the doorway looks like she's going to protest. Then she thinks better of it, and holds her tongue. Jack looks to Harry.

"I really, *really* don't want to touch yours," she says. "Can you search the body? Or at least pick up that knife? Because Mommy and Daddy's credit cards aren't going to work forever—or even that much longer if we keep having to drop out of sight to keep from getting caught in the middle of a coronation—and every little bit helps."

More questions for the car, then. Harry doesn't think he can express how much he doesn't want to touch the dead boy on the floor, how much he wants a way to wash the blood from his hands without going into that horror show of a bathroom ever, ever again, but he nods and moves toward the boy he (*killed*) fought, the boy who might have been the Summer King if he'd been a little bit faster, or stronger, or alone. Harry's smart enough to admit that. He has a healthy streak of self-preservation; he likes being alive, he likes seeing new things and having new experiences. If someone tried to mug him or beat him up, he'd fight back. But would he be able to kill them? Even under circumstances like this one?

No, probably not. If not for the boy's friend going after Melanie and making this all very, brutally real, Harry wouldn't have been able to pick up the knife, much less put it against another person's throat. Had the boy come alone, had the two decided to split up and face their targets one by one, the outcome could have been a very different one.

Jack casts a sympathetic look in his direction as Mel is gathering her things, and he knows she can guess the direction of his thoughts. She plucks the car keys off the nightstand as he digs through the boy's clothes, finally coming up with his wallet. There's nothing else to find or steal, except for a medic alert bracelet around the boy's left wrist. Harry doesn't even glance at it. He doesn't need the boy whose life he ended to be any more of a real person in his memory.

"We're leaving now," says Jack to the unnamed attendants—*God, they're not unnamed,* Harry thinks, *their names are Jack and Jenny.* This is going to get confusing. Does every candidate for the crown have to have attendants with the same name?

Based on the way Jack keeps muttering about "his" missing Corn Jenny, he's going to say probably yes, and much as it sucks, he's not sure there's any choice in the matter.

The stranger that Harry knows so completely looks at them with longing as they exit the motel room, leaving the corpses and the sea of broken glass behind. Melanie still doesn't have her shoes on. They dangle from the fingers of one hand, all but forgotten as she pads down the concrete balcony and onto the stairs, descending toward the waiting parking lot.

Her feet leave no prints, bloody or otherwise. Harry can't stop himself from staring.

Jack loads their things into the trunk as Harry slides behind the wheel, and this, at least, is normal; this, at least, is the way things are meant to be. He starts the engine, and nothing unexpected happens. He's just a boy in a car, taking his girl for a drive.

"Why didn't you put your shoes on?" asks Jack, climbing into the backseat.

"Glass," says Melanie, voice gone dreamy and distant once again. "I stepped on a bunch of it back in the room. I think it's still in my heel."

Harry forces his hands to stay on the wheel, forces himself not to turn and stare at her the way he wants to. Whatever she is, whatever she's becoming, he can't stop it without killing her. Maybe if he were an alchemist in his own right, he'd have a chance, but that's not the world they live in. She's changing, and all he can do is follow her and try to make sure she doesn't get lost in the process.

(In Harry's mind, the word "alchemist" and the word "wizard" are becoming almost indistinguishable, the one bleeding into the other like two shades of paint mixing in a pail. And he's not as right as he would want to be, and he's not as wrong as Jack would happily tell him he is, and so he isn't hurting anything. Not yet, anyway. Melanie isn't the only one who's changing: it's just that the seeds of Harry's own transformation were not planted by human hands, and so they rest more deeply and rightly in his flesh.)

Harry pulls out of the space he parked in, supposedly for the night, and heads for the highway. In the motel behind them he sees lights start to click on, people start to move, as if the world had only been delaying the inevitable long enough for them to make their escape, slipping away like thieves in the night. He doesn't like the thought. Liking or disliking something doesn't do anything to change how true it is or isn't. If it did, none of this would be happening right now: he'd be home in Portland, having spent Saturday night dancing with Melanie in his arms, not here in the middle of nowhere, following the direction of a preteen's finger as she points for the highway on-ramp she wants him to take.

He turns onto the highway, his car blending with a river of others, and they're away; this town has nothing more to offer them.

The cave, which had been dim in the beginning, was growing steadily lighter as their group walked, going from pearl-tinted twilight to something much closer to the rosy light of dawn, as if somewhere in the distance, the sun was giving sincere thought to the act of rising. They walked on, and dawn broke into sunrise, buttery light suddenly filling the air, illuminating every dancing mote of dust, which rose up with their footsteps, chalk and sand and the crushed shells of long-dead marine creatures learning, however briefly, how to fly under their own precious power.

Zib laughed, and sped up, arrowing her footsteps toward a wide archway cut out of the cave wall. The others followed her, the Crow Girl bursting once more into birds in her hurry to see what was on the other side, until they all emerged into the bright, warm light of a seaside morning. They were standing on a beach that glittered like the sugar on a Christmas cookie, all pristine white and stretching out to the horizon both to the left and to the right, but yielding straight ahead to the lapping waves of an endless indigo sea. The water looked warm and gentle, and when it struck the sand it seemed to whisper, Yes, children, good, children, yes, good children to come into me, come swim, come swim, come swim with the sirens and the sea fairies and all the good things that water can coddle and claim. Come, children, come.

"Do you hear that?" asked Avery, suddenly nervous as he inched closer to Zib. She might be loud and wild and unaware of the importance of well-shined shoes, but

she was from the same ordinary town as he was, and she knew that the ocean wasn't supposed to talk. Not so clearly, anyway, and not with such a bright and blazing need as this one.

"It wants us to go swimming," she said, voice dreamy. Then she shook her head and shot him a quick, alarmed look. "How does it want anything? It's the ocean. Oceans aren't supposed to want things."

"This is the Saltwise Sea," said Niamh. "This is where the King of Coins and the King of Cups collide. It's the truest border between their two domains."

"How does that make it so the water can talk?" asked Avery. "Water isn't supposed to talk."

"The King of Cups has the Page of Frozen Waters now, but he used to have the Lady of Salt and Sorrow," said Niamh. "She's the patron of my city. Everyone there loves her so, and she loves us, even if she can't pull herself out of the sea to talk to us any longer. We all know the Page is responsible for her losing her crown and her own good skin, but we can't prove it, because we can't find her bones."

"Has anyone told the King?" asked Zib.

The Crow Girl swirled back into being in front of them, pulling birds back into her body until she was only one thing, instead of many. "He doesn't care," she said, and there was more mourning in her voice than there usually was. "He has the Page, and she doesn't question what he wants or tell him not to do the terrible things he thinks will be pleasant. Maybe they are pleasant, for him. I don't know. I'm just a crow girl, I don't even have a name, and names change everything. . . .

—From *Along the Saltwise Sea,* by A. Deborah Baker

BOOK V

Bay Area

I stand amid the roar
Of a surf-tormented shore,
And I hold within my hand
Grains of the golden sand . . .
                    —Edgar Allen Poe, "A Dream Within a Dream"

There was once a girl
Or maybe more than once
Twice upon a time
Not her time—out of time, anytime
But every single time.

                    —Talis Kimberley, "Time and Tide"

Rest Stop

H arry drives until he starts to shake from stress and fear and delayed trauma, until his vision starts to blur and he knows it isn't safe for him to keep going. But he does anyway, unsure of what else he can do, until Jack leans between the seats and places a hand gently on his arm.

"There's a rest stop in two miles," she says. "Pull off there."

More grateful than he can express to have the responsibility taken away from him, Harry nods, and when the sign appears to mark the offramp, he turns the car in that direction, exiting the flow of traffic. None of the other drivers take note of his departure. For one thing, that's not how highways work; no one tracks anyone else to that granular of a degree. For another, perhaps more important thing, half of them had never even noticed his car, not even when it was in front of them and going so far below the speed limit that it posed a legitimate traffic hazard. Somehow, between the aggravation and the acceleration, they forgot he was there.

They never noticed.

The rest stop is empty, a single brick building bathed in February moonlight. The only sound is the distant yapping of coyotes and the faint buzz of the vending machines near the bathrooms. Harry parks as close to the building as he can, glancing at Mel, who has been silent and still for the entire drive so far.

"Please put your shoes on before you get out of the car," he says, then gets out himself, taking a deep breath of freezing air before he bolts for the bathroom with the little stick figure icon for "male" affixed to the door. Thankfully, the door's not locked. It's late enough that he was a bit concerned.

The toilets are stainless steel, icy to the touch and probably infinitely unpleasant to sit on. He empties his stomach into the nearest one, almost welcoming the smell of bleach and industrial cleaner invading his nostrils. It's better than the blood and bile he's been smelling since they left the motel.

Once there's nothing left inside him to vomit up, Harry straightens, flushes the toilet, and walks to the sinks, which are as brutalist and industrial as everything else in this room, bolted to the concrete wall below a mirror that isn't made of glass, just a sheet of hard-polished metal that throws back a subtly distorted version of his face. He looks at himself in silence for a long, long moment, trying to figure out why he looks so wrong, before he abandons the attempt and starts the faucet, using the grainy pink soap from the dispenser to wash the blood off of his hands.

He's never washed his hands this thoroughly in his life. He scrubs until the blood comes off, and then he scrubs them again, and then again, and again, and again, until the world is not and never has been anything but scrubbing, and look, the blood is back, how is the blood back, he washed the blood off. More soap, more water, and it's so cold, there's no heat in this place (heat costs money, don't want to encourage vagrants and wastrels to spend our state's funds on luxuries like *hot water*), but the tears running down his face are hot enough to make up for it, and he's scrubbing, scrubbing, scrubbing—

Somehow he doesn't see the anxious oval of Jack's face in the mirror until her hands are wrapping around his arm with that same awful frozen-slush feeling he always gets from touching her. But it's soothing now, somehow, cooling, like a damp cloth on his forehead in the summer sun. It feels like it's chasing a fever from his body, and when he breathes again—a deep, shuddering inhale that shakes him from the soles of his feet to the crown of his head—it feels like some terrible toxin flows out of him with that breath, leaving him centered in his body once more.

He looks at the paper towel dispenser, filled with rough brown sheets that will feel like sandpaper on his hands—they had the same towels at his elementary school, where Billy Daniels once swore he got a splinter drying his hands and that was why he couldn't wash them anymore—and decides he'd rather wipe his chapped, raw fingers on his jacket. The fabric's absorbent for a reason. It can handle a little water.

He glances at his blurry reflection again, verifying that there's no blood on his shirt or face, then turns his attention to Jack. "This is the men's room," he says, inanely. "What are you doing in here?"

Jack tilts her face up to look at him, and smirks. "It's the men's room, but we're the only ones in here, sunshine, and you aren't going to call the authorities on me for going through the wrong door. You're not a narc."

That's true enough. Harry has never been one for involving adults in his problems; when he was little, it was out of a combined desire not to upset his mother, who had a genuine gift for looking down her nose and making him feel like he was some nasty thing she'd found crawling in the grass and could put back outside whenever she decided to, and not to draw attention to whatever he'd been doing with Mel, who had no sense of self-preservation whatsoever and seemed to regard gravity as something that happened to other people. She'd never met a tree, or a fence, she didn't want to scale; the one time he'd been able to arrange to have her come on the family's summer trip to Castleview, she'd been up the rose trellis so fast that even the gardeners had been impressed, once they stopped panicking about the delicate little girl with the heart condition being twenty feet off the ground and still climbing.

"No, I'm not a narc," he says, and is almost relieved when he recognizes his own voice, when it still sounds the way it's always sounded, and not like it belongs to a stranger. He *feels* like a stranger right now, like he doesn't fit in his own skin, and his hands are starting to ache. He's scrubbed half the skin off of his joints, and the scabs are going to hurt like anything when they form.

Scabs . . . He looks at Jack with sudden alarm. "Seriously, though, what are you doing in here? Where's Mel?"

"In the car," says Jack. "Don't worry. We're far enough away from anyone else that you'd know if there was another Summer challenger anywhere nearby, and I'd know if there was a Winter challenger, so we're safe for now. They're not going to be coming that quickly at this stage."

"What? Why not?"

"Because there are too many of them."

Harry's confusion must show in his face, because Jack sighs, smiling almost fondly, as she steps away and uses the heels of her hands to boost herself up onto the sink he didn't fill with soapsuds and blood. The cold metal doesn't appear to bother her the way it would bother him. He's not actually sure she can *feel* cold, and that thought just makes him think about Mel's feet again, and the way they didn't bleed when she stepped on the broken glass. He can't think about that right now. Thinking about that opens a door, and there are monsters on the other side of it. Alice didn't want to go among the mad people, Avery and Zib didn't want to go to the Queen of Swords, and he doesn't want to go where the monsters are.

So he doesn't. Right here, right now, that's what he can do, and that's what he's doing. He's not going. He's not thinking about Melanie's feet and he's not thinking about the fact that he just killed a man and he's going to listen to whatever Jack has to say, and she's going to tell him what he needs to know. Yes. And maybe this time, what she tells him will make sense, and he'll finally start to understand what's happening, and why his life has stopped making any meaningful sense.

Jack starts to speak, then pauses and looks at him carefully, studying his face with the long, slow care of someone who's about to change the world, or at least make a solid stab in that direction. Then, to his surprise, she smiles.

"You're getting there," she says. "Those assholes were the short, sharp shock you needed to snap you out of the world you had and into the world you're going to have from now on. This is the world where you either live or die, and it was about time you joined us here."

"What?"

"Look," she says, with exquisite patience. "You were raised pretty much in the real world. The place where most things happen, where two and two always equal four and never rain, or quiet, or thermonuclear destruction. Alchemy and sorcery and things like the seasonal monarchs, they matter just as much as the things you find in the real world—the fact that they aren't part of that reality doesn't make them any less real where they matter. The back of the mirror is always there, even when you're only seeing the surface."

Harry makes a noncommittal noise. He wants her to keep talking, he wants her to keep untangling the mess he's found himself snared in, and if this is the way, then this is the way.

"Melanie was basically half-and-half. She wouldn't exist if not for alchemy; she's an artificial vessel, while you're a natural one. That's part of why you locked on to her and started running in parallel the way you did. She was supposed to join up with her sister, and it gave her a receptive nature that you keyed to without ever even realizing it. I'm not accusing you of anything, don't get that defensive look on your face. I'm just telling you how it played out, because you're finally ready to listen. She never had any trouble slipping through to the back of the mirror, because she was always halfway here. That's the point of the artificial vessels, you see. They're primed to fall. Not like you, not like me. We have to find the wall before we climb over it. She was born already standing on the edge."

"Okay . . ."

"Those assholes back at the motel, though, they scared you enough to break the glass, and now you're on the other side of the mirror. You're starting to see things clearly. You're starting to retain the things your mind was telling you were nonsense or imaginary before. And that's good."

"I'm losing my mind and that's a good thing?"

"No, you're losing what you *thought* was your mind, and that's a good thing. Harry March, high school football hero who's going to go to college and study forestry and land management in order to take over his family's lumber empire, is not the guy we need here. Right now, we need Harry March, Summer King in waiting, the badass motherfucker who's absolutely going to kick contender ass and claim the Summer crown."

"Okay," says Harry. He likes the way that sounds, likes how confident and clean it is, so he squares his shoulders, trying to ignore his aching hands, and repeats, "Okay. So what do you mean, there's too many of them?"

"There are literally hundreds of Ascendants, in all four flavors, although you're mostly going to be dealing with the ones associated with the primary seasons, because we're tied to people like you and Mel. Jacks in the Green and Stingy Jacks, they stand alone for spring and fall, and they either build the labyrinth or keep to themselves when a coronation is going on. I think they're afraid if they get too involved, the system will realize it's unbalanced and manifest Incarnates for them, too. We're everywhere. We're not as common as people with naturally red hair, but we exist in substantial-enough numbers that you've probably met a few of us during your lifetime."

"Okay . . ."

"It's not one-to-one with Ascendants and Incarnates. We're shallower, we take less energy for the season to sustain, and since we can't draw on it as directly, we don't help it assert itself in the same way. All that's stuff you'll need to worry about later, much later, so don't worry if it doesn't make much sense now. Just focus on the math. There are more Jack Frosts than there are Winters, got me?"

"Got you."

"You won't necessarily pick up on every Corn Jenny who crosses your path, because it would be just too much white noise and a lot of them already belong to other potential Summers, which blunts the signal, but you'll know if you get close to another Summer."

"What will that feel like?"

Jack looks frustrated. "I don't know. I'm not trying to bullshit you or confuse you for my own amusement—I literally don't know. I'm not Summer-bound. When I get near another Jack Frost, it feels like someone's dropped an ice cube down the back of my shirt, and when I get near a Winter, it feels like . . . like . . ." She pauses, expression going just a little beatific. "It feels like ice cream on Christmas morning. Everything is cold, but in the best possible way. It feels like a Norman Rockwell painting come to life. It feels like living in a Rankin-Bass special full of talking reindeer and singing snowmen, where your parents never hit you or sold your birthday presents for drug money."

"That's, uh. That's a really specific feeling."

Jack shrugs. "Maybe so, but that's what it feels like to me. Being in the presence of the Winter is like being home, for me. For Mel, it's going to be more like biting down on foil. For you, too, probably. Didn't you feel anything when those jerks broke into the motel room?"

Harry thinks back. "I felt . . . too hot, just before they threw that car engine through our window. So hot I was afraid I'd burn Mel's fingers if she tried to touch me. I always feel warm. It's never been like that before."

"That was the Summer in you reacting to the presence of a challenger. It'll get stronger and stronger as there are fewer of you still in contention for the crown. Right now, there are probably, oh, two or three dozen of you across the continent, every one of them working their way toward wherever the final labyrinth has decided to manifest—Don't ask right now." She holds up one small hand, gesturing for him to be patient. "It would just confuse you, and we'll get there soon enough. Anyway, if there's a potential Summer in Iowa, he's going to have to clear the state, and then fight his way through Nebraska, Colorado, and Arizona, just to hit California. So he's not bothering you. Odds are good he dies on the journey, and you never know his name."

"I already killed somebody, and I didn't learn *his* name," says Harry, and there's a wobble in his voice that Jack doesn't like, a certain element of disconnection and uncertainty. He's got a better grounding in his season than he did before the motel, but that doesn't change the man beneath the manifestation. He's still the person he was before the Summer started coiling through him, and that's not going to change.

Melanie, though . . . where Melanie's concerned, Jack's not so sure. There's never been an alchemical vessel for one of the seasons before. It's been done with other concepts, the Doctrine of Ethos and a few of the Virtues (which means some asshole alchemist has probably embodied a few of the Vices as well, squirrelling them away somewhere in catacombs to wait for the opportunity to ruin everyone's day) and it's worked, for the most part, but from what she knows, it took multiple tries before it worked, every single time. So will this work? On the first try?

She supposes they're going to find out. One way or another, they're going to find out. But will the person Harry knows survive the process? That's the big question. After that's answered, they can move on to asking themselves whether Melanie's an already-broken vessel that's going to shatter when she places the crown on her head.

If that happens, they're screwed. Another coronation will start immediately, and this time there won't be a whole crop of candidates waiting for their chance at the crown. If she has any doubts about Melanie's suitability, she should be undermining her, should be setting her up to fail for the sake of her season.

But Harry's Corn Jenny never came. Harry doesn't have another attendant to keep him from getting killed. And he collapsed the same time Mel did. Jack isn't completely sure—she tries to sound sure when she's talking to the candidates, because she knows she's young, and she knows she looks like she should be clutching a teddy bear and planning a slumber party, not trying to orchestrate the coronation of two of the primal forces of creation—but she thinks if Mel goes down, so does he. They're running in parallel. That gives them certain advantages, and faster access to the deep parts of their prospective seasons. It also means that what hurts one of them can hurt them both.

Losing Mel costs them Harry. Losing Harry seems cruel to the boy, who thought a week ago that he was going to be going on campus tours, and signing up for his first classes at whatever college he decides to attend, and planning a life that's not an option for him anymore.

Poor guy. Jack smiles, lopsided and reassuring.

"You didn't need to know his name," she says. "He was an opportunist. He probably hopped on the first bus when he heard a coronation was being called, made for the nearest small town with a big highway, because he figured a candidate would come through. He wanted to force a confrontation as fast as he could, and when he got one, it was more than he expected."

"Why was he wearing a sweater?" It's been bothering him. He never gets cold because he has the summer in his bones. That other boy did, too. So why did he get cold?

Jack doesn't seem thrown by the question. If anything, she looks reassured that it's something simple this time. "He wasn't as far along as you are. That's the other thing—every one of you is going to be connected to your season by different degrees. You're very connected to the Summer right now, and that means you don't get cold. Once it's officially spring, you'll start leaving little flowers where you walk, and all that other frustrating summer stuff. It's not the easiest gig. Or so I hear."

"So you hear?"

"During true summer, after the spring ends but before the autumn starts, I'm a normal little girl. I can get sunstroke, I can get older, I need to do a lot of things that are one hundred percent optional during true winter. Winter, I'm just shy of invincible. Until the spring starts, even you can't really touch me. Spring and fall, I'm tougher than a normal kid, but I'm either waxing or waning, and I'm not taking many chances. And in the summer, I take *no* chances, at all. I never met the last Summer Queen. She was asleep from long before I was born until the coronation started, and it wasn't worth risking my life to try waking her up."

"Huh," says Harry. Then: "I stabbed that guy."

"I know. I saw."

"Melanie . . . Melanie didn't stab the guy who attacked her."

"I saw that too."

"How did she do that?" He looks at her with the lost expression of a child abandoned by their trusted adults, and for the first time, Jack feels like he's truly present, truly listening, not just going along with things because nothing else made more sense at the time. He's committed now, whether or not he ever realized he wasn't before, and that's going to be a good thing soon.

That might be enough to save them.

"You're closer to Summer than the boy who attacked you was, but Melanie's . . . Melanie's almost all the way to Winter. She could probably walk the scarecrow trail right now if we knew the way to the labyrinth, and that's not necessarily a good thing." Jack grimaces. "Part of the point of putting a human face on the seasons is having it be, well, *human*. And if she sinks too deep into Winter without someone pulling her back, she won't be human at all anymore."

Harry starts to reply, then pauses and sags into himself, looking at his chapped hands again before he mutters, "You keep throwing around terms I don't understand like I should understand them, and it makes me feel like you think I'm stupid."

"No, I don't think you're stupid," says Jack, and she sounds almost gentle, maybe for the first time since he's met her. She's trying to talk to him like he's a person whose opinion matters. It's a nice change. It's one he wishes she'd been able to make a little earlier, when it would have made more of a difference. "I think you're unprepared, and it's not my fault, but it's my problem. Mel's also unprepared, because her father was keeping us from getting to her. I don't know why your Corn Jenny never came for you."

She has her suspicions, but she wants to keep them to herself for now, until she knows whether she's on the right track. All they'd do now is muddy waters already so muddied that they've turned practically opaque. So she smiles at Harry, trying to seem encouraging, when she wants to hurry this along as much as she can.

"Okay," says Harry, gathering himself. "So we have to keep Mel from giving way all the way to Winter, even though she has to be the best candidate it has if we're going to win these crowns you keep talking about, and we have to do it while assholes keep showing up and trying to kill us. So how do we do that?"

"Mostly, I don't," says Jack. "I'm as Winter-bound as she is—not quite as strongly right now, but I'm starting to think that's a good thing—and the deeper she goes, the deeper she'll drag me. I'm her attendant, after all."

She pauses, expression turning wistful in a way that makes Harry think for the first time that there must be something in all of this for Jack, some great and unidentified benefit to being the attendant of whichever candidate takes the crown. He doesn't know what that could be, and this doesn't seem like the right time to ask, and so he tucks the question away for later, swaddling it in all his concern for Mel, which is currently vast enough to overwhelm everything it comes into contact with.

"So if she needs an anchor to the world outside the Winter, it's not going to be me. It can't be me, even if I want it to be. And I don't know if I do. I'm scared of what happens if she goes too deep, but I'm sure candidates have gone too deep before. Maybe what the world needs is a Winter who cares more about the snow than how much they can get for selling it."

"That's not what *I* need," says Harry sharply. "I need Melanie. I need the girl I love to stay human enough to remember that she loves me, too. I need her, not some idea of what the winter looks like in a human body."

"You won't be parallel anymore if she goes that much deeper than you," says Jack. "If you stop holding her in her own skin, she might pull away from you naturally. She might let you go. Then you could renounce without dying on the spot. You could go home."

That's tempting. Harry looks at his chapped hands and thinks of his bedroom, of his parents, of college applications and scholarships and football games and all the things his future has always been built upon. Even, despite his own stubborn insistence that they'd find a way to save her, the absence of Melanie. She's never been a part of those future fantasies, because even as he's been unable to imagine a life without her, he's been equally unable to imagine a coherent future with her.

And now he can finally have one, and if it's the kind of future he would never have imagined on his own, who gives a fuck?

"No," he says, firmly. "I don't want to go home. Not without her. So as long as I can 'hold her in her own skin,' as you put it, I'm holding on. She's staying, and so am I."

"Good for you," says Jack, and smiles.

She's still smiling as he turns and walks out of the bathroom, heading back toward the car, into the freezing night. Only when he's gone does she allow herself to sag, fingers clenching on the edge of the sink. She's fighting as hard as she can to seem like she knows everything, but she's only had this job for a year, and there's so much she *doesn't* know, so much she feels like she *should* know, and so much she can't possibly have known, so many holes in the brief education she received at the hands of a woman who is either missing or intentionally absent but, either way, isn't *here*.

If they lose faith in her, they're going to lose faith in this whole process, and half of what gets them to the labyrinth is faith. She needs them to reach the labyrinth if she wants them to win, and she wants them to win, very, very badly. She wants the time it gives her if they keep the crowns. She wants a hundred years of adolescence. She wants the rules to be different for her, the way they always have been, one way or another.

Jack slides down from the sink, shoves her hands into her pockets, and follows Harry's path out of the bathroom, slowly, giving him plenty of time. Giving him a head start.

Harry steps out of the bathroom and turns, immediately, toward the car. It's still sitting where he parked it, lit from above by the dim glow of the poorly maintained streetlight that's meant to illuminate the parking lot.

There's no one in the front seat.

"Mel?" It's not a shout. It's just a question, quiet and faintly puzzled, like he can't understand what he's seeing. She was in the car when he and Jack went into the bathroom, he's sure of that. He told her to put her shoes on.

Maybe she's in the ladies' room. It would make sense for her to want to clean herself up after what happened at the motel—and at least the cold water won't bother her. He doesn't want to go past the social barrier represented by the skirted stick figure outside the bathroom, but he steps past it anyway, trusting the absence of other cars to protect him from any possible consequences.

There's no one in the bathroom. The doors to both stalls are unlatched and hanging slightly open, at that angle that shows vacancy and not much else, and there are no feet visible under the barriers. She'd have to be standing on one of the slippery metal toilets to go unseen, and she has no reason to do that. If she wanted to go home, he'd take her. Even now, even after everything that's happened, he'd take her, and she knows him well enough to know that. So she isn't here, hiding from him.

"Mel?" The question is louder this time, growing in strength as the panic starts to settle in. He spins on his heel and runs for the door, moving fast now, faster than his whirling thoughts can keep up with.

He's an essentially sheltered person, like any teen with a reasonable amount of personal freedom and parents who knew what it meant to be parents, not jailers or vaguely emotionally abusive peers. He's made his own choices for as long as he can remember, and somehow those choices have almost always aligned with what's allowed by the rules, or at least the ones that made sense to him. (He has never, for example, been able to understand the rules that said he shouldn't spend every spare minute with Mel when she's not feeling well, as if the fact that she might die would make him *less* eager to be around her, when there's a limit to how much time they have.) So he's never actually been at a rest stop in the middle of the night before, only seen them in movies and on the kind of television shows where the credits include listings like "corpse #2" and "kidnapped girl." He should never have left Melanie alone. Not even for a minute. What was he *thinking*?

Outside the bathroom, there's still no sign of her. Harry runs to the car, like he might find her lying down in the seat. That's happened before, twice, when waves of dizziness and exhaustion suddenly forced her to abandon sitting up as a bad idea. (They told her father about the first incident, and he responded by grounding her for three weeks, saying she was too delicate to go out, or even to go to school. That had been enough to teach them their lesson, and they hadn't told him about the second incident. Sometimes, disproportionate consequences teach the wrong lessons.) It doesn't seem likely now, with her heart doing so much better, but if there's any chance at all—

Melanie isn't in the car. But her shoes are, abandoned in the footwell. Harry straightens, a chill running across his skin, just in time to see Jack emerge from the bathroom.

"She's gone!" he yells.

Jack frowns, walking toward him. She doesn't seem worried yet. He's sure that will come, with time. "What do you mean, she's gone?"

"I mean she's not in the car!" He kicks the tire, a little flash of worried violence, and balls his hands into helpless fists. He regrets both gestures immediately, as kicking the tire hurts his foot and bending his fingers hurts his hands. He unclenches his hands, shoulders sagging. "She's not in the car, and she's not in the bathroom. Did someone snatch her?"

"No, she's still here," says Jack. "She's close enough for me to feel her."

People think of eucalyptus and the beach when they think of California, but so far Harry's experience of the state has been pretty solidly in line with his experience of his home state; mountains and evergreens as far as the eye can see. They surround this tiny rest stop, their tight-packed canopy of needles shutting out the light of the sky above, stars (so bright this far from any major city; it's unrealistic how bright they are) and waning February moon alike. A serial killer could easily have dragged Mel into those trees and be taking her methodically apart only a few feet away from here, and he'd never know, or be able to see them before it was too late. Or a bear could have come out of the wood looking for something to eat, and decided that in the absence of any convenient picnic baskets, a bit of succulent girlflesh would do just fine.

"Melanie!" Harry yells. *"Mel!"*

There's no answer.

Jack, tethered to Melanie by the invisible but omnipresent chain of the season they share, manages to keep her calm a little better. She turns in a slow circle, looking around at the parking lot, the trees, the scrubby stretch of green that is the rest stop lawn, no doubt maintained for the benefit of families road-tripping with their canine companions. It's not a very welcoming lawn, made up mostly of weeds and some plants that look, even in the low light, like stickers and thorns, but it's green, and a dog could get in some good running before doing its business. It extends all the way around the back of the building.

Hands still in her pockets, Jack starts walking across the lawn. She's following a hunch more than any actual direction; the winter tells her Melanie's close by and not in any immediate physical danger, but that's all it can do. Now, anyway. For all her talk about worrying what will happen if Melanie forgets what it is to be human and falls completely into what it is to be the living incarnation of Winter, she doesn't know what will happen to her, either, if Mel decides to go that route. The most recent Winter hasn't maintained an Ascendant in well over a hundred years, viewing them as a crutch used to stave up a faltering season; his last Jack Frost died sometime in the nineteenth century, and she's never been able to find anyone who'd actually met the man.

If Mel loses humanity, maybe Jack loses it too. Maybe then she'll always know where the other woman is, and they won't have any secrets from each other. She's not sure she's comfortable with that idea. She likes her secrets. She doesn't have many of them, but the ones she does have are important to her. So she walks slowly around the structure of the rest stop, and when she sees Melanie, she stops, taking a moment to take in the scene in front of her.

She's still standing in frozen—ironic—silence when Harry comes jogging up behind her and skids to his own stop in the dewy grass, eyes going wide and mouth dropping open in a silent O of confusion and mild shock. He probably shouldn't be this surprised; wouldn't be if he'd been better prepared, if she were better equipped to prepare him.

But she isn't, and he is, and there's Melanie, standing barefoot on the disk of concrete poured to support the rest stop's sole picnic table, her hands raised to float at the level of her shoulders, elbows resting lazily by her sides, eyes closed. She looks like a dancer at very sad goth club, one that can't afford lights, or music, or any other dancers.

That's not the strange thing. Neither is the way she's swaying slightly from side to side, unsteady as a reed. That's still within the realm of normalcy, and something Harry's seen her do before, after she had exhausted herself, when she was still trying to pretend everything was fine. No, her pose, while odd, is still odd in a reasonable, rational way. Anyone could be odd like that.

What's not normal is the way the air around her sparkles with tiny points of self-contained light, every one of them glitter-bright and suspended in place. The air a few feet away from her doesn't shine that way, only the air close enough for her to run her fingers through it. Jack starts moving again, approaching her as slowly as she'd approach a wild deer suddenly appearing in the middle of a grocery store, something strange and feral that she doesn't want to shock or startle. Harry stands rooted to the spot, unable to lift his feet or bend his legs.

As Jack gets closer to Melanie, she sees that the sparkle in the air isn't glitter at all. It's made of countless tiny snowflakes, each of them a perfect crystal in its own right, none of them quite falling, even as Melanie stands and sways.

"Mel," says Jack.

Three things happen. Melanie opens her eyes. Melanie lowers her hands. And the glitter starts to fall, a brief dusting of tiny snowflakes scattering over the concrete at her feet. She blinks. "What?"

"You scared us, disappearing like this," says Jack. "You weren't supposed to go anywhere without us."

"Harry didn't say to stay with the car," says Mel, reasonably enough.

Jack glances back over her shoulder to Harry, who still hasn't moved. This would be easier if he'd come over here and back her up. She frowns, trying to convey that thought to him with a look, then forces her face to relax as she turns back to Melanie. "No, but he told you to put your shoes on," she says. "Can I see your feet?"

Startled, Melanie looks down at her bare feet before sitting on the picnic bench. Even the way she sits worries Jack. She sits without care or control, plopping down like a small child whose proprioception is still in flux and needs a certain amount of sharp, swift motion to calibrate it. She was more collected before the motel, more like a girl her own age.

Where Harry vomits and yells, Melanie disassociates. That's good to know. Jack tucks it away for future reference as she closes the distance to the picnic table and kneels in the remains of Melanie's brief, impossible snowfall, reaching out with both hands for the foot Melanie amiably deposits in her palm.

Cupping Melanie's heel, Jack studies the sole of her foot and grimaces. Harry was right to be concerned: there are several slivers of glass wedged there, at least one of them driven in so deep that she can only see the glint of its base between the bloodless edges of the gash in Melanie's skin. She forces her voice to stay level as she looks up, meeting Mel's placid, unprotesting gaze, and says, "You have a piece of glass in your foot. I'm going to need to get it out. Can you sit still for that?"

"Sure."

Jack looks over her shoulder to Harry again. He's still standing where he stopped, still staring at the two of them like he's never seen them before. *Oh, great. Please don't let this be the point where they* both *check out,* she thinks. Aloud, she calls, "Harry, is there a first aid kit in the car?"

"In the trunk," he says. His voice is level and still mostly steady, thank the Wheel. He can do this.

They can do this.

"Can you get it for me, please?" She doesn't let go of Melanie's foot. She needs to keep the other woman from wandering away again.

"Sure," says Harry, with obvious reluctance, before taking two steps backward, then turning to jog around the building toward the car. Jack sighs her relief and turns back to Melanie, who still looks disconnected and disinterested, like nothing that's happening could possibly be relevant to her as a person, or have any bearing on what she does next.

Jack frowns. This is worse than she thought. "Mel, do you know where you are?"

"I'm sitting on a bench, of course," says Melanie, bright and chipper as a preschooler being asked to count to ten. "And you're holding my foot."

"I didn't ask what we were doing," says Jack. "I asked where we *are.*"

"Oh. California, I think. We've been driving for a long, long time." Melanie's smile is wide and glassy. "I like California. Last time we were here, Daddy took me and Harry to Disneyland. I got to ride the Haunted Mansion three times. It was fun."

"Harry's getting the first aid kit from the car so I can take the glass out of your foot."

"That's nice of him. Harry's always so nice to me. He worries about me a lot, you know. Probably more than he should. He ought to spend more time worrying about himself, and less time worrying about me. I think he'd be happier if he could figure out how to do that."

"So do I, but Melanie, I need you to come back now, okay?" Jack squeezes her foot, which is cold, so cold. It would be like holding the foot of a corpse, except that it's so clearly part of something living.

It has tension and resistance, and lacks the smooth malleability of dead flesh. It's just a living thing carved out of ice, rather than a living thing like a human being would be.

"Come back?" Melanie blinks, eyes wide and guileless and still glacier blue. There's no hint of a snowflake pattern in her irises. Do Winter Queens get the obvious branding that Jack Frosts do? Jack doesn't know, isn't sure anyone knows, and she silently damns William Monroe for his selfish refusal to be a part of the Wheel he willingly yoked himself to for so many, many years. They've lost so much here in North America, and they need to get so much back, and she doesn't know how they're going to do that fast enough for it to make any difference at all.

"Come back," Jack repeats. "You're retreating right now, into Winter. It loves you and it's willing to take you as deep as you want to go, but we need you here and now and helping us run from the people who want to hurt you. We need you to stay. We need *Melanie,* not the Winter Queen. She comes later, after Melanie gets strong enough to coexist with her."

"I don't . . ." Melanie blinks again, and the innocence in her eyes cracks like ice on a pond, letting a bit of the panic and terror beyond show through. "I don't want to," she says, voice much smaller. "I don't want to run, and I don't want to be afraid, and I don't want to have to see what's coming. I don't want to come back. Please don't make me."

Jack has one chance to get them through this, and if she takes it, she'll be hurting the woman she's sworn to serve, and if she doesn't, she might be getting them all killed. So she shakes her head, and says, "I'm sorry. You don't have a choice. If you keep going, Harry's going to be all alone. He doesn't have a Corn Jenny. He just has me, and you, and if you go, I'll be so busy trying to follow you that he won't have either of us. He'll be alone, in the middle of a coronation, and the part of you that's already in the Winter knows he won't survive that." It's possible to win without running parallel, but not without a guide. "Come back for Harry's sake, even if you can't stay for your own."

Melanie's eyes clear still further, innocence replaced by despair. Something warm touches Jack's fingers. She glances down.

The foot she has cupped in her palm has started bleeding, the myriad gashes from the broken glass beginning to realize that human people—like Melanie still is—bleed when they get hurt. They don't freeze.

"Thank you," says Jack, as Harry comes running back with the first aid kit, and Melanie begins to cry.

Farmers' Market

Two days of driving slowly through Northern California, two days of stopping at every rest stop and gas station they pass, two days of never staying on the highway for more than a few exits, and now the bright lights of the Bay Area are finally on the horizon, or would be, if it weren't the middle of the day. The sun's still high in the sky, bathing the land in watery light. That's the only watery thing about this place: it hasn't rained once since they crossed the state line, and for two teens from rainy Portland, that's just shy of a terrifying miracle in the middle of February. They don't know what to do with this.

Once again, it's down to Jack to be the worldly one and remind them that it doesn't rain all winter long everywhere you go; there are places where it never rains at all, and since this part of California has been experiencing a drought on and off for the last several decades, it's probably a good thing it isn't raining now. "California drivers have water-soluble driving skills," she says, more than once, until both of them can recite it when half-awake and staggering back to the car after a night spent in a dive motel that makes the first one seem like a resort.

(A little after three in the afternoon the day after getting back on the road, they pull into the parking lot of that motel, Harry half-petrified with fear as he pulls out his credit card and passes it to the clerk, expecting a rejection. Instead, it goes through without a hitch, and they're given the keys to a room so small and grimy that it doesn't even have spiders in the corners; the spiders have standards, and are probably infesting someplace nicer. Like the dumpster. But it has a roof that doesn't leak, and a door that locks, and a shower, even if Mel can't bring herself to use it without leaving the door propped open and talking to Harry the whole time. He still has to come into the bathroom and help her rinse the shampoo out of her hair when her injured feet refuse to let her balance well enough to do it herself.)

(Harry hates to see Mel in pain. He's still a little relieved when she can't balance, when she needs him. The loss of pain seems to indicate the Winter is taking her over, and he wants his human girl more than he wants a frozen doll who summons snowflakes out of the air and doesn't feel it when she steps on broken glass.)

(They sleep soundly if not entirely safely in that little dive motel, and they spend the second night taking turns dozing at the tables at the back of a truck stop food court, alternating naps with cups of strong, bitter coffee, talking about nothing of any importance. Certainly not the cycle and strength of seasons. Harry knows from his own grinding experience that most people wouldn't have heard anything they didn't want to hear, but Jack's exhausted; making her spend another night explaining basic concepts of the universe that she wasn't prepared to teach them both seemed more cruel than kind.)

They're all exhausted by the time they see San Francisco stretched across the horizon in towering steel and glass, all of them worn down and ready to collapse at the slightest pressure. Maybe that's why Jack leans up between the seats, puts a hand on Harry's shoulder, and says, in a low, urgent voice, "Don't go to San Francisco."

"Is there another challenger there?" Harry doesn't feel anything, but he wouldn't, would he, if they were driving toward a potential Winter? Melanie and Jack would feel that, and he'd feel nothing until another Summer candidate joined the fray. They are each their own early warning systems.

"Maybe. We're still too far away for me to tell."

"Then why . . . ?"

"Because Mel's asleep." When Harry doesn't respond with understanding, Jack sighs. "She's exhausted, and you're not any better. *I'm* exhausted. If there's another candidate in the area, they're probably in San Francisco, and it's Valentine's Day. You deserve a break."

Harry looks at her reflection in the rearview mirror with suspicion. "You're the last person I expect grace and understanding from."

"A tired Mel is a Mel who's not buttressing herself against the Winter the way we both need her to," says Jack. "A tired Harry is a Harry who's not prepared to drag her back if she starts slipping. The whole point of this exercise is getting the two of you to *embody* your seasons, not get subsumed by them. Help me help her by helping yourself."

"That probably wouldn't make sense if I weren't so tired." Harry sighs heavily, the sound seeming to travel all the way up from the soles of his feet. "All right, if I'm not going to San Francisco, where *am* I going? And if you say LA, I don't care if you're a kid, I'm going to pull off to the side of the road and kick your ass so hard that you can't walk for two days."

If Harry's threatening violence, he's even more exhausted than Jack thought he was. She leans back in the seat, well out of reach, and looks out the window, reading a green road sign as it flashes past them. "Berkeley," she says, with what she hopes will sound like real conviction. "You're going to Berkeley. Big enough that you'll be able to find someplace to crash for the night, small enough that it's less likely to have a candidate lying in wait for the pair of you."

"Berkeley, sure," says Harry, without much enthusiasm. He's tired. He just wants this all to be over.

More and more, he feels like it's not going to be over for a long time.

I t takes another hour to reach Berkeley. The highway offramp deposits them in a distinctly gentrified-looking part of town, old train depot and chic little shops sitting side by side, surrounded by trees carefully curated to look just a little wild and overgrown. Well-groomed people walk their equally well-groomed dogs down smooth, perfect sidewalks, or gather with them outside the artisanal ice cream shop, and it looks so much like Portland that Harry feels a sudden pang of homesickness.

Well, he'd been considering going to college closer to his grandparents. Maybe this whole ridiculous adventure is the world's way of telling him he's not built for travel. Maybe he's one of those lucky people who grew up where he ultimately belongs.

Or maybe this is just the world saying he can find the place that makes him happy anywhere he goes, and he should head for Castleview, with its wide, beloved halls and its idiosyncratic interiors, as soon as he thinks he can get away with it. He glances at Melanie sleeping peacefully in the passenger seat with her cheek pressed up against the window and her mouth half-open, a thin thread of saliva connecting lips and chin. As long as she's with him, he thinks he can be happy anywhere.

He could be happy here.

There's no parking on these narrow, tree-lined streets, already packed with people who made actual plans for Valentine's Day, who aren't running for their lives in the face of a force too large to fully understand. So he keeps driving, following signs for the local university, a college he'd considered before he'd realized majoring in forestry at a school that had its own biodiversity and conservation club was likely to result in four years of endless harassment by his classmates once they realized he was going to keep cutting trees down. His family tried to be responsible stewards of their land and cut sustainably, but they couldn't run a lumber business without felling a few trees. Berkeley's program was well regarded, but it wasn't for him, despite everything.

He never even toured the campus. He feels a little bubble of excitement work its way up through his chest. This is almost normal life. They're driving down the coast to tour colleges, that's all, and having a little adventure in the process. And if he tells himself that loudly enough, then maybe he can pretend to be a version of himself who's never killed a man, who doesn't know what it feels like to have hot blood on his hands that gets tight and sticky as it cools, who isn't stained, indelibly, by the things he's done.

He misses that version of himself. He didn't even know that *was* a version of himself until after he'd killed him, killed him at the same time as he killed that boy whose name he may never know (whose name, as Jack so casually puts it, doesn't really matter anymore; and she says the Ascendants don't kill, but she took the corpses so calmly that he doesn't quite believe her. She's a child who's seen death before, he's sure of that, and he doesn't know whether she dealt it or simply stood in its path, and he doesn't know how much that matters, and the not knowing is maybe what disturbs him most of all).

The little shops fall away, as do the industrial bones of the old railway tracks, replaced by a sprawling, bucolic series of wooded streets and eccentric little houses that remind him more than ever of home. Home, and not home at the same time—Portland doesn't have this much redwood, this many stairways leading to the doors. Half the houses look unstable, given how often the earth shakes down here, like they were designed by children to be knocked down.

The postage stamp yards are green despite the drought, box gardens bursting with flowers and vegetables. He sees more tomato plants than he's ever seen in February, and thinks the winters must be very mild, for so many things to be blooming already. They've lost all connection to the year, here in California, and chart the seasons more by calendar than by anything else.

Oh, he can't go to school here. The absence of proper seasons would destroy him, whether or not he claims the crown.

Then the university is ahead of them, low and sprawling and dominated by the spire of a clocktower surrounded in scaffolding. It's clearly under repair. All roads seem to lead there, but none in a quite-straight line, and the street he's on forks twice before dropping him in a less boutique, more downtown shopping area. It still has an old-fashioned feel that he appreciates. Sleek, modern cities are too far outside the realm of his experience, and he prefers the places that feel like they grew up organically, like people really *live* there.

He gets lucky after one more turn, and comes on a parking space just as the car that occupied it is pulling out. He slides smoothly into place, turning off the engine, and twists to look at Jack.

"Is this good enough?" he asks.

When she nods, he pulls the keys from the engine and tucks them into his pocket before turning to the sleeping Melanie and shaking her shoulder. Her skin is cold where it brushes against his fingers—not chilly, *cold*. He's not sure he'll ever get used to that.

"Hey, sunshine, wakey-wakey," he says, as jocularly as he can. "We're here."

Melanie makes a small noise, quietly resistant to waking up. He's not sure how she can be so comfortable sleeping strapped into the car, then supposes it's probably not that different from sleeping in a hospital bed. He doesn't like that thought, and so pushes it aside, to join all the other thoughts he doesn't want to have. One day they'll form some vast ur-thought, entirely terrible, too large to be ignored, and then he's screwed. But it hasn't happened yet and it isn't happening today, and so he shakes her again.

"Mel. Come on, honey, wake up. There's a Starbucks."

She opens her eyes. "Real coffee?" she asks. "Coffee that doesn't taste like burning and cat piss?"

"I'm glad to hear that you haven't killed all your tastebuds yet," says Harry. "Yes, real coffee, with so much whipped cream and flavored syrup it doesn't even deserve the name anymore."

Portland isn't as coffee-focused as Seattle, but they have enough independent coffee shops and carts that have survived even in the face of the big chains that he always feels a little traitorous when he goes to Starbucks. But there's a Starbucks in the hospital lobby, and Mel's been addicted to the stuff for as long as he can remember, even with her doctors telling her over and over that she shouldn't go anywhere near caffeine. She sticks to decaf and cocoa for the most part, and defends her love of Starbucks by saying it's the same everywhere she goes, and she deserves a little predictability.

At this point, maybe they both do.

"Jack, you coming?" he asks, opening his door.

"Where she goes, I go," says Jack, and scoots across the backseat to open the door that will put her out on the sidewalk. It's nice when she remembers to pretend to care about her own safety, even if he has no faith at all that she means it. She thinks she's invincible. He supposes that if all this seasonal stuff had started when he was twelve, he'd think that too.

God, if any twelve-year-olds are candidates for the crown, he has no idea what he'll do. Probably just die. He can't fight a twelve-year-old. He still has a heart.

Melanie limps a little as she gets out of the car and puts pressure on her feet, and he hates that he's still glad to see it. If she's limping, she can feel pain, and if she can feel pain, she's still his Mel. He's glad she can walk on her own, even if it hurts her. She's never done well with enforced stillness. Just one of the many reasons her illness has been so cruel.

Now that he knows it's not something she was always going to have to live with but something her father *did* to her, he wishes he'd been less polite to the man. Forcing a confrontation with his girlfriend's father wouldn't have been politic, but it would be so satisfying in hindsight.

Motivated by the thought of caffeine, Mel beelines for the Starbucks, pausing there to let Harry and Jack catch up. She glances over her shoulder with her hand on the door, effectively stopping traffic until they reach her, then smiles like the sun and pushes it open, releasing the smell of brewing coffee, sugar, and baked goods. It's a sweet, familiar perfume. The sight of Melanie beckoning him inside is equally sweet, and equally familiar.

He lets go of thoughts of crowns and coronations, seasons and sacrifices, and steps into the Starbucks. Time for coffee.

The line is short. They move through it quickly, and when Mel reaches the register, she flashes the barista a sunlight smile before she chirps, bright as anything, "Venti gingerbread hot chocolate, extra syrup, extra whipped cream, chocolate syrup drizzle on top, please."

If the barista is distressed by the thought of how much sugar Mel's putting in one cup, she doesn't show it: she doesn't bat an eye, not even when Harry follows with a somewhat amused "Black coffee, large, room for cream and sugar, and whatever she wants," indicating Jack.

Jack adds another horrifying concoction of syrups and sugars, although hers contains actual coffee, and, as if to test him, three different cookies from the display of baked goods. Harry pays, and they wait to pick up their treats, waiting for Harry to doctor his before claiming a table by the window. Jack immediately removes the lid from her cup and dunks her first cookie in the liquid.

"Coffee *good*," she sighs, taking a bite of sodden cookie.

"I'm not sure what you're drinking counts as coffee, and if Mel's drink has coffee in it, they made it wrong," says Harry mildly.

"Don't care," says Jack. "I stand by my statement, because I'm right. Coffee good."

"If you say so." A pair of teens roughly their age has just come in the door, and the girl of the pair has some of the most remarkable hair Harry's ever seen. It's long and white and—if her eyebrows and lashes are anything to go by—impossibly natural, with undertones of cornsilk green. He doesn't feel anything when he sees her, no sense that she's connected to his season in any way, but with that hair, she looks like she *should* be. That's a summer child if he's ever seen one. He glances to Jack, eyebrows raised in silent question. Jack shakes her head.

"I wouldn't be able to tell," she says, voice pitched low out of deference for the fact that they're in a public place far busier and more crowded than the truck stop where they spent the night. "I don't pick up on any season apart from my own. But the boy she's with isn't Winter, if that's what you're wondering. They're not here scouting for their own candidates. If she's scouting for a Summer solo, and she has her friend with her, she hasn't taken them very far from where they started, and they'll be lucky to survive until spring." She manages to make that sound completely reasonable and matter-of-fact, like it makes absolute and perfect sense.

None of this makes sense. Harry sips his coffee, which has lost all flavor, and watches the white-haired girl and her friend approach the counter. They're dressed sensibly enough for the season, flannel shirts and blue jeans; the boy has dark brown hair and a kind, friendly face. If not for their coloration, he'd assume they were brother and sister, and when he catches a glimpse of the boy's eyes behind his wire-framed glasses, he reassesses his belief that the girl's hair is natural, because their eyes are exactly the same, the clear pale brown of honeyed whiskey.

Colored contacts exist, but it's such an odd color to choose that it's easier to believe the girl has access to the only white mascara he's ever seen. They're talking to each other, heads so close together that they're almost touching, and he shouldn't be staring at strangers, but he is. He envies them so much in this moment that it hurts. Their lives are normal. His was normal a week ago, and now it's never going to be normal again.

Either he's going to be dead or he's going to be the living Summer, and that's that. One option ends with darkness; the other ends with him and Melanie living happily ever after, and probably not being allowed to go to college, either together or apart. The future is an uncharted country, and he can't even start to guess at what he's going to find there.

Melanie taps him lightly on the shoulder. "Want to come back to us, or would you rather keep staring at another girl for a little while longer?" she asks, mild as anything.

Harry turns to blink at her. She's looking at him with a half-peeved, half-amused expression on her face, and he knows she's not sincerely worried, just like she knows she has nothing to be worried about. He wrinkles his nose before leaning over and kissing her on the mouth.

Her lips taste like chocolate, like sugar and whipped cream and that ChapStick she uses in ridiculously high quantities. He's never been able to understand how she can eat anything when her mouth is always covered in a layer of peppermint, but after a while, he supposes it just becomes a seasoning.

Melanie laughs as he pulls away. "What was that for?"

"For you. For me. For both of us, being here, together, and not in a hospital room, or dead in some shady-ass motel." He doesn't bother telling her death isn't his biggest concern anymore; that's reserved now for frozen silence, and the sight of snowflakes dancing in the air. He doesn't need to. They've been together for so long that some fears don't need to be spoken to be understood, and she nods, loss and longing in her eyes, before she leans in and kisses him again.

It's longer and slower this time, like they're trading sips of their respective drinks, and when they pull apart, Jack is gone. Her cup remains; they didn't hallucinate her. Harry glances around, finding her by the two teens, talking in low tones. He blinks.

"She's never seemed prone to making friends with strangers before," he comments.

"Except for us," notes Melanie.

"Yeah, but we're all tangled up in the same big ball of metaphysical hoo-ha, so I'm not sure we count." Harry picks up his drink and takes a long sip to cover how nervous it makes him to have Jack out of arm's reach. The last time that happened, he had to kill somebody. He doesn't think an attack in the Starbucks is likely, and doesn't have that all-over feverish feeling, but it's still unsettling, and he's more relieved than he can express when Jack waves to her new friends and comes walking back over to the table.

"There's a really nice farmers' market around the corner, apparently," she says. "California does them all year round, because they're weirdoes and they have the climate for it. Mostly they're weirdoes, though. Anyway, I don't think there's a challenge coming here, and we all need to move around a little. We can't stay cooped up in the car forever."

Harry wants to say that of course they can; it's when they get out of the car that people try to kill them. Since he'd rather not be killed, the car is currently his favorite place in the world. The car is also starting to take on that clinging funk he associates with long road trips, and if he doesn't spend some time in the fresh air, he's afraid his sinuses might actually attempt to crawl out of his face.

He loves the car. Right now, though, a little time seeing other places wouldn't go amiss. "Sure," he says. "Why not?"

Melanie beams. Jack nods, looking pleased with herself.

"Cool," she says. "Kim says it's open for another two hours."

Harry assumes Kim's the girl of the pair, although this is California, so who knows, really? "Hey, did you happen to ask whether she dyes her hair?" he asks.

Jack blinks. "No. Why would I?"

"No reason." Too bad. Well, some questions are destined to go unanswered, he supposes. Melanie stands, and Harry does the same, while Jack gathers her assorted half-eaten cookies and follows them to the door, just as the pair who pointed them at the farmers' market reach the counter and begin to place their own orders.

The farmers' market is, indeed, only a few blocks away, although it's not a straight line from here to there: they have to stop several times to ask for directions. Melanie is lightly dressed even by local standards, and after the second person comments that she must be cold while looking meaningfully at Harry, he shrugs off his jacket and drapes it gallantly around her shoulders. Melanie rolls her eyes.

"You're the one of us who actually gets chilly," she says chidingly, as they walk along what's supposedly the last stretch of road and the park where the market is being held.

"Yes, but we don't want to stand out in anyone's memory once we get back on the road," he says. "We're weird enough as it is."

"This is Berkeley, California," retorts Jack. "I'm pretty sure those people in black we just passed are on their way to spend a few hours chasing each other around campus, pretending to be vampires. We are so one hundred percent *not* going to stand out in anyone's minds after today."

"Picking up any candidates?"

"Nary a one. Relax, Summer boy. It's time to shop."

The farmers' market is ahead of them, gaily striped awnings

fluttering in front of prefab stalls of wood and plastic. Their counters and tables are laden with less of a variety of produce than
they'll see in the summer, but still a dazzling amount for two kids
from Portland. There are even flower vendors, their wares seriously
picked over by this time on Valentine's Day.

Melanie smiles at the flowers but doesn't approach, and when
Harry nods in toward them, she shakes her head and laces her fingers through his, making it clear that she really doesn't want him
to buy her any. He nods and they walk deeper into the market, Jack
flitting from one side of the street to the other as she grabs free samples and admires winter melons. The street has been closed to cars,
leaving it dedicated to foot traffic and fruit sellers. Melanie pauses
to admire a stall selling at least fifteen varieties of apple, and Harry
pulls his hand from hers to drift toward a kettle corn vendor whose
wares have scented the entire market carnival bright and appealing.
He's always liked kettle corn.

There's a vendor selling potatoes next to the kettle corn. Harry's
never considered the virtues of artisanal potatoes before, and doesn't
see why anyone would want to spend five dollars a pound on them,
but he's sure there are things that matter to him that don't make
sense to anyone else, and so he doesn't feel the need to comment on
it. There's a woman looking through the potatoes with the serious
air of someone getting ready to perform life-saving surgery.

That's not what holds his attention about her, though. She seems to
stand in the middle of a flickering kaleidoscope of colors, like someone has wrapped her in one of those sheets of plastic that manage to
be clear and infinitely iridescent at the same time. It's not something
he's ever seen before, and he can't stop himself from staring.

The line for the kettle corn moves forward, bringing him closer
to the register, and the woman by the potatoes glances up, catching his eye. Her hair is very red, save for a streak of white that cuts
from the crown of her head and down into her bangs, forming a
candy cane stripe that hangs just above one eye, and those eyes are a
pale, foggy gray, making her pupils seem to float in a sea of white. It
makes looking at her directly uncomfortable in a way the rainbow

halo doesn't, and so he glances away. The line moves again. He steps forward, ordering one of the large bags. It'll give them something to eat in the car once they get back on the road. The vendor asks for ten dollars, and he's in the process of handing it over when he becomes aware of a presence by his side.

Whoever it is is standing close enough that he assumes it must be Melanie. Accepting the corn and his change, he turns to offer her the bag. "Want some?" he asks, before he yelps, a short, wordless sound of shock.

The woman in the rainbow veil is standing right beside him, perfectly positioned to have been concealed in his blind spot during her approach, making it seem like she simply snapped her fingers and blinked across the intervening distance. He doesn't understand how she could have gotten so close.

The person behind him pushes past, between him and the woman in the rainbow veil. He doesn't seem to see her at all, although he clearly sees Harry, given the way he nudges him aside to get to the counter. "Come over here," says the woman.

It's not a request. But she doesn't feel like summer and she's not trying to kill him, so Harry steps away from the line, clutching his kettle corn, and follows as she gestures for him to do so, leading him to the lee between the potato stall and a seller peddling homemade jams and jellies. Once there, she narrows her eyes and glares at him.

"Who are you and how the hell can you see me?" she demands.

He blinks. The longer he looks at her, the less jarring the rainbow veil seems, the more she's just another woman, if one who's somehow managed to turn on her own private Instagram filter. She's dressed for the farmers' market, blue jeans and a flannel shirt over a T-shirt with a complicated math pun he isn't even going to try to understand printed on the front. There's a wicker basket over one arm, half-filled with produce, including the fancy potatoes she was selecting when he noticed her.

"Um," he says. "Harry? Is me. My name, I mean. Is Harald, but everyone calls me Harry, because 'Harald' is old-fashioned and doesn't suit me as well. That's with an *a*, not an *o*. It's a family name."

"Okay, when I asked who you were, I didn't want a complete etymology of your name. Save it for my brother, he'll care," says the woman. "Let's get back to how can you see me? No one else here can see me. I'm not in the market to be seen."

Harry doesn't know what to do with that. He's heard that Berkeley is a hippie town, but he didn't expect to meet someone who's so high she thinks she can make herself invisible. He looks around, somewhat frantically, hoping to spot Mel, or Jack, or someone else who can extricate him from this weird-ass situation with this weird-ass woman he doesn't know and doesn't think he wants to.

They're about six stalls away, heads together as they bend over a display of local honeys. The teens from the Starbucks have joined them, holding their own drinks, laughing at something Melanie's said. Harry manages not to wave and yell, largely because the woman snaps her fingers, dragging his attention back to her, where she clearly feels it belongs.

"Hey, eyes front," she snaps, voice hard with irritation. "Mr. Harry-is-me, I need to know how you can see me."

"I don't . . . I don't know?" he says. "You're all wrapped in rainbow cellophane. I'd never seen anything like that before, so I was looking less at you than I was at the colors. I'm sorry if I wasn't supposed to look at them. I won't do it again."

She blinks, and cocks her head to the side, like a falcon trying to decide whether or not to take its chances on a neighborhood cat. "You can *see* that?"

"Um, yes?"

"The 'rainbow cellophane,' as you put it, is a shield made of seconds stolen from five minutes in the future," she says. "Pulling them back to me and out of phase with themselves kills them, and when they burn up, they make little auroras. And no one can see them, except for me." She takes a step toward him. "How can you see the seconds dying?"

"Um." There's nothing immediately terrifying about this woman. She's tall, yes, but he's taller, and she's at least like thirty; he's pretty sure he can take her. And somehow she's the most frightening thing he's ever seen. Worse, even, than the sight of Melanie standing in a sparkling haze of snowflakes, and that was pretty frightening. "Lady, I don't know what you're talking about, but it doesn't really make any sense and you're sort of freaking me out right now, so I'd like it if you'd stop, please."

People can't see her, but they can certainly see *him,* and some of the shoppers are slanting suspicious looks in his direction as he stands there talking to the empty air. The urge to wheel and run is getting stronger. He doesn't think she'll chase him. Not if she's here to buy potatoes and not be seen.

But he's not sure he can wager Melanie's life on that, even if he's willing to wager his own, and so he remains frozen and frightened, watching the redhead sweep her eyes up and down the length of his body like he's one more thing to buy at the market, one more thing she needs to check for freshness before she puts it in her basket. There's nothing sexual about it, none of the predatory assessment he's occasionally encountered since he finished puberty and settled into being tall, broad-shouldered, and unquestionably attractive; she's taking his measure as an object in her world, nothing more and nothing less.

He still doesn't like it. "Creepy" is a word that's taken on distinctly sexual overtones just during his lifetime, and there's nothing sexual about her, but the way she's looking at him is nothing short of creepy. He tries to take a step backward, and discovers he can't.

The woman smiles, thinly. "There was a fifty percent chance you'd try to retreat if I got in your face, so I just made sure we were in the place where the other option won out. You're not going anywhere."

"Has anyone ever told you that you're terrifying?"

That seems to please her, because of course it does. Scary women always like to be told how scary they are. "I learned from the best. Now I need you to explain exactly how it is you can see me despite the seconds, and how you can see the seconds at all."

"I'm—"

"And quickly. The market closes in two hours, and I need to finish my shopping."

His throat goes dry and his voice goes dead in his mouth. He can't speak. He can't even squeak. All he can do is stare at her, frozen, like a mouse in front of a snake.

"Hey, Sunshine!"

Even Jack's shout isn't enough to snap him out of it. She runs up, looking more like the child she is than he's ever seen her, a bright hothouse daisy in her hair and honey on her lips, and skids to a stop beside him, reaching for his bag of kettle corn. "Share the spoils, man," she says, and laughs.

The woman switches her cold, reptile's gaze to Jack, not even seeming to blink. For Jack's part, she doesn't acknowledge the woman's presence, or seem to be in any way aware of it. She ignores her like everyone else who isn't Harry as she grabs first a handful of kettle corn, then his elbow, tugging to make him come with her.

"Snowflake was asking about you," she says. "I think she's feeling a little neglected. I need to teach you two the meaning of the word 'codependent,' I think you might find it really useful in the days to come."

"We already know," he says, tongue unsticking in the face of something far more normal than invisible, intimidating women wearing rainbows. When the living servant of the Winter became normal is something he doesn't want to examine too deeply.

"Huh," says Jack. "So maybe work on it? Just a tip."

The woman is still watching them, although she hasn't moved. Maybe her weird invisibility only works as long as she doesn't draw attention to herself? People hadn't noticed her talking to him before, although they'd noticed *him* easily enough; maybe she's staying quiet so Jack won't see her too. But he allows himself to be tugged away, relief stronger than concern as Jack leads him toward Melanie.

"We have a stalker," says Jack smoothly.

Harry glances over his shoulder. The woman is following them.

He wishes that were a surprise, but it's not, and it was never going to be. Quickly, he returns his gaze to the front, resisting the urge to walk faster and get the hell away.

"You can see her?"

"Sure can. Wait, she's not a Summer candidate?" Jack glances back this time, frowning a little. "That doesn't make sense."

"She doesn't feel like Summer to me," says Harry. "I figured she was Winter if she was anything."

"No. She feels like time, but she's not a part of my season. She's . . ." Jack stops. Stops dead, dragging Harry to a halt as her hand tightens on his elbow and makes it impossible for him to keep walking without yanking the smaller girl off of her feet. "Aw, *damn*."

"What do you mean, 'damn'?" But she's ignoring him as she lets go of his elbow and turns to stomp back toward the woman, who looks surprised but not shocked by her approach. On some level, she'd already figured out that Jack could see her too.

Oh, this has the potential to go very badly. He's not sure how, exactly, but he's also not sure how having their guide alone with a woman who steals seconds from the future and murders them so she can go shopping without being bothered can possibly be a good thing. He scans the crowd for Mel again. Despite Jack's claims, she doesn't seem to be looking for him; she's too busy talking to the teens from the Starbucks, both of them clutching paper cups and watching her talk with serious expressions on their faces.

"Guess this is my problem, then," he says, and turns, walking back toward Jack and the woman.

They're eyeing each other warily, two tigers trying to share the same hill. Jack gestures to the woman with her chin. "You get a name off of her?" she asks Harry, as he approaches.

"No," he says. "She got one off of me, but I was a little too freaked out to ask."

"And I've learned the hard way not to volunteer," says the woman. "Information is currency and knowledge is power."

"And you're an adorable bumper sticker," says Jack. "How are you sidestepping the flow of time?"

"Your little sister's about as subtle as a head trauma," says the woman.

"She's not my sister," says Harry. "She's my girlfriend's . . . Fuck, Jack, you never told me how to explain this. 'She's my girlfriend's personal servant' doesn't really work and it makes people look at me funny."

"My name is Jack Frost," says Jack, looking steadily at the woman. "Or at least it is now, but since that's a title as much as anything else, it doesn't give you any power over me. I am my own thing, and you cannot touch me."

"Oh, I could touch you, kid," says the woman, suddenly much more relaxed. "You're all Seasonals, aren't you? That explains a lot. My brother said he was putting the light on for you folks, but I wasn't sure he'd get any Incarnates. Cool that it worked. He's gonna be smug for a month."

"Are you alchemists?" asks Jack, with audible loathing.

"Nope," says the woman. "We're something better."

"Um, where I come from, we don't go around telling kids we can touch them," says Harry. "And I come from Portland, so it's not like it's all that far away."

"Portland . . . Oh my fuck." The woman blinks, less terrifying and more human as she focuses her attention on him completely. "You're not the first Seasonals we've seen in the last few days, although you're the first to include an Incarnate—or two. You're a Summer boy, aren't you?" She doesn't pause for his response as she focuses on Jack. "There's a coronation on, and that's where you're heading, isn't it?"

"Um, yeah," says Harry. "How do you know that, if you're not . . . You're not Summer and you're not Winter, so what *are* you?"

"As you measure things? With your quaint little calendar fetish and everything? I guess you'd call me Time." The woman smiles, baring all her teeth at once, and just like that, she's terrifying again. She doesn't even really have to try. Raising her right hand, she snaps her fingers and says, softly, "Okay, Kimmy, let's go."

The white-haired girl jerks upright, eyes wide, and turns to scan the market until she spots the red-haired woman. She looks surprised to see her talking to Harry and Jack—or maybe she's just surprised to see her talking to anyone, since she's still wrapped in rainbows. The white-haired girl—Kimmy, he supposes—says something to Melanie and starts walking briskly in their direction. Her brother follows.

After barely a beat, Melanie does too.

The redhead sighs at their approach. "Black hair, white skin—did you really have to be that on the nose? I guess the seasons have their sensibilities, but it's a little cliché."

Melanie pauses, blinking rapidly. Then she looks at the redhead with more interest, and asks, "Are you really one to talk? You're one cartoon bird short of an animated special."

The white-haired girl barks laughter before clapping a hand over her mouth and looking, briefly, ashamed of herself. "Sorry," she mumbles.

"I'm sorry," says the boy, adjusting his wire-rimmed glasses with one hand. "What's going on here, exactly?"

"Your mom is a jerk, is what's going on," says Harry.

The boy wrinkles his nose, looking utterly disgusted. "Dodger is *not* my mother," he says. "What a horrifying idea."

"Technically, if I'm anything, I'm his older sister," says Dodger. "Also legal guardian, even though neither I nor my brother have any business being responsible for children. We can barely manage to be responsible for ourselves. They'd never let us have these ones if they legally existed."

"You're responsible for half the forces governing the universe," says Jack, sounding dazed.

"And two teenagers, and ask me which one is more trouble," says Dodger. "You know these people, Tim?"

"We met at the Starbucks," he says. "Kim and I gave them directions on how to get here. I didn't expect them to run into you."

"Meaning you didn't expect them to be able to see me, meaning neither one of you picked up on anything strange about them," says Dodger.

The teens look faintly shamefaced, Kim scuffing her toe against the pavement and looking down, while Tim puts a hand on her shoulder and frowns. Harry can't take it.

"Neither did you," he says. "You didn't notice me until you realized I was looking at you when I wasn't supposed to be able to be. Don't go getting all superior just because you're older."

"Harry," hisses Jack. "She's not acting superior because she's older. She's doing it because she's Mathematical Function Incarnate, fully manifest, and she could edit us out of existence if she wanted to."

"Not quite," says Dodger. "It's nice of you to say, but editing people out of existence is more Roger's thing than mine. I'm more likely to just stick you in a time loop and leave you there—but you might welcome that, huh? Cancel the coronation and let you stay where you are. Anyway, you three better come home with us."

"What? Where? Why?" asks Melanie.

"We don't live far from here," says Kim, apparently trying to be helpful. "Roger and Erin are home, they can probably help explain what's going on. Dodger doesn't explain things so much as she hurls them at you and hopes they don't cause brain damage or mental trauma when they hit you in the head. Which means that of course they do, half the time."

"Oh my God, I am so glad our names don't rhyme," says Harry, glancing at Mel. "Can you imagine? School would be hell."

"Harry and Mary," she says, voice bland in the way it always is when she's preparing to say something cruel. "Or Del and Mel, I suppose, if we assume I'd get to keep my name."

"Can we not twit the *basic fundamental forces of the universe* today, please?" asks Jack, a little desperately. She steals a glance at Dodger, apparently waiting to see how the woman is going to react. If it's poorly, they could all be in a lot of trouble.

Harry doesn't care. This is all stupid. He came to the farmers' market to stretch his legs and forget about weird metaphysical nonsense and murder for fifteen minutes, not to wind up posturing like shaken roosters with a woman who appears to scare Jack shitless just by breathing, who can wrap herself in stolen time and use it to disappear but uses that ability not for anything important or useful, just to get left alone while she buys produce. None of this is what he wanted. None of this has *been* what he wanted since he saw his girlfriend collapse on the football field, and he doesn't have the energy to keep dealing with it. Any of it.

The only good thing about this stupid situation is Melanie, who still looks better than she has in years, at least when she's not falling into weird fugue states and turning into some sort of blissed-out avatar of winter. And she's only done that the once. Maybe it's not something that's going to happen again. If they can just stay away from situations that might make her feel like she has to freeze someone to death . . .

Which there's no way of doing. Not easily. Harry sighs and takes Melanie's hand, offering her the bag of kettle corn at the same time.

"We only have an hour on the parking meter," he says.

"That's no problem," says Dodger. "Anybody got a quarter?"

Looking quietly embarrassed, like any teen whose adult authority figure insists on doing stupid magic tricks, Tim hands Dodger a quarter. She spins it between her fingers before making it disappear into her pocket. "There," she says, somewhat smugly. "Now you have six hours."

"You don't know which car is mine," Harry protests.

"I'm sorry, did I say 'you'? Now every car parked on Shattuck within a mile of the Starbucks has six hours."

"The city uses parking meter money to pay for lot maintenance," says Kim, a sharp note in her voice. "That's technically theft."

"And if the city ever bothered to actually *maintain* the parking lots, I might feel bad about it," says Dodger. "The potholes in some of them are deep enough to qualify as swimming pools for squirrels. Roger nearly broke an axle last week. I'll worry about stealing from the city when the city stops stealing everyone's quarters."

"Like you just stole mine," says Tim.

"Details." Dodger waves his objection away before turning her sharp, gray-eyed gaze on Harry and Melanie. "Well, come on, little seasons. We can't stand here all day, and we shouldn't keep Roger waiting."

"You didn't know you were going to run into us," protests Harry. "How would he even know?"

"You'll be happier if you don't ask," says Tim. "Let's go."

"Do we have a choice?" asks Melanie.

"Not really," says Kim. Calm as anything, Dodger starts to walk away.

The rest of them follow. Anything else would be foolishness.

Stalking

CALENDAR SEASON: FEBRUARY 13TH, 2017: WIN-
TER, WANING WORM MOON.

The lot outside the motel crawls with police, like maggots swarming over a piece of rotting meat. They've cordoned off the whole place with yellow tape, painted orange and green by the flashing lights atop their cars. If there are any guests remaining, they've moved their cars elsewhere. Trevor looks at the parking lot and the number of uniformed officers clogging the stairs and balconies and can't imagine anyone's still here when they don't absolutely have to be. This is a lot of authority looking for someone who needs to be punished. They'll find traffic tickets from twenty years ago, medical marijuana and talking back to your grandmother, and they'll do it with the ruthless efficiency of men who get paid to be right about everything, even the snap judgments they make on the basis of their own prejudices and preconceptions.

"They were here," says Aven serenely. She's comfortable in the front seat of the car, surrounded by candy bar wrappers and empty drink bottles. Their drive so far has been one long process of her starting to figure out what she likes, what she prefers, what makes her happy.

So far, they know she likes chocolate peanut butter cups, Mexican Coke, and taking people apart to see what's inside them. Her first subject was her father, who came apart under her hands like a jigsaw puzzle that could never be reassembled, no matter how hard the surgeons might have tried. Trevor's pretty sure the man was still technically alive when they left the house; Aven has a supernatural knack for flensing flesh from bone and nerve from tissue, and she left parts of her father exposed to air that were never meant to be, walking away with him butterflied across the floor.

If she hadn't found the process pleasant, that might have been enough for her, but she'd enjoyed it sufficiently that she's tried again several times since they left Portland in Trevor's battered old Honda, dismantling two gas station attendants and a woman whose only mistake was stopping at the rest stop at the precisely wrong moment. It's slowed their progress considerably, but Aven isn't worried, and so neither is Trevor. He literally can't do this without her, not without finding another potential Summer who still needs an attendant, and so whatever works for her will work for him as well.

Plus, keeping her happy keeps her knives and rage and endless curiosity aimed outward where it belongs, rather than inward, where he's the only potential study partner she can find. He doesn't want the things he's seen her do to others to be aimed at him, thank you *very* much. He didn't realize, when he decided he didn't *want* to serve the Summer he was meant for, that he'd be swapping Harry March, milquetoast rich boy who had never worked or wanted for anything in his life, for a girl who was half teenager, half toddler, all serial killer in the making.

Aven grew up in the alchemical equivalent of a sensory deprivation chamber, not quite alive and never allowed to die, learning only the things an alchemist thought were important enough to teach. She's not evil: she's amoral, unaware that half the things she does are wrong.

"Can you tell from all the cops?" he asks, frowning. He doesn't feel another potential Summer anywhere nearby. He's pretty good at spotting candidates for the season he already considers his own, although he hasn't been able to lead Aven to any of them yet; the only one he's picked up on since they hit the road was in a car heading for Canada, too fast and on the wrong side of a concrete divider.

Aven hadn't noticed the potential challenger, focused as she was on following the trail of her sister and her self-appointed rival; she'd had better things to worry about, and Trevor had chosen not to point out the possibility of a fight. Aven would have demanded he go after them, and he knows how this works, knows the competition will thin itself out, every individual season throwing themselves against the others, until only one is left standing. He intends to let the fighting die down, then present Aven to an exhausted Harry as a fait accompli, still fresh, still ready to do whatever she deems necessary.

And Aven deems a lot of things necessary. She opens the car door, swinging long legs out to touch the parking lot, and when he grabs her arm to stop her, she merely looks at his hand against her skin, slowly raising one bone-white eyebrow to crest high on her forehead, almost verging onto her hairline.

"Why are you touching me?" she asks, voice very mild.

Trevor takes his hand away. "I do not mean to overstep my place . . ." he begins.

"So don't."

". . . but it looks as if you're preparing to go out there and confront the police."

She lowers her eyebrow and continues to stare at him, eyes flat and cold. At least she isn't getting out of the car. "They were here," she says, as if he might have missed that, as if he might not understand the importance of what she's saying to him. "In this place, they were here. My sister and her Summer boy were here."

"How are you so sure? Maybe a drug deal went badly and someone got shot. Maybe something else happened." Something bad, judging by the number of officers.

"She called down the Winter," she says. "It filled her up with coldness, top to bottom, and she left some of it behind when she walked away. I can feel it. Can't you feel it? It doesn't want Summer to be manifest here. It wants me to go away, and I don't like being told what to do."

It would be impossible to miss the warning in her tone. He's telling her what to do right now. That's not a good way to have her happy with him, and the small part of Trevor that wants to be a good person, that doesn't want to be killing people and breaking things that would be better left unbroken, recoils from that tone. He leans back into his own seat, hands well away from her.

"I can't tell you what to do, but I can tell you what you don't know," he says. "You don't know how the police work. If you get out of this car and start walking toward them, you're going to cross a bunch of invisible lines they've drawn with their authority and their presence, and they're not going to like it. You're a pretty white woman, so you'll probably make it to the motel without anyone shooting you, but then they'll start telling you what to do, and they won't be nice about it. They won't let you see the bodies, if there are any. They won't tell you where your sister went, or anything else you want to know. They won't *help* you, Aven. They won't make this any easier."

"So what do *you* want me to do?" she demands . . . but she pulls her feet back inside the car, and that makes him feel a little better. She's listening. She doesn't always. Sometimes she just *does,* as driven by impulse as any child, and oh, she's exhausting, and maybe he should have stayed with Harry after all.

Maybe not, though, because she's going to win. He can see it in the way she moves, in the way she walks through the world, in the way she excites the air. Pamela could never have given her the space to flower into what she's going to become, a perfect, poisoned posey that will seize the Summer on her own behalf and, by extension, his.

He's going to live forever.

She closes the door and looks at him, mulish and unhappy. "I want to see where my sister was," she says. It isn't a request.

"So we wait until the cops leave, and then we find out what happened here."

"Fine," she says, and folds her arms across her chest. "I want lunch if I can't go inside."

Toddler. It really is so much like trying to control a violent, potentially powerful toddler. "I saw a McDonald's a few blocks back. Let's go get you some fries."

He pulls away from the motel and starts for the McDonald's. As they reach the parking lot, something tickles around the edge of his awareness. Not a Summer, exactly, but something adjacent; something he might be able to use.

Maybe he can give her something to do after all.

The House with the Clocks for Walls

Kim wasn't kidding when she said they didn't live far from the farmers' market. Dodger leads them for about three and a half blocks before she turns down a tiny street that winds like a creek as it heads off into the hills. The houses are narrow and close together, but tall, with more of those high porches Harry noticed on the way in. Most of them are natural, stained wood, or else painted brown to match their neighbors. A few white and beige are mixed into their ranks, but on the whole, it's a quietly dignified space.

Tim catches Harry studying one of the natural wood-colored houses and smirks. "People around here like to be harmonious," he says. "They like to 'vibe.'"

"We get that at home, too," says Harry. "People don't want to be landmarks. They want to fit in. I like the wood. My family's in lumber, so it's nice to see people respecting it for what it is, not trying to turn it into something it's not."

"So you appreciate a subtle paint job?" asks Kim, her voice a mirror of her brother's smirk. "You like it when a house doesn't stick out?"

"It depends on the house," says Harry, starting to feel as if he's walking into a trap. Melanie squeezes his hand, and he brightens. She's not limping badly yet; that will probably concern him later, since he wants her to feel pain enough to be human, but right now, it means he's not dragging his injured girlfriend through residential Berkeley, and it makes him feel better about what's going on. "I mean, my grandparents live in a literal—What the *fuck* is *that*?"

"That" is one of the small Victorian-style houses he's been seeing jammed in amongst the Queen Annes and the ranch houses ever since they crossed the city limits. It's roughly the same size and era as most of its neighbors. It belongs here. And that's where its similarity to the houses around it ends, because if there's a color, it's painted on this house. Every step in the stairs leading up to the porch is different, as is every board in the porch itself, and in the fence that surrounds the garden, which is a seasonally impossible riot of flowers that almost takes his breath away.

The window frames are neon. The windows themselves are patchworks of carnival glass, spattered with an assortment of suncatchers. Even the shingles are painted, no two touching in the same color range, much less the same actual *color*. Harry stops dead, pulling Melanie to a halt with him, and just stares.

There's a car in the driveway, a reasonably new Mini Cooper, parked next to a much older VW van. The van has been painted in tie-dye swirls, as garish as the house. The Mini Cooper appears at a distance to have dodged the six-year-old's fever dream that is everything around it, but from where they are now, Harry can see that the paint is designed to change colors depending on the angle it's viewed from. The car, which looks like a calm, metallic blue, is actually a dozen colors in one.

Just the thought of it gives him a headache.

"What's wrong?" asks Kim. "Doesn't respect the wood? Sticks out too much?"

"It hurts my eyes," says Melanie. "I think it hurts *everyone's* eyes. It would hurt a mantis shrimp's eyes. How is this allowed?"

"Turns out we're at the intersection of three HOAs, and each of them has different rules, and we didn't actually agree to abide by any of them," says Dodger, taking a step back to join them. "The house pre-dates the HOAs, and that means we weren't required to join up. So there's nothing anyone can do to stop us."

"Rules lawyer," says Tim fondly.

"Yup," says Dodger. "You would be too, if you had to live with my cuckoo-bananas brother in your head all the time."

Tim and Kim exchange a glance, and Harry can't help feeling like Dodger has just said something insensitively hurtful, although he can't really imagine what it is. He frowns instead, and asks, "So this is *your* house?"

The woman in her veil of rainbows is far too tastefully dressed to have designed a home like this one, and she doesn't have the look of someone who would spend enough time outdoors to have a garden like that. Her skin's too pale, although she's darker than Melanie; she'd burn to a crisp if she even tried it. Plus her hair clashes with at least half the fence, and she seems too self-possessed to have done that on purpose.

"Yup," she says, sounding smug. "Bought it free and clear when the last owner passed away, gave Roger carte blanche with the exterior, as long as he didn't try to control too much about the interior decorating. Which he didn't, because he's a great guy who doesn't actually care whether the couch is placed at a forty-five-degree or forty-seven-degree angle."

"Forty-seven won," says Kim quietly, to Harry. "Forty-five had too many divisible factors."

"Huh," he says, for lack of anything else to contribute to the conversation. This doesn't make any sense. None of this makes any sense.

"Going through the garden may make you a little uncomfortable," says Dodger to Jack and Melanie. "It's mid-June there, and I'm pretty sure you're not supposed to be awake come mid-June."

"I'm Ascendant, not Incarnate," says Jack. "I'll be fine. Do you have another way in, that won't drag the living Winter through the middle of June?"

"Wait," says Harry, who suddenly wants to be in that garden with a longing verging on addiction, one that doesn't leave much room in his body for anything else. "What do you mean, it's mid-June in the garden? That doesn't make any sense. It can't be one time there and a different time somewhere else."

"Go through the front gate and find out," suggests Dodger. To Jack, she says, "We can take her in through the garage, if you're really concerned, but if the coronation has only just started, she shouldn't be far enough along for it to matter."

"Mel's a special case," says Jack. "Her father took some notes from yours."

Dodger's eyes darken, pale gray turning stormy, in the kind of change that shouldn't be possible. Harry notices, but doesn't wonder about it the way he should; he's already drifting toward the open gate in the multicolored fence around the garden, unable to resist the pull of the magical words "mid-June." Melanie, her hand still in his, follows along, not resisting, even if she doesn't seem to share his desire to see what's in that garden.

The closer he gets, the less ridiculous Dodger's claim seems. Some of these flowers can't be thriving in February, no matter how mild the climate here is. It's not possible. There's a tomato plant in full flower, some of its branches already drooping with heavy green fruit, and the temperature is at least ten degrees warmer than it was on the sidewalk.

Melanie pulls her hand out of his just before he steps through the gate. He's so enthralled by the flowers that he doesn't notice.

Two more steps and he's in the middle of the garden, surrounded by planter beds and the smell of sun-warmed greenery on all sides, and he can *feel* it, he can *feel* the growth around him, as immediate and manifest as the sunlight baking into his skin, and he's never felt anything like this. It's the first time he got behind the wheel of a car and the first time he snuck a beer and the feel of Melanie's breast in his hand, soft and full and perfect. It's every good chemical his brain knows how to produce, and a few hundred it doesn't, that it shouldn't be able to make without outside aid, and it's filling him from top to bottom with brilliant burning, he's on fire, he's on fire and it doesn't hurt, because he's made to burn, just like Melanie was made to freeze.

Winter may be flashier, may be impossible snowfalls and frost-bite, but Summer is just as powerful, in its slow way, and for the first time he can feel that power in every inch of his body. He closes his eyes, turning his face up toward the impossibly warm, impossibly welcoming sun. He's home. This is where he belongs. This is what he's been fighting for this whole time. He's never leaving this garden.

"Huh," says a voice. "Will you look at that?"

"He's not as far along in his manifestation as she is," says another voice. "Melanie's already losing herself to the Winter, for short periods. But the worm moon just passed, and we have until the pink moon before his ascendancy actually begins. So he's sort of hobbled by the time of year, and she's encouraged by it."

"You don't sound disappointed about that."

"I'm her attendant, not his. The only thing that would have made me happier about this whole process would be if it had started under the beaver moon. I don't have the time to get her fully ready for what's ahead. I don't have the tools to get *him* ready."

"So where's his attendant?"

"That's the ten-million-dollar question, isn't it? There's supposed to be one attendant for every candidate, and there was a Corn Jenny where they were, but there weren't any Jack Frosts. I had to be called from across the country when the season found me, and I barely managed to get there on time. If I'd been even a little bit delayed, they would both have gone into this without the proper preparation, and Mel's father would have been able to—Melanie! *No!*"

There's some kind of commotion outside the gate, but anything that happens outside the gate doesn't really matter, not to Harry. That's a different world, a winter world, and things that happen in the winter world are none of his concern. Nothing that happens there belongs to him, and nothing about it can—

There is a heavy sound, like a sack of wet concrete hitting the ground, and a sudden pain lances through his chest, there for a moment before it vanishes again, leaving him strong and warm and filled with light. That moment of pain is enough to snap him out of the euphoria of summer, and he regrets its loss even as he lowers his face from the sun and opens his eyes.

Melanie is sprawled face down on the path inside the gate, one arm extended toward him. She isn't moving. She isn't breathing.

Harry, who has seen her dead twice in his lifetime, knows immediately what that terrible, impossible stillness means. He rushes back to where she's lying, dropping to his knees and gathering her into his arms. "Mel? *Melanie?* Someone call 911!"

"No one call 911," says Jack, stepping into the garden. As soon as she crosses the boundary, she seems . . . reduced, somehow, lessened in an impalpable, indefinable way. Part of him hates it. Part of him loves it, has been waiting to see her brought down to normalcy. That part of him is smaller, but growing stronger the longer he's here in the warmth and sweetness of summer.

Tiny tendrils of green are forcing their way through the cracks between the bricks of the garden path where he kneels, growing with impossible speed, already unfurling minute leaves. He doesn't notice them, clutching Mel to his chest as he turns wide, disbelieving eyes on the girl who was supposed to help her—help them both to survive this ridiculous coronation and claim their crowns.

"What?" he demands. "Why not?"

"Because human medicine can't help her," says Jack. "She's dead, but she'll get better when it's not summer anymore." She looks past him, meaningfully, toward the stairs.

Harry understands in an instant what he's being told to do. It's ridiculous and impossible, but so is everything else that's happening right now. So he gathers Melanie into his arms and stands, carrying her along with him as he straightens, trying to ignore the sickening cold of her skin where it brushes against his own, the absolute dead weight of her against his chest.

"Are you okay with her?" asks Tim, stepping around his sister, eyes on Harry as he moves into the garden.

"I can always carry Mel," says Harry. "She's never too heavy for me."

He's been playing football and training for long enough that he's not lying—not intentionally, anyway—and the summer surging through his veins makes him feel as if he could do anything, like he could walk all the way back to Portland with Melanie in his arms. As he walks toward the steps, she seems to get heavier, and he pauses, adjusting his grip, for long enough to understand that he's moving out of the center of the impossible artificial summer.

Summer ends completely at the bottom of the stairs. He knows as soon as he's stepped outside of its sphere and back into the tail end of winter. Weakness washes over him, and he stumbles, nearly dropping her. She's still not moving or breathing. She wouldn't notice if she fell. But *he* would notice. *He* would know that when she needed him the most, he dropped her.

Straining now, Harry pulls himself onto the first step, and then the second. Above him, the door opens. Feet move on the porch. He can't lift his head. He can't look. If he focuses on anything other than continuing to move, his legs will give out, and he'll drop her.

He can't. He can't drop her.

"Well, will you look at that," says a new voice, with a new accent. Boston. But there's no reason for someone with a Boston accent to be on the porch above him. Harry keeps moving, keeps hauling himself toward his goal. "Dodge? There a reason a boy with a corpse is heading for the door while you just stand there?"

"That's Harry," says the woman named Dodger. She sounds distantly, wryly amused, like this is something that happens every day and never fails to entertain her. "He's a candidate."

"Huh. Erin said the coronation had started. Wasn't sure why I needed to care about that, but I set some snares out anyway, and I guess it's on our doorstep now. Literally. Hey, Harry?"

The Boston voice turns warm, collegiate, friendly, the voice of a favorite teacher or that one children's show host who sets up camp in your heart and never goes away, no matter how old you get, no matter how much you know you should have long outgrown them.

Harry's never heard a voice so appealing in his life. If this man did audiobooks, he'd break the bestseller lists.

"I know it's hard right now, but I also know you can do this. You can carry her as far as you need to. You can make it up the stairs. You've got this."

Harry finds his second wind between one breath and the next, and even though he can't feel the summer anymore—even though the summer's over until it gets here the real way, and that's for the best, really; it's better if things happen in their own time, at their own speed—and he makes it to the top of the stairs without pausing or slowing down again. Melanie's still heavy, but he can carry her as far as he needs to. He always could.

The man is waiting there to meet him. He's a tall, scrawny guy, with slightly overlong brown hair, streaked with white the same way Dodger's is, and eyes that match and mirror Dodger's behind the lenses of his own glasses, which are nowhere near as fashionable as Tim's. He's dressed like someone who was a middle-aged English professor by the time he turned sixteen, brown trousers, a white button-down shirt, and a brown wool cardigan with honest-to-God patched elbows. He's a walking cliché, and he looks like he belongs on the porch of this technicolor nightmare house about as much as the house looks like it belongs to the neighborhood.

He scans Harry and dismisses him at the same time, turning his attention toward the gathering in the garden below. "You could have turned the summer off, you know," he chides gently. "I can always plant more flowers."

"Spoken like the man who just tells the universe what to do and doesn't have to work for it," Dodger replies. "It took me a long time to get those equations exactly right. I'm not taking them down just so strangers can walk across our yard more easily."

"I think these are strawberry plants," says Kim. "Growing right up through the middle of the path like they belong there. Oh, look. They're putting out fruit now."

"It took you *five minutes*," says the man.

"That's a long time!" objects Dodger. She reaches the top of the

stairs, puts her hand on the man's shoulder. Harry sees them together for the first time. If the eyes and the white streaks in their
hair hadn't been enough, their faces would have given the game
away. They have the same bone structure, under all the natural differences created by their being two different people, two different
genders, two different heights. They couldn't have been anything
but brother and sister. Even parent and child would have introduced too many genetic variables.

"Do you have a couch where I can set her down?" Harry asks, a
little desperately. He doesn't want to admit that she's getting heavy,
still feels a bit like that would be failing her, but she is, and he doesn't
want to drop her now. Not after getting her to the top of the stairs
when he didn't think he could. Not after running away from home
when she said they had to.

Not ever.

"Oh, sure," says the man. "Sorry about that. I live with barbarians
now, and it's done a number on my manners. Come on, this way."

He gestures for Harry to follow as he turns and heads into the
house. Harry does, Dodger behind him, grumbling about how some
people come from uncivilized cities where it snows all the damn
time and no one knows how to drive, and maybe they shouldn't call
decent mathematicians barbarians.

Harry is beginning to understand three things with terrible clar-
ity. First, that these people don't come with footnotes: they're so
accustomed to being themselves, whatever that means, that they no
longer stop to explain anything. After several days of Jack's clumsy
attempts at explaining everything, that's almost welcome. Second,
that they're essentially harmless, wrapped up in their own lives and
hobbies and interests to such a degree that there isn't room for much
outside the tiny world they've crafted for themselves. He's known
adults like this before, teachers mostly, people who had decided
having a passion for a profession was the same thing as having a
personality. They've always seemed like useful cautionary tales to
him, people whose choices are so obviously wrong that they make it
easier to make better choices on his own.

Thirdly, and finally for now, that these are the most dangerous people he's ever met in his life. They're too calm, too casual about impossible things. For them, this is just the way the universe works, and if something contradicts that understanding, they'll either change it or dispose of it, and he's not sure which is worse. Even more, he's not sure he'd have a choice if they decided one of those things had to happen.

The interior of the house is old-fashioned, dark and narrow, and contradictorily filled with light. None of the windows are anything other than clear, honest glass, and Harry pauses to blink at one of them, trying to reconcile the exterior with what he's seeing now. These can't be the same windows.

"Dodger lets me do whatever I want to the outside, but she says having rainbows on her whiteboards gives her headaches, and I've learned not to mess with her math."

"Learned the hard way," grumbles Dodger. "He lost gravity privileges for a *week* last time he distracted me while I was trying to work."

The front door opens on a small dining area, with a table that has somehow managed to not attract any clutter apart from a lace table runner and a bowl of fruit. That may be the least realistic thing about this whole place. The man gestures for Harry to follow through the door on the other side, which deposits them in a living room like something out of a murder mystery, walls lined with floor-to-ceiling bookshelves, seating consisting of a couch and two loveseats arrayed around a small fireplace. It should seem heavy and oppressive, like the furniture itself, all of which is clearly antique and made of heavy maple. Instead, it feels homey, lived-in, and alive in the calm, vital way of well-maintained wood. Harry ignores most of it, making a beeline for the couch, where he kneels and stretches Melanie carefully out atop the cushions.

She still isn't moving. He places his hand against her chest, where he knows her heart is. (Harry got in trouble in eighth grade for lecturing a science teacher about human anatomy, when the man made the mistake of claiming the human heart was located inaccurately.

He'd been simplifying for his younger audience. He hadn't anticipated a boy who had all but decided to become a cardiothoracic surgeon solely for the purpose of saving his best friend's life.) She still doesn't move.

"Hey, Mel," he says. "It's winter again. You can wake up now. That weird lady from the farmers' market took us home to meet her brother, and he's going to help us figure out where we're going next. But we can't do that until you wake up, because I'll be honest: if you don't, I'm going to renounce this stupid crown before it causes me any more problems, and head home to apologize to my parents."

Maybe "if you don't stop being dead, I'm leaving" isn't the best way to get his girlfriend to come back to life, but since when have they ever tried to do anything the best way? He takes his hand away and sits back on heels, waiting.

The traditional thing to do here would be to kiss her, but even though he has permission from her a hundred times over, that's always felt a little weird to him, like crossing a line so obvious it shouldn't even have to be drawn. So he just waits, as the others crowd into the room, Dodger and her brother—the threatened Roger, he assumes, and hopes they don't have a third sibling named "Codger" or something—leaning against the wall with a calm self-assurance that he can't help seeing as a little predatory. They know nothing in this place can hurt them, and so they don't worry about it.

He gets the feeling they don't worry about much of anything.

The teens from Starbucks are next, Tim and Kim, placing themselves to either side of Roger and Dodger, respectively, like they belong there. He can see the resemblance between them when they array themselves like that, despite the wide dissimilarity of their coloration and personal styles. They're a family, two sets of twins from decades apart, and he envies them for their obvious comfort with each other and the general strangeness of the situation.

Jack comes into the room after them, and while she looks a little concerned by the sight of Melanie still motionless on the sofa, she doesn't rush to her side, but hangs back near the door, leaving room for the next woman to step inside.

She's shorter than Roger and Dodger, taller than Kim and Tim, with strawberry blonde hair half the girls at school would kill for, and a dusting of freckles across her nose. Saying her eyes are blue is like saying Mel is pale: technically true, but such an understatement that it verges on a lie. Her eyes are like the wings of those weird butterflies in South America, the ones that are dark and light at the same time, and there's no way they're natural. He stops looking at her. She's giving him a headache.

"Why's there a corpse on the couch?" asks the woman he doesn't know. "It seems unhygienic."

"Hello to you, too, Erin," says Roger. "The corpse—"

"Melanie," interjects Jack.

"—Melanie," says Roger, smooth as anything, "is one of the Winter candidates. She's trying for the crown, and she's apparently entangled enough with her season that the shock of stepping into the summer Dodger made for my garden sort of, well . . ."

"Killed the shit out of her," says Dodger.

"You have such a way with words, sis," says Roger.

"Huh," says Erin. "It's not summer in here. Shouldn't she be waking up by now?"

That's Harry's question, too. He doesn't like any part of this, doesn't like the house, doesn't like the people, doesn't like the uncertainty of it all. He wants Mel to open her eyes. He wants to go back to the summer in the garden and stand in the sun and figure out more about what it means, while the season uncurls in his belly like a serpent. He wants to go home.

"This is all sort of new to us, too," says Jack. "I'm her attendant, and I've only been Ascendant for a year. I don't know how most of this works."

"Aren't you both supposed to have attendants?" asks Erin.

"Harry's attendant didn't bother to show."

Harry raises a hand in a brief wave, in case he's somehow turned invisible, but doesn't move from his place by Mel's side. She'll need him when she wakes up, and she *will* wake up, she *will*, this isn't how their story ends. It's too anticlimactic, for one thing. They've been racing through a fairy tale. It can't be over just because a woman wrapped in rainbows decided to make the summer happen in her front yard.

"How did you find them, Dodge?" asks Roger.

"I was scraping seconds from the future so I could shop without anyone bothering me, and the Summer boy *saw* me. He couldn't possibly have seen me, but he did, and so I thought I should look into things a little deeper. Lo and behold, he's in the running to manifest the living Summer, and that makes him sort of our problem. The dead girl, too."

"More yours than mine."

"I don't know. People who are also anthropomorphic manifestations of natural phenomenon are more language than they are math or time. I think they're your problem."

"Pretty sure you're bullshitting me because you don't want the ball," says Roger.

Dodger shrugs. "So what if I am?"

"As long as there's a dead girl on our couch, I think they're *our* problem," says Erin sourly.

"Fair enough," says Roger. He takes a breath, and when he speaks again, it's with that sweet, mellow, best-teacher-in-the-world voice. The one that says he understands, he *cares*, and whatever he says he wants is for the absolute, inarguable best. Harry recognizes it better as a compulsion this time, but it isn't aimed at him; there's nothing to resist. "Melanie? You've had a nice nap, but it's winter, and winter is when you should be awake. Please wake up now, Melanie."

"Please wake up as Melanie, and not as the winter," says Harry hurriedly.

"Please wake up, *Melanie*," says Roger, stressing her name harder this time.

"You know, asking dead people to wake up doesn't usually work unless you're Dr. Frankenstein," says Jack.

Melanie sighs.

It's a small sound. It might go unnoticed if they weren't so focused on her, but they are, and so it's the loudest sound in the entire world. Harry feels her chest rise beneath his hand, and for a moment fancies he can actually *feel* her heart beating, *feel* the confirmation that she's back in the world of the living. He understands a bit more about the man they call Roger now: somehow when he tells something to do something, it listens. Even when it shouldn't be able to listen. Even when he's telling Harry's arms to push past exhaustion and not drop his temporarily dead girlfriend, or telling Melanie's frozen heart to beat. He can talk the world into going along with him.

Harry's earlier impression was correct, then. He's dangerous. They both are, this woman who can bend time and this man who can persuade it to stay bent just by sounding as if it would make him really, really happy. Together, they can remake reality to suit them in any way they like, and the thought is terrifying.

Melanie sighs again. Then she opens her eyes, and blinks. "Harry? Where are we?"

"Inside Dodger's house," he says. Her chest is still moving, but there's no heartbeat; that was an illusion, a phantom of his relief, and she's still dead. She's just dead and moving again, like she's been since the football field. It's good enough for him.

"We were outside, in the garden," she says. "You were just . . . standing there, smiling at the sun, and it was like you were glowing, and I tried to go to you, and then everything was cold and dark and I couldn't wake up."

"You died," says Harry.

"Sort of," says Jack. She finally moves from her place near the door, crossing to the couch. "Remember I told you the price of manifestation would be dying for three months out of the year? It's not death-death, in the sense that you move on to the afterlife, if there is one. But you'll be gone for the duration of the season opposing your own, and you'll wake up when the season that abuts you both begins. So Melanie dies during the summer, and comes back on the first day of fall. If we'd had a Stingy Jack here, they would probably have been able to wake her."

"And you couldn't do it because . . . ?"

"Because I stand for Winter, same as she does, but I don't die during the Summer, I just age like a normal person. So me being here didn't tell the seasons something was wrong and she needed to come back to us."

"Huh," says Harry. "Okay, well, that sucks."

"Wait," says Melanie, pushing herself up into a sitting position and narrowing her eyes at Jack. "Are you telling me that you were serious about one of us being dead for six months out of every year? We only get six months together? That's bullshit."

"I'm serious about most of the things I say, and you'll only have three months apart," says Jack. "Him in the summer, when his season keeps him busy, and you in the winter, when your season does the same. And you get six months together, for as long as you keep your places, instead of spending all your time waiting to die."

"Okay, well this is very John Hughes meets George Romero, and I sort of hate it," says Erin. "Why are you in our house?"

"I told you, I brought them home," says Dodger.

"We found them first," says Kim. "They were in the Starbucks when we stopped for coffee. The little one came over to talk to us. We didn't realize there was anything weird about them, they just looked like people we should talk to . . ." She ducks her head, cheeks coloring red, and Harry realizes they must be very lonely.

Being two seemingly normal teenagers sharing a house with two manifestations of natural forces and one . . . whatever the hell Erin is, can't really leave much room for a normal social life. He wonders where their parents are. He knows enough, despite his own relatively sheltered upbringing, to feel like it's inappropriate to ask.

The thought of making friends must have been intoxicating, for the short while it lasted before they reached the farmers' market and found him locked in unwilling conversation with their terrifying older sister. *Much* older sister. If she weren't so clearly unsuited to being anyone's mother, he would probably still have taken her for their mom. It seems a little unfair for someone in her thirties to represent a pivotal force of the universe. She'll die soon, and they'll have to find a new one.

Or maybe not. His great-grandfather was ninety when he died, and his own father has been grumbling recently about the approach of his fortieth birthday. Maybe Roger and Dodger and their terrible rhyming names will live forever, and Kim and Tim will never be able to make any friends. He'd probably find that a lot sadder if he weren't suddenly concerned about how he's supposed to ever make friends again, if he's busy being dead all winter, and hanging out with anthropomorphic manifestations all the damn time . . .

Melanie has gotten her hair under control, smoothing it with her hands, and is now engaged in a sort of staring contest with Erin, who keeps cocking her head like changing the angle from which she stares at Mel will somehow change the information she's receiving. Finally, she presses her fingertips to her temples and begins to rub in small, concentric circles, glancing to Roger.

They all do that, Harry realizes, even Dodger, checking with him before they decide anything. Roger's the wheel they all turn around, and while they would probably deny it if he said the man was in charge, he clearly is. He wonders if they know it. He wonders if they resent it.

"The boy's natural," she says. "His genetics are as orderly as anyone else's, which is to say they're not orderly at all—he's pure natural selection and chance. But the girl . . . she was *constructed*, Roger, and I recognize the maker's mark. She may not be a sister. She's a cousin, no question of that. An alchemist built her from the ground up, and what we have here isn't the whole thing."

Melanie blinks, looking alarmed. Jack turns on Erin, eyes narrowing.

"What do *you* know about alchemists?" she demands.

"I know I was designed by James Reed and Leigh Barrow, and constructed by Barrow by herself, pulled together piece by piece to be the representation of her smallest and least unfettered desires," says Erin. "Hi. I'm the living incarnation of the force of Order. It's not a pleasure to meet you."

Jack looks nonplussed. "Oh," she says.

Melanie, on the other hand, is sitting up straight and attentive, staring at Erin. "You know Dr. Barrow?" she asks, in that light, airy tone of voice that Harry knows means she's about to bolt from the room.

"Leigh Barrow is dead," says Erin, tone gentling as she shifts her attention back to Melanie. "She's never going to hurt you again."

"I don't remember her hurting me in the first place," admits Melanie. "She would come to see my father sometimes, and it always made me uncomfortable when she did, but she never touched me. I sometimes felt like she wanted to, but I'm pretty good at keeping my distance from adults I don't trust."

"Who was your father?" asks Roger.

"Dr. Roland Cosgrove," says Melanie. "He's probably really worried about me by now. We ran away when we were supposed to be going to a dance at our school, and I—I have a heart condition, I've never done anything like this before. He's probably afraid I've died and Harry's running because he doesn't know how to deal with my corpse, or something."

"Or he's the alchemist who made you, like I keep saying, and he's just mad that his pet science project got away," says Jack. "Your father's probably upset, but worried? No. He's not worried. You're not a daughter to him. You're a thing, and broken things get replaced."

"Cosgrove," says Erin, venomously. "I remember him. One of Reed's little sycophants, always talking about how if we could embody theoretical concepts like Chaos and Order or Hope or Honesty, we should be able to craft perfect vessels for the naturally occurring manifestations. Like the seasons. He shared a lot of his research with Reed, and Reed gave him the seeds all his work was built upon."

Harry and Melanie both stare at her for a moment, struck silent by the size of what she's saying. Melanie finds her voice first.

"I'm sorry," she says. "You know my father?"

"It's a long story, kid, but I did, once, before we stopped changing the world," says Erin. "You and I are probably built from the same seed stock, since Leigh also got her starting material from Reed. But she cultivated me on her own, grew me to contain Order and straight linear lines, and then let them kill my other half—my equivalent of your Summer, or Roger's Math—and left me alone in the world."

Roger and Dodger look uncomfortable at that. "I'm sorry," blurts Dodger. "We tried to push the numbers that far back, but we couldn't do it, not even by sacrificing other pieces. There was no winnable scenario without you, and you wouldn't join us if he was still alive, but we could have kept trying, we could have done more—"

"And I told you, the universe is not a *Mario Kart* game. You can't keep resetting it and trying again just because you don't like how things are playing out. Eventually you have to settle for the high score you have. You saved me. You saved Smita. You couldn't save everyone, and you knew that going in, and if I can forgive you for letting Darren die, you can shut the fuck up and forgive yourselves," says Erin, not unkindly. She keeps her unsettling eyes on Melanie. "Sorry. The terror twins think that just because they represent two of the foundational forces of creation, they get to take responsibility for absolutely everything that happens, ever, to anyone. It's *boring* and tedious and I wish they'd stop."

"But we *are* responsible for everything," says Roger, in a wounded tone.

"That attitude is why you're never going to get laid again," says Erin.

"Sure, it's the attitude, and not the twenty-four seven psychic connection to his sister," says Kim. "Every girl likes to get into bed with a guy who brings his sister along for the party. It turns us on."

Erin shakes her head. "See how it is around here? I'm completely outnumbered. Leigh made me to be one thing and one thing only, and when I stepped up and did it, she called the project a success and went on to doing other things, while they loosed me into the world to serve as Roger's handler. I kept him from manifesting for as long as I could, and when it wasn't possible anymore, I helped him get to the Impossible City and light the beacons to bring the Queen of Wands safely home. And if that doesn't make sense, don't worry about it. It will, if it needs to, and it won't, if it doesn't."

"We know Asphodel Baker was the alchemist who made James Reed," says Melanie, somewhat peevishly. "How does my father fit into this?"

"Alchemists can be born or they can be made. James Reed and Leigh Barrow were made, same as everyone in this room except for your boyfriend and your attendant," says Erin. "Your father was born. He was a normal, natural man who brushed up against the alchemical world and thought, 'Oooh, all that power, all that tyranny, and all I have to do is give up my qualms about taking other people apart for my own benefit? I'm in!' He and his wife were both acolytes of Reed's, when the Doctrine project was still active—before they knew for sure they had a success."

All four siblings look uncomfortable. Harry frowns. There's something here he hasn't quite made sense of yet, and he can't help feeling that once he does, he's going to be even less happy than he is right now.

"I told you that you were constructed to be the perfect vessel," says Jack, voice gentler than Harry's used to hearing from her. "It's why you keep sinking so deep into Winter, even though you don't have the crown yet."

"It means we're probably related," says Dodger. "Reed never met a single cell of Asphodel's that he didn't think deserved the chance to be recycled. He took his failures apart and reincorporated them into the rest of us. He built me and Roger, Kim and Tim, even Erin over there. And, since your parents were building off his research, supplied them with seed stock. Sort of literally."

"Well, that's horrible," says Melanie, with all the inflection she might use to say that something was a less-than-fabulous idea. "What if I'd been a failure?"

"You sort of were, since your mother went into labor when she did," said Jack. "You were supposed to grow up with your sister, each of you secure in your respective seasons."

Roger looks intrigued. Jack shakes her head.

"Later," she says. "I can't believe I'm blowing off the Doctrine of Ethos, but later."

"Just because you underpin the universe, that doesn't mean you get to know everything," says Dodger.

Roger's intrigued expression shifts to annoyance. "I'm aware," he mutters, petulant child in the body of a grown man, denied the one toy he desperately wants.

Harry can't allow himself to be distracted, not when Mel's still staring at Erin with rapt, if somewhat horrified, fascination. Dismayed, Mel asks, "So my father isn't my father? This James Reed asshole is?"

"'Asshole' may be the only title James Reed ever deserved, except for 'monster,' but we can't entirely blame him, any more than we can blame you for having cold hands, or me for alphabetizing the spice section every time we go to the grocery store," says Erin. "He was constructed too, put together by Asphodel herself, and half of what he did in his life was just a matter of following the instructions she left him with when she had to go away. I'm much more inclined to blame men like Roland Cosgrove, who had a choice in the matter. He didn't *have* to be an alchemist, or if he felt like he did—if he was one of those true believers who pursue alchemy because they view it as their duty to keep magic from leaving the world forever—he could still have done something else with his life."

"As if magic could *leave*," scoffs Kim. "It's so entangled in all the manifest vessels that it couldn't slip away if it wanted to. And it doesn't want to. Magic belongs here like everything else does, and it isn't going to subtract itself from the equation."

"Everything evolves. Magic used to be raw and flexible and everywhere, like water. But too many people drowned, and it's just aware enough to realize that if it turned itself into the monster in the castle on the hill, it *would* be burned out. So it became people who could do things that seemed impossible, but were just extensions of their natures within their specific, narrow spheres, and it became alchemists, who could change the world in bigger, more variable ways as long as they followed the rules. The difference between a forest fire and a candle is scale and control, not elemental nature."

"And my father was a candle."

"You're a candle," corrects Erin. "Your father was a little boy with a book of matches. Your mother had a book of matches, too. I remember when Reed and Leigh were discussing the project that made you. If it had succeeded without complication, they were going to use the two of you to force a coronation. The old Winter King wasn't tractable enough for them. He *wanted* things. He made *demands*. Reed wanted the universe made manifest and leashed to his hand."

Harry is suddenly very glad they keep talking about this Reed person in the past tense. If he were here, in the living flesh, Harry's not sure he could resist the urge to break the man's jaw. He's not usually a violent person, but it sounds like all their problems, or the greater measure of them, can be traced back to James Reed.

"Oh," says Melanie. "I don't think I would have liked that much."

"You wouldn't," says Tim. "They liked making people in pairs. That was something Reed learned from Asphodel. People should always have counterparts they care enough about to bleed for, because someone who has something to lose is someone you can control."

Kim leans over and takes his hand, not saying a word, and a little more of their story unfurls for Harry, horrible in its implications, impossible to contemplate with any comfort or ease.

"I also remember how Cosgrove's project went wrong," says Erin. "How's your sister?"

"Dead," says Melanie, not batting an eye. "Maybe you don't remember as much as you think you do."

"Or maybe there's things he never bothered to tell you. They were hoping to salvage *something* from the project, even if they couldn't have their perfectly balanced vessels. Roland and Ariadne were equal partners, according to Leigh; after Ariadne died, he couldn't try again without convincing another woman to be the mother of his children, and fortunately for the women of the world, incubating the vessels of the seasons when they were alchemically constructed for perfect balance meant drinking way too many foul draughts

and doing way too many ridiculous rituals for him to trap an innocent into helping him. There are plenty of female alchemists. Most
have the common sense to not offer their wombs as lab space. So if
he wanted to prove his theories, he had to work with what he had,
and what he had was one little girl the world knew about, who had
effectively and symbolically had a stake driven through her heart
while she was being born, and one little girl the world didn't know
about, who was legally dead and alchemically sustained."

Melanie blinks, eyes going wide and glassy. "My sister didn't
die?" she asks.

"Not unless it happened after I was turned out of the lab," says
Erin. "That was a while ago, and they were still debriefing your father following the death of his wife. I can't say for sure that the
other girl made it out of infancy. But they had plans for her. If she
lived, she was going to be the Summer Queen one day and balance
you in all possible ways."

"That's why it was so easy for you to go parallel," says Jack, sounding relieved, like some terrible mystery had just been resolved. "You
were primed. All the accounts of old coronations say that once two
candidates had joined forces, if one of them was lost before they
were so entangled that you couldn't kill one without losing them
both, the remaining candidate would parallel much more quickly.
They already knew what it was not to be alone."

"Is that also why she's so deeply sunk in the Winter already?"
asks Harry. He wants to grab Melanie and run, wants to tell these
strange, serious people with their devotion to a cosmology he isn't
sure he'll ever fully understand that he's good, thanks, he doesn't
need their specific brand of crazy. But he can't. He's seen too much
to dismiss the things they say as simple delusions: he knows this is
all happening, whether he likes it or not.

And he's not sure Mel would come with him if he tried. The wild
story they're spinning involves her parents, both of them, the father
she ran from and the mother she never met and has hence always
idolized; worse, it involves the twin sister he's always felt like he was
competing against in a small, invisible way, the girl who would have

been Melanie's preordained best friend and confidante, who would have been there for her through everything, always, if she hadn't died at birth. Now Erin says she *didn't* die, and she might still be out there, and if she is, she's also going to be competing to seize the Summer.

He hopes Mel hasn't already made the connection he has, the one that reminds him that only one candidate can seize the season, while the others have to either renounce the crown or die. And he can't renounce right now without killing Mel.

If she were running in parallel with her sister, it might be possible for him to step aside, but since everything else in this wild, self-contradictory world they've gotten themselves sucked into seems to end with death, he has trouble believing that he'd be allowed to simply step aside, even if he wanted to. And he doesn't entirely want to. Does he want to be the Summer King? Well, he can't say that with any certainty. It sounds like a lot, and not the kind of "a lot" where he still gets to go to college, and play football, and take over the family business. His future has always had two absolute landmarks that he can't imagine going without: Melanie, and Castleview. He's been trying to come to terms with the idea of losing the first for years. Now he may get to keep her, but it will mean losing the second.

Getting what you want is hard and surprisingly horrible, and that means that running when it's all he wants to do probably wouldn't work out that well for him.

A hand touches his shoulder. The freezing-slush sensation that accompanies the contact means he's not all that surprised when he looks around and finds that it's Jack, her hand on his shoulder, taller than him while he's sitting down and she's not. The look on her face is sympathetic enough to be jarring.

"Hey," she says. "I think this is going to take a while, and I can see that Mel has about a million questions. You want to go outside with me for a few minutes, catch your breath?"

He starts to protest, then catches himself and stands, looking to

Erin for the answer to his last question. She meets his eyes unflinchingly.

"I don't think you could stop her from sinking if you tied her ankles to the clouds," she says, and that's surprisingly poetic, and not surprising in the slightest. It just confirms what he already knows. Melanie was built to hold the Winter, and he wasn't built to do the same for Summer. She's going to keep sinking. She's going to go deeper and deeper, until there's nothing left of the girl he loves but her face.

If her face was all he wanted, he could go and find someone who looks like her. With the kind of money he'll inherit when his parents die and his trust funds mature, he could *pay* a woman to look like her.

He's already lost her.

"Okay," he says to Jack, and stands, and lets her lead him out of the house, away from the alchemical madness unfolding behind him, back into the sunlight.

M elanie watches Harry leave, hand in hand with her attendant, and wishes she could muster the enthusiasm to go after him. She's exhausted. She's overwhelmed. She needs to understand what Erin's trying to tell her; she suddenly feels, in a very real and concrete way, as if her life depends on it.

"All right," she says. "Laying this out in a straight line, my parents were alchemists who worked for Dr. James Reed. They wanted to create the perfect vessels for the Summer and Winter, and some things went wrong, resulting in me having a heart condition and my sister being presumed dead. She wasn't, and my father has been raising her in secret this whole time, letting me think I was an only child with a genetic condition because . . . why, exactly? And does the fact that my sister isn't dead have anything to do with Harry's attendant not showing up?"

"It could," says Erin. "Your sister, if she's still alive—and I don't know one way or the other, at this point, just that she *was* alive when your father took you home from the hospital and came to make his report to Reed and Leigh—was crafted to be the perfect vessel for the Summer, like you were the perfect vessel for the Winter. With her around, it's entirely possible that any Corn Jenny close enough to come and attend on him would be attracted to her instead."

"Jack said Jack Frosts who tried to get to me had been disappearing for years before she managed to get into my room," says Melanie.

"That makes sense. The last thing an alchemist wants is for their subjects to know too much. Subjects who know things tend to have ideas about them and want them to be handled in the right way, and maybe don't want to be participants in a human sacrifice, or kill people when they don't think they have to, or any of the other things that can be required in order to manifest." Erin shrugs. "Even when there's no guarantee a coronation is ever going to arrive, you're supposed to have at least a little understanding of what you are. What you could potentially become. If your father was stopping the Jacks from getting to you, he could also have been stopping the Jennys from getting to her. And that would mean they weren't around to come to your boyfriend."

"So Harry winds up dropped in this without even a mouthy sidekick to hold his hand and make sure he understands what's going on."

"Yeah," says Erin. "I know this is a lot, and I'm sure your Jack has been doing her best to help you understand it all, but she does it from within the system, and we're outside the system. It has to make things easier."

"I can't take any more of this," says Tim, and walks abruptly out of the room. Kim hesitates, looking torn, before she chases after her brother.

Someone still has the strength to follow the people they love, Melanie thinks distantly, although she assumes the relationship between siblings is stronger than the relationship between high school sweethearts. That's probably what her father's been banking on. All of his attempts to get her and Harry to open a little space between them are taking on a new light, seeming less like the actions of a protective father trying to keep his only daughter from being hurt, more like the actions of a scientist trying to remove an unexpected complication from his experimental field.

He must have been so horrified when she came home from pre-school with the number of another potential Summer written in crayon on her construction paper homework folder. She still has that folder, tucked into the box of keepsakes under her bed. Or she did, before she grabbed what she could carry and ran away from home forever. She supposes she can't really say she still has any of the things she left behind. Maybe that should feel freeing.

It doesn't. It feels terrifying, like everything else about this day. Everything else since the motel, when this transformed from a fun if somewhat strange road trip into a journey through hell. There's blood on her hands, and on Harry's, and she doesn't know what she's becoming anymore, only that when she thought that man was going to kill her, the cold had risen up like a great tide and pulled her under, and she'd watched everything that happened between there and the rest stop where Harry and Jack had pulled her back into herself through a thick, distorting wall of ice, unable to break through, unable to tell them she was still trapped inside.

Is that inevitable now? Is she going to freeze no matter what she does? She doesn't want to die, but she's not sure there's any real differ-ence, if living and taking the Winter crown leaves her in that distant, frozen place, where she can see the people she loves as they suffer, but can't reach for them, can't go to them, can't *be* there for them.

Melanie looks levelly at Erin. "I have to take the crown or I'm going to die," she says.

"Yes," says Erin. "Technically, you died when you were born, but the Winter has been animating you as a sort of backup in case some-thing happened to the Winter King. Well, something happened—from what I hear, 'something' was a massive heart attack—and he's out of the picture now, and Winter needs you. So it's keeping you going. You're the best available candidate."

"Coronations are bloody, right?" asks Roger. "That's what I've been able to gather from the books that actually go into it. There aren't many of them. If you claim the crown, you'll be the first alchemical creation to do so. Alchemists aren't all that interested, by and large, in things they can't control. Once they figured out that they couldn't seize the crowns from the Incarnates no matter how hard they tried, they stopped really bothering with you people."

"That's a nice way of putting it," says Melanie hotly. "You always this politic?"

"He's the living manifestation of Language, and he still manages to stick his foot in it on a surprisingly regular basis," says Dodger. "Like a puppy that never finished obedience school."

"I will leave you speaking Mandarin for a month," threatens Roger genially.

"Do you enjoy having friction?" asks Dodger. "Just checking, since it really sounds like what you're saying is 'wah wah, smarter, prettier, all-around better sister, I'm tired of the laws of physics being willing to speak to me.'"

"Children," says Erin, weary and warning at the same time. To Melanie, she says, "This is my punishment for working with the alchemists as long as I did. I was a trained lab animal, but it still took me a long time to bite the hand that fed me. And my reward is these two, who think they're funny." She casts a thin smile at Roger and Dodger. "They're not funny."

"Come on, now," says Roger. "Your reward was us rewinding time over and over again until we managed to orchestrate a situation where you survived the fall of Reed's lab and you got to be free."

"Uh-huh," says Erin, and turns back to Melanie. "You can answer his question."

"Um," says Melanie. "Jack says they don't have to be. The last North American coronation was three hundred years ago, and it was a bloody one, but people can turn the crown aside. They don't have to take it, and that means they can opt out. Everyone but me. If I opt out, the Winter leaves me, and the shock of the coronation starting kills me."

"Dead girl walking," says Dodger, approvingly. "Nice."

"Do you think you can fight your way to the finish line?" asks Roger. "Are you playing to win?"

Melanie thinks of the frozen place, how much she hates it there in the deep, unbreachable cold. And she thinks of Harry, how much she loves him, how much she'd do to stay with him.

"I don't have a choice," she says.

Strawberry Summer

CALENDAR SEASON: FEBRUARY 14TH, 2017: WINTER, WANING WORM MOON.

It's still summer in the garden.

Harry can feel it as soon as he steps onto the porch, even without going down the stairs. Jack feels it too; she looks distinctly uncomfortable, and when he steps onto the stairs, she doesn't follow, but hangs back in the shadow of the eaves, where it's as close as this space gets to the actual season at play in the world outside this ridiculous, topsy-turvy place.

"Sorry," she says. "If you go down there, I can't go with you. But you should go down, if it helps you feel better. This is a lot for me, and for Mel, and it's happening during our half of the year. I can't imagine trying to swallow all this shit if it had started up during the spring."

"I'm good here," says Harry, and sits. The strawberry plant that sprouted between the bricks of the path when he became enraptured by the summer has continued to spread, now obliterating half the walkway. It's putting out fruit, red and ripe and luscious in the sunlight, and he knows that if he went down there to harvest it, it would be the most delicious thing he's ever tasted.

He did that. Him. He may not have frozen a man to death in a cruddy motel bathroom, but he changed the world to the tune of calling strawberries out of nothingness and bringing a little more life into being. Because he's going to wear the Summer crown, or he's going to die.

The weight of it all is too much for him to carry. He bends forward, putting his hands over his face, and shakes. Not for long; just a few seconds, just long enough to shudder out some of the terror, some of the pressing conviction that the sky is going to fall. He doesn't cry. He almost wants to, but he's not quite there yet. He will be, soon enough, he's sure.

When he sits up again and turns to look at Jack, she's been joined by the kids from Starbucks, Tim's mouth tight and pinched and his eyes grave behind his glasses, Kim watching him with concern. Tim walks over and flops himself down next to Harry, waving a hand vaguely at the yard, the street, the horizon.

"This was all going to be ours," he says. "Only two of the cuckoos from the generation before ours were still around, and they were inherently flawed, they couldn't stay together for more than a few hours without trying to kill each other, and the Math cuckoo had already tried to kill *herself* when she didn't have Language as a target, and we were going to inherit it all. Our father told us so."

"Your father . . . ?"

"James Reed," says Kim. "I know that . . . I know Erin didn't have good experiences with him, but Roger and Dodger never really knew him as a person, not like we did. He was our dad. He made us, and he took care of us, and he would bring us the most magical things when he traveled. He was good to us."

"And then the damn flawed cuckoos figured out how to get along," says Tim. "They started to manifest. They started to yank the Doctrine to themselves, and they didn't leave any for us. They talk to each other, you know. They're inside each other's heads all the time. They don't always remember to talk out loud when we don't have company. So you'll be reaching for the rolls at the dinner table and Roger will suddenly hand them to Dodger, and look confused when you object. Or you'll all be doing homework, and they'll both start laughing like they've just heard the funniest joke in the world. They never have to be alone. They don't understand how lucky they are."

"It was that way for us, before they seized the Doctrine," says Kim. "We each knew what the other was thinking. It wasn't creepy, or weird—at least not to us. It was how the world is supposed to be. Your best friend is inside your head, and you never have to be alone."

"Can't they . . . I don't know, can't they give you a little piece of this Doctrine thing, so it turns back on?" asks Harry. "Like Jack doesn't hold *the* Winter, but she has a little piece of Winter inside her, and that's what makes her Jack Frost."

"No, because our system isn't natural the way yours is," says Kim. "I don't know if we'd get the Doctrine if something happened to Roger and Dodger. I don't even know if something *can* happen to Roger and Dodger. They're more the sort of people that happen to things than the sort that things happen to."

"Things are afraid to happen to them," says Tim. "So we get to be a part of this fucked-up alchemical world, and we're monsters just like all the people we live with, unnatural and unnecessary, but we don't even get the cool superpowers to go with it. Not unless we become alchemists."

"And alchemists tend to make things worse," says Kim. "I mean, you can't honestly listen to all that talk about Melanie's dad and think he didn't make things worse. But maybe he also loved her. Maybe he took care of her instead of scrapping the project and doing something else because when he met his daughter, he loved her. Like our father loved us."

Harry, who knows his current opinions about James Reed are based entirely off the word of people he has no more reason to trust than he does Kim and Tim, nods a little. "So you regret it, then?" he asks. "You wanted to be a part of the alchemical world, and talk in each other's heads, and never be alone again?"

"It's what we were raised to be," says Kim. "Of course we regret it. You can't create someone to be a monster, raise them to be a monster, and then turn around one day and tell them they have to be mortal and expect them to be okay with it. We regret it and we resent it and we should probably hate Roger and Dodger for taking the Doctrine away from us. We were so close to claiming it when they managed to manifest! And they . . . well, they try not to think about it more than they have to. Sometimes I think Dodger actually forgets where we came from, and thinks we came with the house. 'Six bedrooms, three baths, two teens.'"

"We know our father wasn't a good man," says Tim. "He was willing to use us to manipulate each other, and he put us in the line of fire when he didn't have to. He could have moved us to a safe house as soon as he knew the manifest Doctrine was coming, and instead, he set things up to transfer it from its current hosts into us, which meant we had to be on location. He wasn't a good man, and he wasn't a kind man, and he wasn't a generous man. But he still loved us. He did things for us that he didn't have to do. He remembered our birthday, he remembered the name of the woman who'd incubated us, he made sure we were as happy as we could be, in his underground lab where we never saw the sun."

Harry isn't sure that sounds like love. It sounds, in some ways, like a more extreme version of the not-quite-love he'd watched Melanie receive from her father, who sometimes seemed to think raising a daughter with a heart condition and raising a rare orchid were the same thing, like he could solve all of their problems if he just built her a big-enough greenhouse. So he doesn't say anything, just listens.

"The seasons are more generous," says Jack. "They happen all over the world, and so they spread themselves around. Ascendants like me, we don't get enough to force our seasons to happen out of turn. You'll never meet a Corn Jenny who can grow strawberries without seed cuttings, or a Jack Frost who can freeze a car engine solid. But we carry our seasons in our hearts, and they keep us connected to the rest of the web. It's why we can find our candidates. There's not a potential Winter or Summer for every one of us, but we don't fight for them. The candidates are more selfish, because there's only one crown per continent for each season. So they have to eliminate the competition."

"It wasn't always killing, though, right?" asks Kim. "When Dodger came downstairs and announced that a coronation had started, so we might have weirdoes showing up on our doorstep demanding we help them find their missing crowns, she said we shouldn't let them in if that happened, but shut the door and go find an adult." Her lip curls at the end, making it clear what she thinks of that particular piece of advice.

"No," says Jack. "It wasn't always killing. The last Winter King of North America set that tone during his own coronation, when he started killing his opponents, even after they'd renounced their crowns. He thought he had a right to claim the continent, because he was white and most of them weren't."

"Three hundred years ago," says Harry, suddenly disgusted. He looks at his own hands, white-skinned and strong, and scowls. "Colonialist fuck."

"He was," Jack agrees. "It's not your fault where you were born, as long as you try not to be an asshole about it. He, on the other hand, had choices, and all the choices he made were bad ones, and now the shape of a North American coronation looks a lot like a European one. Lots of blood on the barley. Lots of blood on the snow. Lots of bodies to step over on the way to ascending the throne."

"You know, you keep using all this monarchist terminology, but I don't think you've ever explained what it *means*," snaps Harry. "Get better words or provide definitions for the ones you have."

"Until you fell deep enough that you stopped denying any of this was real, it didn't matter what words I used," says Jack. "The crowns are real. They're material objects, and they're kept at the end of a labyrinth made by all four seasons coming together. That's part of why the attendants matter. We craft and keep the labyrinth, and make sure it's always ready, because we don't always know when a coronation will be called. The current one is somewhere in the American South, I think, although I'm not sure exactly where—it would be cheating if I did. The attendants who maintain the labyrinth after it comes together are ones who stand for spring and fall. They don't have any candidates of their own, so they don't have anything to gain by cheating. If we can find the labyrinth, you can enter, both of you together. You can start along the scarecrow trail and make for the Impossible City."

"And that's where your entanglement—what Jack keeps calling 'running parallel'—will work *for* you, instead of working vaguely against you," says Erin, who emerged from the house while Jack was speaking and is now leaning up against the doorframe, arms folded, watching them. "Entanglement means you both fall deeper into your seasons faster, and once you go too deep, you'll forget how to be like normal people. That's what's going on with Roger and Dodger. So much of them is taken up with hosting the Doctrine that there isn't much room left for being ordinary. If you lose your humanity before you reach the labyrinth, you won't be able to stand the sight of each other, and you certainly won't be able to work together long enough to navigate it and claim the crowns. You'll have lost by moving too fast. You still seem pretty human. You're keeping your girlfriend from going under. Eventually she'll start weighing you down, if she keeps dropping the way she has been."

"I don't care," says Harry. "She's my Mel and I love her and I'll keep her from going too deep if it kills me."

"It might," says Erin.

"I still don't care," says Harry, and he means it, completely and utterly and down to the base of his bones.

People keep telling him his love for Mel only seems like the sun because he doesn't have anything to compare it to; that eventually, he'll be able to see it for the candle it truly is, because it will be set against all the other candles he's lit in his lifetime. Maybe they're right and maybe they're wrong, because right now, he's seventeen years old and his love for her *is* the sun, bright and burning and utterly all-consuming, and she loves him the same way, he knows she does, and all he has to do is keep her from freezing so completely that she forgets.

All he has to do is anchor her, the way he always has, the way she's always anchored him.

Erin looks at him carefully, and after a moment, she shakes her head. "I really think you mean that," she says, and turns to Jack. "Keep him alive if you can. I know he's not your problem, or at least not your responsibility, but we've had shitty monarchs for a long time, and that introduces chaos into the system that I don't like. I want this one on the throne."

"Not up to me, but I'll get him to the labyrinth if I can," says Jack. "I can't choose him over Melanie, but as long as they're not in conflict, I'll keep helping him."

"That's all I can really ask," says Erin.

"Labyrinth," says Harry. "Please. There's so much that every time you start telling me what I need to know, you get sidetracked and stop actually answering my questions. What is the labyrinth, and why does running parallel help us there?"

"Right now, it's a solo game," says Jack. "You and Mel aren't in competition with each other, since you're vying for different crowns, which means you can cooperate, but you're in competition with every other candidate for the Summer crown, and yeah, I like you, you've got a good reason to want to be coronated, but they all have stories of their own. There's not another Mel out there, thankfully—as far as I know, Cosgrove was the only alchemist actively seeking to steal the seasons—"

She pauses there and glances to Erin, waiting until the other girl nods before she sighs in relief and keeps going.

"—but there could be Summer candidates with sob stories that would break your heart. You have to beat them. You don't have to kill them if you can get them to renounce, but whenever you meet one of them, you have to walk away the winner, or this is all for nothing. This isn't a game. It's a competition, but it isn't a game."

"I already killed someone," says Harry softly, and looks down at his hands. Is that a fleck of blood beneath his thumbnail? He knows it can't be, knows he's washed his hands too many times since then for it to be blood, but . . . *is* it? It's impossible for him to say. So he takes a deep breath, not looking at Tim or Kim—as people his own age, their condemnation will hurt more than Erin's or Jack's. "I didn't do it with the Summer. I did it with my hands. He was trying to hurt me or make me renounce, and I killed him."

"And no one's come to arrest you for it, even though I bet you made plenty of noise, huh?"

Harry's head snaps up, eyes locking on Erin in a silent plea for her to explain. She shrugs.

"The alchemical world is all around us, just like the magical world was before things shifted. It protects itself. Not completely, but surprisingly well. If someone comes to drop a package on our porch, they'll notice we have a bunch of flowers and vegetables that shouldn't be doing this well out of season. They'll see that we're not entirely bound to the casual flow of time. And then, when they leave, they'll forget. Unless their shell is already cracked a little, they'll forget. If they come back too often, the forgetting will start to take longer, and eventually they'll start to remember, and we'll have to deal with that."

"Our regular deliveryman comes to pick peaches from the tree Dodger has in the backyard," says Kim. "It's always August for the tree, and somehow that doesn't make it stop flowering, just means it fruits year-round."

"Eventually he'll start asking questions," says Tim. "He'll start wondering about the tree, how it can do that, how any of this can be possible, and once that happens, either he'll figure out what alchemy is—or sorcery, I guess, since that's like, proto-alchemy, it's easier—or he'll fall apart and we'll get a new deliveryperson."

"How can you sound so calm about that?" asks Harry. "You're talking about people not being able to see the world around them."

"Right now, it's keeping you from being arrested for murder, so maybe you could have a go at being chill about it, huh?" says Jack. She shrugs. "They don't see alchemical things because they don't want to get sucked into alchemical things. We inhabit the uncanny valley. We look human, almost, most of the time, and we're just enough wrong that we can't be trusted, can't be interacted with, can't be turned away from. The cops aren't coming because the coronation is covering up any sign that you were the one in that motel. It's weird and it's impossible and it shouldn't work, and you need to just accept it, because even if you don't, it's still happening. The more you accept, the easier everything else gets."

"And it's not like refusing to accept changes anything," says Kim, and flounces down the stairs, high-stepping like a cheerleader, a physical tic Harry knows all too well from the time he's spent with Melanie, to the patch of strawberries on the path. She crouches, filling her hands with ripe red fruit, before she comes prancing back. She offers her hands, full of fruit, to Harry. "Here," she says, not ungently.

Harry takes a strawberry. "I know this is all happening," he says. "I figured that out when a dude tried to kill me so he could be the Lord of the Summer, and my girlfriend started making snowstorms for fun. It's real. It's too *stupid* not to be real."

"Summer King, please," says Jack. "The Lord of the Summer is something altogether different and not important to what's happening here and now, so we're all going to forget you said His name."

Harry blinks at her. But the implacability in her expression is unmistakable, and he can tell he won't get anywhere by pushing, and so he doesn't. After a moment of silence, Jack starts to speak again.

"When you reach the labyrinth, everything changes," she says. "It's not a solo adventure anymore. All the candidates who haven't found someone to run parallel with will be frantic to pair up before they go in, and that's when you'll be in the most danger, because they'll try to steal Melanie from you. They can form gangs as the labyrinth looms, packs of hunting wolves whose only goal is to catch a potential Winter for themselves. They can't force a Winter to parallel them, but they can kill you and hope she chooses one of them."

"Why? Is it like some sort of weird murder maze?"

"I don't know."

Harry stares at her for several long, uncomfortable seconds before Jack looks away and continues.

"No one knows anymore. It's been too long since we had a coronation, and the labyrinth is different every time. We just know candidates go in in pairs, and only one pair comes out."

"So why do we have to fight at all?" demands Harry. "If the labyrinth chooses, we should all just be able to go there and let it do its job, not waste all this time killing each other."

"Once you enter the labyrinth, you can't renounce anymore," says Jack. "You're in it until the end. And every candidate who enters lowers your chances. Maybe they're better suited than you are. Maybe the season has managed to sink a little bit deeper into their soul. Maybe, maybe, maybe. And then it doesn't matter, because you're running for that finish line along with everyone else in contention for your crown, and whatever happens there is a mystery to me, but I've always thought it has to be fairly horrible. Only the truly serious enter the labyrinth. And most of them die there."

"So we could all—"

"Entering the labyrinth is a death sentence if you don't win, and the more people you allow to go in with you, the lower your chances become of getting to the finish first," says Jack. "You fight the other candidates to keep them from having a chance to beat you, and because every candidate who chooses to compete does so believing they can win, yeah, most of them will have to die. Some at your hand. You didn't get much of a choice, thanks to Cosgrove fucking with the natural order of things. You refuse, you die."

"But I'm a natural person," says Harry. "You said only Melanie was made by alchemy, and I was just born this way. I won some sort of weird cosmic lottery, and the prize is the chance to die horribly and turn into the Heat Miser from those old Christmas specials."

"You're a natural person running parallel to an unnatural person," says Erin. "If you refuse your claim to the crown, if I'm understanding this all correctly, then the fact that you're tied to her, and she *can't* refuse and survive, means you'll die like any Summer King who lost his Winter."

"You died when the coronation started," says Jack. "I know it's easy to forget that when you feel fine, but it still happened. If you lose your connection to the Summer, you lose your connection to Melanie. If you lose your connection to Melanie, you lose your connection to the alchemy that's keeping you alive."

"Why do I have any more right to live than the rest of the candidates?" asks Harry.

"You don't," says Tim. Harry looks at him, feeling obscurely wounded, like he expected a boy his own age to have an argument for why he, in specific, was special enough to deserve to keep existing when other people didn't get the same chance. "I guess the question is whether you think Melanie has more of a right to live than the rest of the candidates. Because she's not the one out here melting down because she doesn't want to kill people. She'll keep fighting as long as she has to. Only she'll do it while she's sinking deeper and deeper into the Winter, and maybe if she doesn't have you to hold on to, she goes all the way under, and we lose her. Or maybe when you drop dead because you think it's the right thing to do, she snaps and stops even trying to stay human, and we lose her. So it's not a question of your right to live. It's a question of hers. I know she's not your sister, but I'd throw myself in front of a train to save Kimberley. And if there was something I could do to not only save her but restore her connection to the Doctrine, I wouldn't hesitate. Not for a second. Not even if I knew I wouldn't survive." He turns then, looking gravely at Kim. "Not for a second."

She takes his hand, leaning toward him until their foreheads touch, like she thinks she can somehow still push her thoughts into his if she just tries hard enough, and everything is silence, and the sweet smell of summer strawberries, impossibly stolen from their season.

Departure

CALENDAR SEASON: FEBRUARY 14TH, 2017: WIN-
TER, WANING WORM MOON.

"The labyrinth runs along the border of real time and alchemical time," says Jack, when the silence frays and falls away, allowing the sound of the street outside the garden to return. "I guess you people would call it the boundary of the Impossible City, since you're acolytes of Asphodel's and all."

"I'd say Asphodel could rot, except that's either already happened or utterly impossible, depending on which story you believe, so I'll settle for 'fuck Asphodel Baker' and let you keep going," says Erin.

"That's part of why it moves," says Jack. "The Impossible City moves."

"The Impossible City isn't real," says Harry. "It's a story from a children's book. I'm not Avery, and Melanie's not Zib, and we're not walking the impossible road."

"You're right about two of those things," says Jack. "The books were written about two children because almost all manifestations, alchemical or natural, come in pairs; they balance each other. People like me and Erin, we're out of true with our own natures, off-balance because our other half isn't here. Remember how, in the books, any time something happened to Zib, all Avery could focus on was helping her, even when they weren't getting along? And the same for Zib, when something happened to Avery?"

"Yeah," says Harry dubiously.

"Baker wrote the alchemical journey through the four humors of the magical and natural world. Earth, water, air, and fire. Baker mapped them, and then Baum reversed them, and now the whole continent's in a state of constant flux, because people don't know where they are." Erin leans over and steals a strawberry. "So the Impossible City moves, trying to stay true to a map that doesn't stay true to itself, and it sounds like the Seasonal Attendants build their labyrinth on the borders."

"Like bowerbirds," says Jack. "Throwing up our nests where we think they'll be safe until we can use them. Every year, a new labyrinth is constructed, and every year it's torn down, unless a coronation is called. So this year, the labyrinth gets used. And since the Doctrine has embodied, the countries aren't shifting as much, and that makes the South a nice, sold, stable bastion of Air. Air favors Winter, so Melanie will have an easier time making the passage than you will. Sorry about that. If I'd been on the planning committee, I would have asked for Earth or Fire, to give you a little more of an advantage."

"Mel's your candidate," objects Harry.

"Mel's my candidate, and Mel's halfway to being made of snow," says Jack. "She doesn't need any more advantages than her father already blended into her bones."

The front door opens. Dodger appears, looking a little shamefaced, Melanie close behind her. "Roger's making you some sandwiches and there's Rice Krispies treats from last night," she says. "They should still be good."

"You're feeding us lunch?" asks Harry.

"We're throwing you out," says Dodger. "Hey, attendant girl, is it cheating if I give them a map?"

"Not at all," says Jack. "The rules allow for alliances and advantages, as long as you find them during your journey."

"Good. Then we're throwing you out with lunch and a map, but Roger says you can't stay here any longer, and he'd know."

"What, did he stick his head out the window and ask the clouds where they wanted the seasons to go?" asks Erin sarcastically. Dodger doesn't meet her eyes. She sighs heavily. "You know I can't take you people seriously when you pull shit like this. Speaking ev-

ery language there is shouldn't mean having conversations with the
sky."

"Sometimes it does," says Tim. Erin looks at him and sighs.

"All right," she said. "Sometimes it does. But it's still stupid and
I don't have to like it and don't you have homework you could be
doing?"

"You need to head for the labyrinth," says Dodger. "The candidates
are starting to migrate in that direction, and there's not currently
another potential challenger for the crowns within a hundred miles
of here. But there will be soon, and you're not ready to face them,
and that's all I know. So you need to take the sandwiches and the
snacks and get on the road. If you win, come back and tell us all
about it."

"And if we don't?" asks Harry, standing. Kim tips the rest of the
strawberries into his hands, like an apology, or an offering.

"If you don't, I'm betting your Jack will make sure that whoever
does win comes back and tells us all about it, since you don't leave
the closest thing you're going to find to literal earthbound gods in
the dark if you have any choice in the matter," says Dodger. "Come
inside. Get your sandwiches."

Harry starts to rise as the others head for the door. Melanie grabs
his arm, keeping him where he is.

"Wait," she says, voice soft.

Harry pauses. So does Jack, until Melanie looks at her, shakes her
head, and says, "Go."

Jack goes, and for the first time since the motel, Harry and Melanie
are alone.

A dreadful thought strikes him. "How much of that did you
hear?" he asks.

"Not much. We weren't eavesdropping in there. We were talking
about the alchemical world, and how it bulldozes everything, and
what my parents made me for. Harry, I'm sorry." She lets go of his
arm. "I'm so, so sorry. You were dragged into this because of me."

"Not true." He wants to agree with her, on some level, to point
out that his Corn Jenny never came; if not for her, he could be safe at

home in Portland, staying well clear of the coronation, with no idea what was coming. He'd be easy prey for the first Summer candidate to stumble through the city, and he wouldn't even know he was supposed to defend himself. Once the coronation started, safety was never an option, not for him.

But he doesn't know how to articulate all that, so he just looks at her, his Melanie, and feels like he's in the presence of a miracle. She's still pale—she's always pale, and it makes a little more sense now that he knows she was designed that way, this isn't just genetics combining at random to make someone out of a fairy tale—but there's color in her cheeks, and her breathing is smooth and easy, and her eyes are bright, gaze focused. She's not floundering in a sea of hypoxia and medication, she's *here,* with him, utterly and completely here. It's glorious. It's impossible.

It's worth it. Whatever they've done, whatever they still have to do, it's worth it to see her this way, to have her back with him. Even six months apart every year will be worth it—and as Jack says, when she's trying to ease the sting, they'll each only be aware of three of those months. It's a small enough price to pay.

It is. It truly is.

"If my father hadn't—"

"Mel." He seizes her hands. "Being on the yearbook committee doesn't make you responsible for the world. If it did, the world would be better, because you'd make it better. Your parents did horrible things, and they did them without your knowledge or consent. But they didn't make me fall in love with you. They didn't put us in the same place. I'm pretty sure your dad would have been happier if we'd never met. He never liked me spending time with you, he never wanted us to be together, he never quite hit that cliché of 'protective father offers daughter's boyfriend money to break up with her,' but I honestly think that was because my folks have so much more money than him that he figured it wouldn't work. There's Summer in my bones because it was born there. I'm season-stuck because that's how I was made. And if that made it easier to fall in love with you as completely as I did, I'm grateful for it. If we lived in another world, one where we weren't born from seasons, one where we were just ordinary people living ordinary lives, I'd find you anyway. I'd choose you anyway. Over and over again, forever. Don't apologize. Not for being my girl. Not for letting me be your boy. Okay?"

Melanie blinks several times, unshed tears clinging to long black eyelashes, before she pulls her hands from his, makes a small choking noise, and throws her arms around his neck, pulling him close to her while she presses her face into the curvature of his shoulder and sobs. She was terrified, he realizes, afraid learning she was some sort of smug fuck's science project would be the final straw and he'd say "Screw all this" and walk away. He should probably be hurt that she'd think he could do that. Instead, he's just relieved she came to him and didn't let the worry turn slick and septic between them, poisoning everything it touched.

The front door opens. Dodger reappears, a peevish look on her sharp-featured face. "Well?" she asks. "Were you going to come get lunch? Smita should be home soon, and once she gets here, we're going to have a lot more trouble explaining what the hell's going on. She knows about alchemy. She's on the border of becoming an alchemist in her own right. She isn't going to sit quietly while we talk alchemical concepts she hasn't encountered yet, and we're going to wind up needing to explain absolutely everything again, and she'll probably want bone marrow samples from your ice princess here."

"Let's go," says Mel hurriedly, wiping her tears away as she pulls her face from Harry's neck. She's smiling as she turns to face Dodger, a practiced reflex honed by years of cheerleading and being "the sick girl" who needed to seem upbeat at all times if she wanted to be included in anything.

Melanie follows Dodger into the house, and Harry follows Melanie, and somehow that order matters; it matters that Summer is following Winter, while Winter is following Time.

Laughter and chatter lead them to the kitchen, where the others have gathered, assembling truly ridiculous sandwiches in a sort of disassembled assembly line. Tim has several loaves of bread and a whole counter of condiments; Kim calls out what should go on each sandwich, and he applies the desired spreads, no matter how horri-fying the combination. Erin has sacks of pre-sliced lunch meat and cheese, which she doles out at Kim's request, while Jack has some-how taken over the salad station, providing leaves of lettuce, slices of tomato, and more esoteric toppings, like bean sprouts, or straw-berries, or pickled artichoke hearts. Roger is at the table, accepting sandwiches and wrapping them in foil before adding them either to a pile or a bag, depending on whether they're being set aside for the occupants of the house or sent on the impending road trip.

Harry stops to stare. Mel does much the same. It's like a Subway gone feral, sinking its teeth into everything around it as it manifests itself in the world. Dodger pauses next to them, smirking. "Any preferences?" she asks. "It's good to be clear. I told Kim to surprise me once, and wound up with peanut butter, gooseberry jam, ba-nana, bacon, onion, and curry powder. We have just about anything you could want on a sandwich, but precision is key."

"The sandwich is the perfect food," says Roger. "No matter what you put together, you wind up with a meal at the end. The inevita-bility of the sandwich fixes everything."

"Asshole," says Dodger, with perfect fondness.

"Um, roast beef, cheddar, and tomato," says Harry.

"Are those squash blossoms?" asks Melanie. When Jack nods, she says, "Chicken, rosehip jam, honey, and squash blossoms."

Everyone looks at her funny except for Harry, who's had a life-time to get used to her weird thing about edible flowers. He just smiles as she moves across the kitchen to supervise and assist in the construction of their lunches.

"This is really nice of you," he says, to Dodger.

"It's the least we could do," she replies. "I mean, this is all sort of our fault."

"That was the last question I wanted to ask," he says. "You people talk like academics on meth—one topic into the next topic into the next, and if we're lucky, you remember you never finished the first topic before we all forget what you were saying. I think you do it on purpose, at least some of the time."

Roger is listening now too, shoulders tense, head canted ever so slightly to the side.

Dodger shrugs. "Maybe we do. I mean, Roger and I are both academics. He teaches at the university, I mostly do research and short projects for think tanks. Erin's a social worker."

She rattles off their professions like a small child might explain what her Barbies do all day while she's at school. Harry can't believe any of the three of them has actually done a day of work in a long time, if they ever have. And that's okay. He's not here to judge these strange, impossible people. He just wants to understand them, a little, maybe, if he can.

"I just don't quite get some of the things you say."

"I mean, we *are* forces of the universe, and you're more of a force of the world in training," says Dodger. "No summers on Mars. You'd be powerless there. But there *is* math on Mars, so I do just fine."

"Please don't tell me you people hang out on Mars for fun, I don't think I could handle it right now."

"Okay," says Dodger, and goes quiet for a few seconds. Harry lets them stretch like taffy, broken by the sounds of the sandwich makers asking each other for toppings, or the rustle of Roger's foil, or the clank of knives against jars. He gets the feeling silence is something Dodger doesn't handle well, and if he just lets it linger, she'll tell him what he wants to know.

He's not wrong. "What do you want to know?" she asks.

"What did Erin mean, when she said sometimes you have to settle for the high score you have?"

Dodger sighs, heavily, and walks over to take the foil from Roger, who turns smoothly to face Harry. Neither of them says a word as this exchange takes place, although Roger reaches out to squeeze Dodger's shoulder, leaving his hand there as he starts to talk.

"We're like Melanie. We're artificial. Everyone who lives here is artificial, except Smita, and she's not a manifestation of anything, unless she's the natural force of leaving wet towels on the bathroom floor."

"She's not," says Erin. "That would be Chaos or Entropy, and Darren's still dead."

Roger makes a brief, uncomfortable face. "Yes, he is," he says. Then he sighs. "You and Melanie—and Jack—you're supposed to exist. You're pearls the world created when grit got caught inside the way things worked. Pull out a pearl and the oyster makes another one, because it's in the habit. The universe doesn't know how to operate without you anymore. It doesn't matter if some of you are artificial, you're still familiar things. You're *supposed* to be."

"Okay," says Harry, dubiously.

"Me and Dodge, Kim and Tim, we're not supposed to be. We were made by a man who was following a blueprint by a woman who thought forcing things that were never supposed to exist as people into human skins was the way to control them. But what neither of them ever seems to have considered is that once something becomes a person, it can do whatever it wants. If you go outside in December and freeze to death, that's impersonal. If your girlfriend creates a blizzard in your lungs, it's a choice."

"Mel wouldn't do that."

"No, I don't think she would. But if Winter takes her over, becomes her instead of her becoming it, it could choose to do that. It would still be a person, even if it wasn't the one you wanted it to be. Some mornings I wake up and I don't know who Roger Middleton is. He's a stranger, a man I've never met, and I'm just Language, all the way from one side to the other. All I want to be is Language. The thought of going back to being Roger is disgusting."

"So how do you come back?"

Roger reaches up and tugs the white streak in his hair. "I have a sister," he says. "She gets lost too, sometimes, but as long as we never get lost together, one of us is always ready to lead the other home. But that's beside the point. The universe isn't used to us yet. The Doctrine of Ethos has always existed—it's foundational—but it never had the ability to *want* things before. To make *decisions* for itself. That's all new. It's all down to Reed and Baker and them messing with things they shouldn't have been messing with."

"Huh," says Harry.

"Neither of us can live without the other, because we're not balancing each other, we're not opposites, we're literally two halves of the same idea split into separate skins. If you put the whole thing in one place, it never figures out how to be human, and that's not as useful for the people who made us. And Reed forgot kids aren't tools, and they don't automatically want what their parents want. They don't do what you expect them to do because you gave them life and they owe you. We started rebelling almost immediately."

"First time around, we didn't even make it to twelve," chirps Dodger, with almost maniacal cheer. "'Lab accident,' my ass. Leigh Barrow was a monster and she deserved what we did to her."

"Yes, she did," agrees Roger. "We figured out, sort of by accident, that when we're together, we can actually reset time."

Melanie drops her butter knife. Harry blinks.

"Whoa," he says.

"It's not as useful as you'd think," says Roger, a little wryly. "For one thing, we can only go back along our personal timeline. If Dodger had come home and said you'd threatened her or something, and she couldn't live with it, she could have demanded we reset the world to yesterday, and decided not to go to the farmers' market when she got up this morning."

"So it's more of a rewind than a reset?" asks Harry.

"It was, until we fully claimed the Doctrine," says Roger. "We traveled back to whatever fixed points we had in our timeline—usually places where we made big decisions that would have lasting impacts—and then we lived things out again from there, making different choices, not always making the right ones. Not even usually making the right ones. We were flying without any sort of safety measures in place."

"Then I went AWOL," says Erin.

"Yeah," says Roger. "About our five hundredth time through, we made it far enough that Reed arranged for Darren's death. And that changed everything. With Darren gone, Erin was no longer fully under their control. She began to rebel, and allied with us, intending to help us reach the Impossible City and become manifest. Since Erin represents Order, and wasn't part of the closed circuit Dodge and I form together, we realized we could use her to retain things between resets. She could be asked to remember things, to understand things, to help us make the right choices at crucial junctures."

"I am exactly as useful as a hacked Furby," says Erin blandly. "Goodie for me."

Roger ignores her. Harry presumes he has a lot of practice at that. "So now there were three of us trying to get away. And after a bunch more resets and attempts, we managed to reach the Impossible City and become manifest. That's when we found Kim and Tim—Reed had been priming them as vessels for the Doctrine—and learned what we'd been doing to the universe."

"How so?" asks Harry.

It's weird, standing here with this man so much older than he is explaining himself like Harry is somehow capable of judging him. But Roger looks ashamed, ducking his head, as he explains, "Every time we reset, we reset *everything*. The whole world. Maybe the whole universe, although I'd rather not think about us being that powerful."

"It was the whole universe, because the stars never moved," says Dodger. "Every single time."

"Right now is later than it has ever been before," says Roger, ignoring her. "Time didn't start moving forward without interference until we stopped treating it like our personal lifeline, and even once we understood and became manifest, we had to go back and do it all again a few more times."

"They finally got to understand what they'd been doing to me this whole time," says Erin, carrying another sandwich to the table. "They had to go back into their own pasts with full understanding of what was happening, and who had already betrayed them, and who they had to lose."

"My parents were Reed's people," says Roger, and shrugs, oneshouldered and uncomfortable. "They loved me in their way. There was nothing I could do to sway them to our side of things, and telling them I was manifest just forced us to trigger a reset on the spot. They loved their master and they loved the thought of power way more than they loved the weird kid they had adopted at his command."

Dodger puts her hand on his shoulder, and he leans into it. "We sat down and mapped out every important moment of our lives, and then Dodger ran the variables until she found a path through them that did as little damage as possible while still turning us into the people we needed to become. It does us no good to play a perfect game if we come out the other end as Reed's puppets. Our broken places matter as much as our intact ones."

"You let yourselves get hurt on purpose?"

"Yes, but we did it knowing it was worth it. We played the closest thing we could find to a perfect version of our timeline. The first time we managed to manifest, Reed killed Erin, Erin killed Smita, Kimberley nearly killed Erin—it was a mess."

"So we fixed it," says Dodger. "Some bad things had to happen, no matter what, because they were the bad things that taught us how to keep being human."

Harry supposes when you're talking about people who can literally rewind and rewrite time, you want them to be human. Humans are petty and awful and mean and small, but they're also generous and wonderful and kind and the biggest things that could ever exist. Humans matter, and he feels a little better knowing that the kind of people who go to farmers' markets and treat sandwiches like serious business are in charge of reality. It makes more sense than any other theology he's ever considered.

"And once we got it as close to right as we could, we stopped," says Roger. "We're still working on the problem, but I don't think we're going to try again. I think we're already in the best-case scenario."

"There's no way to save Darren and still get Erin to join us," says Dodger. "Roger can't leave her with instructions that go back before she'd joined us, or she relays them immediately to Leigh, and Leigh comes to punish us for insubordination. So until Darren dies, Erin effectively isn't in play. And there's no way to save my parents. If I move them, Leigh finds them. If I move them without their consent, they react badly. And trying again would mean resetting the entire universe to the day we were born."

The thought is horrific. Harry and Melanie are so much younger than the pair of them . . . they'd have to live their whole lives over again, without the benefit of a road map telling them which mistakes to avoid.

They'd have to live through the motel again, and however much of the coronation they get through. He doesn't even want to consider the possibility.

"*Doctor Who* made time travel seem a lot cooler than this, huh?" asks Dodger, amused and sympathetic. "Don't worry too much about it. You have better things to focus on, like the coronation, and getting out of here. We're done being the story. It's your turn. All three of you."

"Just one request," says Roger. "It would be convenient for us to know the local seasonal monarchs. It would make things easier going forward. So if you win, come back and let us know, okay?"

"Okay," says Harry, and doesn't mention that Dodger already asked them to do that. It's sort of reassuring that the twins don't automatically share everything. It means they're still individuals. It means one less thing to worry about.

Dodger hands Melanie a paper bag filled with sandwiches and puffed cereal treats, and Jack steps away from the salad station, and that's it, then: their interlude is ending, and it's time for them to get back on the road.

"Where do we go next?" asks Harry.

Dodger's eyes go glassy and a little unfocused as she stares at a point he can't see. "South," she says, after a long quiet. "You want to head south, and then cut east, and keep going until you hit Alabama. You'll know you're in the right place when they come out to meet you. They'll be able to show you the rest of the way."

"What, she sees the future, too?" asks Jack.

"Who are 'they'?" asks Melanie.

"I don't *know*," says Dodger, looking annoyed.

"She doesn't see the future, she's just looking for the logical out-comes of the numbers as she knows them," says Roger. "Right now, that means your optimal path is south, then east to Alabama. That could change, depending on what you do along the way, but we have to live in the moment, right?"

"Right," says Harry, and he doesn't mean it at all, and that doesn't matter.

H arry carries the sack of food and food-adjacent objects as they walk back toward the car, and finds himself weirdly grateful for lunch. Lunch proves all that weirdness really happened: lunch proves he's not hallucinating. Plus, lunch is a good thing to have. None of them has been eating enough.

(They left the house through the garage to avoid the out-of-season summer, stepping around piles of yard tools and cardboard boxes with unintelligible labels scrawled in Sharpie. It was reassuringly normal after everything inside, save for an unusual number of paint cans on the rack by the door. Kim had paused before opening the door.

"Nothing's ever perfect for everyone," she said. "Don't get so focused on making things perfect for other people that you stop trying to make them perfect for you."

Then she hit the switch and waved at them out the door, skirting around the edges of the front yard, and now the three of them are walking away from the only people they've found who understand any of what they're going through. They just have to keep going.)

"Does it bother you?" Melanie asks abruptly. He turns, only to realize that she's talking to Jack, not to him. "That I'm not natural."

"My mother had this ring she pawned every time she needed to pay for something," says Jack. "Car repairs, groceries, rent a couple of times. We were going to be okay as long as she had her ring. And then the local pawnshop got new ownership, and the guy said he couldn't take her ring anymore, because it had lab-grown diamonds.

He'd sure been willing to take her cash when she was paying off her ticket."

Melanie frowns. "So you think . . . I'm not real?"

"I think her diamonds were good enough to keep us alive until someone decided to be an asshole." Jack shrugs. "I don't care how you happened. You happened, and you're here, and you're my responsibility, and if I have anything to say about it, you're going to win."

There's the car, and true to Dodger's word, there's no parking ticket on the windshield; the meter says they still have almost four hours left. Harry unlocks the doors, and they all get in, and then they're leaving Berkeley behind. What they're leaving it *for* is less clear, but they're on their way. They're on their way.

The future is waiting.

Many things in the Up-and-Under were different from the things Avery and Zib had known in the ordinary town where they were born. It would be a lie to claim otherwise, and it is the job of a narrator to tell as few lies as possible, since the people who listen to us will always assume that we have been telling the truth. It is a mean trick for someone whose job it is to honestly account an adventure such as this one to exhibit an unnecessary disregard for the truth when there is no way to verify what's being said. So I am breaking the veil of the anonymous for a moment to address you, the reader, directly, and make this promise to you:

No matter how strange or improbable the things Avery, Zib, and their friends encounter on their journey through the Up-and-Under, I am telling you the truth as it was seen on those hazy, not-so-long-gone days. There may sometimes be other layers to the truth, things concealed beneath the superficial surface, but I will not say a thing was so if it was not, nor will I tell you a thing was not so when it was. You can trust me on this journey, even as Avery and Zib could trust the improbable road.

It was not long after Avery followed Zib into slumber that the Crow Girl burst into birds once more, flying out the window and finding roosts for herself in the briars and branches of the garden. She filled her many bellies with bonberries, until her beaks and talons dripped with pink juice. And then she closed her many eyes and slept, although it cannot be said whether she dreamt, for the dreams of birds are strange, tangled things, not recognizable as the dreams of children. The Crow Girl was, in that moment, still very close to being lost forever, for all that she was no longer in the cold hands of the King of Cups.

Inside the cottage, Niamh sat in a chair with a clear view of the door, being a silent, steady presence as the others slept. She would rest in her own way when the need came upon her, but the need was not upon her yet, and so she watched with open eyes, waiting to see whether the cottage's owner would appear and object to their uninvited guests.

The sun sank below the long edge of the sea, having put in an appearance over the high wall of the cliffs, and was gone. Darkness followed, first painting the horizon in pinks and oranges, then tucking all the colors away under a veil of indigo-black night. Stars glittered in the high, clear air, and it was good that Avery was asleep, for not a one of them would have been familiar to him, a stargazing boy who enjoyed evenings in the backyard with his book of constellations and his wide-eyed hunger for the universe. Their strangeness would have been yet another offense heaped on his narrow young shoulders, and he was near enough to the breaking point that he needed no more weight.

Zib wouldn't have noticed the strangeness of the stars, but she would have known something was wrong when *she saw the moons, both of them too small and too dark to be the moon she knew, and most of all, each one cleaving close to the other, twins dancing through the darkened sky, and not a Man in the Moon standing elegant and alone. They would discover the sky soon enough, and inevitably; while there are many oddities that can be concealed from the eyes of curious children, an entire sky is not among them. But for the moment, they slept peacefully, too exhausted even to dream.*

And Niamh waited.

—From *Along the Saltwise Sea,* by A. Deborah Baker

BOOK VI

Blow the Man Down

Summer is only the unfulfilled promise of spring, a charlatan in place of the warm balmy nights I dream of in April. It's a sad season of life without growth . . . It has no day.

—F. Scott Fitzgerald

For strength of character in the race as in the individual consists mainly in the power of sacrificing the present for the future, of disregarding the immediate temptations of ephemeral pleasure for more distant and lasting sources of satisfaction.

—Sir James George Frazer, *The Golden Bough*

Into the West

Harry has never driven in this part of California before, but I-5 is a straight line drawn down the length of the state, a spine of stone holding the shifting tectonic plates in place. He knows an earthquake would split the highway without hesitation, but it still feels safer to drive along it, trusting in its strength, its length, its long endurance to see them safely to their destination.

Not that they have a destination, per se. They're heading south, as instructed, and when they reach the bottom of the state, they'll turn and head east, until their wanderings bring them to the inevitability of Alabama. He's never been there before, has a west coast native's natural trepidation and vague concern about the idea of traveling that deep into what might as well be a foreign country for all that he knows about it. They share a government . . . technically. Since every community gets to elect their own officials, he can't necessarily say anyone in a position of authority in Alabama sees the world the way he does, and that's okay! Alabama should be allowed to make its own decisions about the future! He just isn't sure they'll have anything in common. And they share a language, supposedly, but he's experienced the shifts in slang and regional meaning just between Portland and Seattle or San Francisco. He can't say the differences in distance and ideology won't make any difference to their survival.

This is all uncharted territory, and he's trying not to fret about it as he pulls off the highway in a little city called Crows Landing, looking for a place to fill the gas tank. Eventually, Melanie's father is going to convince his parents she's been kidnapped, and they're going to turn off his credit cards, but until that happens, he intends to use it whenever possible. He's less worried about being tracked during his road trip than he is about running out of the cash he's managed to yank out of ATMs and squirrel away, so the longer he can go without touching it, the better.

This doesn't stop Melanie from grabbing a twenty out of the stash in the glove compartment and throwing herself out of the car as soon as he pulls up to the pumps. "Be right back!" she chirps, before running—running!—for the convenience store attached to the gas station.

Harry pauses to watch her go, barely aware that he's staring before Jack prods him in the arm and says, "Hey, loverboy, eyes go *inside* your head."

"It's just nice to see her feeling like she can run," he says without rancor, turning to take the hose from its resting place and select the grade of gas he wants. A sweep of his credit card verifies it's still active and approves him to start pumping. He twists off the gas cap and seats the nozzle, getting it locked into position a bare heartbeat before a sudden feeling of sickening heat washes over him.

It's the heat of sunlight beating down on the pavement during the middle of the summer, of bonfires in July, when they have no business burning, and Harry turns to scan for the source of it right before the baseball bat catches him across the face and everything goes black.

Melanie is at the register with a heart-shaped box in hand, waiting for her chance to pay, when the stand of somewhat-wilted roses catches her eye. She looks at it thoughtfully, weighing the price on the chocolates against the price of the flowers. She'd have to go back to the car and get more money if she wanted to buy both, and somehow that feels grubby in a way swiping the first twenty didn't. She wants to get Harry a Valentine, and yeah, he's technically paying for it either way, but the first twenty was impulsive and a reminder that today is Valentine's Day, even if they didn't celebrate in any of the traditional ways. A second twenty would show intent.

Regretfully, she decides to leave the roses where they are and steps up to the register, putting her cheap box down and favoring the clerk with a smile. He's older, a little worn down by a life spent doing all sorts of things she doesn't know and wouldn't assume were any of her business if she had the opportunity to ask about them. But his face is kind, and when he returns her smile, showing an assortment of yellowed teeth, the expression is sincere.

"What's a pretty girl like you doing in a place like this on Valentine's Day?" he asks. His tone keeps the question from crossing any of the lines into creepiness that it could have merrily gone bounding over; it comes across as genuine curiosity. He really wants to know.

"My boyfriend's filling the car, and I thought I'd sneak away to get him some chocolates to say thanks for everything he's done today," she says. "He's been amazing, I'm the flake."

That's not quite the whole story, but it's good enough for a stranger in a convenience store. The man's smile only grows, and he nods toward the wilted roses.

"You should grab him a bundle of those," he says.

"I can't. This is all the money I have, and we're going to be on the road for a while—he'll appreciate the chocolates a lot more."

"It's all right." His smile turns knowing. "This late on Valentine's Day? No one's coming here looking for flowers. They're on the house." He passes her change back across the counter—eleven dollars and thirty-seven cents—and she stuffs a five into his tip jar before smiling brightly, tucking the remainder in her pocket, and snagging one of the less-wilted bunches of roses with the hand that doesn't hold Harry's chocolates.

"Thank you so, so much," she chirps, and turns for the door. The man calls a bright farewell, enchanted by his own generosity. She steps back out into the diesel-scented evening, breathing deeply from her gifted bouquet, before she trots toward the car.

The pump is still jammed into the gas tank, the cap dangling from its thin plastic thread, but Harry's gone.

So is Jack.

And there's blood on the side mirror, just a few drops, round and red as the roses she has just dropped to the pavement, scattering their petals like confetti for the night wind to take. Her eyes are wide and round as she claps a hand over her mouth.

Not fast enough or tightly enough to stop the scream from getting loose, but enough to muffle it, a little.

Alone, Melanie Cosgrove stands, surrounded by ruined roses, and tries to figure out what happens next.

Abduction

It takes almost five minutes for Melanie to get herself back under control, adrenaline flooding her system and triggering the desire to run in some random direction, arms flailing, until she finds safety. It wars with the equal desire to find Harry's phone, hers having been taken rather catastrophically apart to keep her father from finding her, and calling 911.

She stops screaming and looks, almost desperately, toward the convenience store. The nice man who'd been so concerned about what she was doing all by herself is back to reading his magazine, paying no attention to the little drama in the parking lot. He should have heard her screaming, if nothing else. The fact that he didn't means . . .

Means she's slipped between the edges of the world once again, and whatever happened here was a consequence of the seasons slamming into one another. She doesn't feel the killing cold that would tell her another Winter candidate was nearby, but whoever took Harry made a mistake.

They also took Jack.

She's still holding the chocolates, her fingers digging divots into the cardboard of their box. She tosses them through the open window into the front seat, grateful to Harry for thinking to swipe his credit card first as she disengages the hose and returns it to the pump. Driving away with the car still connected to the fueling station might be dramatic and all, but she's not a very confident driver, and she doesn't want to have to contend with an explosion at her back. She also doesn't want to have to push the limits of the situational invisibility that seems to come from interaction with the alchemical world.

Melanie walks around the car to the driver's side door like she's in a trance, pulling it open and sliding behind the wheel. Harry, not intending to leave the car, has mercifully left the keys in the ignition, and she turns them after she buckles her belt and adjusts the rearview mirror to her own needs. The engine roars on.

Melanie bows her head for a moment, breathing deeply, trying to center herself on the night, which smells of gasoline, yes, exhaust fumes and the nearby highway, but also of the dying winter, the coming spring. She can smell her future in this night, in the melt of distant snow and the germination of sleeping flowers.

California is further into spring than her beloved Oregon, and she wonders, on some level, what that's going to do to her: whether there's a place where the climate ignores the calendar so completely that it'll be like stepping into that impossible garden once again. She's spent most of her life knowing what it felt like to die, to fall down and simply . . . *go,* disappearing into the great absence on the other side of the heartbeat she still doesn't have. In Berkeley, she learned a different way to die.

Stepping into the summer wasn't a fall into the great absence, it was a soft tumble into the forest she visits in her dreams, the bare branches full of icicles and owls. She could spend eternity there if she had to. The thought of spending three months out of every year walking there is less distressing than it could have been, and when that man Roger ordered her back to life, she'd come to with the scent of a blizzard lingering in her nostrils and the sudden, utter conviction that what they're doing is nothing more or less than the right thing.

She can smell the spring approaching, bearing down on their location like a freight train, and nothing she can do can hold it off. Yet. She has a dim idea that eventually, it will be something she can delay, if not postpone forever. Once they manifest, once they know how they fit into this convoluted system, they'll be able to push back a lot harder against the world. They can change things. Not completely— the seasons are a million moving pieces, and she doubts even the number of seasonal monarchs the world contains could be enough to understand them all—but a little bit, when necessary.

So she knows what spring smells like, and winter, and summer. She rolls up the car window, breathes deeply, and coughs. The car smells like three people have been crammed inside it for days, eating and breathing and sleeping and farting. It smells like road trip. It's not the most pleasant thing ever. But she's looking for something, and so she closes her eyes and tries again.

And there, beneath the season they're in and the season that's coming and the scent of snow and dark, frozen woods that seems to seep from her own pores, she finds it. A lighter winter, bright and breezy, not shallow, exactly, but uncommitted in a way that's difficult to articulate. That's her Jack. *Her* Jack.

It's easier to touch the Winter without being dragged under by it when she treats it as something outside herself, something that can be argued and negotiated with. Not a friend, not yet, but a partner. She shifts a small amount of control to Winter and steps down on the gas, trusting it to guide her.

In a matter of seconds, the parking lot is empty save for the forgotten roses blowing off into the wind. The attendant will find them when he cleans up in preparation for the next shift, and will wonder what happened to the nice young girl he gave them to, what made her boyfriend throw such a thoughtful gift away.

He won't notice the blood smeared on the concrete, not even as he sweeps the petals and the broken glass away.

He won't think of the encounter again, not ever for the rest of his life . . . but he'll find the winter winds seem to cut less deeply into his bones, that the chill bothers his arthritis less. He won't connect those things, and it won't matter. The winter will.

The winter always remembers.

Harry wakes slowly, vision blurry when he opens his eyes. His head is ringing, and there's a sharp, coppery taste in his mouth that he guesses must be blood, because nothing else makes any sense at all. He's sitting on something hard—a chair. He tries to stand, and can't, because he's not just sitting, he's tied down.

Well, that's a whole new situation.

The room around him is dark, verging on pitch-black. He's not alone. He can hear someone breathing. Cautiously, he licks his lips, tasting more blood, and croaks, "Hello?"

"Harry." Jack sounds unaccountably relieved. "You're awake."

"For now." Closing his eyes and going back to sleep sounds like the most appealing thing in the whole world. The room is dark and warm, and even sitting up, sleep would be easy to find. He was having a beautiful dream, of a sunlit meadow filled with flowers and fruiting berry bushes, and no pain. No pain at all. It's hard not to give in to the urge to go back there.

"Stay awake." Jack is almost pleading. That's odd. Jack doesn't plead. "Harry, we're in real trouble here."

"S'Mel here?"

"No, she was inside when they took us, but Harry, I need you to *focus*. Stay with me, and stay awake, and focus. Can you do that for me?"

Harry considers for a moment. It feels like a lot to ask in his current, somewhat befuddled state. He hadn't realized how *cold* he's been for the last several days. Even the heater hasn't been enough to counterbalance spending February packed into a car with two avatars of Winter. "I can try," he says, finally, and it feels like a huge concession.

Jack sighs in audible relief. "Great. Thank you."

"Wha' happened?"

"I can't pick up on the presence of Summer candidates the way I can Winter ones. Apparently, this Summer candidate is a serial killer in training. They whacked you with a bat, then dragged me out of the car before I could run, and stood on my chest until I blacked out." Her voice turns a little wry. "Not the first time I've wished I were a bigger person, but definitely the most recent. If I were your size, I'd have bounced the creep off the pavement a few dozen times for hitting you. Still got all your teeth?"

That's an alarming question, although Harry's been playing football long enough that it isn't the first time he's been asked that. He runs his tongue around the inside of his mouth, ignoring the taste of copper, and relaxes when the topology is familiar and precisely as it should be. "I do," he affirms. "Little surprised he didn't break my jaw, if he hit me hard enough to knock me out, but I'll take it."

"The human body is at once ridiculously sturdy and too fragile to function," says Jack. "Can you move at all?"

Harry considers. Harry tries. Harry fails. "Nope," he confirms.

"Should have known. I can't either. This asshole took his time with the knots, which is almost as insulting as it is worrisome. He knew he could be lazy about it. He's got to come back soon."

"Does he?" Maybe he won't. Maybe he's out trying to catch Mel for his little collection, or woo her to becoming his Winter instead of Harry's. He's in for a nasty surprise if he thinks that's going to work, and Harry allows himself a moment's pleasant fantasy about a guy with a baseball bat walking up to Melanie and offering to be her new boyfriend.

The fantasy turns a lot less pleasant when she says no and leaves him with only two ways the scene can reasonably play out. Both the man hitting her and her freezing him are awful things to consider, and Harry doesn't want to. He shakes his head, which only makes it ring harder, and the wave of pain that follows wipes all traces of the daydream away.

His stomach roils. "I think I'm going to be sick," he announces.

"Please try not to. If you throw up, I'll throw up, and then we'll be sitting here in puddles of our own sick, and that won't make anything better, but it will definitely make everything *worse*."

"Things are bad enough that I'm not sure I'd categorize that as making them worse."

"I know what was on my last sandwich," says Jack. "Trust me. Worse."

Harry trusts her, and stops arguing. His eyes are starting to adjust, which means there's light coming from somewhere, although it's so diffuse that he can't say exactly where. There are no visible windows, only plain, seemingly featureless walls. He can't see even the dark shapes of any other furnishings; he and Jack may well be tied to the only chairs in here.

The light getting suddenly brighter doesn't really answer his questions about where it's coming from, only hurts his eyes. He flinches and screws them shut for a moment before cracking them cautiously open.

The new light is definitely coming from somewhere overhead, but is otherwise as nondirectional as it was before. The reason for that is finally clear: the walls and ceiling are covered by great sheets of opaque plastic, creating a smaller space within the room and obscuring everything real about it. More plastic covers the floor. Harry shifts on his chair and hears the plastic crinkle, and wonders how he could have missed it before.

But his head is still pounding, and this is an entirely new, entirely terrible situation. He looks at Jack, and realizes she lied at least a little about how she got here: one of her eyes has been blackened, and there's a bloody scrape down the side of her face that's going to turn ugly as it scabs and heals. They'll have to pick her up some concealer, or people will think he and Mel have been beating the kid.

And that assumes they're getting out of here alive, which is not a safe assumption. That feeling of boiling summer sun is washing over him again, making the room too hot and his skin too tight and everything about his surroundings stuffy and unbearable. Harry breathes in as deeply as he can—his nose is clogged, probably with dried blood, and won't that be fun to clean up once they get out of this—and strains against the bonds holding him to the chair.

If this were an action movie, he knows, this would be the moment where he snapped the ropes and broke gloriously free to save Jack and beat the living crap out of the guy who kidnapped them both. Instead, nothing happens. He coughs.

Something rustles on the other side of the plastic sheeting. Harry turns toward the sound so quickly, his head spins for a moment afterward. Jack does the same, and he sees her wince.

Some of the plastic sheeting is pushed aside, and a dainty woman in a heavy white sweater and ski pants steps through. She's bundled up like she thinks she's about to go snowshoeing in Saskatchewan, not like she's in a well-heated location on a relatively mild February night in California.

She's not carrying any weapons, and she's not the man who hit Harry with the baseball bat. He relaxes a little. "Hey," he says. "Hey, before you freak out, can you untie us? We don't know what we're doing here, and we need to go find my girlfriend—" He's found that introducing the fact that he has a girlfriend as early in the conversation as possible tends to help girls his own age relax around him, which makes sense, given that he's over six feet tall and built somewhat like a brick wall that decided to get up and walk around. Football works its wonders on the physique, even as it takes its toll.

The woman stops and looks at him, patently disbelieving. Her lip curls upward in what he recognizes as disgust even before she speaks. "Ew," she says. "As if I'd help you get back to any girl who'd date an *embodiment*? That's gross. You shouldn't date her. She's gross."

"So what, I should be dating you?"

"No, you shouldn't be dating anyone, because anyone you date is going to be dating an embodiment, and hence gross." She runs her eyes along first him, and then Jack. "The little one's a halfsie, right?"

"A what?" demands Jack.

"You know. Half-embodiment, half-normal person like the world is supposed to belong to? Not quite as gross. Also not the girlfriend, unless he likes them *really* young and has a generous idea of what it means to 'find' someone."

"Not the girlfriend," says Jack. "And if you know all this, you're not a 'normal' person either. But you're not a seasonal. I'm going to go out on a limb and say 'alchemist,' which means you're the living worst. Am I close?"

The girl smiles. It's a thin, sharp expression like a slice along the span of her face, and there's nothing of kindness in it. Nothing at all. "I like you better than the other one. I'm going to enjoy seeing what I can do with the pieces of you."

"The other one?" asks Jack.

The girl just keeps smiling, turning it on Harry without seeming to move her head. "You, on the other hand, it doesn't matter how much I like, I get you for my own. Oh, the rest of my coven is going to be *so* jealous when they hear that I got to take a candidate apart!"

Jack groans. "Coven? Like this is an episode of *Sabrina* or something? Come on, lady, witches haven't been real for hundreds of years. You're an alchemist. Behave with a little bit of dignity."

The girl ignores her. Harry can sort of understand the impulse. "I'll be able to barter bits of you for years, and even if they catch candidates of their own, you'll further my studies incredibly." She looks at Jack, smile fading, replaced by a hard, flat look in her eyes. "You, on the other hand, are a lot less valuable than he is. I know three other practitioners who've managed to nail halfsies to their tables, and they've already pretty well cornered the market on the little pieces of you. I'm still going to harvest, I'm just not going to enjoy it as much."

Jack spits at her.

That always works in the movies, always leaves the villain shamed and disgusted and wiping mucus from their cheeks. In this case, Jack mostly just spits on the floor, well short of her target. The girl looks at it, expression going hard.

"I should make you mop that up with your face," she says coldly, looking slowly back up to Jack herself. "I may, when you're handed over. It would be a nice way to teach you about manners before it doesn't matter anymore."

She turns on her heels and stalks to the spot in the plastic where she entered, bellowing, "Matthew! They're all yours!" before she disappears.

Harry looks at Jack. Jack looks at Harry. The sense of doom in the air is almost overwhelming. Jack still manages to take a breath and say, almost nonchalantly, "I hate the Hot Topic alchemists. They're even worse than the Congressional kind."

"What?"

"The American Alchemical Congress is sort of correspondence

school for alchemists. There aren't enough of them for everyone to have a formal education, no apprentices and masters for the majority, but they'll tell alchemists what to do and how to do it. Formalized alchemy is largely based on sympathetic magic. I'm assuming that's why Reed's pet projects had rhyming names, and it's why all the attendants stop answering to our birth names basically the moment we figure out what we really are. The name I had doesn't even *sound* like me anymore. I played along for about a month before I split, because I didn't really have a choice while I was still in my mother's house, but it would be like me deciding to start calling you 'Michelangelo' all the time. You could learn to respond to it. Doesn't make it you."

"Huh," says Harry. "So you definitely think she's an alchemist?"

"If she's talking about taking us apart and using our femurs to curry favor with her coven? Oh, yeah. The difference between an alchemist and a witch is the difference between Whole Foods and the Dollar Store. Witches don't get proper training, but they can cobble together a lot of the same concepts if they have the time, and they like to share what they know. Hot Topic has a lot to answer for."

"My head hurts," grumbles Harry.

"It'd be weird if it didn't," says Jack. She's tense, her attention focused on the flap cut into the plastic even as she answers Harry's questions. He can't blame her for that. He'd be tense if his head wasn't spinning and he wasn't so god-awful worried about Melanie. As it stands, he can't quite work up the focus for anything more than pulling gently against the ropes holding him to the chair, trying to find some slack in the knots, some leeway.

There isn't any.

"I think you have a concussion," adds Jack, somewhat anxiously. Harry's not her responsibility, but he's the best chance her candidate has of reaching the labyrinth alive, and she wants Melanie to win more than she's ever wanted just about anything in her entire life. She needs to save him if she wants to save *her*, and she knows that completely.

The plastic rustles again. A pleasant-faced young man, appearance dominated by brown hair, brown eyes, and a well-trimmed beard, steps through. His clothes are impossible to judge, covered as they are by a heavy canvas apron, and thick gloves cover his hands.

All of that is obvious and easy to see, and pales in importance next to the saw he's holding in one hand, dangling it with the casual ease of someone who knows precisely how his tools work and has no qualms about using them.

That baked-summer-pavement feeling accompanies him into the room, and Harry is gripped with the sudden, almost overwhelming desire to punch him in the face until those overtly perfect teeth develop gaps and leans, shattering enamel and the lines he probably paid some orthodontist dearly to achieve. The reason candidates fight is much clearer now: if he's going to feel this way every time he meets another contender for the Summer crown, violence is inevitable. It may be the fact that this guy hit him with a baseball bat, but it feels more essential than that, more unavoidable.

It feels as natural as breathing.

"Hello," says the man, looking at Harry, with a small smile on his face. "Will you repudiate your crown?"

So at least this guy knows the basics, even if he's working with a substandard alchemist. Harry didn't know them a week ago, or even what an alchemist really was, and yet he can't stop himself from feeling slightly superior to the man in front of him. So this guy has an inferior alchemist? Whatever. Melanie's father is a good enough alchemist to make *people,* and while he can't necessarily be said to be on Harry's "side," he's definitely not someone to sniff dismissively at.

"No, I don't think I will," he says, words rendered slightly mushy by the swelling in his mouth. He's not sure his head has ever hurt this badly in his life. "It's mine and I'm keeping it."

"Ah, but see, it's *not,* not yet," says the man—Matthew. He hefts his saw. "You have a potential claim to the crown, which is clearly not going to be exercised, since you have to reach the labyrinth alive to go through the trials. And as of right now, you're not going to make it. I'd rather not kill you while you're still in contention, if you don't mind."

"What the fuck difference does it make?" Harry demands. There's no give in these ropes. He can't get himself free. This is not an action movie. Either he buys enough time for Melanie to come and find him—possibly pushing herself deeper into Winter in the process, although he doesn't want to think about that more than he absolutely has to—or he dies here, taken apart by a man with a fucking enormous bone saw.

"Right now, you're tied to the Summer," says Matthew patiently. "Misty likes that about you. She's a little too excited by the idea of getting pieces of the Summer to keep in her spice rack and sprinkle on her casseroles, and I'd rather not help her on her quest for horrifying world domination."

"I can't believe you're hanging around with an *alchemist*," says Jack, like it's the worst thing she can imagine. "Don't you think that's going to backfire?"

"No. Should I?" Matthew shrugs. "You don't get a say in who I hang out with, little Winter sprite. You belong to someone else. Someone I'm *very* excited to meet, when she gets here."

Harry sits up straighter, straining against his bonds. "You stay the fuck away from Melanie!"

"You have a mouth on you, you know that?" Matthew seems delighted by that, like the fact of Harry's swearing somehow justifies everything he's done and everything he's planning to do. "Melanie, you say? Sounds like a cool girl." Then he snorts, amused by himself. "Of course she's cool. She's a living manifestation of Winter. She'd have to be cool. Not like the other Winter we had around here."

His expression darkens, something cold and cruel moving behind the genial mask of it all. Harry has a terrible feeling the past tense in that sentence isn't because his Winter left.

There's a rustle, and then a third person bursts into the room. This one is slightly older than either Harry or the boy with the saw, who also looks to be in his late teens; this one's in his mid-twenties or thereabout, Latino, with short-cropped dark hair and a flannel shirt open over a thin white tee. He looks more anxious than either Matthew or the absent, terrifying Misty.

Jack stiffens, narrowing her eyes and glaring hate at the lanky man next to Matthew. "Traitor," she accuses, mildly enough that Harry has trouble hearing the venom in the word.

The man doesn't. He winces, and asks, "What would you have done, if this was how your candidate wanted to win?"

"*My* candidate doesn't have a saw in her hand. *My* candidate isn't in this to take anyone else apart. She'll kill if she has to, but she won't do it for fun. You've helped yours set up a fucking murder room like something out of a Bryan Fuller show, and you can't tell me it was out of necessity."

Matthew bounces the saw in his hand. "This is getting boring," he says. "Tommy, how many limbs does an attendant need to do their job?"

The man swallows hard, his Adam's apple bobbing up and down like a fishing buoy. Harry can't look away. There's something about this man, who has inspired Jack's hatred so quickly, who's helping someone who intends to kill him, that speaks of home and harvest, of safety in the storm. He's in the presence of a Corn Jenny, whatever the other Summer wants to call him, and he should have been able to feel this man's calming presence since before their current adventure started.

"Tommy?" says Matthew, more sharply, and the Corn Jenny snaps out of staring at Harry to look around and answer.

"Um, there are no requirements in regards to number of limbs. The first Jack Frost I met was a double amputee following her service in the first Gulf War, and she was still fully equipped to support and train her candidate."

"Excellent," says Matthew. "Then I can have her arms, and maybe she'll learn to keep a civil tongue in her head. Or maybe I'll take that, too, and she can figure out how to communicate with no voice or hands. It's all the same to me."

Jack bucks against the ropes as he approaches. He's almost there when the man says, somewhat desperately, "Wait!"

He stops and turns, looking placidly over his shoulder at his attendant. The man stands a little straighter and says, in the same borderline desperate tone, "You promised her to Misty. She's not going to be happy if you do any damage, and you know she takes that out on me. Please don't get Misty mad at me again."

Matthew's look turns curious. "Are you scared of my sister?"

"I have a sense of self-preservation, so yeah, I'm *terrified* of your sister. She'd be threatening to take you apart for scrap too if she weren't so worried about upsetting your mother."

"So instead she just blackmails me with threats of telling Mom about my little workroom," says Matthew, and gestures toward Jack with his saw. "I don't *need* her anymore, except as a lure for someone I'm not sure I actually want to deal with yet. It's better if the Winter shows up to find her Summer already dead and gone. Then we blame Misty for killing him, and she takes care of all our problems in one beautiful swoop." He looks to Harry then. "Surely you can see the wisdom of repudiating your crown. Let it go and I'll let you go."

"No, you won't."

"No, I won't," agrees Matthew, with a sigh. "Misty does want her pound of flesh, and I know how hard it's been for her to resist taking it out of me. Poor little mite. She's a nightmare, you know. Far more frightening than either one of us, at least until we get to the labyrinth. I'm assuming you're traveling with your Winter because the two of you care about each other? She came out of that convenience store with roses for you, and it's Valentine's Day, so that had to mean *something*."

Hearing that makes Harry's heart hurt. Last Valentine's Day, he bought her so many roses that his parents lectured him on sensible uses of his allowance and the other guys on the football team gave him shit for making them look bad. This year he didn't even get her a Hershey bar.

Sure, he ran away with her and fully intended—fully intends—to drive to Alabama for the sake of keeping her alive, but they're the products of a capitalistic society, and it's hard not to see his empty hands as some sort of a failure.

Some of his distress must show in his face. Matthew laughs. "She adores you, whether or not it's mutual, and she's not going to consider another partner while you're alive. I *need* a Winter if I'm going to win. You need to repudiate the crown or I'm going to do terrible things to you. Terrible for you, anyway."

"You're going to kill me whether I repudiate or not," says Harry. If he repudiates, Melanie dies. That's enough to keep him playing at bravery, even while he doesn't feel very brave at all. If he dies while they're linked . . .

Melanie's entanglement is what pulled him under, and he's her counterweight, but she's the reason he's so deep in this shit already. Neither of them had much of a choice about how this was going to go. If he dies while he's still a candidate, maybe the Winter that's slowly strangling her will just change its allegiance to the nearest available Summer.

And since the nearest available Summer has a bone saw and is threatening him, he's not very interested in helping that happen.

"I am not giving up my claim to the crown," he says, slowly and clearly. "If you kill me, you kill me while I'm a candidate, no matter what that does to what you've promised your sister. Because you're right, my Winter and I are a thing. She's been my girlfriend since middle school. You're getting your hands on her over my dead body."

"Is it a cliché if I say that can be arranged?" asks Matthew mildly. "Because it can absolutely be arranged."

"Fuck, this is like watching two dogs try to figure out which one of them is in charge of the front yard," groans Jack, letting her head flop back until she's staring at the plastic-wrapped ceiling. She flexes her hands like she wants to clap them over her eyes, but her arms are tied down, and she can't move. She looks more relaxed, somehow, and Harry can't decide whether that's a good thing or not. "You're both big and impressive and scary as shit, okay? You don't need to bark at each other all night."

"Matthew!" Misty's yell comes from the other side of the plastic wall, loud and shrill enough that she might as well be in the room. "Mom says you have to come take out the trash!"

Matthew gives Jack a poisonous look. "You're lucky my parents are unreasonable," he huffs, and turns to stomp for the exit.

"Bark bark," says Jack mildly.

Matthew looks back at her, and there's no disguising the malice in his face. "I'm going to make you regret that," he says, and it sounds like a promise, not a threat. "I'm going to make you sorry you ever crossed me."

"I'm already tied to a chair while you try to make yourself feel like a real scary scientist by threatening me with a bone saw," says Jack. "Not sure how you could make me sorrier than I am right now."

"She makes a good point," says Harry.

"I wouldn't be helping her if I were you," says Matthew.

"*Matt!*" howls Misty.

Matthew sighs and hands his saw to Tommy. "I'll be right back," he says. "Keep an eye on them."

He stomps out of the room, already pulling off his gloves. Tommy watches him go for several seconds. There's a slam, as if someone has gone through a more substantial door. Jack opens her mouth. Tommy shakes his head and gestures for her to be quiet, and she settles, eyeing him warily.

After another five seconds he drops the saw and moves toward the chairs where Jack and Harry are tied. "He's going to kill you both, you realize that," he says, voice low and tight, speaking fast. "He's already killed two other Summer candidates. The first one was the night the coronation was called. I hadn't even been able to tell my girl that it was happening . . ."

"You're not Matthew's original attendant?" asks Jack.

"No. I belonged with a girl named Sandra. She would have been an amazing Summer. She and Matthew went to high school together. He found her at the Valentine's Day dance, and strangled her in the middle of the dance floor when he realized no one was paying attention to them anymore. I couldn't be there with her."

"Why not?"

"High school, remember?" Tommy gestures to himself. "I graduated four years ago, and while the seasons lend a lot of anonymity to the situation, they're not good enough to keep a bunch of white teachers from noticing the Latino guy in his twenties skulking around the campus. I was with her before I graduated, and I'd been teaching her everything she'd need to know. She'd complained to me about Matthew before, called him the school creeper and said he was way too into her, but she'd never realized he was attracted to her because they were both candidates for the Summer. Then the coronation started and she recognized him, and he saw her as the competition. Not just the competition: she was also the girl who'd rejected him over and over for years. He got his revenge while the DJ played terrible dance music, and I felt her die, and there was nothing I could do to save her. I couldn't even get onto the campus without running into the security guards."

"Did he not have an attendant?" asks Jack.

"His Corn Jenny left a long time ago," says Tommy. "He was smart enough to see the writing on the wall when Matthew was a kid. He warned the rest of us that there was a potential Summer in the area who couldn't be trusted, and so we kept our distance."

"That sounds . . . It's weird for there to be two Summers in a town this small," says Jack. "How many of you are there?"

"This was in Sacramento," says Tommy. He grimaces. "They've moved around a lot. I'm sure you can guess some of the reasons why."

"Arson and torturing small animals, probably," grumbles Jack. "All right, say I believe you. Matthew killed your candidate and your allegiance switched over to him. What about the other one?"

"He was at the bus station," says Tommy. "He was on his way to Texas, I think, with his attendant. They'd heard a rumor the labyrinth was to the south. Matthew caught them before they could board, but there was no way to abduct them. He had to leave the bodies behind. Misty was furious. She's been working for years to become what she calls a 'real witch,' and now her older brother is not only potentially more powerful than she is, he's killing people and not bringing them home for her to harvest."

"Has he killed people before?" blurts Harry.

Tommy just looks at him, flat and silent and disbelieving. Harry grimaces.

"Ew," he says.

"Like I said, they move around a lot," says Tommy.

"Takes a pretty fucked-up family to produce an alchemist," says Jack. "All right, it can't take that long to take out the trash. Now's when you untie us."

Tommy blinks at her. "I'm not going to untie you," he says. "If I turn against Matthew, he'll kill me too. He's killed two candidates and one attendant. I don't want to be next."

"I don't have an attendant," says Harry quickly. "If you untie us, you can come with me. He can't kill you if he can't find you."

Tommy looks momentarily tempted. "I'm not sure . . ." he says.

"We'll call you by your actual name," says Jack. "Jenny."

Tommy jerks like he's just been hit with a mild bolt of static shock.

"I know that other name doesn't fit you anymore; it feels like they're talking about someone else whenever they call you that," says Jack. "Whoever that guy was, he went away a long time ago, and now you're here, but you're stuck with people who don't respect you for who you are. Maybe you were also Tommy when Sandra was still here, but that was before the coronation started. Now that the seasons are spreading their influence over the people who serve them, you're more Corn Jenny and less Tommy every day. That's not going to stop. It's just going to get worse and happen faster as we get closer to the coronation."

Tommy and Harry are united in staring at her. Jack looks at Tommy, expression grim.

"You didn't say any of this before," says Harry. "Why didn't you say any of this before?"

"Because it's not going to happen to Mel, and it's not going to happen to me," says Jack. "I'm at the end of my season, and the two of you are at the start of yours. Mel's already so snow-struck she's basically incarnate already; the coronation is a formality to prove she deserves it. But you and Tommy, you have a long way left to fall. It's a long way down to the bottom, in case you've never been a diver."

"I'm not sure I can be," says Tommy.

Jack shrugs. "That's fine. I can be a diver for us both."

A horn blares outside the plastic-draped room, loud and shrill as a klaxon. Harry turns toward it, trying not to get overly excited by the sound. It's hard not to. He knows that horn, has been hitting it since he and his father drove the car off the lot and into the world.

Mel's here.

His excitement dies almost as quickly as it dawned, sickening and twisting in his stomach. Mel's *here*. Mel's in range of this demented Summer attendant and his creepy alchemist sister.

Tommy moves toward him, faster now. "I'll let you up," he says. Harry eyes him warily. "I will," he says. "Trust me."

"You haven't given me a lot of reason for that," says Harry.

"I couldn't with Matthew in the room," says Tommy. He begins yanking at the rope holding Harry to the chair, which seems counterintuitive until Harry realizes he's pulling so as to reduce the tension on the knots and make them easier to untie. "When he killed my original Summer, he claimed my loyalty. I'm *his* attendant right now. I can't move against him any more than I can move against my own hand, it just won't work. But if you were to claim me . . ." His hands keep working as he looks at Harry, blatantly hopeful.

"Okay, so we're doing this," says Jack. "We just need to get past Murderpants McGee out there. Got any idea how to find his original Corn Jenny?"

"No, not really," says Tommy. "I just know the guy ran, and with the way Misty complains about me not letting her have at least a toe, I figure Matthew didn't manage to catch him before he got away. If I'd realized how much of a danger he was, I would have run before the coronation started. I wouldn't be sticking around if the rules hadn't kicked in when the old Summer Queen died."

Harry nods slowly. "If he's already killed one Jenny, you're in as much danger as the rest of us . . ."

"Now you're getting it," Tommy says wryly, yanking the first knot loose. Harry pulls his hands out of the loops of rope, moving them around to the front of his body and rolling his shoulders as he tries to get the circulation to come back. "He's a malicious little fuck who didn't see other people as *people* even before he understood that he wasn't technically a person. Now he's on his way to becoming the living Summer, and he thinks that means humans don't have to matter at all anymore. The only reason Misty's even halfway safe is that she's as bloodthirsty as he is, and he knows having an alchemist on his side going into this will give him an advantage he can use. Try to hold still, I'll get your feet."

Harry, who hasn't been considering that an alchemist could be an asset in this weird semi-competition, frowns and holds still as Tommy unties his feet. He kicks the rope away as Jack bucks on her own chair, straining against the rope that still holds her.

"Hey," she says. "Do me next."

Tommy straightens slowly from his crouch, eyes fixed on Harry's. "Please," he says. "Claim me as your attendant. You have more of Summer in you than Matthew does. If you lay claim, I won't have a choice. I'll have to go with the stronger incarnate."

It feels uncomfortably like owning people to Harry, who doesn't know quite how to articulate how much he dislikes this idea, or why it rubs him so much the wrong way. Still, he can't mistake the desperation in the other man's face, or the anxious way his eyes keep darting to the door. His freed hands are still filled with pins and needles. He sets one of them on Tommy's shoulder, closing his fingers around the other man's flesh, holding him in place.

"I am Harald March, I am the Summer King, the season incarnate, and I claim you as my Corn Jenny, to serve the season in ascendancy," he says. "When I take the crown, you will stand by my side, and you will be my herald in the world that is to come."

Pulling his hand away, he blinks. "I have no idea where any of that came from. I'm sorry. Can you get Jack free, please?"

"In a heartbeat," says Jenny—says Tommy—says *Jenny*; thinking of him as Tommy has become suddenly impossibly painful, like trying to think of his mother or Melanie as a slur. It's not a word that applies to this man, or ever could have. It's barely even a name.

Jack looks at Harry thoughtfully as Jenny moves to untie her. When Harry meets her eyes, she nods approval. "They came from the part of you that's just waking up, the part of you that calls sunshine the way Mel calls snow," she says. "They came from the Summer. This is all new to you, as a flesh creature of fleshy fleshness, but the Summer knows what it's doing. Sometimes you just have to let it."

There is a clatter from outside, as of someone rolling an empty garbage can back up against a garage wall. Jack's head snaps toward it, shoulders tense. There's been no indication of Melanie's presence since that first blast of her horn; until the clatter, everything was silent. She fought back in the motel.

She fought back because Harry was there, and she didn't want him to get hurt. Now she's alone, and there's no telling what that other Summer is saying or doing to her. Maybe he's trying to convince her Harry's already dead, and she should transfer her partnership.

The part of Harry that knew what to say when claiming Jenny as his own knows Melanie could refuse him as her potential consort and take another Summer in his stead. He also knows it hasn't happened. Knowing things without being told is not the most comfortable thing he's ever experienced; it's sort of like having ants in his brain, busily bringing scraps of psychological sugar to the front of his thoughts.

Jenny has Jack's hands free. She stretches her arms over her head, then reaches down to help with the knots holding her legs, just as the plastic is shoved aside and Misty flounces into the room, ponytail swaying with each bouncy, angry step. "You people are going to have to wait while my brother flirts with some washed-out Snow White–looking cheerleader," she says, before she bothers to actually look at them. Her face goes hard, but there's a feral delight behind those flat, uncaring eyes. "Oooo, Tommy, Matt's gonna be *so mad* at you," she says, with glee that doesn't match her furious expression.

Harry stands, legs only shaking slightly as he starts using them again. It's good to know that all that time in training has left him able to walk through numbness. "His name is Jenny," he says coolly. "He's my attendant. I don't care if your brother gets mad at us. I'm pretty pissed at him."

Misty reaches into the pocket of her cardigan and pulls out a vial full of dark, roiling smoke. It looks like a prop from a bad fantasy movie, and Harry can't stop himself from staring at it. The world stopped making sense when Mel collapsed on the football field and a kid barely out of elementary school started lecturing him about how magic is real and he's a part of it. This is happening, whether he wants it to be or not, and he's come to terms with that, somewhat unwillingly, but still.

Apart from Mel's private blizzard, this is the first thing he's *seen* that he can't dismiss as a bunch of people playing a really weird LARP that they've somehow drafted him into. That smoke is moving with intent, throwing itself from one end of the vial to another like it wants nothing more than to escape.

"You know what this is?" asks Misty, holding the vial up and shaking it like a dance team leader's baton. Jenny freezes in the act of untying Jack's feet, and Jack freezes in the process of trying to shake the ropes away. Harry can tell from their reaction that whatever the smoke is, it's really, really bad, and they don't want it to get loose.

He folds his arms, looking at Misty the way he's learned to look at girls who get a little too enthusiastic with their offers to "comfort" him following Melanie's supposedly inevitable death. Thinking of how disappointed they'll be when they realize she no longer stays dead is one of the only good things about this situation.

"No, and I'm not sure you know, either," he says. "You're waving it around like it's something scary, but if it were really something scary, you'd be treating it with a little more respect and a little less 'look at me, I'm the villain from an anime you've never heard of, I'm so *bad*.'"

Her eyes narrow. "You know, my brother doesn't *need* any of you. He only brought you here because I said I wanted your body for my birthday."

"That's gross," says Harry.

"If it's mine, I can do whatever I want with it," she says, clearly furious, and throws the vial at the floor before running back to the opening in the plastic and flinging herself through. She stops right on the other side of the clear vinyl sheet, a hungry expression on her face.

Not as hungry as the smoke. It boils free when the vial cracks, gathering into a black, horrifying cloud in the middle of the room, much larger than its previous confinement would have indicated. It doesn't wisp or dissipate like smoke should, only clusters more and more tightly together, a dire warning of disaster to come. It looks like a snake getting ready to strike. The roiling continues, and Harry swears he can see faces in the blackness, eyes gouged-out holes, mouths chattering in ceaseless, furious hunger.

Misty looks almost as hungry as the smoke, eyes alight with obvious excited expectation for what she believes is about to come. Jack is free of her chair; she and Jenny are clinging to each other, terrified.

"You promised your brother you wouldn't hurt me!" shouts Jenny, like he thinks it's going to do a scrap of good.

Misty laughs, wildly. "*You* promised my brother you wouldn't betray him!" she calls back. "He's more important than some stupid Seasonal Attendant! There's dozens and dozens of you, and only one Summer King! He's going to win the crown, and it won't matter what happened to you!"

The smoke lunges forward. It surrounds Harry in an instant, swirling and biting, filled with a thousand razored mouths, a million teeth that slash at his skin. He'll be devoured in seconds if he doesn't do something about this smoke, if he doesn't find a way to escape it. His first instinct is to run, but he knows it won't help;

smoke clings. Anyone who's ever known a smoker knows that. He can't roll to put it out, because it isn't burning, only the aftermath of burning, not fire, only the consequences of fire.

He doesn't move.

The smoke continues to swirl. He hears Jack screaming, the loud, horrified shrieks of a child seeing something terrible unfold. She's always seemed so much older than her age, and this is almost more frightening than the smoke itself. Magic is real and magic is terrible and being a part of a magical world isn't enough to protect him from its dangers. Jack's only an attendant. If he can't survive this, what's going to happen to her?

He doesn't move.

The biting of the smoke is starting to become truly painful, like having sandpaper struck repeatedly over his skin. His eyes are closed, as much to protect them as anything else. He takes a deep breath, coughing as he inhales a few flecks of the roiling smoke, and raises his arms, reaching inward, looking for the place he found in the garden in Berkeley, looking for the feeling of utter peace and belonging that suffused him in the summer sun.

It isn't summer now, not here, but he's still the Summer, and for the first time, he fully understands the distinction between the two. The season is temporary and transitory. It dictates his strength, yes, but it's like the joke his father used to tell when his mother scolded him for having a drink before lunch on the weekend—it's five o'clock somewhere. Well, it's summer somewhere, in Australia, maybe, or someplace else on the other side of the world, someplace far away and unfamiliar, where he may never get to go. Becoming a living vessel for the season means limiting some of his adult choices, means not traveling as much as he's always idly wanted to . . . but he'd only wanted to travel so he could show the world to Melanie, and she's never been all that interested. He'll have her. He'll have Castleview. And he'll have the sunlight burning in his veins.

It's always summer somewhere.

It's always Summer where the Summer King stands. He doesn't hold blizzards or the fear of frost, but he has to be Melanie's equal or he can't be her opposing force, and that means he has *something*, especially here and now, during the coronation, when he's finally accepted a Corn Jenny of his own. The season he harbors is complete within him for the first time, and while it's weak this time of year, it still exists.

Matthew didn't know what he was risking when he treated his Corn Jenny poorly. He'll have to tell Mel to be nice to Jack, although he doesn't think there's much risk that she won't be. She's been following the girl's advice and giving in to her demands since they met.

Harry raises his hands toward the ceiling, fingers bloody as they emerge from the cloud of seething smoke, and brings them down hard, as if he were spiking a football. And the summer, unseasonable and impossible as it is, follows his hands, follows the hands of the Summer, and crashes down into the room in a burning wave of heat and dazzling sunlight. Jenny yelps, surprise and delight. Jack's sound of surprise is much less delighted, much more shocked, like a small child who's just put her hand down flat on the surface of a burning stove.

Misty shrieks, short and sharp and quickly cut off, presumably because she's clapped her hand over her mouth. And the smoke screams from all of its hundreds and thousands of mouths, every one of them wailing in brief, eerie harmony before the blazing light shining from Harry burns them away. In less than a handful of seconds, the smoke is gone, and the room is empty again, save for the three of them.

The plastic is melting from the walls. It was designed to keep blood splatter from getting on the paint, not to withstand a sudden blast from the undiluted power of the sun. Misty, shying away from the melting sheet of vinyl that was meant to protect her from her own horror, looks like she has the world's worst sunburn. Her eyes are wide and horrified, and for a moment, Harry thinks she's staring straight at him. Then she moans, and he realizes she can't see anything at all.

He'll think about the ethics of flashblinding someone who just tried to kill him later. Right now, he has better things to worry about. He whirls toward Jack and Jenny, suddenly afraid that he's damaged Melanie's attendant by manifesting the Summer in the room with her.

She's clinging to Jenny's waist, again seeming like her actual age for once, her face pressed against the man's stomach. They must have been like that while Harry was wrapped in the smoke. There's no way they had time to move.

Jenny looks just like he did before the explosion, skin darker than Harry's but not burnt or damaged in any way. He meets Harry's eyes and smiles a crooked smile, clearly able to see the other man.

So at least the Summer attendant is undamaged. Harry crosses the room quickly. He can't forget Misty saying that Matthew was flirting with Melanie. He wants to run out of here more than almost anything. He knows now that his own success or failure will hinge largely on having a supportive attendant; whatever they normally do for their Seasons, it's far more essential now that the coronation is in process. He needs Jenny. He needs to win. He needs Melanie to win, and that means she needs Jack.

Jack pushes herself away from Jenny and turns to face him. She isn't burned. That's the first thing he sees, and it's such a relief that he almost sits back down on the chair behind him, which is thankfully not on fire or anything else ridiculous like that.

"Well?" she demands. "Why are you still just standing here like a big dork? Go get our girl!"

"Watch for the alchemist, she's still standing," he advises.

Jack's smile is feral. If Misty tries anything, she's not going to enjoy the consequences.

That was the last thing Harry needed to do to feel like he could leave them. He turns toward the melting sheet of vinyl between him and Misty, breaking into a run from a standing start. They do this at drills all the time. If she doesn't get out of the way, she's going to get hurt, and right now, he doesn't care. She hurt him. He's bleeding from countless tiny tears in his skin, the bitemarks not having blown away with the smoke. The top layer of blood has dried on his skin and clothing, thanks to the Summer, but that didn't heal his wounds.

A running football player sounds something like a charging rhino. Misty can't see him, but she can hear him just fine; she steps aside at the last moment, leaving him to race harmlessly past. He doesn't pause. Jack and Jenny can take care of her, and she was planning to take him apart, so he's not too concerned about her.

As he suspected, the little plastic-wrapped murder room was constructed inside a freestanding garage. On the other side of the sheeting is a band of empty space, about three feet wide, cluttered with a few yard tools and cardboard boxes, but otherwise clear. He wonders how hard it was for Matthew and his sister to convince their parents they needed full ownership of the garage, to let them clear out whatever debris the place had accumulated in favor of their own projects. He can't imagine their parents know the kids were using the place to construct a murder room; if they did, he's in even more trouble than he thinks he is, because the family that takes apart tourists together runs a horrifying abattoir of terrors together.

The door to the outside is unlocked. He slams through it as hard and fast as he can, racing into the scrubby-grassed yard. Moonlight bathes the lawn, catches glints off the windows of the low-slung ranch-style house that the garage is actually detached from, reflects off the hood of the car in the porch, and off the much newer, cleaner, more familiar car pulled up to the curb.

Melanie is standing outside the driver's side door, an expression of sheer, unquestionable fury on her face. She looks barely short of committing murder. Matthew is between Harry and the car, hands in his pockets, looking utterly and profoundly relaxed.

Harry can't imagine the other man didn't feel him calling the Summer. He can believe Melanie didn't—he didn't feel her calling the Winter back in the motel, and their seasons are opposed enough that he doesn't think there's anything strange about that—but if he can call that much Summer that close to another candidate and not have it register, this system is more self-contained than it has any good reason to be. He skids to a stop, muddy ground squelching under his feet.

"Hey, asshole," he calls, voice low enough not to wake the people in the house, but certainly loud enough to be heard. Melanie turns toward him, her anger melting away in the face of first relief, then horror as she sees the blood all over him.

"Harry!" she cries, and breaks to run around the car.

Which is when Matthew finally moves. Not toward Harry, no; Harry might as well not be here at all. He moves to intercept Melanie as she runs, putting himself firmly between the two and grabbing her by the shoulders, jerking her to a stop.

He's almost the same height she is, built sturdily enough that he's able to pull her to a halt. Melanie struggles against his grip, trying to break free, and he digs his fingers in deeper, keeping her from going anywhere.

"I told you," he says, voice low. "Your little boyfriend renounced his claim to the crown. He can't help you now."

"I did no such thing," says Harry, advancing toward them. "I refused to renounce my crown, because like hell is some two-bit suburban asshole going to convince me to give up on my girlfriend and our quest."

"This two-bit suburban asshole is better equipped to win this than you are," says Matthew, still holding on to Melanie. "I have more assets than you do. I have a Corn Jenny. I have an alchemist. You have nothing to offer her."

"You *had* a Corn Jenny," says Harry. "And there's a good chance you had an alchemist, by this point, since I left her alone in there with both our attendants and they're pretty cheesed off."

"Misty?" says Matthew, finally sounding uncertain. Melanie breaks loose from his grasp and runs to Harry, who opens his arms to receive her as she flings herself into them. He gathers her tight, reveling in the familiar rose-soap scent of her, now underscored, as it always seems to be, by the scent of snow.

"Oh, *Harry*," she half-moans. "I came out of the store and you were gone, you were gone and there was blood on the ground and

Jack was gone and I was so afraid something terrible had happened to you—"

"I'm fine," says Harry.

Matthew makes a face at being referred to as "something terrible," looking unimpressed. He keeps glancing back at the garage, apparently waiting for his sister to emerge. Harry suspects he'll be waiting for a long, long time. He can still feel the Summer bubbling in his veins, effervescent as a bottle of champagne, and it's a relief when Melanie doesn't recoil from him. She feels less cold than she did before, fitting warmly and comfortably in his arms, the same way she always has, where she belongs.

They're back to balance. They're back to being equal. That's a wonderful thing, if an oddly painful one, because it means they've both lost their connection to the world as they've always known it. This is their reality now. There's no going back.

And even that thought hurts a little, because it drives home the fact that until the garage, he could have gone back. All he'd ever needed to do was find it in himself to leave her, and he could have gone back to the bright sunlit world he'd always believed was going to be his one day. Melanie had been lost from the beginning, but he . . . he had chosen to lose his way.

There's a difference. Much as he didn't want there to be, there's a difference.

He pushes Melanie out to arm's length, looking at her gravely, letting her look at him. She gasps at the sight of his face, before raising her hand to gingerly graze his cheek with the tips of her fingers.

"I'm so sorry," she murmurs, Matthew now fully forgotten. He takes a small, inappropriate thrill at that, at the realization that he's the only boy she sees in the world, even when the other option is also Summer-tied, and would balance the cold growing in her veins just as well as he can. "He hurt you."

She turns to Matthew now, and the boy doesn't look very pleased to be remembered, as Melanie's eyes narrow and her skin grows colder under Harry's hands. "He shouldn't have hurt you."

"No, he shouldn't have," says Harry, snapping her attention back to him. "But most of the damage is from his sister, Misty. She's an alchemist."

"Alchemist?" Melanie keeps her eyes on Matthew, her skin getting even colder. "Like my father?"

"A less refined one, I think; your dad never attacked me with flesh-eating smoke." He'd looked like he might want to a few times, but Harry's willing to chalk that up to being the parent of a sick girl faced with the reality of her first boyfriend. Disliking Harry may have been the only normal thing Roland Cosgrove ever did. "She's been working with him to help him target other candidates. Which reminds me."

He pulls away from Melanie, only regretting the motion a little, and turns toward Matthew. The other Summer candidate has shed his ridiculous apron somewhere between the garage and here, presumably inside the house if he had to go there to deal with the trash cans, and his hands are empty. He doesn't have a weapon right now.

He also doesn't have as much of the Summer in his veins as Harry does. The seasons are a push-and-pull situation until one of them claims the crown, and with Harry holding this much of the season they share, there isn't a lot left for Matthew. That's a good thing. Harry's never been one of the football players who think it's funny to pick on people smaller than they are, has always been more interested in taking care of people than threatening them, but he straightens and cracks his neck, making himself look as imposing as possible, before he takes a step toward Matthew. The guy is decently built, and could probably hold his own in a fight, but he's not enormous, and he doesn't have the shoulders of a football player. Harry's pretty sure he can take him in a fair fight, and with the Summer this out of balance, the fight isn't currently fair.

Matthew shies back, but doesn't run. "What did you do to my sister?" he demands, still trying to sound like he has the upper hand here, like this is exactly what he wanted to happen.

"Same thing you did," says Harry. "Left her alone with two pissed-off attendants, and figured she could take care of herself. That was after she threw her bitey smoke at me. I didn't appreciate that part."

Behind him, Melanie gasps, the sound short and sharp and cut off by her hand clapping over her mouth, flesh striking flesh in crisp punctuation. She sounds surprised, not distressed, and so Harry doesn't turn as he continues to advance.

"It seems like doing the same things you did is the way to go," he says. "I want to hear you refute your claim to the crown, and I want to hear it now."

A door opens and closes. He hopes it's the door to the garage, and not the door to the house. Matthew and Misty are young enough that their parents probably still think of them as innocent children, although in his experience, innocent children don't have murder rooms in the garage. The thought of a couple of six-year-olds hanging that much plastic sheeting is almost enough to make him crack a smile.

That, and the fact that their murder room isn't really there anymore. Melting it probably destroyed any forensic evidence the pair had missed, but they'll still have to explain the mess.

Matthew looks at him, false bravado in his eyes, and shakes his head. "No," he says. "I won't renounce my claim to the crown, and you can't make me."

"My dude, I don't think you understand how thin the ice you're standing on right now really is," says Harry.

They're not standing on any ice at all, of course: they're standing on the dead February grass of a muddy lawn. Harry takes that as a good thing. If Melanie gets upset enough, the grass will probably start icing over, and then they'll have to deal with her having another descent into Winter. He understands now, how easy it would be for her to fall. He can see it so clearly it hurts, because his own season is a bright string pulling him into the future, promising him the world if only he'll take it into his heart and hold it close, and burn, and burn, and burn. He wasn't built for this, only born to it, and it's still hard to resist. For her, freezing must already be an addiction.

"I have to mean it if I renounce," says Matthew. "I hoped fear for your life would be enough to make you mean it, to make you give up the crown, but either you've killed my little sister or you haven't. If she's dead, I have to avenge her. If she's not dead, all renouncing does is leave me defenseless with a little sister who already wants to take me apart. So if I renounce, I'm dead."

"That's basically the choice you offered me," says Harry, as footsteps approach across the lawn. Behind him, Melanie squeals, and he hears Jack laughing as the two girls presumably embrace. The other set of footsteps continues to approach, until Jenny is standing beside him. He glances over, taking note of the lack of blood on the other man. "She dead?"

"Unconscious," says Jenny. "I hit her as hard as I could, and she fell down, but she's still breathing."

"Good." Harry returns his attention to Matthew. "Renounce."

"No." Matthew's smile is cold. Harry realizes what he's about to do a bare heartbeat before he does it, pulling in a great breath of air and shouting, "Mom! There are people on the lawn! I think they hurt Misty!"

A dog barks in the distance. All the lights come on in the house, and there's a clatter from inside before the door bangs open. Harry swears and runs for the car, trusting the others to follow. They do, and as the four of them fling themselves into their seats, Melanie not yet questioning why Jenny is with them, the back door bangs open and a man who looks a lot like Matthew charges out, shotgun in hands.

Harry hits the gas and they're away, shooting down the street as fast as his increasingly taxed engine can manage. Matthew is still standing on the lawn, still a candidate, but as he's about to have to explain the garage and his unconscious sister to his parents, he's unlikely to be much of a problem.

Harry hopes.

And Harry drives.

Aftercare

CALENDAR SEASON: FEBRUARY 14TH, 2017:
WINTER, WANING WORM MOON.

H arry, you can slow down now." Mel puts her hand on his arm. Her fingers are chilly again, not frozen; he can feel them as part of a human hand, not an assault on his Summer shell. She's thawing. He's not cooling. That should probably worry him. But the road is long and straight, and they'll be back on the highway soon, heading south before they bend east, heading for the labyrinth, heading for the crowns.

What he didn't realize before—couldn't realize, because it hadn't been made clear to him the way it needed to be—was that he never needed Roger and Dodger to tell them where to go. He only needed to connect to his season. He knows where he's going now. If they lost the car, he could find it on foot. The labyrinth is calling him, calling him to come and claim his birthright, to be the first to take and wear the Summer crown, and he'll kill anyone who tries to stop him from getting there, he'll stop anyone who wants to get in his way.

Mel knew. Mel was already tied into her season, and she knew, even before they were told what it was, that someone had lit a beacon in the east, calling the seasons home. There's no possible way she didn't know. He glances at her pale, well-loved face across the dim cab, and feels a flare of anger stronger than any he's ever felt for her in his life. She's his Melanie, his best friend, his girl, and now his Winter, the opposing number to the fire he feels burning through him like a curse, and she's not supposed to be the one who betrays him. The fact that she has hurts more than anything he can imagine or articulate. They were supposed to be in this together, and she didn't tell him.

Her expression turns concerned, reading the anger in his eyes, but she doesn't take her hand away from his arm. "Harry? Honey, are you okay?"

In response, he hits the gas a little harder.

Jenny leans up between the seats, occupying the space that has traditionally belonged to Jack, and says, "He's still Summer-struck after calling it to him back in the garage. It may take him a while to come back to normal."

Melanie twists in her seat. "Who *are* you?" she asks, and it's not a demand, more like a plea for things to start making sense again, and somehow that doesn't help as much as it should. Harry can't help feeling like she doesn't have the right to ask his attendant anything at all, not when she had an attendant and he had nothing but questions and confusion for so long. Why is he even *here*? He'd be safe at home in his own room, in his own bed, if not for her—

But that means he wouldn't be hearing the sweet siren call of the labyrinth, urging him onward, nudging him toward the best route to reach his future. Mel may have pulled him into something he could just as easily have avoided, but now that he's here, he wants to stay.

He wants to stay so badly that he can't imagine letting go even enough to come back to her.

"Corn Jenny," says Jenny apologetically. "I was attending the asshole from the lawn—his name's Matthew, and I wish we hadn't left him alive, that's going to come back to bite us later—but your boy here was able to claim my loyalties. So I work for him now. I'm going to help and shepherd him toward summer."

"He's my opposite number," chirps Jack, and she sounds so happy about that that Mel yields her suspicion and sags in her seat, hand still on Harry's arm, expression still concerned.

"Well, okay," she says. "I'm guessing he's with us now?"

"You have a problem with that?" asks Harry sharply. "You're allowed to have your attendant and I'm not?"

Mel snatches her hand away from his arm like he's finally started burning her the way she's been freezing him, cradling it against her chest and staring at him with wide, wounded eyes. Jack elbows Jenny in the side.

"You want to be an attendant, attend," she says. "Convince him what we need right now is a human person, and not an incandescent ball of gas shoved behind the wheel of a hybrid sedan."

Jenny looks at her blankly. Jack groans.

"I had to talk Mel down when she sank too deep into Winter before, and he couldn't do it," she says. "You're probably never going to meet people more ridiculously and unrealistically in love than these two, and he wasn't enough to anchor her to being a person. That's my job. And it's your job."

"Matthew never—I mean, I haven't . . ." Jenny stops. "I don't know how."

"I didn't either, before I did it. Right now, he's in a place that's very safe and comfortable for him, that doesn't challenge who he knows he is in any measurable way. He needs someone to help him come back from that. Tell him to come back."

Jenny hesitates. Harry, who's been listening to this whole thing from an academic distance, where it really doesn't matter, keeps his eyes on the road.

"Or don't," he suggests. "I can see the labyrinth now. I know where we're supposed to go, and I didn't know before. I'm happy like this. My mental state is not a problem to be solved."

"Sort of is when it's not your season yet and you're manifesting so hard that you're going to confuse the trees," says Jack. "If you pull down much more summer, you're going to ruin the entire artichoke harvest."

Harry's not sure why he's supposed to care about artichokes, but he knows he likes this fire burning in his belly. He wants to keep it there. So he shakes his head, keeps his eyes on the road, and keeps driving. The GPS says it's thirty hours to Alabama, but that assumes driving the speed limit. He's willing to bet he can make it in fifteen, if these people would just shut the hell up and leave him alone.

"He's *glowing*," says Mel, sounding faintly panicked. "Is he okay?"

"No," says Jenny. "But he still can be."

He's never wanted to be left alone this badly before.

Then he feels a hand settle on his shoulder, and the outlines of the fingers through the fabric of his shirt aren't cold like Melanie's hands, or hot like Matthew's. They're perfectly normal, perfectly neutral, just fingers. Just a friend, reaching out across the burning gulf that's opened between him and everyone else in the world, just a ladder, just a . . .

Just a lifeline.

The small part of Harry that understands how abnormal all of this is, how out of character it is for him to refuse Melanie's offer of support, wants nothing more than to seize that hand and let it pull him to safety. But it's a *small* part, such a small part. When Melanie fell, she fell hard and fast and traumatized, lost almost before she had the chance to understand what was happening. Harry, on the other hand . . . Harry knew he was leaving the safe and narrow path he's walked for his entire life. Harry surrendered to his season with his eyes open and the full knowledge of the choice he was making. That he did it to save the woman he now wishes would go away and leave him alone doesn't change that he did it, him, Harald March. *He* made a choice. *He* called Summer out of the space where it was sleeping in his bones.

He's not sure when the last time he made a choice for himself was. He didn't choose to be a vessel for Summer—the season itself chose that, entering him when he was in the process of being made, natural process mirroring the alchemical one Melanie's parents were undertaking. Roger and Dodger's reassurances aside, he's suddenly not sure he chose Melanie, either. She's the perfect vessel for Winter, built and molded that way, intended for nothing more in this world than the containment of her season. Of course he fell in love with her. He didn't stand a chance. No Summer vessel would have.

So his destiny and his parallel were chosen for him, and when Mel ran, she chose for both of them. One more thing he didn't get to decide, one more thing he didn't get to have a real say in. But he chose to call Summer, and he's almost drunk now, on the glories of being the one who makes the decision for a change.

He shrugs off Jenny's hand. "Don't touch me while I'm driving."

"So pull over," says Jenny. His voice is low and soft and very, very close. "This is important, Harry. You need to let the Summer go."

"I will not renounce my crown."

"No one's asking you to concede your claim to the season. You're going to be the Summer incarnate, if only we can get you to the labyrinth and through to the other side. You have a very strong chance of winning, from what I can see. You'll be able to burn forever, if that's really what you want to do. But right now, I need you to let Summer go. You have to trust that it's going to come back to you if you want to be the one who claims the crown."

It sounds reasonable. It sounds rational. Harry doesn't want to listen, doesn't want to believe a single word applies to him.

Then another hand touches his arm. This one is cool, verging on cold, but still the hand of a living creature and not a corpse, like someone who's been walking outside too long in December without gloves on. He can feel the outline of every single finger, and in that moment the man and the season currently driving him are united in wanting to take the woman who owns that hand into his arms and hold her tight and never, never let go.

"Harry," says Mel, her voice gentle. "You promised you'd never leave me, remember? That no matter how bad it got, no matter how sick I got, you'd never, ever leave me. I've never taken you for a liar. Come back to me, Harry. Come back to me before you go too far away."

He blinks, and the road swims in front of his eyes, becoming blurry and uncertain. He's back on the freeway. Cars zip by at what suddenly feel like unsafe speeds as he puts on his blinker and pulls off to the side of the road, as far onto the shoulder as he can manage without pulling into the ditch. Horns blare as cars rush by, still too fast to follow. Faster, now that they're not moving. Harry plants his hands on the wheel and pushes himself as far back in his seat as he can manage, staring into nothing.

Mel's hand seems to get warmer on his arm, and he knows instinctively that she's not actually warming up; he's cooling down, the two of them meeting in the middle as they were always meant to do.

He coughs. "Am I still glowing?" he asks, not looking at Mel yet, not sure he's still allowed to.

She laughs and throws her arms around his neck and holds him close, and it's okay. They're still okay. They're on their way to the labyrinth, and they're okay.

Really.

Road Trip

They pull into Berkeley just shy of midnight, and Trevor knows they're going the right way as soon as they cross the city limits; they've almost caught up to Aven's wayward sister and her bull-headed beau. This will all be over soon.

He won't have to share a car with a woman who vacillates between murderous mannequin and stubborn toddler, sometimes in the space between two beats of her non-existent heart. They'll catch up to Harry and Melanie, and Aven will do what she does best—what she loves most in the world, what he's beginning to have nightmares about every time he lets his guard down enough to risk sleeping—and she'll go on to claim the Summer crown, and he'll be attendant to the Summer incarnate, and he'll never have to be afraid of anyone again.

He's not entirely sure how yoking himself permanently to this woman is supposed to free him from her, but he's an attendant. This is what he was made for. And unlike Harry, he doesn't have the option to refuse his connection to the crown. The incarnates pay more for what the seasons make of them, but they have more freedom to choose how they pay their bills.

Aven looks sullenly up from her place in the passenger seat, poking at a stain on her sweater that could be ketchup or could be blood (since it's drying gummy and red, not brown, he's banking on ketchup; not always a guarantee with her) and frowning. "Why did you stop?"

"Your sister and her boyfriend were here," he says. "Not very long ago. Can't you feel them?"

Aven's frown deepens, as it always does when he asks her to put effort into something other than murder. She likes taking people apart. She doesn't like looking for them. Then her eyes go wide, frown falling away to be replaced by a look of raw amazement.

"Go that way," she says, jabbing a finger at a seemingly random spot ahead of the car. When Trevor doesn't immediately hit the gas, she glares at him and points again, before repeating, "Go that way. I want you to *drive*."

Trevor has learned not to argue with Aven when he doesn't have to. Pushing back is best saved for those moments when failure to do so is likely to get them both killed. Summer incarnate or not, she can still be done in by mortal means, as the previous Summer Queen so generously demonstrated when she threw herself in front of a plane; he doesn't have a fallback if she fails to claim and keep her crown.

The thought of going after Harry when Trevor has literally committed murder to avoid serving the man is repugnant. Worse, even, than working for a murderess. So he turns the car and he drives, and he keeps driving as she barks command after command, sending him down a series of narrow, twisting streets until she shouts for him to stop in front of the ugliest house he's ever seen in his entire life.

It looks like it was painted by someone with a vague grasp of Lisa Frank's aesthetic, but absolutely no idea what made it appealing to literally anyone, even the small children who turned the woman into an artistic empire and motivated the sales of a million Trapper Keepers, a hundred million eye-searing pencil sets. No two swatches of color manage to get along with one another, and when he blinks, he's fairly sure the afterimages of the house stay imprinted on his eyeballs.

"What the fu—" he begins, and gets no further before Aven is flinging herself out of the car and running for the garden gate. Trevor fumbles to pull all the way over, blocking a driveway in the process. "Dammit, Aven! You can't just jump out of a moving car!"

He stops the car, yanks the keys out of the engine, and follows her, praying the people here in Berkeley are less tow-happy than the ones back home in Portland, or they might wind up having to steal a new car if they want to keep going. This is all a little more bumbling fools than he likes; he'd prefer a partner he can make *plans* with, one who has more impulse control than your average cocker spaniel.

But no, he got murder Barbie, fresh from her father's basement laboratory, and while she's a nightmare when she wants to be, most of the time she's happy to eat fast food, ask inane questions he can't refuse to answer, and point in whatever direction she currently thinks she needs to go. He wonders whether Melanie can feel her the way she can feel Melanie. Is she running from her sister, or just running, not sure how to interpret the feeling at the back of her mind that should tell her where her true partner is and free her from the useless man she's currently yoked to? Does she know she's not alone?

Aven has reached the gate and is yanking on it frantically, trying to get into the garden. Trevor shoves the keys into his pocket and jogs the last ten or so yards between them, grabbing her arm and doing his best to pull her away from her target. He succeeds in one thing: he succeeds in distracting her, as she slowly turns a baleful glare in his direction.

Just yesterday he would have backed off, apologizing in a frantic attempt to keep her from hurting him. He's been with her longer now. He understands that she's not as impulsive as she wants to seem, that she *can* see the consequences of her own actions, and simply ignores them.

Just yesterday he thought there was a way he was getting out of this alive.

"We can't break into private homes," he says, voice low and clear. "Someone else owns that house, and if their gate is locked, it's because they don't want us coming into the yard."

Now that he's right outside the fence, he can feel what caught her attention. For some impossible reason, the garden on the other side of the gate feels like summer. No, like Summer. It's radiant and bright, and entirely out of season, impossible to ignore or deny. There's a patch of strawberries in the middle of the path—which is ridiculous, who plants strawberries where people are going to walk? It doesn't make any sense—and they're actually fruiting, putting out fat red berries that make his mouth water even at this distance. Somehow, the people who live here have managed to harness a season they shouldn't have access to.

Alchemists. They have to be. But he's never heard of an alchemist managing to tap into one of the primal seasons without help, and he's a Corn Jenny, for all that he's worked hard to refuse the title and cleave to his own name and identity: if there were a Summer candidate here, he'd be able to feel them. It's a small party trick. It's one of the only useful ones he has.

A pretty Indian woman in blue jeans and a multicolored patchwork sweater that clashes with the house in a dozen different ways, some subtle, some screaming, is walking down the sidewalk toward them, a white paper sack from a local café in one hand. She pauses at the sight of Aven's assault on the gate, looking briefly nonplussed. When she continues her advance, she does it while saying mildly, "I'm sure our gate has done you some great and grievous insult, ma'am, but I'd appreciate it dearly if you'd step aside and let me go through."

Aven stops yanking, although she doesn't release the gate as she turns to the woman and snarls—literally snarls, like some sort of wild animal, revealing teeth dazzling bright and far more perfect than they have any right to be, rendered dull only by the proximity of her bone-white skin. She doesn't tan. She doesn't even burn. It's like the sun loves her too much to touch her.

"Who are *you* to tell me what to do?" she demands. Trevor winces. He's still working on getting Aven to understand that not everyone she sees is a part of the alchemical world, here to challenge for her position or her territory. If anything, she's the one currently impinging on this woman's territory, which puts the stranger in dire peril if Aven tries to push this to a confrontation.

"I'm so sorry," he says, breaking in before the woman can reply. "We've been in the car for a long time, and my sister fell in love with your garden the second she saw it. I'll get her out of here as soon as I can, I promise—"

"I'm not your *sister*," snaps Aven, abandoning her snarl in favor of glaring petulantly at him. "You're nothing to me apart from a useful tool to be broken and discarded. If you touch me, I'll have the skin off your body before you can pull your hand away." Her eyes dart back to the stranger. "That goes for you as well, woman."

"Ah," she says, wearily. "Another of these? You should have said something. I assume you're here for the cuckoos, then? I can't fetch them for you unless you let me go in. And I can't invite you into the garden, terribly sorry about that, but I don't even have the permissions to call for a pizza. When I order delivery, I have to have it delivered to the corner." Her sigh is exaggeratedly long-suffering. It's clear from the look on her face, neutral, almost amused, that she doesn't actually mind the restriction. "It's what I get for being the only real boy in the puppet theater."

"You're a boy?" asks Aven, sounding baffled.

The woman looks at her levelly. "No. It's a turn of phrase. But this is Berkeley; you shouldn't be making assumptions about people, whatever they look like. I could be a boy if I wanted to."

Aven doesn't look like she agrees. Trevor is about to step in again, even knowing how much he'll risk upsetting her if he does, when she finally lets go of the gate and takes a step back, allowing the woman the room she needs to pass. Not enough room: her shoulders will brush Aven's chest, her body's heat mingle with Aven's own. If he didn't know better, he'd assume Aven was trying to be intimidating. Sadly, he does know better.

He knows Aven simply has no idea that what she's doing is socially unacceptable, or likely to alienate people. The knowledge she was given by her father's alchemy included a million ways to hurt someone, the method for manufacturing a hand of glory and the laws of alchemical exchange, but left out the majority of the social graces. She'd be lost without Trevor.

He was looking for a queen, not someone to babysit. And this child is a danger to everyone around her, and Trevor's only chance at winning this thing, making it impossible for him to do what he most desires and walk away. It isn't fair. It isn't what he wanted.

It's what he has.

The woman smiles—the thin, displeased expression of someone who's only doing it out of politeness. "Thank you," she says, voice clipped, before pushing herself into the gap between Aven and the gate and pulling it open.

It comes easily, not locked at all, and Trevor can't understand why they're still on this side of it; Aven should have been through and into that sunlit strawberry patch before he could even get out of the car. The woman slips through, not glancing back, and heads for the porch.

The patch of strawberries seems to confuse her. She pauses and looks at them, cocking her head to the side. Then she shrugs, bends, and picks a handful of ripe red berries before she continues on her way.

That's too much for Aven. She breaks her stillness like a window, surging forward, through the open gate—or tries to, anyway. She bounces off the empty air where the gate used to be, staggering back a step before her face contorts in fury and she flings herself at the open space again and again, bouncing off every time, like a bird trying to assault a window. Trevor watches in silence even as she starts to snarl, not sure what else he's supposed to do.

The woman looks back over her shoulder at the silent Trevor and the raging Aven before climbing the steps and vanishing into the house. A few seconds pass, and she's replaced by a sweet-faced woman with strawberry blonde hair and a distinctly sour expression, like she's just bitten into the bitter anise center of reality and didn't like what she found there. She folds her arms and leans against one of the porch supports, watching Aven fling herself twice more at the air.

As she gears up for a third attempt, Trevor catches her arm and stops her. She turns to snarl at him, all feral rage and futile longing, and stops as the woman on the porch speaks.

"Nice show you're putting on out here, but if you're doing it for the benefit of our neighbors, they can't see you. None of the naturals can, unless they've already stepped to the side like your boy there. Fixing the wording to allow for natural manifestations was a nightmare and a half. I'm pretty sure the grammar is a hybrid of Hebrew, American Sign, and some dead derivative of Enochian no one else in the world understands. So you can fling yourself at the fence all damn day, it won't make a bit of difference unless we decide to let you in."

The woman from before comes back out, now holding two glasses of lemonade. She hands one to the other woman, before leaning against the support on the opposite side of the porch. The two of them stare down at Aven and Trevor, and he can't help feeling like he's being judged, probably because that's precisely what's happening here.

The new woman is the first to speak. She sips her lemonade, watching them closely, and says, "I don't recall anyone inviting guests over today. I know Tim would have mentioned something, and Kim doesn't really do people like that. So you're not invited guests."

"I certainly didn't get any warning when I went out to see my chiropractor," says the other woman. "And since there's half a sandwich shop spread out around the kitchen, I can already tell I've missed something."

"Oh, we *had* guests today," says the blonde. "They left about an hour ago. Places to go, problems to cause, the usual routine. We would have asked them to stick around so you could meet them if they hadn't been in such a hurry. And it's a good thing we didn't, because the one with the white hair looks just like one of them, and I don't think we wanted to be there for this family reunion."

Trevor goes briefly cold. "Did she have black hair?"

"Black hair, blue eyes, and a perpetually baffled look on her face, like the world had gone from being scripted to an improv show overnight. Sort of like you did, when I didn't stab you." That last is directed at the other woman, who makes a face.

"Not my fault you had a dead man's hand and a knife and a story to sell that didn't make a deuced bit of sense," she mutters. "If you'd wanted me to go along with you without arguing, you should have come up with something that came a little closer to sounding like the truth, and not the result of smoking all Dodger's wacky-weed before coming to my lab."

Aven snarls again, but at least stops trying to assault the air. "You met my sister?" she asks instead, an oddly hopeful note in her voice.

"Met her, answered her questions, and pointed her and her Summer sweetheart toward the labyrinth," says the blonde, taking another sip from her lemonade. "You should run along now. We're *not* going to let you in."

"My apologies for the rudeness, but you don't seem like the sort of houseguests we want to encourage," says the other woman regretfully.

The door opens and shuts again behind them, and a man joins them on the porch, nondescript, easy to overlook, brown-haired and dressed like someone's favorite college professor. He has a coffee mug in one hand; he adjusts his glasses with the other as he looks across the yard to Trevor and Aven. "They can see the house?" he asks.

"That would be why we're talking to them," says the blonde.

"I have no idea what's going on," says the first woman.

"We'll catch you up later," says the man. "Promise. it's been a long, weird day, and it's clearly not getting any less of either." He sips his coffee and makes a face. "Plus, Dodger's been mixing my coffee grounds with decaf again. I don't understand why she thinks that's a good idea. She needs the caffeine as much as I do."

"She just drinks twice as much when she does that," says the first woman. "What have you done to upset her this week?"

"Fucked if I know," says the man crossly. "You try spending all your time with your temperamental twin sister psychically linked to you. Sometimes she gets pissy because I *thought* the wrong thing, and then I have to deal with slammed cupboards and stomping for three days before she tells me what it was."

"You should get better at hiding your thoughts from her," says the blonde, sounding amused.

"I'll take that under advisement, because that's absolutely not something I've considered before," says the man. "Why, wherever would we be without the great Erin to tell me how to organize my thoughts."

"Drinking decaf a lot more often," she says.

Trevor is getting annoyed. Their whole routine feels staged, like these people understand how unsettling and off-putting it is for them to chat away like this, like he and Aven don't matter, like the fact that they're here doesn't matter. Aven is even angrier. Heat is starting to bake off her skin in waves, making the air around her warmer than it has any right to be. This is new. She's tied to her season, but she has yet to make the Summer manifest in his presence.

He'd been sort of hoping it would take her longer. Once she truly manifests the summer, he's going to lose any chance of breaking free of her. He may even lose his ability to remain Trevor, an identity distinct from the Corn Jenny he's unwillingly becoming. He always knew this moment was going to arrive. It's been inevitable for so long that it isn't even a surprise, much as he wishes it could be.

"It isn't summer now," says the man mildly. "It won't be summer for a while yet, and I'd appreciate it if you didn't do any more damage to the garden. It took us a lot of effort to get it balanced just so, and your sister's boyfriend already messed things up pretty badly." He looks toward the patch of strawberries as he says that, and the urge to go through the gate and fill his fists with fruit washes over Trevor, almost overwhelming.

He's not sure he could get through. He *is* sure that if he could, he'd have to spend the rest of his life there, or that life would be very short indeed. Aven isn't the sort of person who tolerates disloyalty. Unless she orders him into the garden, he's staying here.

The man begins descending the steps, one by one, eyes on Aven the whole way. "You must be the other half of Dr. Cosgrove's science project," he says. "Please don't take that as dismissively as it comes across—my sister and I are also part of an alchemist's science project.

Ours was just a little grander in scope, because our alchemist was an even bigger asshole than yours. Boy next to you has flower-petal patterns in his eyes, so I'm guessing that's your Corn Jenny, yeah?"

"He is," says Aven warily, shying back, like she thinks the man might suddenly trade his coffee for a cleaver and attack her. "Roland Cosgrove was my father."

Oh, the subtle joy, the unmistakable gloating pleasure in the past tense. She took that man apart, her first jailer and her first kill, and she has no regrets about it. Trevor is beginning to have enough regrets for both of them.

"Was, huh?" The man sips his coffee again, watching her. "It's not our place to compromise a coronation. We're not part of the system that made you, except for on a macro level, since on a macro level we're literally all part of the same system. We belong to the same cycle you do. We walk the same road. You have your guide, and that's all you need to make this a fair fight. I'm not going to help you. None of us are."

Aven bares her teeth. Not a snarl, not quite; just the threat display of a cornered animal, ready to bite if that's what it takes to save herself, willing to be allowed to slink away. Trevor's never seen her show her throat like this before, wasn't entirely sure that she was *capable* of it.

"You are not welcome here," continues the man, calm and implacable. "Not in our home, not in our garden, not in our city. You're on your sister's trail, and I assume you're hunting the boy who travels with her, the one who shares your season."

"I'll kill him," mutters Aven. "He has no right to Melanie. She's *mine*."

"See, that's the funny thing about sisters. Even when they know you, love you, and don't run away from you, they don't *belong* to you. They're still people, not just the other half of you, and where things usually get confusing is when you stop treating them like they're real enough to make their own decisions." He pauses, grimaces. "And none of this is getting through to you, because you don't want it to. Can't persuade the unwilling."

Aven wrinkles her nose. "You're talking nonsense. Of course she's mine. I'm her sister. I match her better than anyone else could. I balance her out. We're perfect when we're together."

"Does that mean you're imperfect when you're not?" The man sounds genuinely curious. But then, everything about the man seems to have been designed for maximum sincerity. Looking at him, Trevor feels like the world would rearrange itself out of civility and shame if it ever had the audacity to contradict the man for so much as a moment.

It must be an intoxicatingly terrible way to live, afraid to express too strong of an opinion, lest reality rewrite itself to conform. Aven narrows her eyes.

"I am *never* imperfect," she spits.

"Huh," says the man. "Interesting. Well, like I said, you're not getting any help here. You need to get out of Berkeley, because we don't want you. We're sitting this one out."

Aven shakes her head. "Let us through that gate and we'll see who needs help," she suggests.

"You mean you're going to commit violence against me? Is that the only song you know how to sing? My sister's all music, no lyrics, and even she has more songs than that." He takes another sip of his coffee. "Begone with you, Summer girl, and think about what you've done."

"You can't make me leave," snarls Aven.

"Oh, can't I?" The man raises his free hand and snaps his fingers, and there is no man, there never was a man, they're parked in front of an empty lot, construction signs posted around the chain link fence, only bare scrub on the other side. There's no summer, no strawberries, no multicolored porch with women standing atop it gossiping and sipping lemonade. None of that ever existed at all.

In fact, none of this happened in the first place. Trevor shivers like he's trying to shake off a spiderweb or veil of unwanted smoke. Aven, next to him, does much the same. She's radiating heat, feeling like she's on the cusp of summoning the Summer.

"Why did we stop here?" she asks, turning glacial blue eyes in his direction, already slightly narrowed. Her temper's up, and she's ready to share it with someone.

Best to find another candidate, then, for her to focus her ire upon. "I don't know," says Trevor. He turns, then, and points, stabbing a finger deeper into the East Bay. "But I think there's another Summer candidate that way, if you want to find out . . . ?"

And Aven smiles.

Arizona

California is a lot bigger than it looks on the map. It just goes on and on and on for hundreds of miles of farmland and empty space and rolling hills still brown and blasted in the fading winter sunlight, although they sometimes blaze with startling green. Driving through the California hills as winter fades toward spring is an education in the fact that sometimes the calendar and the cosmos disagree, because there's no way the winter holds sway here. There are daffodils by the side of the road. *Daffodils.* That's a springtime flower if Harry's ever seen one.

The second time he points them out, Jack waits for Melanie to head into the truck stop bathroom before she puts a chilly hand on his arm and tells him to cut it out.

"The seasons aren't a precise science," she says. "That's how Mel's predecessor was able to keep yours in abeyance for so long. Every time the world began to thaw, he ran for Australia, where winter was just getting started, and he didn't come back until the world began to thaw again. You're stronger right now than you should be, and she's weaker, and I'd be willing to lay odds that those weirdoes in Berkeley did that on purpose."

Harry blinks. "Come again?"

"You're natural and she's not," she says. "She's more likely to fall too deep than you are. This keeps you in Summer territory, and means if she starts to fall, you're beautifully positioned to grab her and yank her back before she gets lost."

"Matthew was planning to head east immediately," says Jenny. He's been speaking up more and more, his voice gaining confidence as he figures out that the rules are different with these people. Harry frowns, and Jenny explains: "He knew the summer would be strongest along the west coast, and so he was banking on the other Summer candidates staying on the coast as long as they possibly could. Inland, the winter's stronger, but he had his sister, and he had a lot more skill at talking people into going against their own best interests than he bothered showing to you."

Harry blinks. "So you're saying that because the Summer is strongest here, the Doctrine of Ethos told us to stay in it for Melanie's sake, and every other Summer candidate has been heading inland to weaken the competition?"

"Probably not *every* other," says Jack. He can't decide whether her tone is meant to be reassuring or not. Probably not: both the attendants have gotten less reassuring since this leg of the road trip began, recognizing that things are getting serious. If they're moving toward the labyrinth, the other candidates will be doing the same. It's only a matter of time before they converge, and if they haven't thinned their own ranks enough by that point, Harry and Mel will have to fight.

He's not sure he can kill again, not even to save his own life. But can he do it to save Melanie's life? That's the question he can't answer until he has to. He doesn't think either answer is going to make him happy. Either he makes himself a murderer or he fails her.

There's no winning.

"Some of the Summer candidates are probably hugging the coast as long as possible," says Jack. "And any other Winter candidates who started here are likely to be following much the same route we are. If we're lucky, we're not going to run into any of them."

The convenience store door bangs as Melanie emerges, a paper sack in her arms and the white stick of a Tootsie Pop protruding from her mouth at a jaunty angle. She waves to the car, bouncing onto her toes before she trots in their direction, and the wave of fondness that washes over Harry is almost strong enough to pull him into its undertow and sweep him out to sea. His answer is drowning in that wave, and he's drowning with it. He always has been.

Yes, he'd kill if he had to, to keep her safe, and since the only way he knows of keeping her safe is staying with her, if the other candidates find them, he'll kill for her. Hopefully, he'll be able to forgive her if it comes to that. He doesn't really know. He doesn't think anyone could know.

Melanie opens the passenger-side door and drops back into the car, pulling the lollipop out of her mouth and waving it like a magic wand before she begins producing chips and candy bars and microwave burritos from her bag, distributing them appropriately. "They didn't have any plain M&Ms," she says, to Jenny, apologetically. "What kind of gas station doesn't have plain M&Ms?"

"The kind where someone else bought them all already," says Jenny, and accepts his bag of Doritos without complaint. "This is fine. This gets me to lunch."

"Which we're having in San Diego," says Jack. "Good Mexican food for a change. Salsa that actually knows what a pepper looks like, dirty rice that's actually dirty."

"I have no idea what you're talking about," says Harry.

"White boy," says Jenny, with far more fondness than he would have shown at the start of their road trip. Days on days in the car—moving more slowly than they would have been if Jack and Jenny hadn't been ordering them off the highway and onto surface streets every time they thought they detected a candidate—had been guaranteed to result in either friendship or eternal enmity, and thankfully, they were all getting along.

"Yes," agrees Harry. "But Mel's whiter."

"Mel's literally made of snow," says Jack, and Melanie laughs, and Harry starts the engine, and they're back on the road, one more segment in a long chain of short journeys all adding up to one seemingly endless one.

It's not fair, not really, that the attendants can feel the nearness of other candidates while Harry and Melanie can't. The attendants aren't risking their lives, after all: they don't have to kill each other for the sake of a crown, and what little they draw from their associated seasons is apparently small enough that the seasons can sustain them all—hundreds of Jack Frosts and Corn Jennies all around the world, supporting and bolstering their candidates, waiting for another coronation to begin. They don't need to wear a crown or win a competition to stay as they are, they only need to serve when called upon. If Harry and Mel win, their Jack and Jenny will get some additional power from their ascension, but will remain essentially the same. They're risking nothing. They lose nothing if their candidates fail.

But somehow, they're the only ones who can feel the chill in the air when a potential Winter is nearby, or the balm-warm whisper of the wind when a potential Summer moves nearby, unless the candidates are right up on top of each other. Jenny had been helping Matthew sniff out his targets; he'd be willing to do the same for Harry, if Harry weren't so insistent on avoiding unnecessary confrontation. Jack hasn't even bothered to offer. Mel's already too close to toppling over the edge and into the abyss of the Winter, and if she falls while still uncrowned, she could be lost forever. "Let them kill each other and we'll still beat them all to the labyrinth" was Jack's only comment, as she ordered them once more to get off the highway, to allow some hopeful aspirant with stars in their eyes and blood on their hands to go zipping by, off to their own inevitable confrontation and possible destruction. "All that matters to us is gaining ground."

As much ground as possible, one truck stop and gas station and greasy spoon and cheap motel after another. Harry checks the papers every time they stop, but there has yet to be any mention of two missing teens from Portland, or of a sick girl abducted by her desperate boyfriend. Jenny still has a phone, which he takes out frequently, and finds no mention of any disappearances he can connect to the two of them.

Deaths, yes. Plenty of those, and some odd enough that he assumes they chart the movement of the other candidates; they have to be stitched to the seasons by thin chains of wind and time, invisible and unbreakable, their victims becoming apparent to the rest of the world only once enough time had passed to let the veil of nonchalant non-existence blow away. Some of them had apparently been lying in their rooms or in the back lots of shopping malls or whatnot for days before anyone happened to stumble across them, and the final touch of the seasons was that no one thought this was odd in the slightest. One of the deaths he found was in Portland, a childless man named Roland Cosgrove, found sliced to pieces in the basement of his home.

Because the article claimed Roland had no children, Jenny didn't connect him with Melanie, anxiously scanning the paper for any mention of her father setting the wolves on her trail. And because the seasons were shielding her, the article was clear about his childlessness: no question of a daughter, teen or otherwise, or any runaways whatsoever. Jenny put his phone down and focused on his lunch, dismissing the man's death as one more oddity that might or might not be tethered to the seasons in any way. When they left that diner, they did so still blissfully ignorant of what Aven had done, of the fact that no one else would be coming looking for Mel. She and her sister were alone in the world now, even if Mel didn't know it yet.

Sometimes, all ignorance can protect you from is the fear.

Lunch in San Diego is as pleasant as promised, the sharp bite of queso, the sting of peppers, the perfect tenderness of homemade tortillas. Melanie has a white girl's suburban palate and drinks glass after glass of water, panting, while the others laugh at her in giddy delight, as relaxed and unified as any group of teens on a road trip. Nothing about them is remarkable or suspicious. This is San Diego; pretty people come here to vacation all the time, and no one spares them a second glance, save to worry that Melanie may burn bright as a lobster when they hit the beach.

Barely an hour after stopping, they're back in the car, heading for the border that will carry them into Arizona. This leg of their journey is ending.

Harry keeps his attention on the road as he drives, focusing on the long, straight line of it, the familiarity of it all. They've been in California for long enough that this feels normal, despite how different it is from the green hills and tree-lined highways of home. The west coast of North America contains virtually every microclimate the world has to offer, and he feels like he's driven through them all by this point. As long as the tires hold out, he'll keep on going.

The signs say it's less than sixty miles to Arizona, where they'll fully commit to the great eastward turn which will carry them toward the labyrinth in truth. Up until this point, they've been running along a single track: they could go back, if they wanted to make themselves targets for all the candidates who haven't turned inland yet, if he was ready to let Mel go. But they're not going to do that. They're going to keep on going.

They're going to win.

Harry is smiling at that when Jenny's hand clamps down on his shoulder, so hard it hurts,. Harry looks up at the reflection of the backseat in the rearview mirror, eyes wide. "What is it?" he asks.

"Winter candidate coming up close behind us," says Jenny. He twists to look out the back window of the car as Melanie jerks upright in surprise and concern.

"We're in a moving car," she says. "They can't do anything to us."

And that's when the sheriff's patrol car behind them puts its flashers on. They blare red and blue, sending strange shadows dancing through the car. Harry looks frantically around. There's no one else the car could be targeting.

"We're going the speed limit," he says, tone anxious.

"You have to pull over," says Jack.

"Or we could run," says Jenny.

"This is a Prius," says Harry. "We'd never outrun them." He puts on his blinkers, begins drifting toward the shoulder of the road, the police car matching him the whole way.

Jack is all but hyperventilating by the time the car comes to a halt. "Winter candidate right here," she says. "It's the officer. It has to be."

The patrol car has pulled up behind them, the officer getting out and walking along the shoulder toward the driver's side window. There's someone in the passenger seat. A man, not in uniform, an anxious expression on his face. Harry barely spares him a glance, focused as he is on the approaching officer. How are they supposed to fight a man in full uniform in the middle of the day, by the side of the highway? It's not possible. If they try, they're going to wind up on the evening news, and not as heroes. Even with the shielding of the seasons to keep them out of sight, this will have to attract attention.

The officer reaches the car and gestures for Harry to roll his window down. "Do you know why I pulled you over?" he asks, without preamble.

"No, officer," says Harry, as meekly as he can manage with anger clawing at his throat. They were so close! They were going to be out of California by nightfall, on their way across the country to Alabama and the labyrinth, to the next step in this strange journey into madness! They almost got away!

But they didn't. The officer pulls his sunglasses down his nose, looking over them into the car—not at Harry. No, Harry might as well not be there at all for all the attention the officer pays him in that moment, focusing his attention entirely on Melanie, with her bone-white skin and her anxious glacial eyes. He looks at her like he's seeing something other than a person, something beyond a teenage girl, and Harry wants to punch him right in the middle of his faintly sunburnt face.

"I'm going to need you to come with me," says the officer, pushing his glasses back up his nose. "It won't be very far."

"He's taking us to a secondary location," hisses Jack. "Don't let him."

Harry only nods, voice a dry, dead thing in his mouth, unable even to swallow. Jack looks like she's going to throw up. Melanie is fixed and frozen, a girl carved out of ice, eyes fixed on the officer as he turns and walks back to his car.

A moment later, the lights start up again, flashing bright, as the officer pulls off the shoulder and drives around to the front of them. Harry turns the key in the ignition and hits the gas, easing back onto the road, following the officer away.

"That's pretty clearly the Winter candidate," says Jack. "He's got his Jack Frost riding with him; that's how they found us. It's not a bad way to go about things. Pull people over, then convince them to follow you someplace where you can finish them off. No telling how many candidates he's killed already."

"He ignored Harry, though," says Jenny. "Maybe he's not aiming for the Summer candidates."

"If he doesn't have access to a Corn Jenny, he can't spot them," says Jack. "And if he's pulling them off the highway, he's not surveilling them first. Not like Matthew was. He may not realize you two are anything more than passengers on a road trip to hell."

"I'll have to kill him," says Melanie dreamily. Harry realizes with horror that the air in the car is cooling rapidly, like she's pulling all the heat out of it and dropping it straight into a freezer. It's still not *cold,* not with him and Jenny both there, but it will be soon if this doesn't stop. She's retreating into the depths of Winter, into the place where she's less a girl and more a force of nature, and he doesn't know how to stop her.

Descending into his own season wouldn't solve the problem. He's not sure whether or not it would actually make it worse at this point; they balance each other, they aren't obligated to oppose. But he doesn't really see anything else that he can do. "Jenny—"

"You can't."

"Why not?"

"Because you're not crowned yet, doofus." Leave it to Jack to put things as bluntly as possible. The officer is still driving along the highway, heading, it seems, for the nearest exit, which is one of those barely labeled country roads that crop up between cities, reminding anyone who drives this way that much of California is rural. As if the rolling farmlands and crumbling barns lining the road wouldn't already have told them, already made it more than perfectly clear. "Every time you go down, there's a chance you don't come back up. If you both descend at once, we're not going to have any leverage we can use in convincing you to come back to the surface."

The air is getting still colder. The officer puts his blinker on, drifting toward the exit, and Harry does the same, schooled to respond to authority, not sure what good it would do to start a car chase on a crowded highway when he's not driving anything designed for speed. He can't save them this way. He's not sure he can save them at all.

"Once I *am* crowned, will I be able to go down after her if necessary?"

The answer feels terribly important. In the backseat, Jack and Jenny exchange a look. "We don't know," says Jenny. "We haven't had a functional monarchy in centuries. Maybe you'll be able to and maybe you won't, but right now, we know you *can't*. Please don't try."

"If you lose control of the car because you forget how hands work, we'll all die," says Jack more bluntly. "We need you to be a boy right now, not a season in a vaguely bipedal shape."

"I'm all right," says Melanie. Her voice is distant, dreamy, but clear. "Can you maybe try talking *to* me, not just *about* me?"

"Mel, are you sure you're okay?" If she says she's not okay, he doesn't care what their attendants say, he doesn't care if he's supposed to let this run its course and allow her to learn to control her season in her own way and her own time. He needs her to be okay more than he needs to reach their stupid labyrinth or claim its stupid crowns. All those things are problems for someone else, problems for someone who agreed to do this voluntarily, and not for him.

He's just a boy who's spent the better part of a week driving down the coast. He's tired and he itches and his hair smells funny no matter how many times he washes it with cheap motel shampoo. He's tired of lying awake and listening to Jenny snore, tired of wondering if he's ever going home, tired of missing his family. He needs Melanie to be okay.

"I'm fine," she says, and her voice is distant and dreamy, yes, but it's still her own. She hasn't been lost yet. Whatever else is happening to her, she hasn't been lost. "He's trying to take what belongs to me. I can feel him in the frozen places."

"What?"

"Don't worry. You'll understand when you meet another Summer challenger, now that you've gone deep. It only has to happen once for you to know the way through the woods, although I don't know whether the woods are there for you. I suppose they might not be. Maybe you have a field, like the one I see you in . . ."

Her voice slips even farther away, like she's talking down a tunnel, distant and fading fast. Then she coughs and shakes her head.

"I'm okay," she repeats. "I'm fine, and this is all supposed to happen. This has all happened before. I can handle it."

The officer takes the exit. Harry follows, and marvels at how quickly the civilized mask of California drops away, replaced by twisting trees with clawed branches, a rusted-out old rail car, a collapsing bridge. It's like they're driving into farmland as defined by a hundred horror movies, and if someone showed him a picture of this place and asked how far it was from a major highway, he'd say a hundred miles at minimum. He'd swear he was looking at the absolute middle of nowhere, and that this is was one of those places where no one would ever find the body.

The officer pulls onto a wide patch of gravel—he can't charitably think of it as a parking lot—in the shadow of what looks to be roughly half a barn and stops the car. For a moment, Harry considers hitting the gas and jetting away. They've done nothing wrong. Even if the officer hops on his radio, he won't be able to describe their supposed arrest to anyone who might come after them. They can still get away.

He pulls up next to the patrol car and turns off the engine, resting his hands on the wheel and staring straight ahead. It's so cold inside the car now that he can see his breath in the air in front of his face, colder than air conditioning could ever have made it, freezing solid. A fire seems to be stirring in his own bones, refusing to let him surrender completely to the cold, and he does his best to tamp it down. Melanie is falling. He needs to let her fall.

But oh, it hurts to sit here while she moves further and further away from him.

The officer gets out of the car, his passenger once again staying behind as he approaches the car. Harry rolls down the window, putting on his best expression of amiable innocence. He thought he was done playing for the fool for authority figures when they ran away from home, but here he is again, and some things never change.

"What's the problem, officer?" he asks, politely.

The officer snorts. "Don't play dumb with me, son."

"Don't use the word 'dumb' to mean someone who's not acting like you want them to," says Harry, keeping his eyes on the officer as Mel unbuckles her seatbelt, unlocks her door, and oh, God, she's getting out of the car; she's going to confront the man. He can't sit here doing nothing while she does that. He can't just sit by while she puts herself in danger.

He's not sitting here doing nothing. He's keeping the man occupied. He forces his expression of genial incomprehension to stay in place, even as he frowns and continues, almost chidingly, "It's ableist and wrong. You should be more careful with your words. Was I speeding?"

Do police in California usually pull speeding teenagers off the road, leading them down backroads to places that look perfectly designed to serve as body dumps? He knew California was weird. He had no idea *how* weird. He briefly considers vocalizing that question, and decides it wouldn't end well for him, choking the thought back into the dim, dark place where it began.

"No, son, you weren't speeding." The officer seems more exasperated than angry, a state that continues as Melanie gets out of the car. "Miss, get back in the car. You need to stay with the vehicle."

Melanie cocks her head and looks at him. That's all. It's already warming up inside the cab now that she's gone, and part of Harry is grateful for the warmth, and the rest of him hates that part for appreciating her absence even for a moment.

She begins walking around the car, heading for the officer's patrol car.

"Miss, you need to stop right there. You're interfering with an arrest."

"You're not who I'm here to see," she says. "You want us to think you are, but you're not. You have a gun and you think that makes you more important than you are. You're just another attendant." The scorn in her voice hurts to hear. Harry glances into the backseat at Jack and Jenny. They're sitting silently, their expressions unreadable.

Catching his eye, Jack offers the smallest of smiles. "It's okay," she says. "The Winter's ideas and Melanie's ideas aren't always going to be exactly the same. I know what she thinks of me."

Melanie is still walking. She's pretty and she's young and she's female, and all these things are clearly combining to make the officer hesitate. He puts his hand on his sidearm as he turns to fully face her, taking a step in her direction.

"Miss, you are in direct defiance of an order from an officer of the law," he says. "Stop where you are, or I will be forced to charge you with resisting arrest."

Melanie turns and looks at him, and he backs up a step, following it with several more, until his thighs brush the car and he all but sits on the hood. Jack leans forward and says, out the window, "We're not meant to argue with them, you know. Not even when we don't like the things they're doing. Let her alone."

Melanie ignores him. Melanie ignores all of them, walking onward toward the officer's car until she reaches the driver's side and opens the door, sliding smoothly behind the wheel. The man in the passenger seat recoils from her presence, just barely too far away for Harry to see the look on his face as Mel turns toward him. He imagines, from the slant of her shoulders and the angle of her head, that she's smiling.

She's usually smiling when she turns on someone like that.

"They're all feral, the candidates," says Jack to the officer, leaning out the window so he can hear her clearly. "At this stage, they're half human and half incarnate, and they don't know how to handle the mix, because it's changing all the time. Not like us."

The officer glances at her, clearly anxious. Jack shrugs, and continues.

"The seasons speak to us, tell us what we are and what that's going to mean going forward, and then they basically leave us alone. We age slow, we heal fast, our eyes get a little funky, but that's it. It doesn't work that way for the candidates. They're changing all the time. Frost forming in their bones, droughts growing in their hearts. It's hard to carry all that and remember how humanity works at the same time, and maybe they forget we're here too. That we need to keep our jobs, and can't be seen pulling over random-ass teenagers on I-5."

The officer glances at her again. "What are you, twelve? What job?"

"Thirteen, and my job is the same as yours: getting my candidate to the labyrinth alive. Which I think I'm going to do, while you've just failed."

The officer whips back around to face his car. The windows have iced over, blocking all view of the interior. It's not rocking; there's no fight going on. Whatever happened there has already ended.

The driver's side door opens again, and Melanie slides out. The air around her fogs and chills, like she's steaming from nothing more than the cold that radiates off her skin. She's on the border of calling another private snowstorm. The officer pulls his sidearm, aiming it at her as she walks calmly toward him.

"Lay down," he barks. "On the ground, right now."

Melanie ignores him and keeps walking.

"You can kill her if you want to," says Jack. "She hasn't reached the labyrinth, and a bullet would take her down. But consider this: you don't have a candidate anymore. All you'd be doing is shooting an unarmed teenage girl for no good reason. Can you live with that?"

The officer hesitates, and Melanie reaches the car. She ignores him as she walks around it to her door, slides inside, and refastens her seatbelt. The temperature promptly drops.

Her skin has gone even whiter than usual, taking on a bluish cast, like a fresh corpse. Harry can barely look at her.

"Drive," she says, and her voice is brittle and very far away. It belongs to something else, not to his girl. Not to his Melanie.

Harry starts the engine. The officer doesn't stop him, and doesn't move to follow or fire his gun as Harry pulls out and drives away.

They have a long way yet to go.

Road Trip

CALENDAR SEASON: FEBRUARY 18TH, 2017: WIN-
TER, LAST QUARTER OF THE WORM MOON.

A ven is bored.

That's never a good thing. Trevor is starting to worry about getting to the labyrinth alive, much less getting there in one piece. As Aven has been all too glad to demonstrate over the last several days, "alive" and "intact" are not synonymous. People can lose a surprising number of parts before they stop fighting back.

He's seen things he never wanted to see. He'd considered himself hardened and ready to do whatever was necessary to achieve his goals, but he'd also considered shooting a woman to be the height of wickedness. He had never considered dismantling people like they were unwanted toys, throwing bits away until they stopped working altogether.

Aven has no such moralistic qualms. Everything is a curiosity to her, and she views the world with a child's innocently malicious curiosity, doing as she pleases, indulging her own desires.

And now she's bored, and he's probably going to die.

They've been following the trail of her frigid sister and her sister's Summer boy all the way along the coast, tracing the seemingly endless miles of the California highway system, the labyrinth calling them ever southward, a pulsing beacon on the horizon that seems to pain Aven even as she insists that they keep driving down I-5 rather than cutting toward the call. Trevor wants to see Harry dead, wants to see his high school rival introduced to Aven's art and reminded of his proper place in the universe, but he wants to reach the labyrinth even more. He thinks this must be what it's like to be a salmon, endlessly called from the ocean to the spawning grounds where they were born, returning home only to make more salmon and die.

He wants to live. With Aven in the passenger seat, crunching her way through a bag of potato chips with no consideration at all for crumbs, and no interest in closing her mouth as she chews, it seems less and less likely that he's going to get what he wants.

She tenses, and so does he, an automatic response to her showing interest in something he can't see. "There," she says, finger stabbing toward an offramp so small that he hadn't taken any notice of it. "Go there."

He doesn't turn the wheel fast enough, and so she turns her head, slanting a glare in his direction. "I said *turn*," she says, voice growing sharper.

Trevor still wants to live. He turns.

Traffic is light enough that only a few horns blare as he cuts across three lanes to reach the exit, pulling onto a narrow rural road. Aven sits up straighter and drops her bag of chips, scattering crumbs across the footwell. She doesn't seem to notice. Her eyes are narrowed, scanning the scenery around them.

Finally, she says, "There," and points again, directing him toward a gravel parking lot that looks like the sort of place hitchhikers go to die. Trevor swallows, hard.

"Have I displeased you, my lady?" he asks, voice sounding strangled and formal and almost like it belongs to someone else. "Are you . . . Is this where you . . ." He can't finish the sentence. Uttering the words "kill me" would make them real, and real things are more likely to occur.

He always knew this was a possibility. He just thought he'd have more *time*.

"No," says Aven, impatiently. "Shut up. Go there."

Trevor shuts up, and Trevor goes there.

There's another car already parked on the gravel, a sheriff's department patrol car, black and white and tan, the lights on top old-fashioned and exposed. No stealth here; this isn't an ambush predator but a proud hunter, designed to pacify through its mere presence.

A man stands nearby, dressed in a deputy's uniform, looking faintly lost as he gazes dully at the car. The windows are clouded over. Trevor blinks, and realizes that they're not clouded, they're *frozen*, iced over from the inside. The air conditioner must have exploded. That, or—

He hasn't stopped the car yet. He's still rolling when Aven kicks open her door and flings herself into the gravel parking lot, and for one delirious moment he thinks about punching the gas and driving off without her. It would be easy.

He still can't do it. He's hers at this point, her Corn Jenny, and he can no more abandon her in this middle-of-nowhere parking lot than he could abandon his own arm. In his effort not to belong to anyone else, he's become her creature, completely, and so he parks the car while she's running toward the motionless deputy, running like she's never wanted to do anything else in her life.

Trevor can almost admire the efficiency of her run. She moves like a lion in final approach toward its prey, and by the time the deputy hears her feet pounding the gravel and turns, it's already too late for him. Aven is slamming into him, grabbing his shoulders. Trevor hurries toward them. He wants to hear what she says.

"Where is she?" she demands. The deputy looks baffled, and Aven snarls, "My *sister*. Where is my sister?"

"The other Winter," he says, comprehension dawning. Then he tries to pull away, and can't, as Aven tightens her grip. "Miss, it's a felony to assault an officer of the law, and—"

"What's a felony?" asks Aven, with such innocent confusion that the deputy stops, blinking, and seems to recognize the trouble he's in for the first time.

This is not a good place to be. They're in the middle of nowhere. Trevor glances around. This location was well chosen by whoever chose it originally.

No one's going to hear the screaming.

The deputy has realized how much danger he's in. He makes one more attempt to pull away, then says, "The other Winter killed Charles and then she got back in her car and hightailed it out of here. I don't know where they were going."

"East," says Aven. "They're going east. Charles was your Winter?"

The deputy nods.

Aven returns the gesture, expression dripping feigned sympathy. "And now he's gone, and you don't have any purpose anymore, do you, little Jack?"

The deputy blanches. "I have a family."

"So do I. And you let her leave." Her smile is terrible. It belongs on some phantom of the deep sea, not on the face of a pretty teenage girl with cheese dust on her fingers. Trevor shivers, glad that it's not aimed at him. "But don't worry. You won't be without purpose for very long."

Trevor's assumption about the area is proven true when Aven gets to work.

There's no one close enough to hear the screams.

When she's done, she licks a smear of cheese dust off the side of her hand, tongue coming uncomfortably close to a splash of the deputy's blood, and all but dances back to the car.

"I think I want tacos," she says. "They're not very far ahead of us. The ice hadn't melted yet. So there's time to stop for food, and then we'll catch them, and then I'll make my sister sorry she left me."

"Yes," says Trevor. "I'm sure you will."

They leave the deputy—or his body, anyway—behind, next to the shell of his slowly thawing car.

Come Back

CALENDAR SEASON: FEBRUARY 18TH, 2017: WINTER, LAST QUARTER OF THE WORM MOON.

The air in the car is still cold. Not so cold that Harry can see his breath anymore, but cold enough that he's shivering, wishing he had a thicker jacket, wishing there were a way to turn down the air conditioning when the air conditioning is his girlfriend. He glances at their attendants in the rearview mirror. Jenny is also shivering, huddled against the car door with a miserable expression on his face. Jack, on the other hand, seems to be perfectly fine, even content with the reduced temperature in the cab.

She speaks for the Winter, if not as clearly as Mel does. This is probably ideal for her.

Melanie still isn't saying anything. She's staring straight ahead, motionless, radiating cold. Harry's glad he's driving. It saves him from the temptation to look at her eyes, which have changed colors almost completely, like they've iced over from the inside. It's not just unsettling, it's terrifying. She's not his anymore.

Maybe she was never his in the first place. Her father built her to be the perfect vessel for the Winter; maybe he's never been anything but a means of delivering her to the inevitable, of seeing her over the boundaries between any candidate and the labyrinth. It's a heartbreaking thought. It's not as distant as he wants it to be. So he hits the gas harder and keeps driving, turning miles into memories, turning destination into distance traveled, leaving it all behind. Leaving everything they were and are and ever wanted behind.

The future will be there regardless. All that matters is reaching it.

Melanie sighs a little, the first sound she's made since fastening her seatbelt. Harry glances at her, torn between frightened and hopeful. "Mel?"

She doesn't reply.

"Hey, Mel, if you can hear me, can you let me know, maybe? Because you're freaking me out right now, and I get it if you need more time, honest I do, I just don't know what to do with it." If he weren't driving right now, he'd take her in his arms and hold her until she thawed. He has a feeling he might not survive the experience without making his own ascent into Summer, climbing those sharp and burning steps between him and a season that is not yet completely his, but it would be worth it to bring her back to him. It would be worth it to bring her home.

All he's ever really wanted was to bring her home.

Melanie doesn't reply, only keeps staring straight ahead, and the car is so cold, and they have so far yet to go. Harry swallows and keeps driving. He doesn't know what else to do.

T his has to be your story too, or there's not any point."

The woman looks exactly like her, white skin and black hair and a face designed to get her out of trouble, pretty enough to deflect blame without being pretty enough to attract it (and that's on society, both parts of it: beauty is not virtue, and not an invitation to vice). Only her eyes are different, black slices of star-speckled sky instead of glacial blue, and Melanie knows they've never met before, and Melanie knows they've been together since before she began.

It's a lot. Then again, everything is a lot. When she closes her eyes even for a moment, even long enough to blink, she sees the other Winter candidate sitting in the police car, struggling to scream as his skin iced over, as his fingers turned black. Death by frostbite can be swift, but it isn't the clean transmutation the movies would make it out to be: it isn't flesh becoming ice, untroubled and clear. It's painful and it's brutal and it's a terrible way to die.

She doesn't think she *can* die that way anymore. Not with this much Winter surging inside of her. But there are always other ways, and one of them will find her if she's not careful.

The forest around them is all black trees against white snow, and the woman who looks like her is the only splash of color she can see, wearing a purple-and-yellow cheerleading uniform that could have been stolen from Melanie's own locker. Since she's fairly sure this is all in her head, maybe it was, or at least from the memory of her locker, the idea of it, the place where she keeps all the best parts of her high school experience.

She was never supposed to live long enough to make it here. She was the sick girl, the dying girl, the failed experiment, and the fact that her father spent so much time and effort on keeping her alive proves he loved her, at least enough not to let her go. That could be a comfort, even here in this frozen place. It isn't, not yet.

The world began fading into forest, into this black-and-white illusion, when she killed the man in the police car. She never knew his name and now she never will, and it hurts her to realize that it doesn't hurt her more. She could have asked. She could have said something beyond "Are you trying to challenge me for the crown? Will you refuse your claim?"

She could have done something beyond grabbing his arm with her cold, cold hands when he shook his head and answered no. She could have found another path. She could have refused to engage. Harry faced his second Summer candidate without killing the man, even after he'd kidnapped and assaulted Harry and Jack. She failed. She failed to find a safe way through this change of seasons, and they're all going to pay for it. She's already paying, because she's down so deep that she can't even find the comforting numbness that greeted her on her first descent; all she can do is feel, and fall.

She feels as if she's falling still, even standing on this snow-covered ground and facing the woman who is and is not her, the woman with the stars in her eyes. This is the forest of her dreams. She isn't dreaming now.

"You can't opt out and still claim the crown. If you stay down here with me, you'll be safe and home, but you'll never be coronated."

Melanie blinks, suddenly interested. She has an option other than victory? Jack never presented that to her. Jack made it sound as if she had to win or all was lost. This is something new. She focuses on the woman, who lifts her eyebrows in apparent surprise.

"Oh, that's what gets your attention? Do you plan to evade the crown somehow? Because it doesn't really work that way. If you stay here, you'll be safe, but you won't be able to keep me. Someone else will do that. And part of why we tolerate the deaths of all the little possibilities who don't win—why we didn't step in when you started murdering each other the way you always do these days, it's quaint, really, although I don't entirely understand why you need to be like that—is because you're all dead already. Every single one of you."

Melanie blinks, frowns, stands up a little straighter. "What do you mean?"

"I know *you* know you're dead, because you went and did it in the most dramatic way possible. Having your heart burst inside your chest is definitely a way to announce your candidacy. And you pulled Harry down with you because the two of you have been running in parallel for longer than anyone ever had the reason to realize. He would have died on his own as soon as the season turned. Probably not as dramatically; some candidates don't even notice when it happens. But immediately. You're corpses from the moment the coronation begins, going through the motions of living while the crowns sustain you.

"Any seasonal monarch is a mass murderer from the moment they're coronated, because claiming the crown cuts all the other candidates off from what it offers, and means they stop being sustained by the season. Don't look so horrified, little girl, you've already killed two of them, and you didn't even know what you were doing."

"But when . . . when we challenge them, we're supposed to give them the option to refute their claim to the crown."

"Yes, and if they take it, they'll die." The woman—the Winter—looks at her calmly. "They'll be cut off, and they'll die. Not immediately. It's not as quick or as clean as losing a challenge, but it's just as inevitable. I'm sorry. You should know all this. My last regent held the crown so long that things got lost, got forgotten, that should never have been overlooked."

Melanie blinks, several times, trying to reconcile this with what she's learned from Jack, the careless way the younger girl has spoken of surrendering claim to a crown. But Jack's said other things, too, hasn't she? Things about the turn of seasons . . . "I don't believe you."

"You don't have to believe me. You could always repudiate your own claim to the crown, or convince Harald he should give up his. All you have to do is mean it, and accept that there's no taking it back. And die, of course. Everything that's mortal dies. Even seasons die. We just keep coming back after we go."

Melanie stares at her. "This is horrible. It's *horrific*."

"Yes. It can be described as both those things."

"It's inhumane."

"Little girl, whatever gave you the impression I was human?" The Winter moves closer, skirt rustling around her thighs, and nothing about her is young or innocent or pristine. She's an insult to the uniform she wears. Melanie wants to rip it off her body, to deny her that common comfort, even as she knows the Winter is appearing like this only so she can comfort *Melanie*, so Mel can hear what she's being asked to hear.

"I was here before I learned to wear a human face, and I'll be here long after. When all humanity is dust and ash and evolutionary legend, I'll still be here, on every planet that turns on an axis, on every world that experiences seasons. There's a phrase in your mind: 'Life finds a way.' It doesn't, always. But winter, on the other hand . . . winter always finds a way."

Melanie shies away from her, frightened and transfixed in equal measure.

"Some of you are born naturally—not made, as you were—with

seeds of seasons already sprouting in your hollow hearts. That's where your own humanity was meant to flourish. As you grow, so do we, and when you reach fruiting age, we put forth our flowers. For the attendants, the soil they offer is fertile but not as nourishing as we'd like. We grow in them, but twinned with the seeds of human nature, unable to claim and conquer what rightly belongs to us. They retain some of their humanity even after the blooming. You, little flower, do not. You are only and entirely what you were made to be, and the sooner you surrender, the happier you will be."

Melanie stares at her. "Jack said if I went too far into Winter, I wouldn't be able to claim the crown. And you just said I couldn't stay here with you, even if I wanted to."

"Coronation requires a small measure of humanity," says the Winter, waving her hand like she's brushing away a particularly annoying gnat. "As long as you cling to scraps, you'll be able to take me. And if not, then when someone else is crowned, you'll fade peacefully, as so many have done before you came. I hope not, though."

Melanie blinks. "What?"

"You were made for me," says the Winter. "A pretty toy for me to dangle on a string. I like the thoughtfulness that went into your construction. I like knowing you exist because someone thought I might want you. Of all the candidates in this batch, you're my favorite, which is why you're getting so much of my attention. I am inevitable. You are not. So fight me enough now to give in to me later, and stay with me as long as you can. We can do wonderful things together."

Melanie backpedals from the frozen woman with her face, smiling so sweetly, so coldly. She doesn't want to be here anymore. She doesn't want to be in this dark, cold place, where nothing thrives and nothing grows and nothing is reborn. The woman walks toward her, and she keeps retreating, keeps running, until she turns to flee, and the cold snaps around her like a branch from one of the skeletal trees. The cold shatters, and the winter shatters with it, as broken as a window, and she's clawing her way out of the wood, she's not there, she was never there at all—

Back in the car, Melanie jerks upright in her seat, sucking in a great, gasping breath of air. Harry, who was the only one of them to have realized she'd stopped breathing some five minutes back, hits the brakes and stops in the middle of the highway. It's safe right now, or as safe as that sort of thing can ever be; there's no one ahead of or behind them for miles, and the sides of the road are just a great emptiness, sand and scrub and hardpacked dirt broken by the distant shapes of looming mountains.

He unfastens his seatbelt and all but lunges across the car, taking her into his arms, and does what he's been doing since they were children, since the first time he realized that sometimes Melanie, much as he loves her, can be surprisingly fragile. He holds her closely while she cries, and he presses his face into her hair, and he doesn't say a single word.

He just holds her.

Acceleration

There's a lot of America out there, and Harry doesn't think he's ever fully appreciated just how *much* before trying to drive it. Even without dawdling the way they did in California, he's been driving for hours without end, and according to Jenny's GPS, they're still at least two hundred miles from the border between New Mexico and Texas. They'll be driving for days yet, and not even the growing sense of urgency that comes over him when he looks up at the dark, star-speckled sky, devoid of any trace of moon, can make them go any faster.

Jack emerges from the rest stop, wiping her hands on the legs of her jeans, and stops next to him, head tilted upward at the sky. "Worm moon's officially gone," she says. "We start moving toward the sprouting grass moon now. And once she's fully in the sky, that's it: winter's out of ascendency, out of decline, even, and the spring is here."

Harry shoots her a worried glance. "You said Mel and I would both be awake during the spring."

"And fall, yeah," says Jack, in what's probably meant to be a reassuring tone. She doesn't quite make the mark. She doesn't seem to care as she shrugs and continues: "But that assumes you've claimed your crowns and been coronated. This is my first coronation, too.

I don't know what happens if there's a change of seasons while it's happening."

"Not making me feel better."

"Didn't know that was my job." She shrugs again before she pats him on the arm. "She's not going to drop dead at the stroke of spring any more than I am. She's just going to get a little weaker. Maybe that's not the worst thing that could possibly happen."

"Yeah," Harry agrees, somewhat morosely, and gets back into the car.

It's been almost a full day since the Arizona border, since the Winter candidate who sparked Mel's plummet into her own personal freeze. She hasn't slipped back under since coming back to them, has been clinging to the present and her own existence as a flesh-and-blood person with both hands, smiling and laughing and talking with as much enthusiasm and vigor as she can dredge up, but Harry knows her. He's seen her put on his routine before, when she had to be hospitalized again, when there was another surgery scheduled and she wasn't sure she'd be coming home. This is her brave face. She's not doing as well as she wants everyone to think she is, and while he can't fault her for trying to seem like she's all right, he wishes she didn't feel the need.

But then, it's not like they've known Jack or Jenny long enough for trusting them to come naturally, or easily. He mostly manages it, because he's exhausted and he's scared and now that they're off the coast, he's constantly on edge, waiting for the next attack, but it's not because he really *knows* them, not the way he knows Mel.

It's a little odd, how quickly and completely Jack seems to have shed the girl she was before the Winter chose her. Jenny at least acknowledges his old name, even if it doesn't fit him at all, like trying to make someone put on the shoes that fit their feet when they were a toddler. Jack seems to have decided her life began the day she ran away from it, and while he wants to ask her more, he's also a privileged child of a remarkably stable and healthy family, and he knows better than to cross certain lines. It may have taken him years to learn, but no one has ever said that Harry March didn't retain his lessons once they were beaten into him.

Mel emerges from the rest stop, a low concrete building with signs on the walls exhorting travelers to check for scorpions before they lower their trousers. It's American brutalism, same as it was in California, in Arizona, all the way back up the coast, and he loves it a little. For the rest of his life, he supposes that when he thinks of safety, he'll think of public rest stops along the sides of America's highways, solid enough to double as storm shelters, no frills and no decoration, broken glass in their parking lots and ancient vending machines sputtering by their sides.

They're certainly more like a slice of safety than the motels they keep cramming themselves into, all four of them in a single room for the sake of security; splitting up would mean twice as many doors to watch, twice as many windows to barricade against attack from outside. Harry's only hope is that once they reach the labyrinth, they'll be able to relax. He's traumatized. He knows Mel is too. They need to catch their breath and find a way to go home.

Her father may be an alchemist, but he can't fight her once she becomes the Queen of the Winter, and he won't control her, not when she has a full court, a crown, and those weirdoes in Berkeley on her side. They can get through this. They have to.

Melanie waits by the rest stop until Jenny emerges, and the two of them walk back toward the car with their heads close together, gossiping about something Harry can't hear from where he's sitting in the driver's seat.

He's never been the jealous sort, but having a girlfriend with an attached expiration date has always made the other boys a little more respectful of his relationship than they might have been. They can snipe and swipe from one another, but not from him; Melanie is off-limits. It would be only natural if he looked at Jenny with Mel and felt jealousy stirring in his chest, waking from its long slumber. But he doesn't. On some level, he recognizes Jenny as an extension of himself, a valid surrogate in almost all situations.

Some of the things he's coming to quietly understand as this goes on are unnerving and even frightening, but he doesn't see where he has a choice.

The pair of them reach the car and get in, Mel leaning over to kiss him on the cheek before she fastens her seatbelt. Her skin is cool but still a reasonable temperature, given the chilliness of the night, and he knows she kissed him just for the reassurance of letting him feel her, and he's grateful for it, even as he starts the engine and pulls out.

They're getting closer to the labyrinth all the time. It's only going to get worse from here.

After another eighty miles he pulls off at a motel that looks like something from a horror movie, all one level, hugging the ground, with a flickering neon sign out front and too much cactus in the landscaping. The room costs less than half of what he'd expected, and comes with less than half the water pressure. But there are two beds, and none of the four of them can feel any other contenders close enough to pose a threat, and the road to the labyrinth is clear. Harry climbs into bed and is asleep almost before his head hits the pillow, Melanie curled up close and lukewarm against him, smelling of soap and stillness.

The room is quiet.

Harry opens his eyes on a sunlit meadow, green grass and blooming flowers all around him, and the air rich with the scent of strawberries. He pushes himself into a sitting position, then clambers to his feet, looking bemusedly around. He's been here before, in his dreams, but this doesn't feel like a dream. This doesn't feel like a dream at all.

Slowly, he turns. There is nothing but open meadow as far as the eye can see. As a child of the western mountains, this doesn't feel like his dream landscape. Something should be breaking it in at least one direction, something should be varying the horizon.

He has time for that thought to coalesce into something coherent and then his next turn brings a distant mountain into view, one he certainly didn't see before, black and white against the sky. He stops turning to blink at it. The idea of a mountain appearing just to make him more comfortable is ridiculous, but that doesn't mean it didn't happen.

He's getting more and more accustomed to the idea that sometimes things happen because they want to, and not because they make any sense at all. Making sense is not high on the priority list for the universe. Maybe that's why he doesn't jump, or flinch, or even really blink when he turns one more time and there's a man standing there, a man with his face and his build and his, well, everything; the only reason they're not identical is that he's dressed in jeans and a woefully stained shirt—this road trip has been hell on his normally strict standards of grooming, and while Mel's just becoming more and more charmingly disheveled, he's starting to look like he has questionable personal hygiene—and the other man is wearing Harry's football uniform, purple and yellow and pristine. No grass stains. No mud or sweat either.

So he's not a football player, and this is a performance for Harry's benefit. Harry knows about performances for someone else's benefit. He slaps an amiable smile onto his face, assuming the sort of relaxed posture he takes with adult authority figures, and meets the man's eyes for the first time.

This time he *does* flinch, although he'll be proud of himself later for how well he manages to keep it together, because the man's eyes break the impression of identicality: his eyes are like a slice of high summer sky, blue and clear and inhuman, streaked with skidding lines of fast-moving cloud that blow in some unfelt, internal wind.

"Guh," says Harry.

"It's almost spring," says the man. "The Wheel's turning. The sun's coming back from its long celestial journey."

"Actually, the Earth rotates around the sun," says Harry, not sure why pedanticism seems like the correct response in this moment.

The man laughs. "Actually, the sun rotates around the galaxy, but it took a long time for the humans to figure that out," he says.

"For centuries you thought the sun revolved around the Earth, and one of your only failures was not believing it hard enough that the universe reordered itself to make it so. Human belief is a beautiful, terrible thing."

"Mel's told me about this," Harry says, folding his arms. "She says sometimes when she sleeps, she dreams about a forest filled with black trees and snow and a woman who looks like her but with midnight in her eyes. That's how she talks to the Winter. So I'm guessing you're the Summer, then?"

"Most candidates take longer to reach that conclusion," says the Summer. "I'm impressed, or I would be, if you weren't running in tight parallel with a frozen maiden. You have certain advantages you didn't earn."

Harry shrugs. "Seems to me they're balanced out by the disadvantages. If you're talking to me the way Winter's been talking to her, does that mean I'm closer to claiming you?"

"We aren't singular the way those people in Berkeley were singular: for them, there's only one at any given time. For us, there's more than one of everything. If you claim my crown, you'll be one of seven Summers walking the world. You'll need to be able to be comfortable with them. You'll need to work with them, even when what they want is to burn."

Harry blinks. The idea of climate by committee should be ridiculous . . . but then, haven't the oil companies been doing effectively that for decades? They make decisions that impact the whole planet, and they do it in boardrooms filled with stockholders who are innately biased, because doing the thing that kills the coral reefs or raises the sea level or whatever will also make them buckets and buckets of money. He's aware, in the way of someone who has never needed to worry about money in his life, that worrying about money is a major source of stress for most people. He wonders how many of those people would be able to look at a report explaining that their comfort and absolute security would come at the expense of a bunch of marine mammals they've never met, and not choose the option that keeps them where they want to be.

Probably not many. So this system is as fair as any other. It's as fair as any system humanity has been able to come up with on its own. He still frowns at the Summer.

"You didn't answer my question. Am I getting close?"

"You are," says the Summer. "Which is why I need to get you comfortable with me, human man. If you claim my crown, you'll never be alone again, never be free of me—or of your frozen maiden. She'll walk with you all the days of your life. Consider carefully before you make any final decisions."

Harry's seventeen, too young to be thinking about marriage with any seriousness (despite his childhood determination to marry Mel when they both turned twelve), but he's always known that one day, those thoughts would become a part of his mental landscape, and all her objections about her probable life expectancy aside, he's always known that when that happens, he'll be thinking of Mel. She's his girl. It's that simple. One day she'll be his wife, if they both live that long. So he shrugs and answers Summer's warning with "So? I figured that out when I was like eight. You're promising me a world where we get to stay together. How could I do anything but agree?"

"You realize she's not entirely human, even now?"

"You mean, do I understand that her dad's some sort of Dr. Moreau asshole who built her in a lab so she'd be a better incarnation of the Winter? I'll be honest. That sounded like bullshit when Jack started saying it, and that's even with everything else that was already going on, which was . . ." He pauses, sighs, shakes his head. "So much. This is all so much. You get that, right? Human belief is big, but individual humans are small, and 'Hey, you have to kill each other to win a crown that turns you into an anthropomorphic personification of a season and means you don't get to be a person anymore, hope you're cool with that' is a little much to take."

Summer blinks, slowly, looking at Harry with that level, cloud-streaked gaze for a long moment before he says, "Is that what they told you? Because that's not entirely true."

Harry jerks upright. "What do you mean? There's a way to opt out?"

"No. But you don't have to kill anyone. All you have to do is claim the crown."

Harry's confusion fades into a frown. "I don't understand."

"You can't kill what's already dead. Any candidates still standing when the crown is claimed will go away, swept out of the path of the new monarchs by the wind of their manifestation. And technically, you're not killing anyone."

"No?"

"As I said, you can't kill what's already dead."

Summer says this like it's perfectly reasonable, something Harry should accept without question, and it still makes him want to sit down in the flowery field, to dig his hands into the grass and scream. He's known Mel was dead since her heartbeat disappeared. He's been trying to ignore the little signs that say the same thing about him. The way he sleeps but doesn't tire, eats but doesn't hunger, sees habitually to the needs of the flesh that don't trouble him at all, as if they were chores to be checked off a list before he can go and do something he'll find more enjoyment in.

His body still functions the way he expects it to, if not slightly better; he's hardly been sleeping for days, eating nothing but truck stop specials and diner food to the point where even his teenage boy's digestion should be starting to object. He doesn't have a headache. He doesn't have so much as a case of the sniffles. He's sleeping easy, waking easy, walking through his days without pain, driving for hours without eye strain or shoulder stiffness . . . really, if this is death, he should have died years ago.

Except he knows that death doesn't usually let people off this easily. So he stares at the Summer in silent shock, unwilling to fully accept what he's hearing, even though he knew most of it already. Mel's been dead since this began. Mel's the product of a mad scientist's lab, because that's what alchemists are, really, call them sorcerers and wizards all you want, like this is some kind of bullshit fantasy world, but he knows a mad scientist when he sees one. He isn't going to lie about what they are.

"The ones who refuse their crowns keep me with them for a little while, as the attendants do," says the Summer. "They have time to return to their homes and families and settle their affairs. And then the fragment of me that's been animating them since the coronation began fades back into the whole, and they fade with it. It's a death adjacent to the seasons, so their loved ones remember them, unlike the ones who choose to fall still fighting for my favor." He laughs at the look on Harry's face. "Oh, did your attendants not inform you? I suppose they may have forgotten, and there's little point, as it changes nothing, but your parents aren't looking for you, because at this point, they don't remember you enough to realize that you're gone."

Harry supposes that isn't more of a surprise than learning that he's a dead man. The seasons have been hiding so much, so many things, even things that could have gotten them into serious trouble, what's one more on top of that? "Will they remember me when I win the crown?"

"Yes. You need be absent only as long as no human will shapes my steading on this continent."

Harry frowns a little as he puzzles his way through that sentence. Finally, he sighs. "You could talk a little less like a faux-deep Instagram post, you know."

To his surprise, Summer laughs, long and loud and utterly without shame, like that's the funniest thing he's ever heard. When he gets himself back under control, he shakes his head and says, "No, I can't. Not yet. When I am you and you are me, I might be able to. But I was William Monroe on this continent for the better part of three hundred years, and he was a small, petty man who chose cruelty whenever he had the opportunity, and never spoke with me enough to let me keep pace with how the world had changed."

"How did he do that? If you were him, shouldn't that have been enough?"

"Normally, it would have been. But he thought himself better than his season. He was the first on this continent to kill as a first choice. Before him, when the change of faces came, they fought, yes, they would compete gloriously and well, and they knew full well that loss would mean their death, but when they lost, they lost with honor. Not William. He was determined to win at any cost. He abandoned honorable challenges and fought to slaughter in every case. I am crueler from my time with him. I hope you can teach me to be gentle again."

It sounds like a sincere desire, and so Harry only blinks, and says nothing. This is a lot. He knows it's a lot, and he's willing to keep listening as long as the season that will hopefully soon belong to him wants to keep speaking. What else is he supposed to do, run away into the meadow? Try to reach that bleak and frozen mountain in the distance, where for all he knows, Melanie is having the same conversation with her own season? No. Better to stay and listen and prompt where necessary, to keep the conversation moving forward, strange as it is. He's learning things. He needs to know them.

"How much of you is you and how much of you is whoever wears your crown?"

"I'm a concept, a side effect of the natural world. Seasons exist because the planet rotates on its axis as it moves around the sun, or because an ancient goddess of the harvest cursed the world to win her daughter back from the lord of the dead, or because humans wanted their crops to come back and sacrificed their own on the snow. It's hard to say. I'm all those things at once, and it doesn't matter which you think is truer than the others, because they'll all carry the same weight for you. Even if you decide one matters more, it won't. One Summer soul isn't enough to change the whole universe, no matter how much you may wish it were. But I'm not a person, Harald. You need to accept and understand that now, while we're still distinct from one another, because you're close enough to the labyrinth that you could win at this point, and once you claim the crown, you can't set it aside. Not without killing the girl you claim to love."

Harry blinks. "We're parallel."

"Yes, but you're not tied to each other the way you will be when crowned. This is the birth of the alchemical marriage. There's no backing out once you say you'll do it, not unless you want to trigger another coronation and start the whole process again."

Harry looks at the mountain in the distance for a long and silent moment before he shrugs and says, "Okay."

"Okay?" echoes Summer, sounding baffled.

"Yeah, okay. I came this far, and I'm already dead, which makes this whole thing a kind of wacky afterlife, right? I can think of way worse afterlives than one where I get to keep having hands and legs and walking in the world, and stay with Mel at the same time. That's just the cherry on top of the sundae of the nightmare my life has become. As soon as we're not stuck with two other people all the time so we can make out more and start getting naked, it'll be perfect. And if you're going to say something shitty about how we're both going to be dead for three months out of the year, don't. I already know that whole part, I don't need you to rub it in."

Summer looks at him, a slow smile canting his lips upward until he's smiling broadly. It's not Harry's smile, for all that he's wearing Harry's face. It's something altogether different.

"Oh, I think I'm going to enjoy being you, Harald March, if you can only make it to the end," he says. "I'll see you in the labyrinth."

"What do you—"

The meadow falls away, and Harry opens his eyes on another dark motel room. Jenny is snoring gently from the next bed over; Mel is curled against him, her head resting on his shoulder, her hair dangerously close to winding up in his mouth. Again. He blinks sleep-crusted eyes, then smiles as he looks down at her.

They're almost there. And they're going to win.

He's never been so sure of anything in his life.

The fog was still there, hanging thick and cottony among the brambles and branches, but it had pulled back enough that she could see the flowers on their stems and the cobwebs glittering with morning dew. The garden had returned as the sunlight pouring down from above in great, buttery shafts came to burn the fog away. There was so much fog in the air that everything was still dim and gray, like it was twilight rather than morning.

More and more crows were beginning to stir. Zib looked at the one that had come to her first, seated on her shoulder with its beak still sticky with bonberry juice.

"I would like it if we could have a conversation, and if you could help me pick berries to take inside for Avery and Niamh," she said. "Crows are wonderful, but you're not so good for talking to, unless I want to really be talking to myself."

The crow cocked its head, regarding her for a moment before it made a small croaking sound and flung itself into the air. Zib had never seen birds that took flight the way the Crow Girl did. She flew as if she was attacking the sky and expected to be repelled at any moment by the creatures that actually belonged there. All across the garden, crows took wing, crashing toward each other and finally colliding a few feet away from Zib in a great cacophony of wings and feathers that consolidated into the shape of one skinny teenage girl in a black feather dress.

"Are there other things like you?" blurted Zib. It was a rude question, but she wasn't sorry to have asked it. It felt like the sort of thing that needed to be answered, either now or in the future, and she was growing increasingly tired of pushing things into the future rather than handling them in the aching, immediate now.

"You saw the rest of the flock when the King tried to take you," said the Crow Girl.

"No, I mean, I know there are other crows, but are there other things?" Zib frowned earnestly, her hands busying themselves with the picking of ripe pink berries. "Are there boys who are also knots of toads, or girls who are a camp of bats when they don't feel like walking on

two legs? I know you traded your name for feathers. Can people trade for other things?"

"Ah," said the Crow Girl, and "Oh," said the Crow Girl, and "Yes, and no," said the Crow Girl. She began her own berry-picking, clever fingers clearing branches in seconds as she pulled the fruit into her palms. She kept her eye on the bush, not looking at Zib. "That was where I had the idea, you see. There was a boy, when I was younger, and he could become a whole shoal of salmon when he didn't want to think like a boy did, when he wanted to swim freely and be left alone. I had the idea that maybe I could be like him, if I tried hard enough. That I could have freedom when I wanted it, and a cage, when I wanted that instead. So I went looking. I slipped away from the people who were meant to keep watch over me, and their faces went with my name, so now I don't even know who I left behind." . . .

—From *Along the Saltwise Sea,* by A. Deborah Baker

BOOK VII

Alabama

Dreaming of spring I can almost taste
Pomegranate, peppermint.
But then I wake, and I hear the wind
Moaning and lonely for her.

—Dr. Mary Crowell, "Change of Seasons"

A candidate for the priesthood could only succeed to office by slaying the priest.

—Sir James George Frazer, *The Golden Bough*

Red Clay

CALENDAR SEASON: FEBRUARY 28TH, 2017: ONE
MONTH TO SPRING, NEW MOON BETWEEN THE
WORM MOON AND THE SPROUTING GRASS
MOON.

They crossed the border into Alabama a little over an hour ago, and they're so close to the labyrinth at this point that Harry's not sure he's safe to drive. The road seems to gleam iridescent ahead of them, so bright it's barely possible for him to focus on it. Melanie can't even look at it anymore. She's leaning back in her seat, eyes closed and face tilted toward the ceiling. Jack and Jenny are pressed together in the back.

"The improbable road has us," says Jack, in a hushed tone.

"Not helping," snaps Harry.

"We can't get lost now," she says. "I don't think it's possible anymore."

"Still not helping, and I can't descend all the way into a children's book without losing the *actual road,* and then you both die." He's come to terms with the fact of his own death over the past two days. It helps that Melanie's dead too, and she doesn't care. All he has to do is claim the crown and he gets to have everything he's ever wanted. This is the definition of a perfect win.

He can do this. *They* can do this. Harry drives on, and Mel pretends to doze, and the road unspools, and then they're passing the city limits of a town called Huntsville, and it's like static electricity dancing across his skin, he can feel it, he can *feel* it, close and bright and burning. The labyrinth. They're almost to the labyrinth.

He keeps driving, no longer looking at the map or asking Jenny for directions—not that the other man could provide them. The GPS was set to take them to Alabama, but not anything more specific than that, and it hasn't said a word since the Mississippi border. He's following the call of the labyrinth, which is part beacon on the horizon and part siren song and entirely inescapable. It has him. He couldn't escape at this point if he wanted to, and he no longer wants to.

Then he pulls onto a residential street, white-walled houses popping up around him like a prayer to suburbia, and the labyrinth disappears.

Harry hits the brakes immediately. The car screeches to a stop. Melanie makes a sound of protest before she sits up, opens her eyes, and blinks.

"Where did it go?" she asks.

"I don't know," says Harry. "I was following the trail, and then I turned on this street, and it wasn't here anymore."

"Pull over," says Jack abruptly.

Harry looks up, meeting her eyes in the rearview mirror. "Do you know something?"

"I know I'm picking up on something I haven't felt in a long time, and you need to pull over."

Harry shrugs, and steers the car to the curb in front of a white house exactly like all the others around it, surrounded by a wide green lawn. There are two holiday inflatables anchored there, one of a large and friendly cartoon rabbit, one of a cartoon dog driving a car shaped like a carrot straight toward the rabbit. He turns off the engine and pockets the keys, twisting to face the attendants in the back.

Jenny has an expression on his face that almost mirrors the one on Jack's. Confusion mixed with longing so powerful it could be used as a weapon. The door to the house opens, and a woman's silhouette appears, backlit by the room behind her. She doesn't come out of the house, but she raises a hand and beckons for them to go inside.

Jack is out of the car like a shot, not waiting for Melanie to tell her she can go, off and running across the lawn without paying any attention to where she's going. She hooks her foot on one of the lines holding the inflatables in place and goes sprawling, facedown in the grass. Jenny, who's running after her, helps her to her feet, and the two of them run on together while Harry and Mel are still getting out of the car.

The woman in the doorway has a laugh like smoky bourbon, smooth and peaty and rich and a bit intoxicating. She laughs as Jack reaches her, and laughs again at something the younger girl says, leaning down to gather her into a hug Harry can tell, even from a distance, will feel like home. Then she lets go of Jack and gathers Jenny into the same, motioning both attendants inside.

She hesitates before following them, looking over her shoulder. "Well, are y'all coming?" she asks. Her voice matches her laugh, flavored with a sweet Alabama accent. Melanie starts walking faster, and Harry hurries to catch up.

The woman is still in the doorway when they reach her, a smile on her painted lips and a faintly amused look in her eyes. Harry looks at her and thinks she's lovely, in an "old enough to be my mother" sort of way: her short, dark brown hair is cut to cup her cheeks, her eyes match the whiskey depth of her laughter, and her face is finely constructed, beautifully symmetrical. She's wearing a black V-neck sweater over yoga pants, completely comfortable, completely at ease with this sudden delivery of strangers to her doorstep.

The reason why comes clear when she catches sight of Melanie. She pulls away from Jack and Jenny and curtseys, as deep and low as a lady of the court greeting the queen.

"My *lady*," she says, and when she straightens, her smile is even broader than it was before. She looks from Mel to Harry, seeming to take note of him for the first time. "Oh, my husband will be pleased to see that you've made it as well. A good omen, starting out with parallels. How entangled are you?"

"They dropped dead at the same time," says Jack. "As soon as the coronation began."

"You were monitoring her?" asks the woman, glancing back to Jack, who nods. "Well, that's going to have contributed to them making it as far as us. They always do better when they have someone to watch over them, or so I hear. One of my dear ones is in England, and she helped with the last coronation, saw the new Summer Queen through her challenges and all the way to the throne."

"I'm sorry," says Harry. "Are you a Corn Jenny?"

"Oh, heavens, no," says the woman, and smiles at him like a roaring fire in the middle of a July night, s'mores and hot dogs roasting over her flames. He would follow her to the ends of the world for that smile. He would follow her anywhere she asked.

He has the feeling he's going to be following her to the labyrinth.

"I'm a Stingy Jack," says the woman. "But y'all can call me Carolyn. Now let's get inside before we give the neighbors a show, shall we?"

Harry takes Mel's hand, holding her tightly, and holds onto her still as they follow the woman through the door, into the bright warmth of her hallway.

She hangs back, and closes the door behind them.

C liff's at work right now," she says, bustling around the living room as they perch on the couches and watch her with expressions ranging from the wary and weary to the worshipful. Carolyn doesn't appear to notice, or if she does, she doesn't appear to care; she's busy getting coffee poured and dumping fresh scones and Oreos onto a platter, which she brings out and sets on the coffee table with all the ceremony of a priest presenting the crown jewels.

Melanie claims a scone and a cup of coffee, leaning back into the cushions and tracking Carolyn with her eyes as she continues to move around the room. "Are you going to sit and join us?" she asks.

"Are you asking it of me, my lady?" asks Carolyn, in return. When Melanie looks nonplussed, she sighs and says, "I'd love to, but you've tracked mud all over my floors, and if I don't get it cleaned up soon, it's going to stain. Can you wait until I've fulfilled basic hostess duties *and* not ruined my floors?"

"Um, sure," says Melanie, expression shifting to embarrassment. She cups her mug between her hands, scone resting on her knee, and continues to track Carolyn as she retrieves a Swiffer mop from a closet near the kitchen and begins wiping mud off the floor.

It would seem a little rude at home in Oregon to prioritize mopping up mud over spending time with guests, even uninvited ones. But the mud here, where Mel can see it sticking to her shoes, is an alarming shade of rusty red, like dried blood. It would absolutely wreck a carpet. Cheeks flushing hot, she ducks her head and asks, "Should we take our shoes off?"

"Little late now, hon," says Carolyn, smiling sweetly. "Mud's already in the house. But it's all right. My mama always said no one with any sense would have a floor that couldn't be cleaned. And I needed to mop up anyway."

"Did someone get murdered in your yard, ma'am?" asks Jack, still with that faintly worshipful tone.

"No, honey, this is just how the dirt is here in Alabama. Something about the soil makes it come up red, and when you get clay on your feet, you can track it just shy of everywhere you go. Once it dries into a thing, whether it's fabric or wood, it stays forever, so you have to get it up while it's still wet. Like blood, in a way, even though there hasn't specifically been a murder."

"I'm sorry," says Harry, sitting up straighter. "You said your name was Stingy Jack. I know that means you're like the Jack we've been traveling with, but for autumn instead of winter. Why haven't we seen anyone else by that name? Why do you still have a proper name, not just go by 'Jack' the way our, um, Jack does?"

"Let me finish mopping before you start asking me the big cosmological questions, please. I've sent Cliff a text, he'll hopefully be back by the time I'm done, or close to it, and then we can all get caught up at once. We've been waiting for you."

"Are we the first ones here?" asks Jenny.

you and when to ask for permission, and he's always done his best to be polite when dealing with adults he's not related to. But this—all of this—is unfamiliar ground, and he's got no idea what he's doing. Melanie looks similarly uncomfortable, and her coffee is starting to ice over. He wonders if she's even noticed.

Jack and Jenny are still watching Carolyn raptly, as enchanted as children who've just been put in a room with a real-life Disney Princess. And there's a trace of the cartoon princess to this woman, an unearthly air of pleasant sweetness. Harry would absolutely believe her if she announced that woodland creatures helped her do her hair every morning, and he's dating Mel, who is basically Snow White in blue jeans. Maybe she's not real. Maybe none of this is happening, and they're all sitting in a Waffle House right now, waiting for a disinterested waitress to bring them toast and eggs. It's so hard to tell anymore.

"I'm not dead, if that's what you want to know," says Carolyn. "None of the attendants are. We're living people with a little too much of the season inside us to live normal lives, but we're alive, and we have to deal with all the things living people do. We have jobs and mortgages and children—if we're lucky—and allergies and sometimes sensitivities to gluten. Mine's not so bad I have to stop baking, thankfully. I know people who can't have a crumb in the house without the risk of getting awful sick, and I'm not sure I'd have been able to prioritize my physical health above my mental health like that even if I'd wanted to."

Harry blinks again. Then he turns and presses his face to Mel's shoulder, eyes closed. "Can things start making *sense* again?" he asks plaintively. "They don't have to make a lot of sense. They don't even have to make good sense. But any sense at all would be a nice change."

Mel pats him on the shoulder. "It's okay, honey. The nice lady stands for the fall. I can feel her, although not very strongly, and I don't think she wants to hurt us."

Carolyn blinks, tilting her head to the side, so the dark wing of her hair cups her cheek. "Fascinating," she says, and glances to their attendants. "This your doing?"

"They were like this when I found them," says Jenny. "Harry isn't my first candidate."

"Mel's mine," says Jack. "And they were like this when I found them, too. They've been running parallel since before the coronation started. She's . . ." And she hesitates there, like she's about to admit something unwise. Swallowing, she finishes: ". . . she's Cosgrove's Winter girl."

"Roland Cosgrove? The alchemist?" Carolyn stiffens. So does Harry, pulling away from Mel at the tone in the older woman's voice. He doesn't like it. She sounds, suddenly, less like she's welcoming them in and more like she's looking at something unpleasant that's bubbled up in her drain. He shifts positions on the couch, very slightly, preparing to shield Mel if he has to.

"He was my father, ma'am," says Mel. "I know he made me to be a better vessel for the Winter, although I'm still not entirely sure what that means."

"He didn't make you to be a *better* vessel, from what I hear told; he made you from top to bottom, snips and scraps, with nothing natural in the process," says Carolyn. "You were a project, same as it used to be, and leave it to the alchemists to stumble into the way things were in their rush to change the way things are. They used to make vessels for the Summer out of roses and sunlight, and for the Winter out of owl feathers and snow. There was nothing human in them, and they were cruel. They reigned all out of control of mortal hands, and the world was poorer for it."

Harry stares at her, suddenly feeling like she would have poisoned Mel's coffee if she'd known where Mel came from before she served them. There's something steely and resolutely unforgiving in her eyes. "Mel's as human as anyone," he says. "She loves me, and you have to be human to love someone."

"Anyone who has a dog would argue with you about that," says Carolyn. "Lots of things experience feelings that look like love from the outside. No way of knowing what they actually feel unless you can read minds, and most people can't, thankfully. That's the sort of terrible party trick that's best left to the gods."

"I love him," protests Mel. "I've loved him my whole life. I know what I feel, and I know I'm a real person. Even if I wasn't supposed to be, something went wrong while I was being born, and I'm a lot more human than you want to give me credit for being."

"Bet a dog would say they felt love for their master, if a dog could talk."

"Bet it wouldn't make a bit of difference if they were wrong," snaps Mel. "If the dog says what they feel is love, and feeling love makes them *behave* like they're in love, makes them protect and look after their master, makes them want to be near the person they've given their whole heart to, does it matter if what the dog feels isn't actually what a human being would consider 'love'? The actuality and the appearance matter just as much under the right circumstances."

For a moment, everything is quiet and tense. Then Carolyn laughs. "Oh, I *like* you," she says. "I don't know if you have it in you to win—I suppose the labyrinth will answer that—but you're only the second parallel set I've seen, and you're definitely the deepest-rooted into your seasons. You're the first full package to come rolling up."

"Full package?" asks Harry warily, not sure if this is another piece of terminology he doesn't have the background to understand.

"Both seasons and their attendants, at the same time."

"I thought you were an attendant too."

"I am, silly. But I don't *belong* to anyone." Carolyn wrinkles her nose, like the very idea is ridiculous, and looks over her shoulder as the familiar sound of a garage door rolling upward rumbles through the house. "That'll be Cliff. I'm glad. We can get this all sorted out."

"Yes, ma'am," says Melanie. None of them rise. A door opens and closes again, and a man emerges from the kitchen, presumably having used a heretofore-unconfirmed back door to enter. The air in the room gets . . . fresher, almost, like a good cleansing wind has just blown briskly through. It's hard to look at this man and not trust him. It's even harder not to like him, and so Harry doesn't even make the effort.

The newcomer is tall, broad in the way of men with sturdy builds, rather than the way football players tend to accomplish the shape, wearing teal hospital scrubs. He just needs a stethoscope slung carelessly around his neck to complete the image of the genial Hollywood doctor. He has a pleasant, friendly face, and a completely hairless pate that catches the light like it's been polished. Maybe it has been. Harry has wondered whether bald men shine their heads to get them so reflective, replacing the rituals of haircare with something more applicable.

He pauses at the sight of them, a broad smile covering his face. "Well, hello, y'all," he says. His accent is, if anything, heavier than Carolyn's. "Care, there any more of those scones?"

"On the counter," says Carolyn. "Grab yourself a cup of coffee too and then come join us. I was just about to tell these nice kids how to get to the labyrinth."

"Oh, that's a speech I should be here for," agrees the man. "Hold tight, and then we'll handle introductions." He ducks back into the kitchen.

Carolyn returns her attention to her guests, smiling placidly. "Cliff doesn't function well without his coffee," she says. "He needs caffeine to keep more than two thoughts in his head at a time. Like a Labrador that thinks he's a pediatrician."

"Didn't you just try to convince us that dogs can't feel love like people can?" asks Mel pointedly.

Carolyn's smile sharpens as she redirects it toward Melanie. "I may have said something of the sort, yes," she says. "But you countered me nicely, and I suppose it's rude to contradict one's guests."

"Are you married, ma'am?" asks Harry quickly, before Mel can turn the sudden tension he feels in her into an assault on their hostess, whose capabilities are still unclear, but who is unquestionably connected to the labyrinth they have to navigate if they want to survive the season.

"Twelve years this October," says Carolyn, with a hint of pride. "We met when Cliff was fresh out of college, before medical school. He'd just awakened to the strength of the living Spring, and he didn't know up from down, the poor lamb. Not sure he'd have made it if he hadn't found me to tether him when he did. Or maybe I'm being full of myself, and he'd have been just fine. He's a surprising man, my husband. Tends to throw people off their balance."

"That, and God talks like me," says Cliff, emerging from the kitchen with a scone and a cup of coffee. He plops down next to Carolyn on the couch, grinning too widely, like this is the most entertaining thing that's ever happened in his home, like he can't wait to see what happens next. "Welcome. My name's Clifford. So you kids are looking for the labyrinth? What do you think you're going to do when you get there? I bet the crowd around the gate's ten deep by now. You'll never hit the center before you get overrun."

"I think we're going to enter the labyrinth, and we're going to claim the crowns and take our thrones," says Mel, in an exaggeratedly pleasant voice. "What's more, I think if you're a Jack in the Green to balance out the Stingy Jack next to you, the two of you are going to be working for us, so it would be nice if you could stop with this little 'good cop–overly polite cop who cares more about propriety than anything else' routine and tell us what we need to know."

Clifford raises an eyebrow, holding his ridiculous grin for another beat before it falls away and he turns to his wife, commenting in a much more natural tone, "I think I like these ones."

"Came right to the door," confirms Carolyn. "Just . . . pulled up to the curb like it wasn't anything at all to find us and come to the house. They tracked mud on my floors, but they apologized for it when I pointed it out, and I think they're a bit distracted."

Harry and Mel both stare at her as she speaks, not saying anything at all—not sure what there is they *could* say. Interestingly, it's Jenny who finds his feet first.

"Wait, so that was all what, a routine? Is it not your job to welcome us?"

"Oh, it is," says Carolyn. Even her tone has changed, still warm, but less artificially formal. She's relaxing. "We constructed this labyrinth."

"We've built six out of the last eight," says Cliff. "Not easy to fit in around everything else we have to do, but it's necessary. Once this one actually gets used, we'll burn the remains, and then the alternate team will put the next one together. Hopefully it won't be used, and then year after, we'll get to build another one."

"Why do you hope it won't be used?" asks Harry.

"Labyrinths are only used during a coronation," says Jack. "They'll keep building them every year, forever, because that's what the Spring and Fall do, but none of them will be used until the two of you die."

Harry pales. "Oh. Well, let's not do that."

"No, let's not," says Mel. "I know you people are excited to have new folk around to tell all about your weird, secret alchemical world, and I respect that: if I had a whole reality almost no one got to see or experience, I'd want to talk about it too. Maybe in five years, once I'm used to being the Winter Queen, I'll do the same thing. But right now, we're in a hurry, and we need to know what you need us to know."

"Blunt little thing, aren't you?" asks Clifford, and sips his coffee.

"She's the Cosgrove girl," says Carolyn.

"What, really?" He lowers his cup, turning to stare at Mel. "I didn't expect that particular science project to make it this far. Are you sure?"

"Unless literally everyone I've met, including the living spirit of the Winter, has been lying to me, then yes, I'm sure," says Mel coldly. "Yes, my father was an alchemist and he built me and trying to save his experiment is what killed my mother and yes, I'm supposed to be the perfect vessel for the Winter, and from what she's said so far, I think he got that part right, but it's not going to make a damn bit of difference unless I'm the first one to put on that crown."

"The Cosgrove girl," breathes Cliff. "I remember hearing about you from a Jack in the Green who used to work at the hospital. She said they'd been trying to get to you and your sister, to help with your medical needs, but your father wouldn't let them. If he was going to craft perfect vessels, they wanted those vessels to grow up sheltered by the seasons, prepared for the responsibility and reverence that might one day be theirs to carry. He turned them all away, except for the ones who disappeared and were never heard from again."

"Jacks in the Green stand for spring; they tend to be attracted to positions involving growth and nurturing," says Jack. "Lots of nurses. Lots of doctors. Lots of teachers, too."

"If being a season comes with a profession, what does being a Jack Frost get you?" asks Harry. "Lots of truancy?"

"Oh ha ha, you're hilarious."

"You're both getting away from the point," says Mel. "What do you mean, they wanted to offer medical care to me *and* my sister? She was stillborn. There's nothing there to care for. You can't provide medical care for the dead. My father was sustaining her with alchemy, not with medicine."

"Oh, but you're dead," says Carolyn. "And I'd say from looking at you that you've been dead a few dozen times since you were born, but your father who made you, he thinks like an alchemist, which means he thinks like a human, which means he thinks it's better for things to be alive when they can. So he kept finding ways to bring you back. That's a good thing for you, and probably a good thing for us, if you're as suited to your season as you seem; even a coronation wouldn't have been enough to call you back if you'd made it past the border of your season. But you've been dead before and you're dead right now. What makes you think your Summer sister can't accomplish the same trick? That's just silliness."

Mel blinks, quiet as she sinks back into the couch. Harry takes the coffee cup out of her hand before she can spill it. If Carolyn gets upset about mud on her floors, he doesn't know how she'll react to coffee on her couch.

"What do we do now?" asks Harry, eyes fixed on Clifford. "How do we get to the labyrinth, and what do we do when we get there?"

"It's so close that you'll be on the scarecrow trail as soon as you step out the front door," says Clifford, with more gravity than he's exhibited thus far. "All you need to do is keep moving forward. All the other candidates will be there, and their attendants, and they'll probably try to kill you, but you can keep each other safe until the doors open. Or you can snipe the competition, it's up to you. Once the doors unlock, you'll all be able to go in and start moving toward the center. Whoever gets there first will be able to attempt to claim the crowns. They'll have winnowed all the unsuitable long before you reach that point."

"So it's sort of like a relay race, only with murder?" asks Harry.

"Now you're getting it," says Clifford. "And no, we don't know when the labyrinth is going to unlock. It does that on its own time."

"We're entering alchemical time once we step inside," says Jack. "That's how this works."

Harry shoots her a sharp look. "I'm getting a little tired of 'that's how this works' as a way to excuse things that don't make any goddamn sense. Just so you know."

"Suck it up, buttercup," says Jack, more gleefully than is probably called for. She takes one more sip of her coffee before she leans forward and places it on the table. "Well, if we're almost there, I suppose it's time for us to get this show properly on the road."

Carolyn looks at her levelly and clears her throat. Jack blinks, clearly confused. "Coaster," says Carolyn.

Jack moves her mug onto a coaster, now looking shamefaced, and stands. "Thank you for your hospitality. We know you didn't have to offer it, and we're grateful."

"You're welcome, and if it helps at all, I think you stand a pretty solid chance of making it to the end. Cosgrove did his work well, and you're the most seasonally aligned pair we've seen so far."

"That's . . . encouraging." Harry's not sure it is, as he stands and offers Mel his hand. She puts her coffee down—on a coaster, earning her an approving nod from Carolyn—and rises, staying close beside him. "If walking out the door puts us in the labyrinth, can my car stay where it is?"

"You're parked on the street, yeah?" asks Carolyn.

Harry nods.

"You should be fine for a week or so, and if the labyrinth hasn't spat you out by then, it's probably because you've died inside. The glow's been getting stronger and stronger, shouldn't be long now before it's mature. We don't know for sure. We've never had one wake up before." Her smile is both sudden and dazzling. "I bet we're about as excited as you are to see what happens when she wakes up."

"Yeah, there's a good chance we're all gonna die when that happens, so you'll forgive us for being less excited," says Harry blandly.

"Now, come on, your attendants will probably live," says Clifford. He stands as well, stretching. "The labyrinth isn't trying them. Most of the candidates left theirs behind, assuming they ever had them."

"My contacts in Europe said a lot of attendants don't survive the coronation," says Jack. "Traveling with your candidate puts you at risk, since it's hard to tell the difference between an Incarnate and an Ascendant when they're right next to each other, so they draw fire when a challenge begins."

Harry turns to stare at Jenny in slow horror. Somehow, he'd managed to ignore that facet of the power structure until this moment, even when they met the Winter attendant on the highway, even when Jenny changed his loyalty from Matthew to Harry with such quick ease. Jenny makes a small expression of regret mingled with acceptance and nods, confirming Jack's words as truth.

"They don't," says Clifford. "It's part of why I've always been glad to stand for a part of the year that doesn't have to train anyone up to challenge for the crown. Now, I know it's tempting to spend the night here chatting with me and my lovely lady wife, but it's time for you to move along. If you're not back in a week, we'll have your car towed. Until then, we can tell the neighbors you came to visit our daughter. She's away at college, she'll never contradict them."

"We were so worried she'd be called to serve, but no, the seasons skipped over her," says Carolyn, sounding smug, like she had somehow managed to convince the seasons they should skip her girl. "She's off studying agriculture and computer science."

"I was planning to go into land management and forestry," says Harry.

"A man who likes the trees? That's always nice to hear," says Clifford. He leads the group back to the front door, pausing with his hand on the knob. "Y'all ready? There's no coming back once you're past this point."

"Not sure it matters at this point," says Mel.

"No," he agrees. "It doesn't."

Labyrinth

The door doesn't open on the lawn, with its attendant inflatable guardians and the comforting outline of Harry's car parked on the street. No, it opens on a long tunnel with a floor of hard-packed earth strewn with straw that has clearly been walked on recently, flattened strands pressed deep into the ground. The tunnel walls are made of corn, tall and green and clearly at the very height of its growth, every stalk dripping with fat golden-tipped ears that smell so sweet it makes Harry's mouth water. You could feast forever in this tunnel, just sit down and gorge yourself on raw corn until you burst.

Harry glances to Carolyn, walking beside him, and flinches as he sees how her attire has changed, ordinary clothes becoming a gown made of red, brown, and yellow leaves that somehow lay almost flat and still move like fabric despite the fact that he can see their individual edges and hear them rustle as she walks. She catches his eye and smiles languidly, inclining her head. "No title for you yet, but I won't be shocked if I'm calling you 'my lord' in short order," she says.

"Um," says Harry.

He's seen other things that prove the alchemical world and the magical world are the same thing viewed from slightly different angles, has had more than enough proof presented to make him accept that all of this is actually happening, he isn't just having a weird LARP road trip with his sick girlfriend and a couple of hitch-hikers, but somehow Carolyn's impossible dress is a step too far for him. He stops walking.

"Nope," says Harry.

"Oof," says Jenny, who has just walked straight into him, too distracted by the walls of corn around them to notice the other man's stillness. "What's wrong, boss?"

"People don't change clothes when they walk through a door-way," says Harry, pointing a shaking hand at Carolyn. She tilts her head and looks at him, clearly amused. They've all stopped now, a little cluster of people barring the way for anyone else who happens to come along.

And hey, if anyone else happens to come along, they're probably looking to kill everyone who's already here, so maybe inconveniencing them isn't such a bad thing.

Melanie still looks the same. So do Jack and Jenny. Clifford's clothes have changed in tandem with his wife's, becoming a suit of green oak leaves, fresh and bright and new. He even has a crown of woven branches. He smiles at Harry, a little lopsided, and gives a small half-bow.

"As she says," he says. "Things are progressing as they ought."

"I am not okay with this," says Harry. "This isn't normal. This isn't . . . this isn't *right*." The world isn't supposed to work like this. He can handle hearts that restart on their own, strawberries that grow too fast and out of season, women who wrap themselves in veils of rainbow light, even snowstorms summoned out of thin air, but this is too impossible and too blatant and too much.

"*This* is where you dig your heels in?" asks Jack. "Really?"

Everything is silence save for their voices, and even that's not right; there should be sound, the rustling of the corn if nothing else. The chirp of crickets or the calling of twilight birds. Not this . . . quiet. The path they walk along is as well lit as any store aisle, but the sky overhead is dark, filled with the distant silver shine of stars. That would be fine if the light had any source, but it doesn't, not that Harry can see. Unless it's coming from the corn.

There is nothing about this that he doesn't hate, and nothing about it that's right, or fair, or possible.

"Really," says Harry. "None of this is happening, and I want to go back."

Clifford looks at him solemnly. "Remember, you have a way out," he says.

"No he doesn't," says Jack, voice sharp.

Clifford turns to look. "He can renounce his claim to the crown," he says. "Candidates are always permitted to renounce."

"He and Mel are running parallel," says Jack. "He can't."

"And I can't because if I renounce, I die immediately," says Melanie. "My heart stopped when the Winter took me all the way over the edge. I'm not a person anymore. I'm an idea a season had about what personhood looks like, and it's not perfect, but it's what I have, and I don't want to give it up."

"All candidates die if they renounce," says Harry. When Carolyn and Clifford exchange a look, shifty-eyed and silent, he shakes his head. "Summer told me. All candidates die, because something inside us got shoved out to make room for our season. It just normally takes a little while for us to . . . wind down, I suppose is the best way of putting it. Once we say we won't wear the crown, we're dead people walking. Mel and I are just in a slightly tighter scrape than most of our peers. You can't tell me to renounce the crown like it's a reasonable request."

"Then what *do* you want to do?" asks Carolyn. "We can't stand here forever. You'll have to enter the labyrinth eventually."

"You mean this isn't . . . ?" Harry gestures around himself with both hands, encompassing the walls of towering corn.

"Not at all," says Clifford. "This is the scarecrow trail. A line. A labyrinth is, by definition, a bunch of lines, all of them squiggling together and into each other, a whole big mess. Like a dungeon in D&D."

Carolyn gives him a sharp look. "Hush, you."

"Nope," he says, looking briefly smug. "Won't. Anyway, the labyrinth's ahead. But the house is behind, and you have to either go forward or refute."

Harry looks to Mel, who looks back, pleading with her eyes. He knows that his refusing the crown would be her ending, and his own. He'd be leaving her, and for once it would be of his own accord. Maybe it's silly. Maybe it's childish. But he still can't do that, either to her or to himself. Even after all this time, he can't leave her alone.

"I won't refute," he says, almost sullenly, and starts walking again. Mel hurries to catch up with him, sliding her hand into his. The rest of them follow.

The corn watches.

The tunnel ends as abruptly as it began, feeding into a wide delta of open space, the ground still sharp with stubble where something has been recently brought to harvest. It doesn't make much sense, given that the tunnel of corn was very much a springtime phenomenon, but this is a place of deep and profound harvest, of autumn sliding into winter. Harry stops, blinking, and Melanie stops with him.

There is a wall ahead of them, plain gray brick, stretching in both directions for as far as their eyes can see. There are people as well, lounging on the ground or on bales of hay, standing in small conversational clusters. It's not the murderdome they were threatened with. Half of the people are shivering in the nippy fall air. The others look perfectly comfortable, like this is precisely as air should always be. The Jacks and the Jennies, then, distinguishable by which season sings to them.

This may not be a murderdome, but there *are* bodies, most of them shoved up against the corn that curves around the whole scene, out of the way. Their necks are broken, their throats slit; their lives ended. They've already been removed from contention.

There is only one entrance, closed with gates made of twisted branches tied together and shaped to look like the ornate curlicues of wrought iron. More people cluster around the gates, although "cluster" may not be the right word. They're all giving each other space, five to ten feet in some cases, and none of them are close enough to grab any of the others. All of them look like they've been through the wars, bruised and dirtied, with blood on their cheeks and tears in their clothing.

"The other candidates," says Jack, confirming Harry's guess as she steps up on Melanie's other side. Jenny steps up on his, and they're a straight line, unified against what's ahead of them. Harry doesn't even have to glance back to know that the other two are gone, somehow taking the exit with them. They've reached the labyrinth.

Everything that happens from here is as it was always going to be, and there's nothing left that any of them can do to change it.

Melanie squeezes his hand, her fingers cold as ice against his own, and begins walking forward. Harry matches her step-for-step. Jack and Jenny are slower, falling quickly behind, allowing their Incarnates to take the lead. Harry feels like he's following a script he's never seen before, one that tells him where to put his feet and what to say. He feels like everything that's happened since the football field has been part of the same performance, all of it designated, all of it designed.

It's not a good feeling. It means nothing he's ever done has mattered, that he was always going to wind up here, no matter what he said or did, how hard he tried. If this was all going to happen anyway, did he really fall in love with Melanie when they were kids? Or has his single-minded fixation on her been the result of the season in his soul telling him what to do, who to love, who to *be*? Free will suddenly feels like as much of a fairy tale as this impossible plain, the wall in front of them, the spired city he can barely see rising in the distance on the other side—

We're standing in the shadow of the Impossible City, he thinks, and that has never been more true, and he has never been more afraid.

Melanie squeezes his hand again. He glances to the side. She's looking at him, and when he meets her eyes, she smiles, and a knot in his chest loosens, making it easier for him to breathe. Maybe this was all preordained somehow and maybe it wasn't; maybe it was always going to happen and maybe it's all happening the way ordinary things happen, one piece at a time, one action feeding into another. It doesn't really matter in the end. They're here, now. This is what they have to live with now. This is the moment they have made.

And he would have loved her no matter what. If she'd been an ordinary girl and still Melanie, if he'd been an ordinary boy and still Harry, he would have loved her. They never needed the seasons to bring them together. They only needed the world to line up long enough for them to meet, and there was never a chance they'd do anything but fall in love once they knew it was an option.

She was made for him, and from the way she's smiling at him, sweet and warm and welcoming all at once, he was made for her.

The crowd around the gate murmurs as they notice the four approaching, eyeing them warily. Harry and Mel are still fresh and they're all battered to hell, and while the other candidates look tense and unhappy about their presence, they're already damaged enough not to engage before they have to. Jack and Jenny peel away, going to join another group of attendants around a hay bale, and it's just Harry and Mel as they approach the gates, hand in hand. None of the other contenders are holding hands, Harry notices; they're all leaving space between them. He doesn't see Matthew in the crowd.

Maybe the man didn't make it this far. Maybe Misty, thwarted and furious but still alive, decided if she couldn't take Harry apart, her own brother would do, and removed him from contention before he could leave California. Harry's a little surprised to realize he doesn't care. The man hurt him and scared Melanie. If he died before he got here, that's just what he deserved.

There's a flash of white at the corner of his eye. He doesn't turn toward it. He's too busy watching the gate, waiting for the moment when the labyrinth decides they've all waited long enough and lets them step inside. It's a waiting game that could turn into a race at any moment, and you don't play football as long as he has without developing at least a little bit of a competitive streak. He wants to win this.

He wants to claim his season's crown and stay with Mel and figure out what normal looks like when he's dead for three months out of the year. Colleges have summer programs. If he can work things out correctly, he can still get his degree; this doesn't have to change anything if he doesn't let it. It's only going to change everything, because he'll have Mel forever, and the two of them can be happy. The only thing standing in their way is the rest of the candidates, and now that he knows they're all dead already, it's a lot easier to think about hurting them.

If he has to "kill" them to get them out of his way, he thinks he can. After all, the seasons killed them first; he's just helping them realize what their bodies already partially know. And then, at the end, his own half-life gets to continue.

He's young enough to believe on some level that he's immortal, and to know down to the bottom of his bones that the world began when he was born and will end when he dies, and nothing he's experienced in the past few weeks has been enough to dissuade him, so he holds fast to Mel's hand and steps up to the gates, and all this is good and right and exactly as it's meant to be; all this is perfectly fine—

Something hits him, hard, in the back of the head, and he goes down hard, collapsing to the earth. His hand is yanked out of Melanie's. He hears her shriek, fear and indignation, and then he hears nothing at all, and the darkness is all.

Melanie grabs the person who just hit Harry, yanking them away before they can finish bending down to do . . . something . . . to his prone form. "Get away from him!" she snarls. Then she freezes, staring at the woman in front of her.

Her own reflection stares back.

Aven

This girl looks exactly like Melanie herself, save for her hair, which is a brutally stark white, like a sheet of new fallen snow. Mel has time to think that it would have made more sense for her to be the one with the white hair, what with her being tied to Winter and all, before the girl—her sister, it has to be her sister, nothing else makes sense—drops the knife she's holding, grabs Mel by the shoulders, and slams her forehead into Melanie's hard enough that Mel sees stars. The girl lets go almost immediately, dancing out of reach before spinning around and delivering a brutal kick to Mel's midsection.

Mel stumbles backward. The girl goes in for another kick, but before it can land, Mel grabs her foot and yanks, pulling her assailant closer.

"Hi," she says, in a blithe, almost perky tone. "I guess we haven't been introduced, huh? I'm your sister. My name's Melanie. What's yours?"

"Aven," snarls the white-haired girl, and launches herself at Melanie again, fingers hooked to grab and claw. She moves like a predator, smooth and elegant, with none of the reservations or awkwardness of someone who'd been socialized according to normal rules; she's never learned not to bite, not to kick or claw. She fights to kill.

Melanie sidesteps her easily, and slams a knee into the small of Aven's back as the other girl's momentum carries her past. "See, here's the thing," she says. A bruise is forming on her forehead, stark and purple against the pallor of her skin. "I'm a cheerleader. Do you know what that is?"

Aven turns and looks at her blankly. "No," she says, finally. "And I also don't see why it's relevant."

Melanie steps on Aven's knife, foot pinning the blade to the dirt, and smiles placidly at the girl who should have been her best friend, not a distorted and distorting funhouse mirror. She's going to suffer for this later, she can already tell, not just with the monster headache she feels building in the corners of her skull, but with the kind of hysterical panic that comes from confronting the impossible and truly accepting the fact that every ludicrous story she's heard has been the truth.

Her father was Dr. Moreau. Her mother, sainted icon of her girlhood, never loved her, never wanted her as a mother wants a child, but as a scientist wants an experiment to succeed. She was not born from love. She was born from obligation and from hubris, and her sister, who she's always believed was dead, has also survived to grow into this half-feral girl who introduces herself by attacking, who has a stain on her sweater that could be ketchup or raspberry jam or any number of other things. This girl who radiates Summer almost as strongly as Harry does, whose skin is hot under Melanie's fingers, like brushing against a stove that's just been turned off. She's not quite hot enough to burn. She's far too hot to be entirely human.

"It's relevant because you don't become a cheerleader without learning to take a few falls," says Mel, voice low. "We live on ice baths and arnica." *And you should have been living there with me the whole time, climbing the same pyramids, learning the same tricks.* "You may be a badass, but unless you're willing to kill yourself in the process of taking me out, you're not going to beat me. And you're not touching Harry again."

She looks up, looks around at the circle of candidates surrounding them, most of whom are splitting their attention between her and the gate, expressions resembling the vaguely disinterested focus of people waiting for the mall to open on Black Friday. She sees them, maybe a dozen in all, and in that moment she hates them without reservation. They're here to take what she's already thinking of as rightfully hers. They're here to put her in the ground.

Well, she's not ready to go.

"That goes for every damn one of you," she says, voice loud and carrying. "If you touch him, I don't care if you're doing it because you're challenging for the Summer and you want to claim the crown, I don't care if you're doing it because he looks like the kid who used to beat you up and take your lunch money, I don't *care* what your reasons are. I will *end* you."

She has no way of knowing whether the Summer candidates will listen to her, and the Winter candidates are more likely to come gunning for her. She doesn't care about that, either. She just glares at Aven, silently challenging her sister to come at her again, to come at Harry again, to give her an excuse.

"This isn't how I thought this would go," says Aven, sounding almost ashamed. Like she really expected to kill Melanie's boyfriend and then share a sisterly hug. "I dreamt about you."

"Yeah, well, I buried you. Before I could even remember that you'd been there."

"Our father—"

"I know the whole story," spits Melanie, and Aven has the sheer gall to look disappointed, like the truth about their origins was going to be the thing they could bond over, the thing that united them. Like learning they weren't real girls was supposed to be the thing that swayed Melanie to her side. Mel learning it from someone else and having time to process that fundamental, foundational betrayal . . . that wasn't supposed to happen.

Aven takes a step backward, out of range. "I'm going to kill him," she says, almost serenely. "In the labyrinth, I'm going to kill him, because you and I, we're meant to be together. Don't you feel it? We'd be the most perfect marriage of the seasons the world has ever known. If we took the crowns together, our reign would be endless."

The worst part is that Melanie *does* know it, on some level; the Winter in her bones sings in Aven's presence, even more loudly than it sings in Harry's. She could pull away from him and run parallel with her sister instead, Roland and Ariadne Cosgrove's grand experiment finally complete, ready to play out against a stage of millions. Part of her wants to.

Most of her knows that Winter doesn't get to make her choices, not yet, and if she let go of Harry, it would be for the sake of Winter, to make the season stronger, and not for the sake of *Melanie*. Fuck that. She's doing what she does next for the sake of Melanie, because Melanie still matters. Melanie will always matter, even when she allows the Winter in her broken heart to spread through her entire body, even when she gives up on being human to become something else and other.

"Go fuck yourself," she says pleasantly, and bends to retrieve the knife from under her foot, looking at it for a moment before snapping the blade shut and sliding it into the pocket of her jeans. "I am not your sister. The same man may have manufactured us both, but if you were my sister, you'd know me, and if you knew me, you'd know not to touch my boyfriend."

Harry is stirring, trying to push himself up onto his elbows. Melanie crouches, sitting on her heels as she offers him her hand, eyes still on Aven.

"Go away, little Summer girl," she says. "I'll fight you if I have to, and maybe I'll win and maybe I'll lose, but I'm pretty well matched to you, and whether I win or lose, I'll slow you down enough to take us both out of contention for the crowns. You know what happens to the candidates who don't claim a crown, don't you?"

"Of course she does," says a voice, surprising in its familiarity. Melanie glances toward it and recoils, almost losing her balance. Only Harry's grip on her wrist keeps her from landing on her behind. He sits up, still holding on to her, and they're on the same level as they stare at the man now walking toward them, familiar and out of place and . . .

"Trevor?" squeaks Melanie. "What are *you* doing here?"

"If you Incarnates cared enough to learn how to spot attendants instead of trusting us to come looking for you every time you needed to do something, you'd have figured me for a Corn Jenny a long, long time ago," says Trevor stiffly. "But you were always too self-involved to care about what's happening around you, and too busy focusing on your own lives to notice what was going on with mine."

"Corn—*you're* the one who was supposed to be preparing Harry?" She stands, pulling Harry with her, and takes a menacing step toward Trevor. Aven is all but forgotten, dismissed in the face of an even better target for Mel's anger. "*You* were supposed to be his attendant?"

"Surprise," says Trevor, smugly.

Melanie glares at him. "What the fuck, Trevor? You decided you didn't like him because of some stupid fight you had in the sixth grade, and so you went with my dead sister over your own teammate?"

"You said you were my friend," says Harry. "You said we were cool. I asked you and you said we were cool."

"Yeah, well, you're not the only one who can lie," snaps Trevor. "And it wasn't sixth grade. It was eighth grade. Before the Spring Fling dance. Remember now?"

"No," says Melanie flatly. Harry, on the other hand, stares at Trevor in slowly dawning comprehension, followed almost immediately by horrified dismay.

"Really, dude? *Really?* You left me unprepared for the coronation because I told you I was going to ask Mel to the dance? We'd been going out for *years*. Everyone knew she was my girl! The *teachers* knew!"

"Only because you were the first one to ask for her homework when she was out sick," snaps Trevor. "If you'd given the rest of us half a chance—"

"You would have what? Convinced a Winter girl that someone was better for her than the Summer boy she'd been in love with since she was a kid? Come on, man. You could have gotten me killed. You could have gotten Mel killed. That was bad fucking form."

"I knew about Aven," says Trevor, ignoring Harry's words. "The Corn Jenny who trained me, she knew about the Cosgrove experiment, warned me to stay well clear of their house. 'There's nothing we can do until she wakes up, and every Jack Frost who goes there disappears.' That's what she said. She told me not to worry, she'd handle the sleeping princess if she ever got the chance to open her eyes, and I could have the golden boy. Said that was how the seasons 'settled.' But I didn't want you." His smile is slow and cruel. "I didn't want to stand in your shadow, Mr. Quarterback, perfect little rich boy with the perfect life and the perfect girlfriend and everything. There was never going to be a coronation. I'd just be your weird sidekick for our entire lives."

Harry spreads his arms, indicating the impossible landscape around them, the endless wall, the shadow of the Impossible City. "Never going to be a coronation, huh? Got any more great predictions about the future, Nostradamus?"

"I hope you like head injuries," says Trevor, smirking, just before the rock Aven has scrounged up from somewhere hits Harry in the temple and he goes down again, crumpled in the dirt.

Melanie steps forward, the air around her beginning to plummet in temperature, moving fast toward Arctic. Her eyes are icing over, a manifestation of the amount of cold she's yanking into the world, pulling it from . . . somewhere else, from wherever it is Winter lives when it isn't walking in the world. The other candidates, who have been watching this little drama with the disinterested eyes of athletes studying the competition before their first match, fall back, and a boy with snowflake patterns in his irises mutters, "I can't do *that*," in the wounded tone of someone who has just seen the year's new hot toy whisked away by an uncaring parent.

Melanie keeps moving toward Trevor, and if she even realizes that this leaves Harry unguarded on the ground, she doesn't pause or acknowledge it. The part of her that cares about other people is very far away right now. She's focused entirely on the cause of her anger, even if she doesn't understand what that anger means right now. The Melanie who understands what she's feeling and why is not currently in control.

Harry groans and rolls over, narrowly avoiding Aven's foot as it comes crashing down on the spot where his head was just resting. He stares up at her and she smirks down at him, at least until he grabs her leg and jerks her forward, bringing her crashing to ground level with him. She scrabbles in the mud, trying to recover her rock, and he hammers a fist into her solar plexus, knocking the air out of her.

He's going to have nightmares about this moment forever, maybe longer than he has nightmares about anything else, the still-nameless boy in the motel room, Misty and her cloud of biting, stinging smoke, the sight of Mel surrounded by a delicate snowstorm of her own making, none of them are as terrible as looking into the face of a girl who looks exactly like the woman he loves most in all the world and seeing nothing but wild loathing reflected there. She hates him. She doesn't even know him, but she hates him, because in her eyes, he's the one who took Melanie away from her.

Not their father, who somehow kept Aven alive and isolated for all these years, cut off from the people who should have been her foundation and family. Not Trevor, for leading her here and filling her head with who knows what nonsense about her sister and her sister's Summer boy, who exists to challenge her in a very concrete and personal way. Harry. Somehow, he gets to be the only one she hates. Maybe because in her eyes, he's already challenged her once and won, when he stole Melanie's affection.

As if Mel could ever have belonged to a sister she thought was dead before she ever even met him. Before she ever even met *herself.*

Aven lunges for him again. He brings his knee up, slamming it into her stomach and knocking her away. Feeling around behind his head, he finds the rock she threw at him. *Mel, I'm sorry,* he thinks, and pegs it at Aven's forehead with all the strength and accuracy he's built up over four years of high school football, and seven years of rec league football before that. It hits her squarely between her eyes, which cross, like she's trying to look at her own nose. Then she goes down in a heap, hard, and Harry scrabbles away from her before picking himself up off the ground.

All this time, Melanie has been advancing on Trevor, who at least has the sense to back away, hands raised defensively. When she raises her own hands to strike, they leave trails of freezing vapor in the air, so cold that Harry knows her touch will burn the boy they both went to school with, the boy who is, after all, only a Summer Ascendant and not a Summer Incarnate.

Trevor hates him. More than he ever understood. The fury over "losing" Mel, when she was never his to lose, has grown deep and poisonous, putting roots down well below the surface. And none of that matters, because they're still teammates, and teammates don't let each other die of frostbite. Harry jerks to his feet, nearly blacking out as his injured head reels and the world spins around him, then catches his balance and lunges after Mel, arms outstretched to grab her and pull her back.

It hurts when he clamps his hands around her upper arms, cold lancing into his fingers and up his own arms until it hits his shoulders. She snarls and struggles against him, a wild thing restrained. "Mel, Mel, hush," he says, lips close to her ear, pulling her back against his chest and holding her there. "Mel, it's me."

She struggles a little more, eyes on Trevor. Harry kisses the top of her head, lips going briefly numb from the chill, then looks to Trevor, his own eyes narrowing.

"Dude, uncool," he says. "You could have made this all so much easier, and you went with making it harder because Mel didn't want to go to a stupid dance with you?" They hadn't even been real dates back in middle school, much as they'd felt like it, ripe with newly released hormones and bright with the lack of other experiences to compare them to. They'd just been an excuse to put on clothes that were slightly nicer than usual—not much of a treat for a kid— and hang out together in the cafeteria, with all the tables folded up and stacked against the walls like that would somehow be enough to make them disappear. Harry and Melanie had been together in their innocent, childish way before that dance, and if Harry had been a more violent child, he would probably have given Trevor a good reason to hate him long ago. But he's never been the sort to settle conflicts with his fists, and he doesn't like that this situation is forcing him to start now.

It's not fair.

Melanie struggles again, and Trevor takes another step back.

"You had everything," he accuses. "Money, the football team, even a girl who was always way too good for you. And then the Summer chose me and the other Corn Jenny found me and taught me what that meant. She promised me when I met my Summer I would know, and I'd be able to serve. I'd be able to do something glorious and important, even if there was no coronation. The incarnates serve the seasons even when they never get to manifest, and I was going to support my Summer. But then one day I turned around and it was *you*."

His lip twists. He looks so disgusted that Harry nearly recoils, his grip on Melanie slipping momentarily. She doesn't break away, only squirms and remains against him, apparently giving up on the idea of escape. That's something, anyway. He's not going to lose her.

"You and Melanie were out by the swings, and I could see how much you wanted to run, but you weren't running, because she couldn't. You were just sitting in the grass, leaning on your hands, looking at her like she was a cake you wanted to eat and a bug you wanted to squash at the same time." Trevor spits every word with focused fury. This is something he's been carrying for a long, long time. "You *resented* her. She was sweet and beautiful and perfect and she cared about you even when you were your stupid self, and you resented her for being sick. You made her feel even worse, because all her illness meant was you not getting to do exactly what you wanted, exactly when you wanted to do it."

"That's not how I remember things," says Harry carefully. Melanie isn't struggling now, but she's still leaning against him, her shoulders pressed to his chest, letting him maintain the pretense that he's holding her against her will. "The only time I remember sitting with her by the swings was right after the first time she had open-heart surgery. They cut her open and they did things to her insides, and her father wouldn't let me come see her. Said I was too young to see her that way, too young to understand how important it was for me to do exactly what the doctors said and follow all their rules, even if I didn't like them. If I resented anyone, it was her father, and the doctors, and the people who were keeping us apart." Mel wasn't too young to cut open. He shouldn't have been too young to be with her when she was alone and scared in a strange place, and maybe hurting.

He'd been sitting with her because she was back at school and he was so overwhelmed with being able to be near her again that the thought of getting up and going off on his own had been impossible. Most of the time, he spent his recess racing around like the wild thing he was, and if she was feeling well enough, she did the same. They might have become attached to each other earlier and more intensely than was normal, but they were still kids. Girls still had cooties, boys were still icky, all the little prejudices and gender roles of the playground had still reached the two of them, but the lure of each other's company had been strong enough to let them come back together every time. He'd been with her because he'd been without her longer than he could stand to be, and if he'd looked resentful, it was aimed at the adults who'd worked so hard to keep them apart, not at Mel, who had done nothing wrong.

"I stayed with her because I loved her," says Harry, and that's exactly right, that's exactly true, that's exactly why he did the things he did, made the choices he made. "I still love her, and that's why I'm staying with her now, and why I'm not letting her kill your ass. We've both accepted that we have to fight the other candidates—we can't avoid it, and it wouldn't matter if we could. Our dice have been rolled, our fates are set. Attendants, though . . . you can still go and have a normal life. You can walk away from this. She'd blame herself forever if she killed you."

"She's not going to kill me," blusters Trevor.

"Dude," says Harry, flatly. "I can barely hold her, she's so cold, and I'm incarnate. You're just ascendant. If she touches you, you'll shatter like a snowball against a wall. I don't want to put that on her."

Melanie pulls away again, and this time he lets her go. She stops after she's gone a foot or so, looking at her hands with wide eyes. They're still steaming cold, fingertips blackened and bruised with frost. She looks back up, at Harry. "Really?"

"Really," says Harry. "I mean, maybe not. I wasn't there when you killed that other dude. But I think probably yeah. It seems like the sort of thing this screwed-up system would do."

Melanie looks beyond him to her sister, still crumpled motionless on the ground. A trickle of blood has run from the cut the rock made on Aven's forehead, thick and dark and drying on her pale, pale skin.

"Is she dead?" she asks, voice hushed.

"I mean, technically, we all are," says Harry, and has to bite back a gale of laughter that would definitely come across as inappropriate under the circumstances. "But she's breathing, and I think she'll be okay."

He hit his head hard enough that he should be vomiting and seeing little green men from Mars by now, but he feels fine. Better than fine. He feels like he just woke up from a good night's sleep, like he could run a marathon and finish an exam and play a solid game of football before dinner. He thinks it's being this close to the Impossible City. He's been feeling better than he should since all this started; why shouldn't that feeling be magnified when they're this close to the place that apparently powers and belongs to them all?

"Thank you," says Melanie, and touches his cheek with her blackened fingertips. He shivers a little but doesn't pull away, and her touch doesn't burn. They balance each other. That's not a way that she can hurt him. "I know neither of us knows her, not really, and she was trying to hurt you, but . . . thank you." Her smile is quick and fleeting, there and gone in a moment. "She's still my sister."

"For now," he agrees. "I'm not giving up my claim to the crown for her sake."

It's a cruel thing, to put it so baldly and out in the open like that. He feels it needs to be done as quickly as possible, because eventually, once they've claimed their crowns and taken up their places, she's going to realize what his survival means. She's going to realize that it was him or Aven, and he chose himself.

Telling your girlfriend you're sorry you're going to have to kill her sister should probably be harder than this, but given everything else that's happened, Harry feels like this was precisely hard enough.

"I know," says Melanie, and leans in, and kisses him.

Harry kisses her back, and for a moment, it feels like the whole world lights up in answer. Then he realizes the light is real, it's coming from outside his body, it's coming from outside his closed eyelids. He opens his eyes and turns.

The wall around the labyrinth is lit up like the Vegas strip, burning bright white and lambent against the darkness. The other candidates are rushing the still-closed gates, all save for the motionless Aven, who remains where she fell. Melanie pulls away from him, sliding her hand into his. "I think it's almost time," she says.

"I think so too," he agrees.

The gates begin to unravel, the branches receding one by one, like the unweaving of a lover's knot. It's a slow, deliberate process, and it hasn't stopped by the time the two of them finish strolling over to join the crowd, leaving the speechless Trevor behind.

Then the last briar retracts, and the gates are gone, and the labyrinth is open, and the candidates pour inside.

In the Dark

CALENDAR SEASON: FEBRUARY 28TH, 2017: ONE MONTH TO SPRING, NEW MOON BETWEEN THE WORM MOON AND THE SPROUTING GRASS MOON.

Harry loses hold of Melanie's hand as they cross the threshold into the labyrinth, and in an instant, he's alone. Not apart from her; alone, completely and utterly alone, standing in a long hall formed from shaped topiary, with none of the other candidates anywhere in view. He turns. The gate is gone. The wall is gone with it, leaving only unbroken green behind.

Well, they told him it was a maze. Harry begins to run, until he comes to a juncture. In two directions, more halls of glowing green, waiting for him to charge headlong down them. In the third, utter and absolute blackness. He remembers something about the rule of lefts applying in labyrinths—always turn left and you'll find the center, or maybe the way out. He's not sure which, but he doesn't have a better plan, and so he turns left and keeps running.

The next two junctures are more of the same, two green and open options, one square of void. He turns left each time, not slowing, scanning his surroundings for any sign of the others. The fourth juncture is the first to present a problem.

There, the left turn is the void.

Harry hesitates, shrugs, and runs into the black.

He emerges in a frozen forest, snow on the ground and skeletal, leafless trees in all directions. He doesn't let the transition throw or disorient him. He just starts walking through the snow, eyes fixed on the horizon, already beginning to shiver.

He wonders if he'll reach the forest's edge before he freezes. If this is the forest Melanie talks about visiting in her dreams. If she's here for him to find.

And just as that thought finishes forming, someone else—something else—moves in the trees.

It steps from shadow to shadow, indistinct and hard to focus on, like a being made of smoke or ashes. He stops walking and squints at it, watching as it comes closer, until proximity alone forces his brain to organize it into a shape he can understand.

It's bipedal, vaguely humanoid, but long and skeletal and almost insectoid in its lanky, stretched-out alienness. It looks like something out of *Star Trek*. It doesn't appear to have substance, but to be made from vapor and from glittering particles of snow suspended in the air. He knows it on sight. He's been holding hands and sharing kisses with it, in another form, for the greater part of his life. It may not *look* anything like Melanie, but it *feels* like Melanie, and he knows this for the secret test at the center of the labyrinth, the one the attendants couldn't warn him about or prepare him for, but that he really should have expected.

This whole process has been about arguing with the universe, convincing it to help them—or at least not to hinder them—to let them move along to the next stage in their journey, to stay together. Maybe that's what natural forces get out of wearing human faces. They get stubbornness, and the ability to argue. So it seems only right that this should be the point where they argue with the seasons for their right to claim the crowns. The actual race isn't about getting through the labyrinth. It's about who steps into the void and makes their case the fastest.

He wants to start the process, before someone else can beat him there. He wants to get this over with. He knows, purely and profoundly, that rushing the Winter at this stage isn't going to help him. So he stands, somewhat antsily, and watches as the skeleton shape of the season comes closer and closer.

It's not trying to hide itself from him. It doesn't really need to. It's so thin and so defined by the absence of substance that it could disappear if he stopped looking at it, or if it stopped moving for more than a few seconds. It's just coming, one step at a time, and the cold comes with it, the temperature in the already-frozen wood plummeting like a stone, falling into the deep negatives with a surprising and terrifying speed. Harry holds his ground. He's survived so much to get here. He's pretty sure he can take a little frostbite.

The Winter moves to a point not three feet away from him, so close he could reach out and touch it if he wanted to, if he was feeling brave and wanted to risk losing a few fingers, and stops. It has no face. He still gets the direct impression that it's looking at him, studying him, taking his measure.

Whether or not it finds him wanting, it's going to have to deal with him, because he's not going anywhere. The time for going anywhere is over. He folds his arms and raises his chin, standing as tall and confident as he can manage while slowly freezing in a landscape that doesn't feel like it belongs to him, that doesn't feel, in the end, as if it ever could.

Then the Winter speaks. Its voice is lower, distinctly male in a way he can't quite name, and carries an archaic, only half-familiar accent, shaping the way it forms its vowels. "So you come to challenge for the crown, little Summer boy who does not flinch from me?"

"Yes," Harry replies. "If the challenge is as yet ongoing, I would like to be considered as a candidate."

"Clever boy." The Winter doesn't sound pleased, precisely; it's making a statement of fact, not a judgment. Harry doesn't think he'd enjoy being judged by Melanie's season. It is, to be a little too on the nose about things, cold. "You are the first to reach me, and the only with a partner already in place, to let me see your heart more clearly. Two more have entered the wood since your arrival, but I think they can wander the trees a little longer before I speak with them." It looks smug, if a shimmering distortion of the air can look smug. "One of them is crying. I will not, I think, have him for a partner. The other gathers firewood. If she ignites it somehow, I will be most displeased. Your time is short. Make your case."

"Make my . . . Okay." Harry catches his breath, tries to pull the veil of serenity back over himself. It doesn't come easily. For a moment, he's not sure it's going to come at all. "I'm not here to challenge for the Winter."

"You think I don't know that? Bore me, child, and our time together is done. I have little patience for mortal fools."

"The Summer and the Winter haven't been a unified force for three hundred years, but they're supposed to be," says Harry hurriedly. "The alchemical marriage. Balance. Unite them and open the way to the Impossible City a little more cleanly, a little more directly. I'm *not* here to challenge for the Winter, because the Winter already has my heart."

"You, Summer boy? I have nothing of you."

"You have my Melanie." He looks the Winter dead in what he hopes corresponds to its eye. This will all be a little awkward if he delivers what he believes will be the winning argument to its collarbone or its forehead. "She's belonged to you since before she was born, since you're the season she was born to become, and I've belonged to her since basically the day we met. She's mine and I'm hers and she's yours and that means you're already mine. I'm not trying to invite you in. I know I couldn't survive you. I'm a Summer child, and my bones burn better than they freeze. But I'm here to win the Winter all the same, because I intend to spend the rest of my life making Mel happy. I plan to spend the rest of my life making *you* happy."

"My counterpart may not select her," says the Winter. "What then? What when I approve you and you find yourself sworn to some frozen stranger? Will you complete the alchemical marriage then, or will you do as William did, and abandon your responsibilities rather than face them?"

"There's a forest," says Harry. "It belongs to my family, as much as any land can belong to anyone, and we take care of it. We make sure the trees are healthy, so we can cut the ones that need to be cut, and we make sure the land endures. I know what it is to carry a legacy, and what it costs to refuse it. If the Summer chooses someone else to carry Winter's crown, I'll stand by them all the same. I may not serve as long as I could have done without a broken heart, but I'll serve."

This is why the ones who run parallel do so much better in the labyrinth than the ones who don't. It makes so much sense now that Harry can't quite understand why he didn't see it sooner. The candidates who make it this far must be acceptable to both seasons, not only their own, or they'd never have survived to make the attempt for the crown. What value is there in having the Summer look at him again and say "Yes, I like this one," when he and the Summer both know that already?

This is the Winter checking to see whether he represents something it can live with, and he can only hope he does.

The air sparkles with frost, swirling and gathering until the spectral shape of the Winter is blown away, and Melanie stands in its place. Not quite Melanie as he knows her; this is a colder version, eyes filled with midnight sky, jeans and sweatshirt replaced by a gown of purest snow. He still takes a half-step forward before he catches himself.

"You'll do," she says, inclining her head slightly toward her chest. She smiles, and it's both beautiful and terrible, both unfamiliar and beloved. This is the Melanie who lives where Winter walks, and he wonders if she's meeting the same version of him, the one who walks in sunlight always and doesn't know what it means to freeze any more than she knows what it is to thaw.

He hopes so. He gets the feeling not everyone who reaches the Winter is going to get this much time.

"Does that mean I can continue toward the crown?" he asks.

"What? No. Don't be ridiculous. If you're not at least a *little* clever, boy, I'll tire of you much sooner than I would prefer. William and Diana held their places for far too long. Human hearts aren't meant to contain three centuries of seasonal fears. But I'd like you to last at least as long as you would have lived if left alone."

She reaches toward him, palms open to the sky, and a crown forms there, of braided black branches supporting snowflakes the size of his hand. It's beautiful. It's impossible.

That really describes everything about the past few weeks.

She walks toward him, crown still balanced in her palms, and stops a few feet away. "Well?" she says, impatiently. "Kneel!"

He kneels. The living spirit of Winter, draped in the face of his girlfriend, sets her crown upon his head, and for all its cold starkness, it is not the crown of Winter; this is the Summer crown, this is the weight and wonder of a season pulled slightly apart from itself, slightly beyond itself, into the bright and open space where everything is impossible and nothing is improbable.

Harry's eyes go wide as the forest falls away and he finds himself standing in a twisting alleyway, cobblestone ground giving way to perfect masonry and brickwork, the sky alight with banners and with birds. He blinks, trying to take it all in at once, because he knows, on a deep and essential level, that this place is not for him; however much he may want to, he cannot stay. But he can come here again, perhaps, in dreams.

Harry March stands, the summer's crown upon his brow and living Summer burning in his bones, and beholds the Impossible City.

What Comes Next

All too soon, the city disappears, as he always knew it would have to, and Harry is standing alone in a wide clearing defined by topiary hedges on all sides save one, which opens into the stubble-strewn field. He can see some few of the attendants milling there, watching the wall, waiting for their candidates to emerge.

He reaches up to feel his forehead. There's no crown there, not even a circlet, but he doesn't need there to be, because the weight of it remains. He was chosen and he made his choice and the seasons did the same, the Summer before he came here, the Winter once he arrived. He looks behind him. There is no one else. He doesn't know the rules of this place, he doesn't know the consequences of lingering, but he remembers what Jack said:

The coronation doesn't end until the winning candidates emerge from the labyrinth. He hasn't truly won as long as he's standing here, and so he turns toward the exit and begins making his way toward it. He's stiff and cold and truly tired for the first time since this all started; until the process is complete, he feels like he's finally human again, finally the person he always believed himself to be.

Harry steps out of the labyrinth and onto the field unchallenged. The attendants all turn toward the movement. One of them—Jenny, *his* Jenny—whoops and punches the air before running toward him, Jack trailing behind. The other attendants look at him with varying expressions of disappointment or regret. One puts her hands over her face, shoulders shaking, and while he's too far away to hear, he has the distinct impression she's started to sob.

Then Jenny is reaching him, flinging his arms around Harry's shoulders and spinning them both around with his momentum. "You made it through!" he exclaims—yells, really, jubilant and unrepressed. "You survived. Man, did you *win*?"

Harry looks at the man who has been his attendant, the Corn Jenny who went through three candidates before reaching the labyrinth, and his throat is empty. There are no words left in him. Not until the coronation is done; not until Melanie comes out.

She will come out. She has to. The Winter chose him because he would balance the coming Summer; the alchemical marriage works best with two willing participants, not a participant and a sacrifice. He defeated Aven. He was the better Summer soul.

But he doesn't know the other Winter offerings. Maybe Mel won't be what the Summer approves; maybe there's someone warmer, someone less damaged, someone more suited to the whims of his home season. So he shakes his head and pulls away from Jenny, shivering.

Jack puts a hand on his arm. "Harry," she says, voice low and urgent. "Do you know where Mel is? Did she not make it through?"

His lips are dry, but he can answer questions about something other than himself. He swallows, and says, "We got separated as soon as we stepped inside. I think . . . I think you really had to *want* to find someone else to navigate the labyrinth anything other than alone." If Aven hadn't been unable to resist the urge to attack him on sight, she could have come after him in the labyrinth. If nothing else, she could have slowed him down enough for someone else to receive the Winter's blessing to proceed. She could have kept him from the crown.

"So you lost her?"

Put like that, it becomes a blow, an accusation he can scarcely weather. Harry closes his eyes and swallows, fighting to get his head to stop spinning. When he opens them again, it's to answer, in a mild tone, "I didn't lose her. I didn't have her. Not once we entered the labyrinth. Everyone enters alone."

Jenny grabs his elbow. "But did you *win*?"

"I think so." Harry's voice turns thoughtful. "The Winter said it could stand my company. Then it put on Melanie's face, and it crowned me. The crown disappeared when I came out, but I still feel it. I think I won."

"If you won, we'll know soon," says Jack. She turns to look at the labyrinth. "We wait to see who else comes out."

Harry turns as well, and sees only the wall, and the distant shape of the Impossible City beyond it. "How can they come out? The exit's gone."

Jack gives him a bewildered look. "No, it's not. It's right there."

Ah. Well, that makes sense. He thinks he'd die for another glimpse of those streets. If there were an easy way back into the labyrinth, he'd take it, just for the chance that he might be able to find his way through to the wonders on the other side. The Impossible City is not for the living or the mortal, and he's both, right here and now; it can't be his home.

Not yet, anyway.

"Not for me," he says. "I'm not allowed to go back in."

"Sucks to be you," says Jack. "I'm not allowed to go in at all."

When Melanie appears, it's by stepping straight through the wall. No gate opens for her to pass through, no exit he might use to re-enter. Just the wall, and then just her, looking dazed, hands crackling with cold as she walks toward them. Harry takes a step forward.

She sees him. Her head snaps around, and she begins to run. He answers in kind, and they meet in the middle of the field, locking their arms around each other and not leaving enough space between them for a single snowflake, a single blade of grass.

They just hold on.

The Queen of Swords has a reputation for making monsters, and most of the Pages are monsters in their own

*way, but she does not forge most of them, nor have any-
thing to do with their creation. Each ruler crafts their own
Court, claiming them from the resources of their land. A
Consort, when desired, Lord or Lady; a Knight, to carry
their will across the protectorates; and, at times, a Page,
who serves as living weapon for their regnant. Many Con-
sorts will refuse to share space with a Page, for so many of
them are monsters.*

*The Pages are heartless, all of them, even the kindest,
you see. They act according to their own ideals, and not to
the ideals of the gentle or the merciful. The Page of Frozen
Waters is the worst of them, and always has been, having
been crafted from ice and the drowned, but without the
natural mercies to which those ordinary things are heir.
And if the Page of Gentle Embers is the best of them, it
is only because the Queen of Wands could envision no
cruelty when she crafted her companion. They are not human. They are monsters, and that the Queen of Swords
is forever blamed for the making of monsters when the
Pages exist is one more piece of proof that the world is
ever and always essentially unfair.*

*But all of them, once they have the scent of something
to be destroyed, will return again and again, and to make
an enemy of a Page is to make an enemy of the elements
themselves, in their rawest, cruelest form.*

*Avery and Zib walked on, all unaware that both the
wind and water were set against them now, in different
ways, or that their journey was so very far from over as to
be barely begun . . .*

—From *Along the Saltwise Sea*, by A. Deborah Baker

BOOK VIII

Coronation

Winter's not gone yet, if the wild geese fly that way.

—William Shakespeare, *King Lear*

I rode a white horse over Uffington Hill
And the Moon lit the valley below
Wolves ran ahead of me, scenting the prey
I followed their tracks through the snow
The circle of seasons was turning again,
Winter would soon lose its hold
But moonlight appeals to me, snow has its charms,
And my kind do not feel the cold.

—Talis Kimberley, "Uffington Hill"

Funeral Faire

He thought only the winning candidates would come out, but that seems to be another thing that's gotten distorted by three hundred years without a coronation, because the other candidates begin to emerge from the labyrinth not long after Melanie. Some of them come out with bloody hands, or with wounds already clotted and scabbed over. Others come with clear signs of frostbite or sunburn, having run afoul of some hunting candidate from the other side. Most are unscathed, save for their eyes, which stare endlessly into the empty middle distance. All look back, gazing longingly at the outline of the Impossible City.

Harry stays where he is, keeps his arms around Melanie. She's no more inclined to let him go than he is her; they cleave to each other as if they fear nothing more in this moment than separation. She says nothing. When he presses his lips to her ear and murmurs, "Did you see the Summer?" she looks at him and nods, starlight and shadows in her eyes.

He can't decide whether that means she won or lost, but in the moment, it doesn't matter. None of the other candidates seem to shine in a way he would associate with them having won.

Aven never comes out. Neither, he's relieved to see, does Matthew.

After what feels like an eternity has passed since the last candidate emerged, the wall begins to fade. It doesn't reveal the topiary, or a clear path to the Impossible City; it just vanishes, leaving empty field behind. Most of the candidates who've emerged are with their attendants now, some weeping, some being consoled. None of them look particularly victorious.

Harry holds on to Mel. It's the only thing he can think of to do, until a throat is cleared behind them. He turns, arms still around her, and there are Carolyn and Clifford, in their ridiculous, impossible seasonal attire. He doesn't say anything, only stares at them and waits.

Carolyn smiles at him, as warm as an afternoon in August, and Clifford bows, deep and low, expression solemn.

"My Lord," he says.

That's the moment when Harry knows for sure. That's the moment when, between one breath and the next, color comes back into the world. Carolyn shifts her gaze to Melanie and inclines her head.

"My Lady," she says.

Harry laughs abruptly, moving his grip to Melanie's waist and picking her up as he spins her around. She joins in the laughter, both of them rejoicing in the moment, in their success, in the sheer impossible reality of their survival and their victory. When the spin is finished, they wind up facing each other. Melanie stares at him, eyes very wide. He can see traces of frost beginning to curlicue through her irises, which are still a deep, glacial blue, but different now. He's sure something about him is equally transformed. You can't dance with the seasons and come away unscathed.

When he kisses her, her lips taste like peppermint ChapStick, like a stiff wind on a cold winter day, like snowfall and the freeze. They also taste like firelight and warm socks and hot cocoa, and it shouldn't be possible for one kiss to carry so much, but it does, because when she kisses him willingly, he's kissing the entire living, beating heart of Winter. They did it. They made it through the labyrinth. They won.

"Winter gave you her crown," says Mel when they break apart. Her voice is hushed, her eyes bright.

"Summer gave you his," says Harry, and traces her lips with his fingertips. She's not going to die. Neither is he. They get as much time as they want. They get the whole alchemical marriage, and someday, when time comes for them to pass the crowns along, they'll have the Impossible City. They may be too human now to claim citizenship, but time is the greatest river of all; it will erode their edges, and give them time to settle into new shapes.

Together. As long as they do it together, nothing else can really matter.

He turns back to Clifford and Carolyn. They're all still in this vast and impossible field. That means this isn't over yet.

"Now what?" he asks.

Clifford smiles.

The stage, such as it is, is small and restrained, and has been assembled from untreated wood planed and sanded to a satiny finish that has nothing at all to do with paint or varnish. This is all natural, sweat and hard labor alone transforming it into something beautiful. Two posts have been erected, one to either side, garlanded with flowers Harry knows don't grow in the same place or the same season. Carolyn and Clifford lead him and Melanie to the dais, all the other attendants and candidates following, forming a small crowd around them.

"Forgive us," says Carolyn. "This used to have more pomp and ceremony, back when it happened on something resembling a regular basis, but these days, we're out of practice. Even the people who taught us had never seen it happen."

"Seen what happen?" asks Melanie.

"The coronation," says Clifford.

Melanie looks at him blankly. "I think you misunderstand," she says. "We've already been crowned, by our Seasons. There's no coronation to perform."

"Ah, but that was for you, and for them, and for the alchemical world," says Carolyn. "This is for your peers."

For the would-be Winters and practically Summers who will now fade into their graves, severed from the vital connection to the seasons that have been keeping them alive since the coronation began. For the Jacks and the Jennies who have only just begun to mourn, some of whom will be losing childhood friends and trusted colleagues. It makes a certain sense. It's less rubbing things in than it is . . . affirming.

Affirming that the choice was truly made, and that it was, in fact, made correctly. So Harry and Melanie follow to the stage and walk up the stairs together, hand in hand, before they turn to face the crowd.

Aven is there, scowling viciously. She made it out of the labyrinth after all, if she ever even went in. Trevor is nowhere to be seen. Either he's smart enough to have stayed away from his losing candidate, or he wasn't, and she's already killed him for the crime of not preparing her well enough to win. Either way, while she glares, she makes no move to approach the stage, so Harry discounts her.

Matthew isn't there. Neither is Misty. That's not much of a surprise. Much more surprising is the presence of five familiar faces. Harry nudges Mel in the side with his elbow, and when she glances his way, points into the crowd. She follows the angle of his finger, blinking at the little group. They're wrapped in a veil of rainbow mist, all five of them, and while people have made a space for them to occupy, it doesn't look like anyone else can see them. They've stepped between the seconds, and the people surrounding them are no longer tied to the flow of time in the same way.

Dodger raises her hand and waves when she sees Harry and Mel pointing in their direction. Roger turns a heartbeat later, and raises one hand in a thumbs-up. So it seems the Doctrine approves of this outcome, or at least its component parts do, because here they are, at something they can't possibly have predicted and probably weren't invited to.

Harry's pretty sure it wouldn't do him any good at all to point that out. This is happening.

Carolyn approaches Melanie, while Clifford approaches him. It feels like it's less about gender and more about place in the seasonal progression: spring comes before summer, autumn before winter.

Each of them carries a platter of the same wood as the stage, polished and sanded until he can read forest legends in the whorl and pattern of the grain. It's beautiful. It's impossible. It's all happening.

On each platter is a crown. The one Clifford carries appears to have been made from braided barley and corn, studded with small red flowers, like red, red rubies. The crown Carolyn carries is black branches and panes of ice, decorated with frozen red holly berries. Harry bends to allow Clifford to place the crown atop his head. Carolyn does the same to Melanie.

The air changes.

Or maybe only they change; maybe the air is the same. Still, Harry breathes in and it's sweet and warm and tastes of the coming spring. He can smell the thawing of the earth and the blooming of the flowers, and feel the imbalance caused by both his predecessor and the carbon that humanity has been pumping into the air. The climate has changed, and the role of the seasons is changing with it, in ways that may never be undone. Still, the world lives with humanity, and as long as the world lives with humanity, it will put faces to the seasons. Summer's shape may have changed. It still needs a head to wear the crown.

Harry straightens and turns to Melanie. She looks, impossibly, even paler than she did a moment before, with a thin edge of weariness he recognizes all too well from years of watching her health like it was his own. Her season is over, her time waning, and soon she'll sleep the summer away, dreaming while he reigns alone.

But she'll wake up. When his time is done, she'll wake up, and they'll be together again. He can handle that. Out of all the prices the world could have asked of them, he can carry this one, at least for now. And if that ever changes, they'll both have had the time to grow weary enough that they can set their crowns aside and go to the Impossible City without regrets. The thought of dying in service of the seasons isn't so bad now that he knows where they'll go when this phase of things is finished. There are some rewards for service, after all.

Looking into his eyes, Mel laughs, a sound that trends into

almost becoming a sob, and leans forward, and presses her lips to his, and kisses him like she's never been allowed to kiss him before and might never be allowed to kiss him again. Harry slides his arms around her waist, holding her against him, and her body is cool to the touch but alive, so very *alive*. She gets to stay.

They both do.

Clifford steps to the front of the stage. "My friends, following the first North American coronation in over three hundred years, I present to you our new reigning monarchs, the Summer King and the Winter Queen, who will carry us into a better future. Long may they reign!"

The cheers that answer from the crowd aren't entirely sincere. Too many of the gathered observers hoped to claim those crowns for themselves or for their loved ones; too many of them will die by inches as the season seeps away from them, and there's nothing that can be done to stop it. Harry can feel that now, through all the Summer souls. A seed unsprouted does no damage, but once it begins to grow, it can't be reduced back to what it was before. There's no way to dam up the hole it will leave when it withers. Like a dandelion pushing through a crack in concrete, the Summer has grown up under their foundations and broken them, and they'll die, just as he was told they would.

He feels bad about that. Maybe there's a way to change it going forward; maybe the weirdoes in Berkeley who rewrote their own ending can find a way to rewrite the endings for the future Incarnates who fail to catch the crown. Or maybe not; maybe that would just leave too many challengers for the throne, make it impossible for anyone to ever truly relax into the role. And he needs to. He can feel that, too. He and Mel aren't here to control the seasons they represent so much as . . . shape them. Summer will be gentler in the hands of someone who actually likes the world. Winter will be less selfish, and hence less brutal.

Seasonal monarchs can't reverse climate change, or the other continents would have resolved it long since, but he feels like having a balanced system back in place will help things, at least a little.

Down in the crowd, Jenny puts two fingers in his mouth and whistles, sharp and piercing, while Jack laughs and applauds with enough sincerity to make up for all the people around her. Mel pulls away and Harry lets her go, but holds on to her hand.

Holding on to her has gotten them this far, after all. They've won, and now they're going home.

They just have to figure out what that means.

No Forwarding Address

After the coronation, Carolyn steps to the front of the stage again, clapping her hands for attention. The crowd settles down. Admittedly, it isn't that much of a change.

"Now, I know y'all have been enjoying our pretty hay maze and our smashing hospitality, but I'm going to have to ask you to head on back now," she says. "The way is open: you can leave. The labyrinth is closed." These are somehow two different things. It's a bit of a relief when full understanding of what she means doesn't immediately pop into Harry's head, supplied by the presence of the season. The labyrinth is the responsibility of the liminal Ascendants, and they'll continue to see to it as they dutifully build it and tear it down year on year, tracing the borders of the Impossible City, whatever those currently happen to be.

The presence of the City is why the monarchs can't be involved. They would never be able to resist the urge to storm the walls, to try to claw their way inside before it was time for them to go. Once or twice, sure, but for the length of construction, every year, forever? No. Better to leave this process in safer hands.

"Thank you for coming," continues Carolyn, as if they'd had any choice in the matter. Her smile is dazzling. Harry wonders, somewhat abstractly, whether she did pageants as a child. Maybe, or maybe she was in a sorority, one of those flocks of perfectly groomed women who wander the campus of Portland State University, a sealed sisterhood that seems to fashion its members even more expertly than Mel's beloved cheerleading squad.

"Now, we have to go, and once we do, the walls will start to come down," she says. "I'd recommend not being stuck here when the access ends, as it won't open again even for us until there's another coronation. Or, to put it more bluntly, your bodies will never be found." Her smile turns thin-lipped and tight. "Thank you for listening, and have a lovely day."

She turns quickly, pushing between Harry and Mel, and whispers as she passes, "Follow me. Don't ask questions, don't look back."

"Listening to her is the best idea under most circumstances," says Clifford. He also steps between them as they follow Carolyn, slinging one arm around each of their shoulders, forming a line between Summer and Winter through the body of the spring.

Harry wonders whether thinking of people as abstract concepts will ever stop giving him a headache, and more, if it will be a good thing if and when it does. But that's a question that can't be answered until it happens, so he focuses on descending the stage with Clifford's arm to guide him, and as he steps back onto the dirt, he realizes how *tired* he is.

The Summer in him burns so much bigger and brighter than it did before he was crowned that it would be easy to miss that it's no longer sustaining him the way it has been. The first phase of frantic growth has passed. What comes now is slow unfurling and maturation into something stronger, something that can endure. Instead of ivy, an oak. Instead of dandelions, a redwood.

He understands forestry. He understands why he's exhausted. The other Summer candidates must be feeling it even more than he is, as their formerly shared season rips itself out of them one fiber at a time.

For their sake, he hopes it doesn't hurt. For Aven's sake, he almost hopes it does. It's a painful contradiction to carry, and he carries it all the same. Someone has to. Better him than Mel.

Jack and Jenny join them as they walk toward the wall of towering corn that has returned, across from the vanishing labyrinth. Carolyn leads their little pack, guiding them to an opening in the corn wall, and when they step through, they're back in the tunnel that brought them here, back on the scarecrow trail.

None of the other candidates or attendants follow. Mel gives Clifford a blankly curious look, and he laughs.

"They came through other routes. You were the only ones to use our house. It's been three days since you entered the labyrinth, by the way. Car's still where you left it. No one asked, and we didn't need to have it towed. So you'll be able to head back to where you came from, after you've had a hot shower and something to eat, and maybe a good night's sleep."

"We have multiple guest rooms," says Carolyn. "And my mama would come back from the dead to beat me blue if I turned you out without making sure you were ready to go."

"It might be dangerous," says Harry uncertainly. "If the other candidates come for us . . ."

"If you're a weak enough King that you can be killed by a failed candidate when you're coming into your season and they're being stripped of theirs, it's better for it to happen quickly, before the labyrinth comes down and the world adjusts to what it has now," says Clifford. "It'll be fine. Let us cook for you and take care of you. You can take time to figure out what you're doing next."

It makes sense. It's reasonable. It still makes Harry worry a little, about someone else getting hurt because they let him into their home. Still, the walk down the tunnel is long, and by the time they reach the end, he can barely keep his eyes open. He dimly remembers Carolyn ushering him, and Mel, into a guest room painted an almost violent shade of purple, handing them a stack of towels, and telling them that she'd see them in the morning.

He doesn't remember undressing, just falling facedown onto the bed, already asleep before his head hit the pillow.

The sunlit meadow is familiar, but there's no figure there to greet him this time, no mirror image of himself. Harry walks among the flowers, and realizes two things. The mountain that loomed on the horizon is gone, replaced by the outline of a magnificent city, and the forest where he once walked with the Winter now looms at the meadow's edge, bare branches reaching toward the sky.

The third thing is slower to come, and arrives only as he wades through the tall grass toward the forest. The other him isn't here, because he doesn't need to be; because this isn't his anymore.

It's Harry's.

He claimed this land when he took the crown, when he became the Summer King, and one day it will be his responsibility to sit with Melanie's successor and interview them for the right to take her place. That's going to hurt, when the time arrives, but it will be the hurt that comes after long service and laying their burdens down.

He'll come here once a year for as long as he reigns; once a year and no more, when he sleeps the deep, slow sleep of the dead. He knows that too, a feeling that only grows stronger as he gets closer to the tree line and sees the snow on the ground, the line of bare earth between it and the meadow's edge. Snowdrops and crocuses push through the snow at the very edge, but beyond that, the only color is from the fruiting holly bushes that stand silent sentry in the shadows. This is a place for transitions.

It always was, but before, they were always changing, becoming new people on an annual, if not monthly, basis. They were growing into the people they would eventually become, the ones who would be strong enough to shelter an entire season, and so they needed to walk on the edge of the Impossible City again and again to learn how to grow in its shadow, to find out if they even could. Maybe there are people who carry the seeds of seasons who don't become attendants or candidates, because they don't thrive where the City can see them, and so the seasons let them go.

So he won't come here often after this, and Melanie won't visit her own seasonal landscape, and they'll live their seasons in the real world, and once a year, when they sleep and end and begin again, as seasons always have, they'll come back to this familiar place and walk alone. There are worse possible futures.

They almost lived through so many of them.

Harry stops about ten feet from the edge of the wood and cups his hands around his mouth, shouting Mel's name. He shouts it again and again, but she never comes out of the trees. When he finally gives up and lowers his hands, he's still alone amongst the flowers.

But they won. They're supposed to get the happy ending. That's how this works, right? They won. They get whatever they want now, forever. They won.

M orning is heralded by the ringing of a doorbell loud enough to belong in the Addams Family home. Harry groans and peels his face off the pillow, scrubbing at the sleep that's formed in the corner of his eyes. The other half of the bed is disheveled, clearly slept in, but Melanie is gone.

That finishes the process of waking him up, knocking him back to consciousness as quickly as a slap. He sits up on the bed, surrounded by soft pillows and warm blankets, still fully dressed, although someone—Mel, probably—has helpfully removed his shoes for him. That's good. He doesn't want to think about how Carolyn would react to mud on her *sheets,* given how upset she'd been about the mud on her floors. "Mel?" he calls.

The room must be very well soundproofed, because it swallows his voice without any of the echo he'd expect, the faint magnification from bouncing off the walls. That begs the question of how he heard the doorbell, but he can't dwell on that right now.

"Mel? Are you here?"

The door across from the bed opens to reveal the guest bathroom he vaguely remembers Clifford mentioning the night before, and there's Mel, wrapped in a towel, drying her hair with another. She's clean and bright-eyed and looks as healthy as he's ever seen her . . . which is healthier than she's been in a long time.

Seeing her like this drives home how bad she'd gotten in a way that nothing else ever will. Harry slides out of the bed and walks toward her.

"Shower's open," says Mel, as he wraps his arms around her waist and pulls her close. She puts a hand over his mouth before he can kiss her, smiling serenely as she holds him at arm's length. "Not until you brush your teeth," she says amiably. "I've been up for an hour, and we were out for at least twelve before that. Everything's in the bathroom."

"Everything?"

"Pretty sure Clifford raided our car. He apologized when I went upstairs looking for coffee. Do not drink the coffee if he's the one offering to make it for you, by the way; he thinks it's some sort of religious ritual thing that needs to be performed just so or you'll offend the beans. Carolyn's coffee is way more normal."

Harry looks at her blankly. "Really?"

"No." She laughs. "He just does this weird routine with a French press and vacuum-filtered water and it takes forever. Go brush your teeth. I'll get dressed, and we can go upstairs."

Harry doesn't want to go upstairs. This is the first time they've been alone and not in fear for their lives in almost a month, and he wants to do some of the things her father doesn't approve of, that they couldn't exactly do in front of company. But they're in someone else's house, and he doesn't want to upset their hosts, so he smiles and nods and lets her go, heading into the bathroom.

By the time he emerges, Mel is tragically dressed, in jeans and a rust-colored sweatshirt, her wet hair braided down her back. "I borrowed this from Carolyn," she says, plucking at one sleeve. "It's dyed with actual dirt. Like, from the red mud we saw outside. Isn't Alabama wild?"

"Sure is," Harry agrees. He took the time to wet his hands and run his fingers through his hair. His clothes, while wrinkled, are surprisingly clean for having been slept in; it'll do. "You said coffee?"

"And muffins. Come on." Mel leads him out of the room and up the stairs, which deliver them to the kitchen.

There is, in fact, a platter of fresh-baked apple muffins on the counter, next to a pot of coffee. Harry pauses to pour himself a mug before following Mel out of the kitchen to the living room, where a conversation is going on.

Then he stops, blinking. Not only their hosts and their attendants are present; the five people from Berkeley are there as well, standing and chatting, muffins and cups of coffee in hand. Roger is the first to notice their appearance. He turns, smiling, every inch the genial high school English teacher excited to hear how his favorite students did in their debate tournament.

"Hope you don't mind us swinging by before we head home," he says, tone as easy as his smile. "We just wanted to check in, see if you needed anything, before we hit the road."

"It'll take us at least two hours to get back to Berkeley," says Dodger, viciously bright. "I'd like to be home before the sun goes down."

Harry blinks again. It took them *days* to drive from California to Alabama, and yeah, they weren't hurrying, but they weren't trying to walk all that distance, either. There's literally no possible way two hours puts these people and their weird van back in their driveway. Then again, Harry considers, this is a woman who had actual, literal summer in her front yard because her brother wanted flowers.

Roger gives Dodger a sharp look. "*Some* people respect linear distance," he says.

"Some people need to learn that miles are just numbers on a map, and all numbers can be negotiated with," she says, and takes a bite out of her muffin.

"See, she doesn't understand that for normal people, driving across the country in an afternoon is impossible, and she sounds like she has a head injury when she says things like that," says Erin, stepping around them to walk over and offer Mel her hand. "Congratulations."

"Oh, um, thanks," says Mel, and takes the offered hand, shaking. "I saw you at the coronation. I didn't expect you there."

"We didn't expect your coronation to involve the Impossible City," says Dodger. "That's why we thought you'd have to come back and tell us."

"We always know when someone enters the Impossible City," says Roger. "We're sort of a part of it, linked to it. We were supposed to make it manifest by existing, and maybe we did in some way. I don't know. I asked the European Summer Queen if she'd seen the Impossible City before her own coronation, and she asked me if I'd seen all the wonders of the Kalos region. I'm pretty sure she was making fun of me." He sounds affronted and impressed at the same time, like it's hard for him to believe anyone would make fun of him, at least to his face.

Behind his back, Kim and Tim roll their eyes in eerie unison. "It's the setting of the most recent Pokémon game worth playing," says Kim.

"Huh," says Roger. "Learn something new every day." He takes a swig of coffee. "And before we get on the road, I want to learn what you did to this coffee, because it is *excellent*."

Clifford preens. "You put some salt in with the grounds," he says. "It brings out the nuance of the beans. And of course, the beans matter more than anything."

"Of course," agrees Roger.

"Congratulations to you, too," says Erin, turning to offer her hand to Harry. "I'm pleased that you both made it. I don't think either of you would have enjoyed ruling alone."

"What does that mean, 'ruling'?" asks Harry. "I know we're, like, royalty and all now, but do we have jobs? Is there something we're expected to do?"

"Just live," says Erin. "Live like people do, and give the season something it can anchor itself to, something that will remind it that humans have to live in this world and carry the consequences of its choices. Get a job, start a family—probably easier for the two of you than for most seasonal monarchs, since you're already a thing, but what do I know?—and live. You won't age, and you won't die of natural causes as long as you wear the crowns."

"What are unnatural causes?" asks Harry uncertainly.

"Each other. Walking in front of a moving plane. Decapitation and fire have both been known to work, under extreme circumstances. I've heard rumor that drowning will do it, but no one seems entirely sure about that, so I'd chalk it up to hearsay and people wanting another way of taking you out. Any Incarnate can kill you. Given your place in the alchemical food chain, I'd be willing to bet your attendants could kill you if they really set their minds to it."

Jack pales. Mel glances at her, eyebrows lifted.

"Something you want to tell us?" she asks.

"No," says Jack quickly. "No, ma'am. We helped you reach the labyrinth because we wanted you to win. What would be the point in killing you now? We can't claim the crowns, and it's not like we've had time to prep another candidate."

"What would happen if another coronation was triggered right now?" asks Mel, turning to look at Carolyn. "I mean, now-now. Not tomorrow, not next month, *now*."

"You mean if I'd poisoned the muffins or something uncivilized like that?" asks Carolyn. "Well, I'd be a bad hostess, and we'd be back to my mama dragging herself out of the grave to punish me for it. Why are you so determined not to let my mama rest in peace?"

"Not if you killed us," says Mel, exasperated. "If Erin strangled me or something. She's an Incarnate, she should be enough to take me out."

"Oh," says Carolyn, blinking several times. "Well, I don't rightly know. I don't think it's ever happened before. But it must have, at least once, or the mysteries wouldn't call for the new monarchs to be taken away for their own safety before the rest of the candidates can recover from their shock. So there has to be some sort of a problem that only happens if we *don't* get you away quickly enough."

"Let's ask Mr. Wikipedia," says Dodger, and elbows Roger genially in the side. "Hey, nerd, what are these 'mysteries' Lady Autumn's hinting at?"

"Sacred mysteries are common to most religions and belief systems," says Roger. "They're usually things that don't make a lot of sense or are difficult to explain to the uninitiated, and while I'm not sure 'I am a literal living manifestation of a season, ask me anything' qualifies as a belief system, it makes sense that some things about it would be hard to explain to people who aren't tethered to the alchemical world."

"Okay. Does that infinite brain of yours include anything about *why* they'd need to get the winners away from the losers so quickly? Do people start throwing tomatoes?"

"Severing the candidates from their season kills them, but not immediately," says Roger. "They wither and die, like a limb that's been cut from a tree. There's still enough sap in most tree limbs to keep them alive for quite some time, which is why grafting is a popular form of agriculture, and why trees who lose limbs in storms can frequently be repaired. Vegetable death is a slower process than mammalian death in almost all cases and—" He pauses, taking note of the way Dodger is looking at him. "And that's not what you were asking, sorry. I get distracted sometimes."

"Roger doesn't *know* everything," says Erin. "It's more like he can answer any question, but he doesn't always have the answer before you ask him. Roger, why do they need to get the winners away from the losers so quickly, if the winners carry the seasons and the losers have been severed? What is the specific danger if they don't?"

"Oh," says Roger. "That's easy. Grafting."

Everyone looks at him blankly except for Harry, who has been studying trees in preparation for taking over Castleview since he was a little kid. He stares at Roger in wordless horror as Roger smiles, triumphant in his sudden understanding, and explains:

"If a coronation results in a crowning, and one of the losers kills one of the winners quickly enough after the coronation, they can take the crown even without the blessing of the season. It's happened before, Africa, 1812, Australia, 1704, and Europe, about eleven times during the ninth century, and then twice in the fourteenth. North America never had any assassinations before colonization shifted their coronation structure to the more European model, and since this is only the second coronation since then, this continent has a clean record thus far."

"So a failed Summer candidate could kill Mel and claim the Winter?" asks Jack.

"Exactly," says Roger.

Harry and Mel both turn to glare at Carolyn and Clifford, who look as stunned as the rest of them. "A little warning would have been nice," says Mel tightly.

"We didn't know," protests Carolyn.

"You knew we needed to get out of there."

"The mysteries tell us to extract the new monarchs so they can sleep in safety and align with their seasons without being disturbed," says Carolyn. "They don't tell us that they might be murdered if we let them sleep out in the open!"

"This whole system is stupid," says Mel. "Why did we even bother going through the labyrinth and getting the approval of the seasons if we could have just stayed at Waffle House drinking coffee until it was all over, and then killed somebody and taken all their stuff? It's stupid and it's not fair."

"But it's the way things are," says Roger.

"Well, I don't like it," snaps Mel.

"We can't go home," says Harry. "Aven never made it into the labyrinth. If anyone's going to try to find us and kill us before the withering hits her, it's going to be Aven. So we can't go home. How far is it from here to Wisconsin?"

"You could drive it in a day if you didn't take a lot of rest stops," says Clifford. "It's close to straight up."

"Then we go to Wisconsin," says Harry firmly.

"What's in Wisconsin?" asks Dodger.

Harry looks at her as if she's just asked the silliest question in the world. "My family castle, of course."

"Of course," echoes Dodger. "Of course the weird kid with the Summer crown and the dead girlfriend has a family castle in *Wisconsin*. Where else would you keep a castle? It makes perfect sense."

"It does," says Harry. What he doesn't mention is the strength of the Wisconsin winters: it should still be cold enough there to keep Melanie from sliding too far into Spring, at least for a little while. They'll have to see about colleges in the area, too. Anything to keep her awake for more of the year, as long as he still gets sufficient time awake to manage the family business.

They've had illnesses in the family before, and he's sure they can find a way to make this work. Maybe it's happening a few years sooner than originally planned, but it's not like this wasn't the idea all along, in one form or another.

"We can't go back to Portland," he says, reasonably enough. "Aven didn't die in the labyrinth, and if the attendants didn't know about this . . . grafting . . . thing that failed candidates can try for, she probably didn't die on the coronation field, either. Out of all the remaining potential Summers, she's the one most likely to come for us."

"You think she'd kill you?"

"I think she'd kill either one of us." Harry shrugs. "Mel rejected her. I 'stole' her sister. She didn't strike me as the kind of person who knows how to handle being told no."

"If she was in an alchemically induced coma for most of her life, she probably never learned emotional regulation," says Jack, voice slow and thick with horror. "So she'd see Mel's refusal to break her parallel as a rejection. The only question is which of you she's angrier at."

"So it's settled," says Harry. "We go to Castleview. It should only take a day for us to get there."

"Actually," says Dodger, "we can help you with that."

Castleview

With Dodger's help—which makes no sense at all; distance isn't something you can *argue* with, distance is distance, it's fixed and immutable, and one weird mathematician with candy cane hair making a few notes on a map before programming a specific and arbitrary route into the GPS can't change it—they make the drive from Huntsville to the absolute top of Wisconsin in under an hour, and that's *with* a stop at Starbucks to get Melanie a nightmare concoction of sugared syrup for the trip.

He wouldn't believe it if he weren't behind the wheel, but even as the GPS beeps and announces "Destination is ahead," the road curves and there's the sweet, familiar shape of Castleview, cupped by the sheltering hand of the forest that surrounds it, all gray stone walls and towering battlements.

It's not a Barbie dream castle or anything else so straightforward and simple: the people who sold it, in Scotland, had inherited it from a long line of ancestors who paid for its walls and masonry with blood, and who probably wouldn't approve in the slightest of its new home. But this *is* its home now; like the people who brought it here, it has put down roots. Maybe not as old or as enduring as some of the trees around it, which were here before the land was developed in any way, and will be here long after, but deep enough that the castle isn't going to move again without human intervention.

Which means "never" as far as Harry's concerned. He pauses on the road, creating a traffic hazard, to smile mistily up at the castle that has been his heart's true home since he was a little boy. All his dreams, big or small, complex or simple, have come back to Castleview, and the future he was going to have here.

"Holy *fuck* me," says Jack, sounding awed.

"Not for a long, long time," says Jenny, half-amused, half-stunned. "You're going to look like a kid for the next decade."

Jack sticks her tongue out at him. He snorts.

"That doesn't help. But I'll echo the sentiment: holy fuck. Harry, when you said we were going to your family castle, I thought you meant just a really, really big house. Something unreasonable. Not a *castle*."

Harry blinks. "Why would you think that?" He's used to everyone at school knowing about Castleview, having seen pictures during show-and-tell sessions or heard him read from the endless tedious essays about what he did over his summer vacation.

Melanie rolls her eyes and pats Harry on the arm. "Not all of us grew up in your house, sweetheart. Just drive, and they'll get over it."

"If you say so," grumbles Harry, and presses down on the gas, resuming the leisurely glide along the road. Can't speed here, not in the shadow of Castleview; the castle pre-dates the current outline of the road, which was planned and paid for by the castle occupants, meaning it conforms to their ideas about visitors (largely unwelcome) and how fast cars should be able to safely travel (not terribly).

By the time they reach the drive, the door is open and Harry's grandmother is standing on the step, flanked by bronze lions and beaming, her hands clasped above her heart. She at least waits for Harry to stop the car before she launches herself in their direction, moving with the easy spryness of a woman who may be in her early sixties but still lives an active outdoor life. She was the only one who laughed instead of worrying when they found Melanie literally climbing the walls that first summer, and she lights up when the passenger door opens and Mel herself emerges.

"Mel! It's so *nice* to see you, sweetheart, Harald didn't tell us he was bringing you to visit." She pauses to shoot a mock glare at her beloved grandson, who is getting out of the car on the opposite side, already shaking his head as his grandmother sweeps his girlfriend into an embrace. "I wasn't sure when we'd be seeing you again, after everything that happened. I'm so sorry for your loss, my darling."

She lets go of Mel and bustles toward Harry as Jack and Jenny get out of the car, leaving Melanie to blink after her in bewilderment. She can't mean Aven, can she? Aven isn't so much "lost" as "temporarily and unintentionally found," and they're hoping to lose her permanently by coming here to go to ground. Jack and Jenny come to stand beside her as Harry's grandmother hugs him and fusses over him, calling him tired and too thin.

"—told us you were on your way, but we expected you a few days ago," she says, and Harry blinks.

"My parents told you I was coming *here*?" he asks.

"Of course they did. We're old, Harald, it's rude to surprise us. And speaking of surprises, who are these nice folk you have with you?"

"Jack, ma'am," says Jack.

"Jens," says Jenny.

"It's lovely to meet you both," she says. "I'm sure Harald has told you what to expect here in our humble family home, but I'm Eliza March, and I'm delighted to host you. My husband is at the office for now; we didn't know when Harald would be arriving, and had no warning that he'd be bringing guests"—her pause promises punishment in private, in that way only grandparents can—"so I was waiting for him by myself. You'll all have to follow me."

"Keys are in the ignition, Grandma," says Harry, getting his bag out of the trunk.

"Antonio will move your car to the garage," she says, and heads inside.

Jack and Jenny exchange a look, perhaps beginning to understand the scope of the wealth involved here, but when Melanie follows the woman inside, they do the same, with Harry bringing up the rear.

The foyer is as large as many apartments, walls paneled in polished oak and kept from becoming oppressive by a wide assortment of family photos, some featuring a younger Harry, many featuring a boy who looks a lot like him, but with darker hair, who grows older picture by picture until Harry begins making his earliest appearances. The teens crowd together in the space as Eliza gestures to the stairs, saying, "Harry, dear, your room is ready; I'll have Penny get three more guest rooms suitable for use while we're eating dinner. Setting a few more places shouldn't be a problem."

The airy way she dismisses the addition of three extra bodies to the table is clearly baffling to Jack, who looks to Mel for help. Mel shrugs in a "just go with it" sort of manner before turning to Eliza.

"I'm sorry, what did you mean before, about 'after everything that's happened,'" she asks, politely.

Eliza stops fussing over Harry and turns to Mel, eyes wide and face going pale as all the blood drains away. She puts a hand over her mouth. "Oh, dear girl, I thought . . . Well, that is, Harry's father believed . . . We thought Harry had left Portland to come to us because we all know he runs to Castleview when he's upset, and it seemed . . . I am so sorry. I thought you knew."

Harry moves to stand behind Melanie, putting an arm around her shoulders. "Thought we knew what, Grandma?"

Eliza looks truly miserable as she replies, "That her father's been killed. There was some kind of home invasion, and the police . . ." She keeps talking, but Melanie doesn't hear any of it. All she hears is a sticky buzz, like a television that's been left on while the cable was down.

Her father is dead.

Her father, Roland Cosgrove, the man who raised her, the man who she always believed loved her, the man who made her in a lab, the alchemist who consigned her to this unavoidable, inescapable version of her own future, that man is dead. That explains why he never came after her like she'd been afraid he would. None of the people she's met since this madness began has said anything about raising the dead. Worse, she doesn't know if she'd wanted them to if they knew how. So he's dead, and he's going to stay dead.

Eliza is still talking as Mel drifts to the stairs and sits, hands dangling between her knees. Harry grabs his grandmother's elbow, stopping her from following, and says something tight and angry. The static in Melanie's head continues.

The static continues for hours, as Harry's grandfather comes home, as they all sit down to what may be an excellent meal but tastes in her mouth of dust and stale air, as Eliza shows her to the room she always uses when she stays here, pink and perfect and a little feminine for her tastes, but the Marches never had a daughter, and it seems to make Eliza happy to treat Mel like a princess. She smiles and murmurs something she still can't hear, and puts herself to bed, where she lies awake, staring at the shadowed ceiling.

It's the farthest she's been from her traveling companions in almost a month, and she can feel spring nibbling at her edges, leeching her power away. She won't know what it means to truly embody the Winter until it rolls around again, because the coronation came so late; she'll dwindle through the Spring, feeling the way she always has, and then sleep through the Summer.

With a three-month nap in her future, it's perhaps no surprise that sleep doesn't find her easily. She tosses and turns for the better part of an hour before she rises and drifts to the balcony doors, opening them and stepping out into the cool night air. She's never loved this place the way Harry does—that would be virtually impossible—but she loves it all the same, and has always known that one day, her heart allowing, she would call it home. They may still be a few years away from that, but she's still comfortable enough to relax as she leans against the stone rail keeping her from toppling into the rose gardens and listens to the static in her head.

A month ago, she would have been devastated. A month ago, she would have been inconsolable. Now . . .

Now the world is different, much bigger and much smaller than she ever thought it could be. Somehow, that thought brings comfort. She leans forward, rests her chin on her arms, and smiles. She's not sick anymore. She's going to be fine, and Harry's going to be fine, and maybe life isn't going to look exactly like they always thought it would, but they'll spend it together, and that means they can handle anything it wants to throw at them.

And they'll handle it in a castle, which is more than most people get.

Melanie starts to giggle. She's still giggling when she hears a rustle in the bushes below her and claps a hand over her mouth, squinting down into the dark. It gets very dark this far from the city. She doesn't see anything.

A raccoon, probably, or a deer. She turns, going back inside and shutting the door. She doesn't get cold, but she doesn't want to get mauled by a bear just to show off her ability to withstand a Wisconsin spring.

She's sitting on the edge of the bed when the balcony door edges open and Aven slips into the room, moving as quietly as she can. Melanie tilts her head.

"What was the plan?" she asks. "Kill me, dye your hair, take my place?"

Aven freezes.

"Our father's dead, and you're dying. Hasn't there been enough damage done already?"

"I know he's dead," snaps Aven. "I killed him."

Melanie should be angry, hearing that. She should be enraged. All she feels is tired, and softly mournful. "Then I guess I'm all you have left. Can you really kill me?"

"You chose *him* over me, so now he gets me instead of you."

"That's not how you unify the seasons," says Mel sadly. She stands. "You can steal the Winter if you're quick, but you'll always be Summer-tied, and two Summer children with a stolen Winter won't be balance. It'll be a mockery."

"I don't care."

"You should, if you want to carry the weight of Winter. It's not light, you know. I had to walk the world and learn to be human while you slept; I lived with a broken heart that kept on breaking every time it beat. I got stronger. You didn't."

"You don't look stronger now," spits Aven.

"Maybe not. But I know the layout of this castle, and you don't."

And Melanie bolts.

The hallway outside her room is long and straight, carpeted in soft runner rugs that swallow the pounding of her feet. She runs, hard, for the room at the end, where she knows Harry will lie sleeping. If she can reach him, if they can come together—

She doesn't know what that will do. She just knows she'll be braver if she's not alone. So she runs, even as she hears Aven come crashing along behind her, running hard and fast and knocking into walls. Aven doesn't care about waking the rest of the house. So Melanie runs, changing her mind at the last possible moment and flinging herself hard to the side, to the stairs, which are tall and steep and have lots of opportunities for someone unprepared to slip and fall.

She grips the banister tight as she descends, smooth wood stretching under her hand like the ribbon of the road that brought them here. She reaches the ground floor without the feeling of fingers in her hair or grabbing her arm, and she whips around to look behind her, a fleeting glimpse, before she bolts for the front door.

Aven is there, avenging phantom of Summer, her long white hair a banner behind her, unmissable in the gloom. She looks furious. She looks ready to kill.

Melanie isn't going to give her the satisfaction.

The front door of Castleview is almost never locked. What would be the point? The castle contains valuables, yes, but it's in the middle of nowhere, and most would-be thieves would crash if they tried to drive along the twisting approach in the dark. Mel hits the door, wrenches it open, and flings herself through.

The air outside is wickedly cold. She feels better immediately, stronger, more awake. She keeps running, gravel of the driveway biting into the bare soles of her feet. She can hear Aven running behind her.

Maybe going outside wasn't the smartest choice she's ever made. But Aven doesn't know Castleview. Aven doesn't know *her*. She doesn't know how much Mel loves to run, or that she loves a boy who loves this place like he loves her, truly and completely and to the bottom of his soul. Mel's only been here the once. She still knows the grounds like she knows the back of her own hand. And so she runs, rounding the corner of the castle, racing toward the trellises.

Aven knows they're there. She must, since she climbed one of them to get to Melanie's room. But she won't know them as well as Mel does, having not had the time to go up and down them recreationally, or to be pried off them by helpful, panicked gardening staff.

The smell of roses assaults Mel's nose, and she keeps going, heading into the tangle of thorny branches. They snag her hair and the fabric of her nightgown as she keeps going, Aven's footfalls close behind her, and hopes the roses will slow the other woman down.

When she reaches the base of the trellis, she grabs hold and begins to climb, nimble as a squirrel, heading for the outline of Harry's balcony. A hand grabs her hair, and she kicks out, knocking Aven back a step.

"Go *away*," she snarls, without turning. "You *lost*. Go and die somewhere."

"Why do you get to live when I don't?" Aven demands. "It's not supposed to be a race! We're supposed to be sisters!"

Mel keeps climbing. "I'm sorry. I'm sorry I was born first. I'm sorry I got to live and you didn't. I'm sorry it had to be this way. But it's our parents' fault, not ours! Not *mine*."

Aven grabs for her again, catching her ankle. Mel half-turns on the trellis, glaring down at her. Then she pauses, thawing a little. Aven looks so small, and so sad, hanging there below her. She never really had a chance. The labyrinth, and the crown, had been her only opportunities to live.

Harry had gone in with every advantage he could have had, and Aven had gone in with none of them. It's not fair. It was never fair.

"You got it all, and I got *nothing*," snarls Aven, face distorting with rage. "You deserve *none* of it, and I'm taking all of it away."

Melanie's sympathy melts in an instant, as she jerks herself away and resumes her frantic upward climb. "You're not taking anything!" she shouts. She's hoping she's been loud enough.

Not yet. When she reaches the balcony, the doors to Harry's room are still closed, and no one's moving on the other side of the glass. She scowls and runs the few short steps across the balcony, grabbing for the door handle.

This time, she's lucky. The handle pushes downward and she shoves the door open, diving through. She slams it behind her, so hard the glass rattles in the frame, almost hitting Aven in the face.

Harry sits up in bed, eyes wide. "Mel? You know Grandma doesn't like you in my room after—"

"Quiet!" Mel grabs hold of the door handle, using the full weight of her body to hold it closed. "My sister's here."

"What?" He slides out of bed, moving to join her. "You're sure?"

"She's right out there, so yeah, I'm sure." Mel jabs a finger at the distorted image of her sister on the other side of the glass. "We're pretty well matched, too. Think the season will cover it up if we kill her?"

"That's cold."

"I'm the living Winter. I'm allowed."

Harry looks at her for a moment, wide-eyed. Then he nods, and reaches for her hand. She lets him take it, and together they step back, away from the door.

It slams open almost instantly, as Aven bursts into the room, glaring wildly around. She focuses on Mel instantly. Harry doesn't step to the side, and Aven shoves forward, surprising him with the strength of her shove to the side. Mel smiles at her, the air crackling with cold as the Summer rises in Harry and calls the Winter in her up to the surface. The rising cold should be a warning. Somehow it isn't. Aven reaches for Mel's throat, hands hooked to grab and squeeze, only for her lunge to halt as Harry puts his hands to either side of her head.

One sharp twist, one sharp crack, and it's over. Aven falls silently. Melanie sighs and shakes her head, stepping around the body of the sister she never really knew and mourned for years ago in order to slide her arms around her boyfriend.

They stand together, watching as Aven's fallen form crumbles into rose petals and thorns and blows away in the breeze from Harry's open balcony doors, and it didn't have to be this way, and it was always going to be this way, and the alchemical marriage is complete. For good or for ill, the crowns have been passed, and the circle of seasons turns endlessly on.

ACKNOWLEDGMENTS

And here we are again, back in the alchemical world, which is not as new but is in some ways no less confusing; I promise I understand what's going on, and I very much hope that at this point, you do too. Like *Middlegame*, *Seasonal Fears* is a book that people who've been with me since the LiveJournal days will probably recognize from the rolling project list I used to maintain, or they might know it better under its previous name: *Pretty Poison Apples*. The first draft was written in the dead of winter, which may explain why Harry took so much of the narration away from Mel. She was otherwise occupied.

Once again, Diana Fox and Lee Harris have helped me to smooth and present an idea and a world that's been with me for a very long time; Mel's wood is much like my own Babylon Wood, and what walks there walks alone.

Talis, Wes, and Mary all fed deeply into the spirit and structure of this story, and talking through large portions of what it would be with them shaped it on an ongoing basis. Phil and Shawn also buttressed everything I did. I am happy to know them, and proud of everything they helped me to achieve.

Kate Secor is one of my best friends, and was very pregnant while I was writing this book—her daughter was born two days before I turned it in. Welcome to the party, tiny human! Thanks for hashing so many things out over Indian food and bad television, and for being a rock I could cling to when the waters got too high.

Thanks to Chris Mangum, Tara O'Shea, and Michelle "Vixy" Dockrey for being the best pit crew and general support system I could ever have wanted. Thanks to Jennifer Brozek, for being a shoulder to lean on, and to Ursula Vernon for identifying weird birds when asked. Thanks to Amber Benson, for her glorious audio narration. Thanks to Whitney Johnson, for being a delight. And thanks to everyone on PFER, who have helped me to stay sane through lockdown. You make the world better.

We have all weathered if not yet survived a pandemic together, and while not everyone who was here at the beginning is here now, the season is changing. Things are getting better. We'll see the summer soon.

Amy . . . I love you. I am so very glad to have you in my life, and I'll walk the improbable road with you any time.

Finally, thank you all, for reading. I couldn't tell these stories without someone who wanted to listen. The Impossible City isn't far from here, and I can take you, if you'd like to go. Just take my hand, close your eyes, and trust me.

I know the way.